FRANK JU

MW01123057

Created & written

by

"Frank Julius" Csenki - (Author)

www.frankjulius.com

Copyright © 2016 Frank Julius Csenki. All rights reserved.

Reproduction of this book or parts in any format is prohibited

without the written consent of the author.

This book is a work of fiction. All the characters, organizations,

and events portrayed in this novel are either products of the

author's imagination or are used fictitiously

Published by

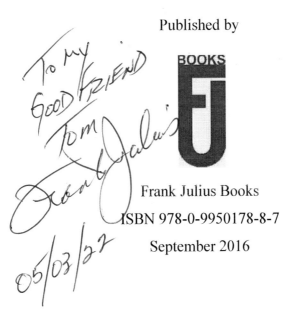

BOOKS

Frank Julius Books

ISBN 978-0-9950178-8-7

September 2016

FRANK JULIUS BOOKS

www.frankjulius.com

THE HOTEL/CASINO THRILLER TRILOGY

BLOOD DICE (Book 1)

(ELDON AND KIMBERLEY TAKE ON THE CIA)

THE RED JEWEL (Book 2)

(ELDON AND KIMBERLEY vs THE KGB AND MAFIA)

INN FORMATION (Book 3)

(ELDON AND KIMBERLEY FIGHT TERRORISTS)

****

BORDER HOUSE (Book 4) Spring 2020

(Eldon and Kimberley address the US Border Crisis)

****

MOSAIC LIFE TILES

(Autobiographic Anthology Series 1)

MOSAIC LIFE SQUARES (coming spring 2020)

(Autobiographic Anthology Series 2)

****

CANADAQUA

Suspense Thriller– (coming 2020)

(AMERICA'S THIRST FOR CANADA'S WATER)

FRANK JULIUS

THE RED JEWEL

Dedicated in loving memory

to

my mother and father

Izabella and Frank

I love you both forever.

***

Author's Note

I wish to thank two colleagues with whom I had the pleasure of working in the hotel business, right around the time the setting of this novel takes place. The two colleagues are Roman Mezibroski and Tim Winter. Both fine gentlemen, Hoteliers in their own right, helped me in reviewing the processes, procedures and challenges we faced with hotel operations in the newly formed Russian Federation during the early nineties. It was an exciting time to be sure. In addition, I wish to thank the wonderful people I met and got to work with in Russia. Everyone, whether knowing or not, took part in making my Russian experience so memorable.

For me; it was an especially ironic set of circumstances, being a Hungarian Refugee as a result of the 1956 Hungarian uprising, and fast forward, thirty-five years, finding myself working and living in the country whose former government had our family fleeing for our lives.

The winds of changes blew strong in those days, and history moved forward. I think I might be right in saying that my expatriate friends, colleagues and I, do share some incredible memories. With the writing of this book, the sequel to BLOOD DICE, I took advantage of the writer's creative license theorizing fictional liberties of how some things were and might have been, behind the scenes of the newly formed and emerging Russian Federation of the mid 90's, and I give you... THE RED JEWEL.

THE RED JEWEL

Prologue
Reflection

In late November on this Friday mid-morning in south Florida it was an unusually hot and humid day. The sun beat down on the manicured dark green Bermudagrass at The Gardens of Palm Memorial Cemetery in Pompano Beach. Already so early in the day, there was a mugginess in the air which usually signaled an upcoming shower, but there was still time.

Time is what brought Eldon to this moment, standing over Linda's grave holding flowers to be placed into her permanent headstone vase.

It was the time when his world shattered, finding Linda's blood soaked body. That was five years ago. Today, Eldon stood looking at Linda's name carved into her headstone. He stood motionless thinking to himself of the deep love they had for one another and Cathy. Even after these passing years, Eldon harbored an element of guilt deep inside his core, blaming himself for not having ensured tighter security. As time, marched on he eventually learned how to compartmentalize this guilt allowing him to move on with his life, finding new love with Kimberley and to raise Cathy in a loving home environment.

It was not often that Eldon visited Linda's grave. He promised himself to visit at least once every six months. These graveside visitations brought him a certain sense of peace and shedding of guilt by momentarily being at his murdered wife's side. He stood for a while longer, gazing, thinking, smiling a little as memories of their wonderful life flashed through his mind. Standing by her graveside, looking at her name he did his best in holding back his emotions, but it was not to be. He felt his throat tightening, letting out a falling tear and a deep sigh, as he stood over her grave grieving but smiling.

He bent down and took a knee, with his left hand he reached out and placed the flowers into the vase, brought his right hand up to his lips, kissed his fingers and touched her headstone, not moving his hand but feeling Linda's presence and everlasting love for him and Cathy.

Eldon stood and turned, his mind even now racing with current events unfolding as he walked towards the parking lot back to his car.

The south Florida sky had turned almost black with torrential rains blowing in from the Gulf, now just minutes away. As he opened the door to his Jag and getting inside, his car phone rang. He answered.

It was Viktor Orlov; The President of Russia.

***

Chapter One
In building a smooth road surface
one must first remove boulders.

Number 10 Spasopeskovskaya Square, better known as "Spaso House" the residence of the United States of America Ambassador to the Russian Federation is in the middle of the Arbat district of Moscow, an area center to the arts and tourism region of the city, with its famous pedestrian walk of Arbat Street.

Kimberley Ashton-Davis drove her "Beemer" up to the Gate Guard situated outside the perimeter of the US Ambassador's residence and greeted the young Russian Government Guard stationed at the entrance to the huge mansion.

"*Dobroye utro Ofiste*r" saying "good morning officer" in perfect Russian.

Kimberley spoke fluent Russian, having studied linguistics in university with her major being in languages and political sciences. She showed her ID along with her official pass to the residence of The Ambassador of the United States of America.

The young Russian officer replied with courtesy. "*Dobroye utro* Missis Devis."

He then performed an external vehicle inspection including an under-chassis mirror examination, asked her to pop open the Beemer's trunk and hood.

Having completed his inspection routine, he

then handed her ID and pass back to Kimberley. The guard thanked her, "*Spasiba*" and motioned for Kimberley to drive on through as the gate opened.

It was autumn in Moscow and as much as the fall and early winter could be harsh in Moscow, it also had a certain charm and proper atmosphere about the city that could only ever be experienced in Moscow. Even upon her very first visit to Moscow many years back, she welcomed the fact that it had been in the winter time.

Kimberley had this absolute fantasy of sleigh rides in the Russian countryside, in a traditional Russian horse-drawn sleigh, being wrapped up in warm woolen blankets and bear-skin throws, with the sound of sleigh bells and the heartfelt strings of a balalaika playing "Lara's Theme" reminiscent of a scene from the movie Dr. Zhivago. She imagined herself gliding over the fresh snow through a birch forest, and finally arriving at her dacha. Kimberley was a romantic at heart, with a perfect mix that more than suited her former foreign affairs postings with the United States Government.

The US Government no longer employed Kimberley. Kimberley now represented Holiday Jewel Hotels and Casinos International. Kimberley's mission this morning was to visit with Ambassador Ferenc "Frankie" Albert.

The Ambassador had cleared his agenda for this morning's 11:AM meeting and was expecting her arrival. Kimberley was today paving the way for tomorrow afternoon's main gathering with Moscow city officials and select members of the Russian Duma. (Russian Legislative Assembly)

Even as Kimberley made her way to the US Ambassador's residence, Eldon was flying across the Atlantic and scheduled to land just after midnight at which time Kimberley would brief him on the latest news and developments here in Moscow concerning the progress of their anticipated hotel opening date. Kimberley's involvement was key and crucial in the success of their expansion. Her connections had proven invaluable in making things happen.

She parked her car and made her way to the main entrance where she was greeted by a US Marine guard stationed on the inside perimeter of the mansion and was once again asked to present her identification. The US Marine checked Kimberley's ID and passport, asked her to place her valuables onto the tray and to walk through the x-ray machine.

She was cleared to proceed.

Spaso House was extraordinarily lavish in both architectural style; having been built and completed in 1914 in the "New Empire Style" along with its treasured collection of furnishings. Even during the Nazi invasion, somehow this mansion had escaped bombardment having come through the entire Second World War with only a few broken windows while neighboring buildings and theaters were reduced to nothing more than rubble.

As Kimberley walked through the building, she sensed the presence of history in the air with eighteen former US Ambassadors having occupied these halls and rooms dating back to the first in 1933.

Kimberley walked through history this morning and was about to have her first official meeting with US Ambassador Albert in the next two minutes. She walked down the hallway, approached another young US Marine standing guard to Ambassador Albert's doorway leading to the small foyer that was occupied by an Embassy staffer sitting behind a counter/desk acting as both receptionist and aide to Ambassador Albert.

Approaching the US Marine, Kimberley flashed her pass and proceeded into the foyer where the Staffer was already expecting Kimberley and greeted her with a friendly hello.

"Good morning Mrs. Ashton-Davis, The Ambassador is expecting you, allow me to advise him of your arrival."

The Staffer announced Kimberley's arrival on the intercom to Ambassador Albert's office. Having done so, he looked up at Kimberley and smiled in a very polite manner. As he was about to let Kimberley know that The Ambassador would be with her momentarily, Ambassador Albert opened his office door and immediately extended his warm welcome.

"Kimberley, how good to see you this morning. I am so very much looking forward to this meeting and our time together. Please, won't you come in?"

Ambassador Albert was a very disarming man, having a way about him that could put the devil himself at ease. In this case however; there was no need for his special social skills. He and Kimberley already knew one another albeit from two previous brief but revealing meetings allowing for their comfort level and mutual respect for one another to have been established.

Ambassador Ferenc "Frankie" Albert; *the new guy*" on the block had just recently been appointed and confirmed as the new Ambassador to the Russian Federation, being the nineteenth Ambassador to Russia with a unique set of circumstances allowing for an understanding and perspective of the former Soviet Union, its people, and its culture.

Ambassador Albert was affectionately known in diplomatic circles as "Frankie Albert" with "Frankie" being the English endearing translation of his first name "Ferenc" from Hungarian to English.

Ambassador Albert was a Hungarian National, born in Budapest Hungary in 1947 but then with history moving forward found himself as a naturalized American Citizen after his family's escape from Hungary because of the 1956 Hungarian Revolution.

Frankie grew up in the United States, became American and thirty-seven years later found himself sitting in the United States of America Ambassador's chair to the Russian Federation.

Frankie Albert knew of things, things not knowable to others who had not lived through the times of Soviet aggression with Poland, the "walling in" of East Berlin and further uprisings in Czechoslovakia and Hungary. Ambassador Albert approached all his dealings with the new Russian Government with a grain of salt and secrecy known only to Frankie Albert. Those secrets; stemming from the former Soviet Union that in his mind being of a "personal nature," could never be revealed, and yet in spite of it all, now having to manage events of recent history while holding to and honoring longheld arrangements made in the past.

Prior to his posting here in Moscow, Frankie Albert was the US Ambassador to the eastern bloc country of Hungary for five years, where he met the love of his life; Marika. Yes, it was late in life for Frankie, but nevertheless found Marika a native Hungarian during his posting as Ambassador to the Hungarian nation some four years ago.

He had met Marika one evening while attending a concert of Franz Liszt's famous works, performed by the Budapest National Symphony Orchestra in which Marika played her favorite musical instrument; the violin. Yes, Marika was a musician in a symphony orchestra and he was so very proud of her, still very much in love.

With Frankie Albert's background and birthplace being Hungary, his posting made a perfect match for the needs of the USA, especially since Hungary was soon to be admitted and welcomed into the North Atlantic Treaty Organization, (NATO) as the newest member nation. Already for the past couple of years even before application into NATO, Hungary had been granted and enjoyed special status with early cooperation in military exchange exercises with NATO in the former eastern bloc countries. These, however, were now new times. New chapters in history would be written in these next very important and decisive days, months and years to come, here in the largest country of the newly formed Commonwealth of Independent States.

Kimberley reached out her hand in greeting Ambassador Albert.

"Ambassador Albert, thank you for seeing me this morning. It is very nice to visit with you again, and I am sure this meeting will clear the way for our interests to move ahead here in Moscow. We are most excited about moving things forward. I cannot tell you how much your help has allowed us to progress in removing seemingly impossible obstacles."

Frankie Albert motioned for Kimberley to take a seat in one of the 19th century French provincial Napoleonic chairs, situated around a large coffee table. Russian aristocracy had always been obsessed with anything French especially architecture and furniture. The Hermitage in St. Petersburg spoke volumes to that testament.

"Thank you, Ambassador," Kimberley said and took a seat in the exquisite chair.

"Please call me Frankie, Kimberley it's high time we did away with the formalities. We need to get things done, and those formalities just get in the way."

Kimberley smiled back with acknowledgment and started in saying; "as you know Ambassador, my husband "Eldon" will be flying in for tomorrow's meeting; however, I don't expect him...."

Her sentence was cut off. A deafening sound of explosives shook the entire mansion. Kimberley jumped off her chair and hit the floor, sliding underneath the heavy coffee table. No sooner had she slid underneath the table, Ambassador Albert was there next to her, and then covered her body with his, shielding Kimberley as the building shuddered. Both suddenly bewildered as to what had just happened. More explosions creating shock waves from nearby battle tank shell firings rumbled through the building with the added screaming of artillery shells flying overhead above Spaso House.

The US Marine guards came running into The Ambassador's office grabbing both The Ambassador and Kimberley forcefully up off the floor. The Marines reacted with emergency evac protocol, immediately taking them both into the bunker area of Spaso House. An atmosphere of terror and confusion with a concern for their lives filled the air.

As the Marines were evacuating the two of them to Spaso House bunker, Ambassador Albert looked at the Marines and asked in amazement; "what in the hell is going on?"

The Marine replied, "far as we know Sir, the Russian Army has just opened fire on segments of its government."

Kimberley heard the Marine's comment, and Kimberley shouted out over the tank firing.

"I'm not surprised at that, something had to give," as they ran down the corridor for nearby cover.

Spaso House was not under attack, the shuddering and vibration that rumbled through the mansion were from shock waves because of battle tanks firing "HESH" (high explosive squash head) shells into a nearby government building a quarter mile from Spaso House. They were safe for now, but apparently, all hell was either breaking out, or all hell was soon to end.

These were days of turmoil in Moscow. The "old guard" consisting of lingering communist power brokers still resisted ouster, and things were now being done. Russian Military loyalty was to the new government and no longer tolerated communist holdouts. The thundering shock waves from the Russian Army battle tanks unleashing their firepower and the screaming overhead artillery shells was crystal clear evidence of that policy to both Kimberley and Ambassador Albert.

History was alive and breathing fire today in The Russian Capital; just a few yards outside the doors of Spaso House.

***

Chapter Two
Nectar attracts the bee
while the bear claims the honey.

The control tower at L.F. Wade International Airport in Bermuda had just given clearance for takeoff to private corporate jet HJHC01.

Pilot Billy Simpson taxied the Challenger 650 onto the runway and prepared for takeoff. It had been a busy day here on the Isle of Devils, so aptly named for the three hundred plus named shipwrecks resting at the bottom of the turquoise blue waters that surrounded these magical islands. Ironically the tragedies of the past five hundred years of lost sailors and their vessels had become a lifeline for the local modern economy attracting divers from the world over contributing to the immense success of the hotel business as fuel for the economic engine that powered Bermuda into being one of the most desirable vacation destinations in the world.

Holiday Jewel Hotels and Casinos owned and operated two five-star resort properties here on the island, one on the south shore in Paget Parish embracing breathtaking views of the colorful Atlantic with its pink sand beaches, and another in St. Georges at the northern tip of the island overlooking the main shipping channel. St. Georges was the oldest town in the western hemisphere, its old-world charm, narrow streets and nautical history of *olde* England echoed daily in the town square with the bell ringing and "*oyez, oyez*" attention calling voice of the Town Crier.

The interior of the Challenger 650 jet was fit for a king. The craftsmanship accentuated with plush leather seating and interior aircraft light weight mahogany wood finish lining the curvature of the fuselage. Billy Simpson made sure its avionics, electronics, and communications were always state of the art and of course; that the bar was at all times fully stocked.

Eldon settled into his seat sitting back anticipating Billy's take off in the next minute or two. He glanced over at Felix his close friend and confidant. The current time was 6:05: AM. Eldon, Billy, and Felix had only gotten about five hours sleep and it looked to Eldon that Felix was happy to grab a few extra winks on this Atlantic crossing. Felix and Billy had become like brothers to Eldon.

Over the past five years, their closeness and bond had become unbreakable, and they were now a team of four; Billy, Felix, and Eldon's wife; Kimberley. Yesterday morning the three of them had left Florida where Eldon's company's head office for Holiday Jewel Hotels and Casinos was located in Ft. Lauderdale and flew to Bermuda on their eventual way to Moscow. Eldon especially wanted to address a nagging matter here in Bermuda that had once again bubbled to the surface concerning hospitality labor union matters. He had to make sure it was nipped in the bud before it had time to fester. Everyone was good now after their meeting yesterday afternoon with the Minister of Labor and the head of the local hospitality labor union. Eldon took care of matters and both the labor union leader and the Minister of Labor were now happy campers.

Eldon would not need to worry or address matters here for at least another four years. Certain matters called for unusual handling and Eldon knew what to do with whom and at which precise time.

His two Bermuda resorts, along with the rest of the resort hotel business would be out of the woods for the foreseeable future. Eldon felt good about what had just happened yesterday on this little island in the sun. It was a solid solution and one that benefited all four sides of the commercial box. The local government would have their resort taxes remain in place with an anticipated increase.

The employees would be happy to have received an unexpected increase in hourly wages holding the labor union at bay for the next four years thus allowing the resorts' business models to be modified with confidence now that hourly labor costs were identified and fixed. Business was good in Bermuda and Eldon was making sure it would stay that way.

Eldon's company being as huge and expansive as it was international, of course did not set the rules for other hotel operators and owners in Bermuda, or for that matter in the rest of the Caribbean. But Eldon's moves within the industry would set the pace for others to follow and in most cases Holiday Jewel Hotels and Casinos not only had its own best interest in mind but usually provided best practices and principles in setting the example for the rest of the industry to follow. Eldon's reputation within the industry was unquestioned, with most competing hotel companies striving to follow his lead even if not admitting to it.

Felix had settled in as Eldon thought he would and was already asleep as Billy increased power on the Challenger 650. Eldon looked out his window watching the runway lights flickering by as the jet picked up speed for taking off. As Eldon watched the Bermuda ground lowering beneath him, his on-board interior cell phone came to life. He thought this most unusual, only a handful of people had his corporate jet's cell number. Another three minutes and they would be out of cell range, so he answered the call right away.

"Eldon Davis." It was Louis James his Senior Vice President of International Hotel Operations.

"Eldon, it's Louis. I wanted to catch you before you were off the island. I have some urgent news for you." Eldon was used to urgent news his entire life and most of it was rarely good. He felt this time would be no different.

"What is it, Louis?" Eldon asked.

Louis answered. "Eldon I'm not sure what to make of this all now but the Russian Army over here has just opened up with tank fire and artillery on some of its own government members located in one of the Duma headquarters buildings on Arbat Street. Eldon's heart suddenly accelerated.

"Arbat Street, that's where Kimberley is this morning, at The Ambassador's residence, she had an 11: AM meeting with Albert!"

Eldon's immediate concern for Kimberley was clearly evident in his response, and Louis jumped on it right away to let him know that Kimberley was safe

"Eldon I'm calling to tell you that Kimberley is unharmed. She's been evacuated to Spaso House Bunker as a safety precaution only. Apparently, the mansion was rattled by shock waves, but all is intact at the home of the US Ambassador. I have been in contact with Embassy staff, and I am assured that Kimberley is safe along with Ambassador Albert. From what I am told, they were both shaken up somewhat, but we have nothing to worry about concerning their safety. But Eldon, with this, happening today in Moscow, I'm not sure if this is a good or bad thing, only time will tell. Eldon at the moment I'm…" and the cell phone connection was dropped.

Eldon had lost Louis; they were out of cell phone range. Bermuda's cell communications towers were enough just to service the island with only two locations on the island and another five miles offshore. The main thing was that Eldon knew Kimberley was safe, so Eldon was relieved, but still Eldon decided to act.

Kimberley's ongoing safety and his being with her as soon as possible were now foremost on his mind. Billy's flight plan would have them flying from Bermuda to Heathrow for a refueling stop and then continuing to Moscow's Sheremetyevo International. The total flight time and refueling stop along with a quick airport coffee shop meeting with his British hotel managers at Heathrow would see him landing in Russia thirteen hours from now making his arrival around or after midnight, factoring in the six-hour time difference.

Eldon got up out of his seat. He then thought of waking Felix, but just as quickly decided not to. There wasn't anything Felix could do about things at this point, so Eldon let him sleep. Felix would be invaluable later no doubt, but for now, it was Billy he needed to talk to and went up front to the cockpit, swiveled the co-pilot's seat around to face Billy and sat down

"Hey Eldon, decided to come up front and keep me company?"

Eldon responded, "Billy I wish it was just that, but something's come up in Moscow. We need to get there as soon as possible, and that's why I have come to talk to you."

Billy looked at Eldon with concern in his eyes and asked. "What's going on Eldon?"

Eldon leaned over resting his elbows on top of his knees while facing Billy and said, "Billy it seems like all hell is breaking out in Moscow. President Viktor Orlov has apparently ordered the army to take out the communist holdouts; some hard-liner deputies of the Duma hunkered down inside one of the Parliamentary buildings. The Army just opened up with tank fire and artillery into the building."

Billy looked over at Eldon in disbelief. "Holy shit," Billy exclaimed.

"Yeah, can you believe it?" Eldon said. "But I think I can figure Orlov's angle on this one, he had to take decisive action, he had to make the call notifying the world that he was in charge once and for all; I can see his reasoning." Eldon took a deep breath, sat in silence for a moment allowing for the impact of everything to sink in.

"Kimberley is now in evac status along with the US Ambassador at Spaso House, she's been shaken up, we need to get to Moscow without delay."

Within a millisecond of having heard what Eldon just finished saying, Billy already knew what had to be done. Eldon knew as well that Billy would be in tune with Eldon's thoughts, sometimes it was almost like the two of them used the same brain.

Billy continued, "Eldon I can have us in contact range with the airport in Ponta Delgada in the Azores. It would save us huge time refueling in the Azores instead of flying into Heathrow."

Eldon then cut in saying, "that's exactly what I was thinking Billy, change our flight plan to the Azores, we can request a priority refuel arrangement just as soon as we are within radio contact range, and be back in the air within a half hour and back on our way directly to Moscow."

"Eldon, flying into The Azores will eliminate the high air traffic we would have to contend with in London. We can fly directly in, no holding pattern and be out immediately not having to line up behind thirty other flights waiting to take off."

"That's it Billy, reprogram the flight computer for Joao Paulo Airport in the Azores, and while we are there it will allow me to talk with Kimberley. The Azores has good communications capabilities. We need to know just what the status is on the ground in

Moscow. I'm sure Kimberley will be waiting for my call."

"Eldon, the flight computer calculates just under three and a half hours to The Azores. We should be in contact range with the tower a half hour out from the airport. If we can get back into the air within another half hour after landing, we should be in Moscow between ten and eleven PM their time."

Eldon reached out and patted Billy on his shoulder.

"Thanks, Billy; fly this bird as fast as she'll go, let's get to Moscow before Orlov decides he wants to declare martial law."

"Roger that Eldon."

Eldon walked back from the cockpit to the salon. He couldn't help thinking to himself about his latest venture into Russia. He was certainly taking a huge gamble, but at the same time the potential rewards stood to be very satisfying and meaningful. This was a good business decision; he couldn't deny his burning desire to pioneer into new territory.

Nevertheless, he thought of himself as the busy international bee, flying around the globe, taking nectar from every business opportunity he could find, while perhaps in this case, the Russian Bear may well end up destroying his hive and stealing his honey.

He went to the kitchenette coffee dispenser and poured two mugs of coffee, came back to sit across from Felix and placed the two mugs onto the table between them.

He reached out across the table and tapped Felix on the side of his knee. "Felix, wake up."

Felix stirred, opened his eyes while stretching out, taking a deep breath and responded, "Eldon, yeah what's up?"

***

<u>Chapter Three</u>

**Now that the hammer and sickle are no longer
Gives me the freedom to bug you even stronger.**

The Federal Security Services, (FSB) formerly known as The KGB, is for all intents and purposes still The KGB but now with a name change to complement the newly formed Government of the Russian Federation. The great irony in this facade is that the new Federal Security Services (The FSB) headquarters are still located in the same building with the same offices, the same prisoner torture cells and for the most part the same individuals holding the same positions and job descriptions as they've always had with The KGB.

There is one new change to note however, and that would be the appointment of the new Director of Federal Security Services, Sasha Bebchuk, close friend of President Viktor Orlov and 1981
Afghanistan war hero of the Soviet Union.

Bebchuk and Orlov formed an unbreakable bond when both were stationed in Afghanistan fighting the Mujahedeen Guerrillas. He and his gunner; who sat in the front seat of the two-seater were flying support mission along the Salang highway just outside Kabul. While piloting his Hindheli assault gunship, they were shot down by an American CIA supplied man-portable Stinger missile.

The crash had Orlov severely wounded and then captured by the Mujahedeen. Sasha Bebchuk; his gunner was unhurt and had evaded capture. Later that day single-handed, Sasha tracked the Guerrillas to their hideout, and with surprise on his side, took out all the combatants, rescuing Commander Orlov.

Sasha carried Viktor; his commander, out on his back and shoulders to temporary safety. Bebchuk then called in air support which allowed for their extraction from the Mujahedeen stronghold.

Viktor Orlov owed his life to Bebchuk and throughout the years their friendship had grown solid with their powers growing in strength together from the same stem.

They were a team of two, partners in politics, tactics and power brokers with a progressive understanding of the need for changes in government, doctrine and the future for The Russian Federation.

FSB Director; Bebchuk, well knew the inner workings of the former KGB, understanding that its legacy would not allow for overnight changes within the newly named Federal Security Services. The same rules and tactics were in place as were before but now toned down with some programs permanently mothballed. His prowess, however, was not to be denied or underestimated. Just a few days after the newly formed government, and Sasha's appointment as Director he and Viktor talked about certain events taking place in Moscow.

These coming days were in need of forwardlooking planning for events unfolding at lightning speed in Moscow and throughout Russia. The main immediate concern was to be focused on events emerging in the major urban centers; Moscow, St. Petersburg, Novosibirsk, Samara, Omsk, and right across the former Soviet Union clear out to Vladivostok on the Pacific coast. The rural areas at this time didn't configure much into the mix in any significant way; it was the major centers that needed the attention.

"We are facing new times Sasha. Even as I sit here behind the walls of The Kremlin here in my Senate building residence, safe and in power, I fear that in our infancy as a new government we must take steps to compensate for our country's lack of laws and regulations needed to govern our newly found freedoms. Are you with me on this, do you know what I am talking about Sasha?" Viktor Orlov looked at his closest friend and enforcer Sasha Bebchuk in a very meaningful way.

Sasha nodded, taking a long drag on a US imported Cheyenne cigarette. There were some things American for which Sasha had developed a liking. Two being Cheyenne cigarettes and Kentucky Bourbon whiskey on ice, which he sipped from a Kremlin rock glass.

He looked back at his friend and President saying, "I understand Viktor that we will need to make certain moves ensuring our dominance and our country's best interest in all newly formed joint ventures now with the growing investment by
Western corporations."

"Precisely Sasha, precisely," Orlov responded. "Sasha, I need you to consider our vulnerability at this time with us not having appropriate laws in place, we cannot be taken advantage of. When the country was governed by unquestioned power, The Soviet required no permission nor validations for whatever decisions were reached, we were a power unto ourselves but now Sasha, we will need laws that the rest of the world can embrace and that will take time."

Sasha listened carefully to what Viktor Orlov was alluding to exactly.

Viktor continud. "So, we will do what we must until the Duma has had time to enact the laws needed to satisfy our country's needs as well as encouraging new investment into our Russian Federation."

That initial conversation had taken place just shortly after Viktor took power in the newly formed Federation.

On this day, almost five years later, Sasha Bebchuk and Viktor Orlov met again in the Kremlin and continued on with the same subject at hand.

"Sasha I am glad you understand and that you are on the same page with me, there cannot be any other way at this time Sasha. I have been thinking of late about Moscow Mayor Anton Marat's comments to me about the sudden overwhelming rush of interest by companies from the west applying for joint venture business licenses. Marat tells me that these applications have numbered into the thousands, mostly smaller entrepreneurial types, import-export businesses, and then there are the large multinational corporations that stand to make a huge impact on our emerging economy. Sasha, let me ask you something."

Orlov's friend and Director of The FSB listened in earnest.

"When driving down our main roads throughout the city specifically closer in towards the Kremlin, what strikes you as the most noticeable changes to our city Sasha?"

Bebchuk took a long drag on his Cheyenne, exhaled and said, "well that's an easy one Viktor, it's the many construction cranes throughout Moscow. But it's the same in St. Petersburg and Samara, Omsk, everywhere Viktor. Our major cities are experiencing resurgence in the building of new hotels that are to welcome and act as venues for business deal negotiations; it's really quite remarkable."

President Orlov nodded saying; "you have that right Sasha, things are moving very fast, building and business permit applications have reached record numbers, more than ever in our history. Sasha, we need to stay on schedule with project "Black Bear", we need to know more of what is being discussed behind closed doors in these new hotels being built. Sasha, I had discussed this issue with you a number of years back, and you assured me that you would attend to our needs. I know when we decide on something you are one to take action and follow up. Where do we stand Sasha?

Bebchuk was about to impress Viktor Orlov now.

"Mr. President, you appointed me to assure the security of our Motherland. I hold that responsibility to heart with every breath I take. That includes our national security of known State enemies and potential enemies as well as newcomers to our economic development. Mr. President, I am well aware that our infancy in this government has left us in a difficult situation dealing with international and multinational corporations now that we no longer have the protections or convenience of the Soviet. We will have to abide by contract law which we currently do not have in place, and Viktor, we still do not have enough lawyers or accountants in Russia to meet the growing needs of the country. Our Soviet system did not require it. Everything was owned by the State, now potentially nothing will be owned or is owned any longer by the State, and Mr. President, most of our people, have no idea as to what a bank checking account is.

Mr. President as you are aware, Russia until just recently had no credit cards, this has been a huge learning curve and change for our people. I know this is an issue of paramount importance that needs to be addressed immediately. I have considered these obstacles and have made arrangements that will allow for our needs in understanding and knowing the dealings that go on behind closed doors."

Viktor looked at Bebchuk reaffirming his continued approval for Sasha's forward thinking.

"Sasha, I am glad you have taken the initiative needed in addressing these issues. I will want you to file a top-secret report detailing all the steps you and your people have taken along with the progress in your surveillance and intelligence gathering methods for all the newly built hotels we talked about. I want a detailed analysis outlining your results to date. Your report should be ready for next week's Presidential briefing sessions.

As for the goings on with the events of yesterday, you know Sasha, just over thirty-five hours ago, Russian Federation Army General Boris Kutosev was sitting in that very chair you are in.

I ordered General Kutosev to rid the hard liner holdouts from the Parliamentary building they have occupied. I told him to use all means necessary and to send a message to the world. Do you know what he asked me?"

President Orlov did not give Bebchuk time to respond; he continued on.

"Sasha, he asked me if he should keep going till the building was rubble. I told him to go as far as needed to flush those rats out into the open so that your people could arrest them and hold them for further questioning. Sasha, the army and the entire armed forces of the Russian Federation are solidly behind us now. The old guard is no more, we are a new nation Sasha, but we have some history we need to take care of with which we need to be very careful.

Viktor Orlov stood up from his chair. That action signaled the meeting with The FSB Director had come to an end. Bebchuk stood as well.

"Sasha, good talking with you, I look forward to your report next week. We have some work to do in the coming days. The Motherland depends on us. *dos vidaniya* Sasha."

"*Dobroy nochi*, good night Mr. President."

Sasha Bebchuk left the Kremlin. His FSB limo drove through the gates of the Kremlin walls and headed out into the Moscow night traffic. Two minutes later driving through traffic, the blue strobe light flashing on top of his vehicle moved traffic aside allowing for his clear sailing.

Sasha thought to himself about the two new major high rises in Moscow with one of the two high-rise buildings already dominating the Moscow city center skyline. He opened the glass partition to speak to his driver.

"Slow down at the next intersection and proceed slowly until we pass the construction site."

"Yes, Director Bebchuk."

As his car came up alongside the construction site, Sasha's car window opened, and he took in the view of the towering skyscraper hotel set to open within weeks.

The bright red neon sign advertising the upcoming opening of the new hotel read in English:

OPENING SOON - THE RED JEWEL.

The hotel was being built on "*Krasnaya Ulitca*;" Red Street.

***

Chapter Four
To Russia with Love

Eldon looked over across the table at his close friend and right-hand man. Eldon pushed the hot mug of coffee towards Felix saying, "there you go, fresh coffee you're going to need it. What's up you ask? What an understatement of a question that is. If you're not fully awake now, you will be in a few seconds." Eldon responded to Felix's waking question.

Felix reached down for his mug of coffee, "thanks for the coffee," feeling its heat as he grabbed hold of its handle, taking a sip focusing on Eldon with inquisition.

Eldon continued. "Felix, you and Billy and I have gone through a hell of a lot over the past five years; I fear we may be facing some of the biggest and most challenging obstacles now more than we have ever had to deal with in all the years we have worked together."

"What's going on Eldon, what do you mean?" Felix was not at all prepared for such words this morning; this was totally out of the blue for Felix, but Felix knew well that when Eldon spoke as he did now, it was serious.

Eldon continued on to say, "things are happening already, and we've only just been in the air a few minutes. Just as we were taking off I got a call from Louis in Moscow; you won't believe this at first when you hear it, but...well… listen up." Eldon had Felix's attention there was no mistaking that. "Louis called telling me that the Russian Army had started bombarding one of their own government buildings. Inside are hardliner communist holdouts occupying the offices and refusing to move or negotiate after five days. Apparently, Orlov ordered the Army to open tank fire and artillery on the building until the hardliners came running out surrendering or failing that, have them all killed in the bombardment. Sections of the city near the area of heavy shelling have been shut down. This would be the first time in modern history that the Russian Army has openly attacked members of its own parliamentary body. This action would be equivalent to the US Army shelling Capitol Hill and the members of the United States Congress.

"Holy crap," Felix let out.

Eldon went on. "Looks to me Felix that although the Soviet Union is no more, the establishment of democracy and the accommodation for dissent will be a hard struggle in this new era of freedom. But having had some time here in the last few minutes to reflect on how this will be viewed by the world, I am thinking this move by Orlov will end up being a positive one."

Felix started nodding his head in agreement with Eldon. "Yes, I think you are probably right about that Eldon."

"Right, but what hit me right away was Kimberly's location. She had her visit with Ambassador Albert this morning at Spaso House, and that's just a quarter mile down from where the artillery shells were landing. It turns out Louis has been in touch with Kimberley; she was shaken up but is unhurt.

36

Albert and Kimberley were whisked away to the residence bunker by Marines, so I'm glad of that, which reminds me, we should be getting close to the Azores by now; we will be in cell phone range soon. Yes, "Lix" I had Billy change our flight plan, we are now skipping London, instead refueling in the Azores and continuing on to Moscow. We should make it there well before midnight. As soon as I can,
I'll be making a call to Kimberley."

Felix looked across at his friend and boss. "Eldon, the four of us have gone through some unbelievable times over the past three years. We have faced murder, kidnapping, government corruption, CIA deceit, Prime Ministerial overthrows, labor union hardball, and Eldon the list goes on. I'm afraid we are about to enter into a new arena of political power struggles in this new emerging economy and society in Russia. When I took on this job as your PR spokesperson and adviser I honestly had no idea where the road you travel would take me, but let me assure you, Eldon, this has been a most incredible journey thus far enriching my life beyond my wildest expectations. I am with you Eldon, as I am certain Billy is. He's up front now flying us into the unknown; I wouldn't want to be with anyone else in this adventure than you Billy and Kimberley." Felix looked at Eldon with his life's confidence and assurance.

Eldon felt it. Felix's words hit home. "That's why I have you by my side Felix because I can trust you with my life and you can trust me with yours. Whatever adventures this business of mine takes us into and has us facing in this new Russian Federation, I know that there is nothing we won't do or tackle in making certain that The Red Jewel opens as planned. My hotel will act as the new shining star of business and hospitality. We will welcome the world's business and corporate giants at The Red Jewel Felix; it will shine its light of international cooperation upon Moscow and Viktor Orlov sitting in the Kremlin just across the street." That it will Eldon, that it will, it's just a few weeks away from opening," Felix said reassuringly.

Eldon continued, "I'm thinking this action taken by Orlov will end up helping us. Orlov has set a clear path. He's announced to the world his presence and decisiveness. There can be no question any longer as to who holds real power, and he's made his announcement in no uncertain terms. I believe we are good to go Felix."

Eldon's mind then keyed in on Kimberley and just as his mind went there, Billy's voice came on the intercom.

"Eldon, we will be within cell range of Ponta Delgada shortly." With the time difference added to it was now almost 11: AM. Eldon's plane was about ten minutes away from locking on to a good cell tower. Billy had already contacted the airport in Ponta Delgada on radio and was arranging for immediate refueling services. The air traffic controller told Billy he could taxi close up to the fuel depot at the far end of the runway he was to land on saving time in the refueling process. There would be no deplaning; it was just a pit stop for fuel. Billy would provide the airport management with HJHC's international fueling, and landing fees account to be charged, and they could be back in the air within twenty minutes.

At 11:10 AM, Eldon tried the cell phone service and entered Kimberley's number into his plane's phone. They were still five minutes out from the island, but Eldon was anxious, he had to try. It was ringing, he was getting through. Billy Simpson brought the Challenger 650 in on its glide path to Ponta Delgada International Airport. Although the Azores was located out in the Atlantic Ocean almost a thousand miles off the coast of Portugal, there were times when air traffic would need to line up.

This morning's traffic was light, and Billy was cleared to land without having to circle, his glide path was direct. As it was most flights to and from the island were from Lisbon Portugal. The Azores was not a huge international destination, as things were turning out, their plan was working just fine.

"Oh Eldon, honey it's so good to hear your voice."

Hearing Kimberley's voice on his cell took the weight of the world off Eldon's shoulders. "Kimberley, tell me you're okay." were the first words out of his mouth.

"Eldon, I'm fine, I'm just fine. Ambassador Albert and I were whisked away to safety just as the Tank shells were being fired off, the Marines here at the embassy had us in safety within a minute after the shooting started, baby I'm fine, just get here as soon as you can, I need to be with you and missing you so much.

Eldon all hell's broken out down the street from here. There are further developments; I can fill you in when you land baby. Things have quieted down now, and traffic is starting to move. What's your ETA?" She paused a moment but before Eldon could respond, Kimberley desperately said, "I'm not sitting still, I'm coming to the airport to meet you. I will be there! I need to feel your touch holding me tight in your arms."

Eldon was so relieved Kimberley was safe and sound.

"Me too, I'm coming as fast as this bird will have us there. We're just about to get refueled now in The Azores. Billy should have us back in the air within the half hour. Sweetheart it's just over a fivehour flight time, plus the four-hour time difference will put us over Moscow just around 10:00 PM. I'll be holding you in my arms soon. I love you, Kimberley, I'll be there."

Eldon was starting to calm down having heard Kimberley's voice and reassurances, but on the other hand, his burning desire to be with his wife was greater now than ever before in their almost fiveyear relationship and just being over three years of their love filled marriage. This was the first and only time when Eldon thought Kimberley's life had been at risk.

He'd already lost Linda five years ago, and because of that loss, he found Kimberley. Cathy now had a new loving step mommy. Eldon's world was once again complete. His darling Cathy was safe at home in Jupiter Florida with Kimberly's mother and father, her newly adopted grandparents.

In these past three years, their married life had seen them apart for long periods of time all having to do with their business dealings. Kimberley's contacts would have her flying to Europe and Russia often whereas Eldon's attention was needed in the Caribbean or his research and development facilities in Florida. They were a loving couple, dedicated to one another but cherished every bit of time they had together. They both felt that once the Moscow hotels were open and running, it would be a good time to take a break for a while and spend more time together as a family, Eldon, Kimberley, and Cathy.

With Kimberley, having come into his life, she had become Eldon's greatest acquisition both into his personal life and his business world. Kimberley's international connections and background opened doors for Eldon's company; Holiday Jewel Hotels and Casinos that Eldon would have been hard pressed to make come about as quickly as Kimberley was able to break down barriers winning over the powers that be.

It never ceased to amaze Eldon how Kimberley could fast track negotiations with politicians that opened business opportunities the world over. It had become crystal clear to Eldon that not only did the old cliché "its not what you know but who you know" applied to things back home, but it was so true in international circles even more-so.

Kimberley had been a State Department career diplomat. She knew members and delegates of the

European Union and to top it off she was acquainted with Viktor Orlov through his wife Svetlana with whom she had a personal friendship since her college days.

Svetlana Orlov, (Svetlana Marin, as she was known then) back in University, was a visiting student at Rutgers University in New Brunswick New Jersey for one semester. She was studying American History in the same class as Kimberley. Turns out Kimberley at the same time was also studying Russian at Rutgers and the two of them hit it off becoming close friends over their semester together.

As the years passed, both ended up in public service with Kimberley entering the diplomatic corps and Svetlana marrying Viktor Orlov. Svetlana was now The First Lady of the new Russian Federation. Kimberley's connections couldn't have been better in the negotiations and dealings with the new Russian government.

The shovel groundbreaking ceremony that kicked off phase one of The Red Jewel construction was as much the result of Kimberley's work as it was of Eldon's.

The two of them had become a force in the international hotel and casino industry. They worked together well with dedication, perseverance and love for one another that transferred to a mutually shared excitement in growing Eldon's global hotel empire. Eldon was the business brain behind it all and Kimberley was turning out to be the broker of Eldon's ever expanding business plans.

The US Marine Commander charged with Embassy security for both the US Embassy building and Ambassador Albert's residence Spaso House gave the "all clear" announcement in person to Ambassador Albert.

With that Kimberley and Frankie Albert left Spaso House bunker and returned to the offices they had just run from two hours ago. The next hour was spent discussing what had happened out on the streets of Moscow. The US Embassy had a straight diplomatic line to the Kremlin and was advised by Kremlin officials that all aggression had ceased, and the hardliners had surrendered.

The Russian security forces had taken control of the building that the communist hardliners occupied and all order in the street was being restored, and calm had returned to the Arbat. The street was still cordoned off to the public, but all else was continuing on as normal.

"Well Kimberley, I would say that was enough excitement for today. I am certain the remainder of my day will be filled with priority communications between The Kremlin, and Washington, The Pentagon as well as the White House." Ambassador Albert said to Kimberley.

"Mr. Ambassador my coming here today was to mainly verify our talking points for tomorrow's meeting with my husband, and city officials." Kimberley began to say.

Albert cut in. "Well, Kimberley at this point we cannot be certain of what tomorrow brings but since for now apparently things outside are mainly over, the events of today may not have affected our plans for tomorrow. I suggest we touch base in the morning to determine if our meeting is still a go."

Kimberley responded. "Ambassador I will check with you in the morning."

"That will be fine Kimberley, let me arrange for a Marine escort vehicle to see you back to your hotel."

Kimberley appreciated The Ambassador's thoughtfulness and thanked him for his cautionary move.

"I will arrange for a Marine driver for your car and a backup Marine vehicle for our driver to return in."

"Thank you, Ambassador; I will be in touch in the morning."

The US Marine came to accompany Kimberley out to her vehicle and to take over the driving. An official US Humvee follow-vehicle with US Flags fixed to the front fenders was to tag along behind Kimberley's Beemer.

Walking out the front doors of Spaso House, everything seemed normal. Light snow was falling this afternoon. There was just the faintest trace of a strange but pungent smell in the air. It was the smell of nitroglycerin mixed with cordite that still lingered in the air. The wind was blowing towards Spaso House from where the Tanks had opened up on Parliamentary Building number 2. There was a stillness that accompanied the falling snow that brought strange calmness with it. Maybe it was just because the shooting had stopped and an eerie silence followed. Like a calm before a storm, but exactly opposite. Kimberley took a seat in the back and allowed the young Marine to take the wheel; they made their way out through the security gate and into the city.

Kimberley settled into the back seat of her Beemer. It wasn't her first time sitting in the back of her own car. Usually, Kimberley was required to have bodyguard protection with her at all times just to stay on the safe side. The bodyguard presence had become a necessity a couple of months after she and Eldon had started in on their first few trips to Moscow. In the early stages, their visitations focused in on exploring business proposals and opportunities which then subsequently lead to Holiday Jewel Hotels and Casinos successful contract negotiation for expansion into Russia.

The first year or so after the birth of The Russian Federation there was no need for such security measures. Russia and Moscow along with all other major Russian centers had been essentially free of major crime. In addition, the presence of western corporate executives driving its city streets; very rare.

The situation was changing and changing rapidly. Cases involving corporate executive kidnappings were on the rise all over Russia, from its oil fields in the Siberian wilderness to its major centers, Russia was undergoing an unprecedented growth of the "Russian Mafia."

This organized crime element had grown in prominence overnight proving to be ruthless and very dangerous, taking every and any opportunity in collecting money for hostages. Capturing visiting corporate executives was quite simple in the beginning since most westerners were unaware of these local unexpected dangers.

The Russian Mafia as it was being called operated mainly in Moscow and St. Petersburg and their aim was not just targeted at corporate executives. Complete convoys of eighteen wheelers had been known to disappear. These convoys made up transports of supplies from countries like Denmark, The Netherlands, Germany, France, and Poland. The convoys would be commandeered by thugs carrying Kalashnikov weapons on deserted sections of the highways. The trailers were systematically emptied, the goods then sold on the black market, and the drivers held for ransom.

Their ruthless dealings and activity did not stop there. Russian Mafia was most famous for their involvement and proliferation of human trafficking of underage women into sex slavery servicing to bars, hotels and strip clubs run by the criminal element all throughout Russia, Eastern Europe and extending to the western countries throughout the European Continent. Crime had rapidly become a huge concern in Russia. Contributing to the growing crime rate was the lack of laws that would have enabled law enforcement to deal with such criminal activities but compounding that effort was the sheer fact of local police being outgunned by Mafia thugs coupled with poor policeman's pay which usually lead to the officer taking a bribe to look the other way.

Although Kimberley usually traveled with security this morning she had decided to forgo having her bodyguard drive her. She felt like going solo for a change. It was only a few miles to Spaso House and almost a straight shot through town. Before leaving for Spaso House, Kimberley let Louis James, HJHC Senior VP know of her appointment with Ambassador Albert for 11 AM. She left her hotel, The Holiday Jewel Danamo which had just recently opened a year ago, and was happy to drive in peace alone to Spaso House. Once she was there, she would technically be on US soil so security this morning wasn't so much an issue for her.

Now on her return to her hotel, it was prudent to have the Marine accompany her with all that had happened just a few hours ago. Holiday Jewel Hotels and Casinos employed several security personnel in Moscow to act as bodyguards to Kimberley, Eldon, Louis James, Hotel General Managers and Financial Controllers.

Sitting comfortably in the rear of her vehicle and riding with the security of the Marine driver and following US Humvee, Kimberley looked out her window at the passing buildings. As her car approached the bridge to cross the Moskva River, Parliamentary Building number 2 came into view. It hugged the shoreline of the Moskva River; it was a massive ten-story structure, now the eyesore of the city after having been bombarded; it was still smoldering. Huge gaping holes had been blown into the sides taking out entire sections of the building with one corner completed having collapsed onto the street.

They continued driving further up Leningradsky Prospekt it would be another ten minutes before she would arrive back at her hotel. Kimberley looked out her window, not really looking at anything in particular, just gazing and thinking to herself of how things had come to be what they were. She had discussed these things with Eldon several times. With Kimberley's diplomatic background and connections, and with Eldon's need to expand his hotel empire, they agreed that a venture into the new Russian Federation would be an exciting and pioneering move. So, they went with it, and here she was... now looking out at Moscow, just having driven by a blown-up government building, with Army Tanks in the street. It was too late to retreat now; the game was on.

Kimberley sat looking out while thinking about it all. "The Soviet Union ceased to exist just a few years ago. With the coming down of the wall in East Germany in 1989 and the subsequent events that were unstoppable throughout Eastern Europe along with the free flow of information, the days of the Soviet Union as the world had come to know it were numbered. Inner turmoil lead to the collapse of communism, it was an assured eventuality.

On the surface, it all sounded and looked pretty good from afar. Kimberley would never forget how Europe and the world celebrated the coming down of the wall in East Berlin. Shortly after that, The Soviet Union was finished with virtually overnight. But what was the country to do now that it was a different country with new rules or perhaps better said no rules? The old rules and regulations of the former Soviet Union no longer applied. Was there to be a burn-in phase? Were some laws still in effect and some others thrown out? Who was to make those decisions, the police, the sworn communist deputies of the Duma? Well, there was no communism any longer and just what exactly then were those sworn deputies doing in power still?

The change came about in baby steps, and one change had taken place today. The tank fired shells that demolished part of the Parliamentary building was a clear sign of change having taken place. Another hurdle in the emergence of this new society had been overcome. There were other issues however still lingering that guns could not solve. What about the currency, and what about international banking?

Things were still evolving and it would take time. Even to this day, three years after the arrival of free enterprise in Russia, Russian currency was still not acceptable for payment of your hotel account, it had to be hard currency, either US Dollars, Deutschmarks, or British Pounds. Russian Rubles were considered worthless, and to top things off, Russians weren't allowed to stay at Holiday Jewel Danamo Hotel nor any of the other western run joint venture properties. Much was still left to be done in this country. Both she and Eldon loved a challenge, this, however, might turn out to be a larger challenge than they had bargained for."

"Thank you for your escort Corporal Manning," Kimberley said as the young Marine driver pulled the car up to the hotel's port-cochere.

The valet parking attendant took over from the Marine and Kimberley was on her way to her permanent suite on the top floor of Holiday Jewel Danamo Hotel. She was back home. A temporary home away from home that is; her and Eldon's residence while and whenever they were in Moscow. She had arrived back home just in time to receive Eldon's call from the Challenger as Billy was bringing the plane in for the refueling stop to Ponta Delgada Airport in the Azores. Kimberley answered her phone.

"Oh Eldon, honey it's so good to hear your voice."

***

Chapter Five
Changing of the guard? Not so much.

Ever since its construction in 1898 the large yellow Neo-Baroque building known as Lubyanka designed by Alexander Ivanov had been and still was a landmark structure in Moscow. Its original purpose was to be the head offices of the All-Russian Insurance Company but following the revolution in 1918 the building was taken over by the Bolsheviks and became the Headquarters of the State Secret Police, better known back then as The Cheka. With its newly established identity as the State Secret Police Headquarters, it took on a life of its own, not ever reinventing itself, only changing up its initialism in becoming the feared KGB (*Komitet gosudarstvennoy bezopasnosti*) during the Soviet era and now the reinvented FSB (*Federal'naya sluzhba bezopasnosti Rossiyskoy Federatsi*) under Viktor Orlov and the new Russian Federation.

The building had become a rock and symbol of Russia's international power for snooping and global interference. Its reputation as a ruthless, diabolical and terrifying interrogation facility noted the world over had preceded and masked its real capabilities as an international spy agency. It was the mirror image of America's CIA (Central Intelligence Agency) although the CIA vehemently denied ever using enhanced interrogation techniques; torture to be precise, but both agencies acknowledged a healthy dose of respect and caution for one another's capabilities. The FSB's specialty was international espionage as was the CIA's along with covert operations in foreign lands.

Technology was fast becoming a central focus point for The FSB and when it came to technology the major advances were being accomplished in private enterprise with military contracts and cooperation. The FSB had recently created a new sector specifically in this area which concentrated on corporate espionage and the procurement of specialized weapons and surveillance technology.

During the Soviet era, any foreign diplomats or for that matter any foreigners visiting Russia were pretty much guaranteed to number one, be followed by KGB agents and two, their accommodations were sure to be bugged with listening devices. These were given elements of traveling to Russia and conditions that all westerners understood well. Not only did the Soviet Union spy on visitors but, of course, their own people spied on one another. This trend had seen a backing off of sorts over the last few years of the Soviet Union, but one could still be assured that nothing was clean and free of secret surveillance.

Sasha Bebchuk's aim was to infiltrate as many western businesses, joint ventures as possible with clean surveillance, undetectable no matter how deeply the detection sensors probed. The decision to bolster former information gathering capabilities of The KGB was made in lieu of the new nation lacking laws, and this would be a workaround to know just exactly who was doing what in this new open society. It was becoming obvious that the need for national clandestine information gathering methods was even more vital now in this new era than it ever had been in the past. Thus, this national FSB effort became a major project code-named "Black Bear" sanctioned as a go-ahead soon after President Orlov came into power. Sasha was given total autonomy.

After almost five plus years since the initiation of "Black Bear," Sasha was sure he had solved the complexities that came with such a task. The FSB's internationally placed assets had confirmed the existence of classified high tech cutting edge audiovideo surveillance capabilities that was virtually undetectable and indeed available.

It was sensitive to be sure in terms of acquiring the hardware, but it could be gotten, and it could be done. This new surveillance tech known as "RUL" utilized a combination of three technologies and sciences. RUL combined radar tech, ultrasound, and laser technologies, thus named RUL. The CIA had a certain sense of humor at times and had code named it *RaUL*, giving the technology a Hispanic human name, "*Raul*". This then later became an inside joke "*Raul* heard and saw it all" and *Raul* cannot tell a lie, so it must be true.

Raul was classified and still deemed experimental, but that classification according to his FSB assets in the field, was strictly cosmetic cover up in nature to prevent unauthorized distribution. The procurement of *Raul* had to be obtained over a prolonged period to avoid any suspicion arising from bulk ordering since the supplier was governed by certain export restrictions. That was over thirty months ago since the first order had been secured, and today Sasha sat back in his FSB Director's chair taking a long drag from his American Cheyenne cigarette, smiling and thinking.

"His FSB agents had already successfully implanted a good number of *Raul* surveillance units into all newly built hotels opened in the past two years. Although not all hotel guest rooms had received the modifications, the hotels had most of their suites, hospitality suites, and boardrooms equipped with *Raul*. By Sasha's estimation, close to eighteen hundred units had been secured and were either already deployed or designated for installation with more than half of the current installations having become operational over the past two years.

The last six months, however, had presented problems with the availability of additional units having become very limited and thus most of The Red Jewel's hotel rooms, hospitality suites and boardrooms escaped the modification process, but not all. Sasha was happy that he was able to allocate a hundred units for modification. By Sasha's estimation, approximately four hundred units were allocated to the three Holiday Jewel Hotels and the rest, already installed throughout the city.

Holiday Jewel Danamo had all its hospitality suites and two of the four boardrooms modified as well as one hundred of its guest suites. The remaining two hundred units still to come were slated for The Holiday Jewel Moskva, but that was still over a year from opening.

"The Red Jewel" Just thinking about the new hotel and it having the word "Red" as part of its name;

Bebchuk recalled the conversation he and Viktor had about the naming of Eldon Davis's new hotel in the center of Moscow.

Somehow it didn't sit right with Orlov to have the largest new hotel in Moscow carry the name "Red". It signified the past and contained a double meaning.

Eldon Davis had insisted upon it. Eldon explained to Orlov, Bebchuk and Marat, the Mayor of Moscow that the hotel's name "The Red Jewel" would be a perfect marketing tool that would bring in tremendous business and after all, it was located on Red Street, so what was the problem? Yes, "red" did have double connotations, but now it was a "jewel", and along with it "the red jewel of Moscow". Orlov finally agreed and bought into the concept, and The Red Jewel naming of the hotel was approved by the Moscow City Council.

Bebchuk had to agree with Davis; it was a good name; it was a great name, simple and very catchy. Bebchuk had respect for Eldon Davis, as did Viktor Orlov. They would watch Davis and his moves, they wanted him to succeed but on their terms, not Davis's terms.

Bebchuk took another drag on his Cheyenne. This audio and video surveillance accomplishment he thought would be the "jewel" in his crown.

Installation had gone well. *Raul* was being installed without any of the on-site construction crew or building inspectors knowing about it. RUL technology was already part of the newly arriving windows at the construction site. The shipment of windows coming from The Netherlands in the last three years had been making short pit stops at an FSB warehouse location just outside of Moscow at a Russian military optics factory where night vision and high-powered binoculars were still being made. Here, certain select designated window panes and television sets were fitted with the sensors. The process was the same for the windows destined for The Red Jewel construction site.

The great irony of it all was that the technology itself was not Russian, not Korean, not even Chinese but American and it was technology that was only available from a Pentagon vendor, a supplier of high-tech to the US Military and that company was Davis International, which also happened to have a wholly owned subsidiary by the name of Holiday Jewel Hotels and Casinos. This was the reason that the procurement had to be spread over a lengthy period, not to cause suspicion due to bulk ordering of sensitive and restricted technology. The ordering and procurement steps and procedures were also a very sensitive and tricky matter, one that had to have the highest of high approval and Bebchuk was being mum about that.

Bebchuk laughed to himself. "This was absolutely perfect!" Bebchuk thought, "even if the surveillance technology was to be discovered or uncovered or somehow tripped upon, how was Eldon Barnes Davis ever going to explain that it's his own product in his own hotels?"

Bebchuk figured it was genius. This was a perfect piece of Motherland security ingenuity; textbook

KGB-FSB. As to how it got into Russian hands and the further installation well, that secret was not to be touched. Not at this point. At this juncture, Bebchuk had not yet discussed or disclosed how he secured the procurement of the technology even to Viktor Orlov and Orlov wasn't interested anyway, so long as things were moving forward, he was happy.

Bebchuk's reasoning to keep The President out of the loop only added to The President's immunity in The FSB's information gathering and procurement methods. There was no reason for his close friend and The President of the Russian Federation to be mixed up in the finer details of FSB's tactics, especially since this information dated back several years to KGB assets still in play to this very day. Yes indeed, it was a smart play to remain mum about that."

Sasha Bebchuk had one person and one person alone to thank for this vital capability in securing the highly guarded and secretive surveillance technology and that person was his half-brother Alexander Mitkin. What made it even more interesting was the information provided by Mitkin, had nothing to do with the surveillance technology. Mitkin's guarded secret information that he passed on to his halfbrother only provided the avenue for securing the information but not the information itself. In other words, Mitkin provided the roadway and the means. As to what items or nature of things actually traveled on that roadway, well that was all up to Bebchuk.

Bebchuk called his assistant into his office. "Sergei, get in touch with Karmalov and have him come to my office in the next fifteen minutes."

"Yes comrade Bebchuk."

Bebchuk then began to admonish his assistant, with a stern voice but condescending, like he was reprimanding a child.

"Sergei, if you refer to me as "Comrade" one more time, I'm going to take you down to one of those cells in the basement and pull out your fingernails myself! The days of Comrade are over... get used to it and don't forget it!"

Sergei stood there in front of Bebchuk almost letting loose into his trousers, but Bebchuk started laughing as a joke. He understood that it was difficult to teach old dogs new tricks. Sergei had been with The KGB his entire career and at 55 years of age, he wasn't about to change.

"Now get out of my office and get Karmalov for me."

"Yes, Director Bebchuk" Sergei said, in an apologetic tone.

Bebchuk waved him out with a flick of his wrist.

Sasha stood up from his chair and walked over to his office window from where he could see clear down Lubyanka Square and out towards the center of Moscow. Towering over the city's central core was the new high rise hotel The Red Jewel. It stood 360 meters tall with 94 floors. At the top of the building, the electronic lettering marquee had already been installed. It would rotate electronically at the top of the building with a brilliant red ruby shaped jewel in the center of the circle on top of the lettering. It was truly an epic name. Bebchuk heard that on the day of opening the red ruby would come alive.

Although the hotel hadn't even opened, it was already the talk of the town by every Muscovite. Sasha thought to himself, "Eldon Davis and his wife Kimberley" they were the epitome of western capitalism. They had arrived in Moscow with force and their impact on the city was being noticed and most definitely felt. The coming year will be interesting, to say the least."

Bebchuk's intercom came to life, "Director Bebchuk, Officer Karmalov is here as you requested sir." Sergei announced.

Sasha was already standing looking at the city view outside his window, he called out, "come on in Vasily."

Vasily Karmalov was The FSB special agent whom Bebchuk had charged with the responsibility of heading up the audio-video surveillance installation process for all new hotels coming under construction in Moscow over the past thirty months.

"Black Bear" was a top-secret FSB operation. All personnel who worked on the installation of the technology including the workmen on the construction site were exclusively FSB agents. In most cases, not even The FSB agents on the construction site were aware of the nature of the project or that even a project was in progress. Bebchuk took the extra precaution of having his agents on the construction site as an added filter due to the sensitivity of the project. It was overkill, but better to overkill than be exposed.

All information was strictly on a need to know basis. The FSB employed thousands of Russians and foreigners in countries throughout the world, fully trained in many skills and vocations, from cooks and chefs to doctors, surgeons, school teachers, professors, sanitation workers, to millwrights, and rocket scientists. There was no area of expertise that The FSB was not involved in. This variety of expertise was not only utilized within the Russian Federation, but The KGB had for decades grown its tentacles reaching into all governments the world over including the USA, as did the CIA no doubt into the former USSR and now Russia. This was what spy agencies did. Their storefronts had always been and remained openly disguised as Embassies with Ambassadors who were in reality both spies and diplomats. The agents assigned to work at the Red Jewel construction site were not stupid and knew never to ask questions; they understood that it was a construction site having significant importance to the agency, but it was not unusual for agents to be left in the dark. Everyone reported to Vasily; he was a trained engineer and electronics expert, a lifelong career KGB and now FSB top special agent.

"Director Bebchuk, good day to you sir." Vasily and Sasha were on first name basis, but Vasily felt better addressing Sasha formally when at FSB headquarters. They had often shared a bottle of vodka between them in the past on a number of boar hunting trips. But at work, Vasily kept it formal. Sasha did not need to; he was The Director.

"Good to see you, Vasily, I don't need much of your time, my main interest is a quick review of how we are coming along with the hotels Vasily. Can you give me an update?" Sasha knew full well that Vasily was the most prepared agent in The FSB. If Vasily did not have the information that Sasha was looking for, there would be a monumentally good reason, and that had not ever happened in Vasily's past.

"Absolutely, Director Bebchuk." Vasily opened his briefcase and extracted a file folder, and was about to hand it over to Sasha.

"No, it's perfectly fine Vasily, just tell me verbally where we stand, I can remember, I have a memory like a computer, or should I say elephant?" Sasha, let out a small chuckle, just to put the air at ease with his colleague, employee, and friend.

Vasily appreciated the tension relief and replied, "thank you, Director."

"Go ahead just read it off for me," Sasha said.

With that, Vasily continued in. "Director Bebchuk, as of today, all joint venture properties have FSB operatives as their Directors of Engineering or as Directors of Security and in some cases, Russian Nationals as Human Resources Directors. Over the past two years, we have been successful in placing our agents into these high-level positions in all the joint venture western interest properties. As you know Director, one of the conditions of the joint venture agreement for all hotel building permit applications was to guarantee exclusively Russian construction crews and engineering. One of two key positions upon opening to be Russian Nationals if possible, being that of Security Director or Chief Engineer. We have been successful in that including the soon to open Red Jewel which has its Director of Security a Russian National; one of our agents."

He continued, "Director Bebchuk the modifications to the building materials with RUL technology has remained on schedule, but of course, we could not move faster than the materials windows being shipped by the manufacturer from The Netherlands and various other sources. Because of the sensitivity of this protected and restricted technology, the modification process at our topsecret facility has been a slow process, but we are on schedule."

Sasha interrupted Vasily. "Yes, yes, of course, remember the entire ordering process timetable had come directly from me, so no need to remind me of that, but I appreciate your thoroughness." Vasily was allowed to continue.

"Over the past two years Director, eight new hotels have opened for business in the city. The first property to open was just twenty-three months ago, being The Patriotic Hotel, a three hundred fortyseven room hotel out by the airport. It mainly attracts business people, and it gets heavy use by airline crews. It's classed as a full-service corporate hotel with two restaurants, but it has no convention facilities."

Director Bebchuk then interrupted Vasily again. "Vasily, just get to the point Vasily, tell me which properties are ready to go, I don't need a complete property description."

Vasily always provided more information than was necessary.

He continued on.

"Yes, Director, the following list of hotels are equipped, and most have been online for the better part of two years. As you know director, although the technology has been installed, the fiber optic connectors from the various properties to our central facility are constantly being upgraded as each new property comes online, that process requires temporary data collection interruptions from previously connected properties. In the last six months, we have actively brought another four properties online enabling city-wide coverage with the upcoming opening of The Red Jewel. The properties are, as I mentioned;

The Patriotic Hotel, one hundred ninety rooms, suites and boardroom combinations are currently being monitored daily with ongoing live data collection. The others are:

Universe Lodging Hotel, four hundred rooms – two hundred units live.

The Bestinn Hotel, five hundred rooms. - two hundred units live.

Sunwood Hotel, seven hundred rooms. - two hundred units live

Royal British House Hotel, six hundred eighty rooms.- two hundred units, live.

Holiday Jewel Danamo Hotel, seven hundred ninety rooms.- One hundred rooms live.

The Red Jewel, eight hundred ninety-nine rooms. - One hundred units to be brought online upon opening.

Whilton Manor Hotel, five hundred thirty rooms. - two hundred units live.

The Harriatt Hotel, seven hundred ten rooms. - two hundred units live."

Vasily finished reading off the list of hotels and status and added, "and the yet to be completed, third Holiday Jewel Hotel to be built in the city currently under construction Director, The Holiday Jewel Moskva Hotel and Casino. That property Director Bebchuk as you know stretches two hundred meters along the shores of the Moskva River situated directly across from the Kremlin. We will have two Holiday Jewel Hotels with The Red Jewel opening in a few weeks, looking down and across the river at the Kremlin Director.

The Holiday Jewel Moskva Hotel and Casino complex will have one thousand two hundred rooms, but not slated for completion for another year and a half Director. It will have two hundred units equipped upon opening and brought online. There are no other hotels planned at this time for the city." Vasily actually got through the list without too much elaboration.

"So, then Vasily… we have roughly five thousand rooms spread throughout the city of which almost eighteen hundred will be under our surveillance capabilities. You and your people have done an outstanding job on this project Vasily.

When I gave the orders to go live with each hotel being completed, I knew your progress had been on target. Soon, we will be city-wide with the completion of the remaining properties. Vasily, as I instructed I wanted all the information gathered to be dissected, analyzed and cleaned. That has been a twenty-four-seven year round operation in your newly created FSB Department, "The Department of Internal Foreign Data". That is where your line of responsibility ends Vasily. You and your teams gather the information, as to what we do with that gathered intelligence is none of your concern. Tell me Vasily, do you have adequate resources in terms of technical expertise on hand? Is there anything I can do for you?"

Bebchuk was now reaching out to Vasily, offering his genuine help and understanding in making things better for Vasily Karmalov's department. Vasily was pleased.

"Yes Director Bebchuk, we are good to go."

"Good Vasily, that will be all for now, but make sure your department has everything you need. The order to go live with Black Bear surveillance at The Red Jewel will be earlier than anticipated. My sources tell me that The Red Jewel's opening has been moved up to a much earlier date since construction and training of the opening staff has gone much better than expected. My "go live order" will come a day or two before the grand opening of
The Red Jewel."

Vasily was dismissed by Bebchuk and started making his way out of Director Bebchuk's office. Vasily was not one to ask questions of his superior. Questions were never welcome by The FSB Director, nor was it ever tolerated in the former KGB, it was looked upon as second guessing The Agency and The Director's reasoning and decisions.

The way things worked in The FSB; all scenarios were played out by "gaming and strategy teams of experts". After all conceivable consequences of potential actions had been considered with relative probability confidence level outcomes; those results were then presented to the Director for his final decision.

Once The FSB Director issued his orders and directives, no further discussion on the validity or soundness of the decision was to be made.

Vasily, however, couldn't help wondering how the information, the audio/video captured over the past thirty plus months could be used in this new spirit of cooperation between the new Russian Federation and the new corporations doing business in his growing city of Moscow. This to Vasily seemed to go against the grain of establishing this new-found trust between Russia and "the West."

This he could not figure out as of yet, but he was sure the reason would become clear soon enough. He thought to himself. "Director Bebchuk is smart and cunning, no wonder President Orlov appointed Sasha Bebchuk to head up The FSB."

The bottom line in justification of it all in Vasily's mind was the simple fact that this was the Russian

Intelligence Service, The FSB, and that is what they did, were in fact mandated as an organization, to spy, locally, domestically and internationally.

Vasily was not in any way shape or form an "original thinker". He was the product of a culture that usually picked and selected your path in life, where during all of your Soviet career development you were at all times "told what to do" and when to do it. You as a citizen worked for the State and your contribution to the overall effort as defined by the powers that be and the powers that were, resulted in your loyalty and dedication in being that one cog in the giant wheel turning the economy. People such as Sasha Bebchuk, well they were the wheel designers and people such as Vasily were the lubricants that kept the wheel turning without loud squeaking.

Bebchuk sat back thinking about how events had unfolded in securing the surveillance hardware and software. He was certain that once he had obtained a few units that his FSB I.T. Department, would have no trouble reverse engineering the software and reproduce as many units as he needed, which would potentially number into the thousands to equip every room in every new hotel that had been built in the city over the past three or so years. Much to Sasha's disappointment the software was so tightly written and programmed that it was virtually impossible to break into the code.

Turns out that each line of code written was itself encrypted, and each segment of each line of code was also encrypted, so not only the source code was encrypted but each segment of each line. Breaking the code was in fact almost impossible.

The CIA had done its job well. It would take several weeks for their FSB supercomputers to possibly break one segment of encryption, and there were literally thousands of segments of encryption. Eldon Davis's R&D Pentagon Vendor was state of the art to be sure, but Sasha was not giving up, he had his top code breakers working around the clock and there was word lately that a breakthrough may be in sight. Once that happened, the technology could be replicated, and he'd be off to the races.

***

Chapter Six
Service with a smile

Eldon, Felix, and Billy had just completed their customs process. The three of them had experienced no complications coming through Sheremetyevo Airport, they had all been through at least a dozen times over the past two and half years, they knew the drill and always made certain to have proper documents in hand. All three additionally had priority Russian Business Visa Documents which sped up their entry process. The only luggage they had with them was carry-on. Billy, Felix, and Eldon had everything they needed at the Holiday Jewel Danamo Hotel, where they lived while in Moscow.

Kimberley always had a driver who doubled as a bodyguard any time she needed to venture out of the Hotel after 5:00 PM. Tonight her car was being driven by Oli Andropov, her trusted bodyguard and most careful driver she could ever ask to have. Driving in Moscow could be somewhat of a harrowing experience even in the daytime and driving at night, well anything was possible. Oli Andropov knew how to handle local police and local thugs. He was ex-Russian Military and took no guff from anyone. Tonight, Oli Andropov had a wing man, the car behind following Kimberley was his partner, Yuri, who was to pick Billy and Felix up at the airport and drive them back to the hotel.

Eldon had already called Kimberley prior to landing. Kimberley was waiting for Eldon at arrivals,

Oli and Yuri had the vehicles waiting along curbside at arrivals and would be wasting no time.

Eldon, Billy, and Felix, they all walked out through the sliding doors from Russian Customs Clearance together into the terminal's arrivals hall. Kimberley spotted the three of them right away. She could hardly wait to put her arms around her husband. Eldon reached out to Billy handing him his briefcase, as Kimberley ran into his arms, he held her kissing her.

"Oh, I'm so glad you're here baby." She then went over to hug Felix and Billy. Eldon's team, the four of them, were together again.

"Oli and Yuri are just outside, waiting for us," Kimberley said.

"Eldon, we'll see you and Kimberley back at the hotel," Felix said. The four of them then walked out to the curb, got into their cars and drove off back to Holiday Jewel Danamo.

"Eldon, you can tell me all about it when we get home. I know you must have had one hell of a day.

"It's like the Wild West here Kimberley; let's hope the new Sheriff in town has made the right moves." Eldon held Kimberley as she snuggled up into his arm in the back seat of her Beemer. They drove along the main thoroughfare; traffic had started to thin out, it was now 10:33 PM. Up ahead there was an extra brightly lit area of the road. As their car approached closer, it became apparent that the light shining onto the road was a reflection coming off a huge building. The closer they drove, it now became visible and obvious what was going on. There was a bank of floodlights; high powered floodlights that lit up Parliamentary Building Number 2.

"Look at that babe," Eldon said to Kimberley. "Look how smart Orlov is, he is a master at telling the world that the old boys are out, and he is in. To light up the building like this is brilliant!"

The floodlights were in the colors of the new Russian Flag. There was a row of super intense white light along the top of the building spanning its complete width. Underneath the second row was bright navy blue and the bottom row brilliant red. The holes blown into the building were visible to the whole world. The street in front of the Parliamentary building was filled with television remote news crew trucks. Video crews and reporters were conducting interviews and commentary. Orlov had pulled off the biggest PR move of his political career. The building lit up with the Russian Flag said it all. "Don't mess with Viktor Orlov; the old days are gone forever!"

Eldon then said to Kimberley. "That is a brilliant PR move by Orlov, just brilliant, now let's see how the events of today impact our meeting with the officials tomorrow."

"Far as I can tell babe, that meeting is still a go," Kimberley responded, still snuggled into Eldon's side.

"Good, that meeting isn't till later on in the afternoon, right?"

"That's right, not till I believe 3:00 PM but I told Ambassador Albert I will reconfirm with him in the morning to make sure it's still on," Kimberley said.

"Okay, well that still leaves most of the day before our meeting with the city; I want to get a few of us together in the morning. Louis, The GMs for both The Red Jewel and The Danamo and I want the company HR Director Irina Sopov and Regional Director of Finance Jennifer Paige, you know what let's get as many of the executives together we can, including the new director of sales and marketing, security as well, everyone we can get. I believe it will be in our best interest to speak to as many as we can right away in addressing what has just happened."

"I totally agree Eldon; it will be vital for them to know that we are in tune with ongoing events. In addition, they will appreciate our concern, it will strengthen their loyalty Eldon, it's the right thing to do. It is a new world out there Eldon, and we're going to play a major part in shaping it." Kimberley let out a big sigh.

"I'm so glad you're here Eldon. I spoke to Cathy earlier on this afternoon when I got back from Spaso House. I needed to hear her voice. She sounded just wonderful; she's taking part in her school play. Eldon, she sounded so excited, can you believe it, she's going to play the part of the Evil Queen in Snow White! They will practice for six weeks, and the play will be a Thanksgiving event."

"She's playing the Evil Queen? Well, that's different, but I'm glad she's all excited. I think we can probably work around that and be there for it." "Oh yes babe, we can't miss that one. Mom and Dad are good too Eldon, I had to call to put them at ease, I'm sure they heard all about what happened here today. You know how Dad is always glued to VNN and all the 24-hour news channels. They are good babe, they are good. I told them you were flying in today, so that calmed them both down, they send their love baby."

"Come here." Eldon pulled Kimberley in closer. "I love you Kimberley," Eldon whispered into her ear, wrapping his arm around her shoulders.

Oli drove the Beemer up to the valet parking attendant at the Holiday Jewel Danamo Hotel. As the valet attendant was opening the door Eldon said, "Thanks, Oli, we'll probably see you tomorrow, have a good night."

"Thank you, Mr. Davis, good night Mrs. Davis." Billy and Felix pulled up right behind them. The four of them were greeted by the doorman, finally some "service with a smile", after all, that had happened today, it was good to be back at the hotel. Saying good night, Felix and Billy went off to their suites located in the west wing of the hotel. Eldon and Kimberley walked arm in arm through the marble lobby, nodding to the smartly dressed desk clerks on duty. "Good evening Mr. and Mrs. Davis, nice to see you back."

It wasn't that late yet, just after 11:00 PM, the lobby bar was quite busy, and the concierge was attending to some hotel guests' needs. It was a welcome greeting from Eldon's hotel employees, looked to him like the service training was coming along just fine.

Everyone who worked at the Holiday Jewel Danamo knew very well who Eldon was. Eldon could not help himself, with the events earlier on today, Eldon walked up to the front desk and told one of the front desk clerks to make sure she spread the word around with the staff that Eldon would be addressing the staff tomorrow concerning events of today. He needed to get the juices flowing. Having lit the fuse, Eldon said goodnight to the front desk clerk. He and Kimberley walked into the east wing elevator and up to their private key access only section of the hotel. Eldon and Kimberley were finally home together in Moscow.

***

Chapter Seven
Room Service

The eight newly opened hotels in Moscow over the past two years all shared one thing in common; they were all joint venture business arrangements. In order for a non-Russian company, individual or corporation to conduct business in Russia, it would have to be done with a Russian partner. That was the basic requirement. As to how the financing arrangements were put together in the fine details of the joint venture agreement, well, that part was open to negotiation, so long as the business agreement was a joint venture, not too much else mattered as to the covenants of the joint venture agreement.

Almost all the non-Russian partners were initially involved on a management contract fee basis, meaning that the Western interest had no ownership of the building or land, and only provided management expertise and therefore ran hotel operations, hired employees, paid the employees, and provided all the necessities to generate a profit. To acquire the joint venture, the western partner contributed a substantial capital investment into construction of the hotel that was to be paid back to the Western partner with interest over a specified number of years on top of the management contract fee. These joint venture agreements also contained some sort of a "buyout clause" whereby either party after a number of years, once having satisfied the joint venture sunset period, reserved the legal right to buy the other partner out, and take over complete ownership of the building, sometimes including the land. However, at this stage of the game, no one was quite sure as to whom and how the land ownership would transfer to, be they corporations or individuals since all the land in Russia had been owned by the State until just three years ago.

Real estate and ownership of real estate, land in particular was still to be decided on as to how that would come about and of course appropriate laws still needed to be written and passed by the legislative body, and then enforced through the legal system and lawyers which at this point were still very scarce or non-existent. This problem not only affected existing businesses and new ventures coming on board, but it was a huge problem among the general population as well. Almost all Russians, Muscovites, in this case, lived in apartment buildings within the city and had always paid a minuscule amount in monthly rent to the government agency running and managing their particular building, but no Russian citizen actually held a deed to their domicile or residence, they only ever had a "permit to reside" but never ownership. How was the average citizen to acquire ownership of their residence when in theory the State owned everything but the next day nothing? So, this was still being worked out throughout the entire country and it was a mess. It was one thing to say it was a mess for the average citizen, but it was a colossal nightmare for large corporations or for that matter every new joint venture start-up business, especially in the first year or two after the collapse of the former Soviet Union.

A very simplified scenario to highlight the problem and difficulties would have a situation whereby a disagreement would come about between the partners in a new business, for example, a newly opened bakery, the Western partner might have invested a million dollars to launch the new enterprise but then for some reason, the Russian partner becomes dissatisfied with the operation and decides to rip up the contract, locks the Western partner out and refuses further contact or settlement. The western partner has now lost his investment and has no recourse to sue the Russian partner since there is no current avenue to pursue resolution through the court system regarding joint venture and contract law. This scenario of course could also be a problem equally for the Russian side of the joint venture. With such a vacuum in legalities throughout the business community, a ripe opportunity presented itself to the criminal element that was quickly being filled by organized crime. Simply put, what the government's legal system could not address sufficiently the newly emerging and fast growing Russian Mafia could without any difficulty address most efficiently because they had no problem killing you if you wouldn't comply with their demands. That may have sounded a bit drastic but in fact, that sadly was the case. Up until about a year and a half ago, the new hotels that had opened were largely spared from Mafia intrusion. With the dozen plus trips that Eldon had made to Moscow and the countless meetings with regional city government officials, it was becoming clear that progress in enacting the new laws and regulations required in dealing with contract and real estate covenants was a very slow process. In addition, street-crime was becoming a huge problem throughout Moscow with sudden shakedowns occurring daily on the streets, and highways, not only by thugs and organized crime but sadly becoming routine practice by underpaid police officers.

A very common and dirty trick was for a street policeman on foot, to wave down a late model Mercedes, BMW, Porsche or Cadillac after sundown, and claim that the front headlight was broken. When the officer was challenged by the driver, that there was nothing wrong with the front headlight, the officer would take his baton and smash it, saying "It most definitely is broken, and your vehicle is deemed unfit for the road." At that point, the vehicle would either be towed to a holding compound, and good luck getting it out or you could settle with the officer there and then for a few hundred dollars.

One obvious and in your face change Eldon, Kimberley, Louis James, and his other hotel executives had to undertake was that of personal protection in the form of hired bodyguards. This was a troublesome new element but an unfortunate daily requirement for all western business people to be holding any sort of perceived power or wealth. Eldon and Kimberley had begun bodyguard protection services over a year ago and luckily no incidents yet other than the headlight trick one time with Eldon and his bodyguard driver. Eldon's driver Maxim was former Russian Military and later, former KGB. His driver now earned ten times as much working for Eldon than he ever earned with The KGB and was very happy to look after Eldon's safety. When confronted by the corrupt police officer that evening, he knew what the game was, and what to expect. Eldon remembered very clearly, after being pulled over, Maxim jumped out of the vehicle and immediately started scolding and screaming at the officer, taking out his now expired KGB badge but nevertheless putting the fear of God into the officer. Maxim got back into the car, and they drove off leaving the officer behind on the side of the road thinking how lucky he was that Maxim didn't lay a beating on him right there and then. The old ways of the Soviet Union and KGB agents still had powerful effects on citizens of Russia, be they police officers or not.

Just because the Soviet Union was no more that did not mean people who once were in power had lost it all. No as a matter of fact, the upper class of Russian society within totalitarianism was mainly made up of hard-liner communists who over the years became rich in their own rights with their private summer dachas in the countryside, annual trips to Sochi on the Black Sea, and extravagant dinners and hunting parties held at upper class country clubs, not open to just any commoner. One such Russian Citizen formerly in high places was ex- KGB Assistant Director Alexander Mitkin. Mitkin served in The KGB and was a protégé of the former Director of The KGB who was forcibly retired from serving with Viktor Orlov having become President and Orlov subsequently naming the successor to be Sasha Bebchuk heading up the national spy organization. Orlov believed that replacing the former Director of The KGB with Sasha Bebchuk, a lot of KGB history and questionable deeds would be retired along with the former Director. That, in fact, was the case; deeds were retired, but history could not ever be. Some of that history Sasha had learned from his half-brother Alexander. Alexander had given this tightly held knowledge to Sasha as a gift, hoping that Sasha would remember him when the time came to perhaps call in a favor, if there ever was a need.

History could only be changed erroneously or revised for nefarious reasons, and sometimes truth itself could bring about greater harm with KGB seeds having been planted years ago, now watered and nourished to bring forth desired results. Those seeds of the past were planted by Alexander Mitkin and Mitkin now divulged the location of those seeds to his half-brother Sasha who was already doing some very serious gardening. Those KGB seeds he planted long ago were now being watered by his half-brother Sasha Bebchuk, giving him the roots to grow even stronger as The FSB strengthened daily. Alexander handed this information over to his halfbrother Sasha Bebchuk in good faith.

When Alexander Mitkin was born, he was his mother's second child. His father; Boris was his mother's second husband after having divorced her first husband Vladimir Bebchuk who had abandoned his mother and half-brother Sasha just five years after their marriage.

Alexander was born two years after his mother remarried to his father, Boris Mitkin. Sasha Bebchuk and Alexander Mitkin grew up as half-brothers under his mother's roof. As the years passed, Sasha developed a military career and Alexander found himself a career as an officer of The KGB where Alexander excelled to that of Assistant Director but decided to step down from The KGB when Orlov named his half-brother Sasha to the Director position of The FSB.

Alexander was rewarded handsomely with a KGB government pension even at his young age of 53 by Orlov for his service, and all concerned believed it was in everyone's best interest to leave nepotism out of the newly created FSB leadership. Alexander decided to become a business man and recruited some of his most dedicated former KGB agents to work alongside with him in his newly formed business enterprise, better known in common circles as The Russian Mafia. He was counting on his half-brother Sasha not to be asking too many questions about his new business dealings, perhaps an understanding of sorts, a show of appreciation between brothers for the information now in Sasha's possession.

Alexander was looking to operate his new growing empire without interference from anyone, and that included his half-brother, head of The FSB. Every good criminal organization of any worth needs a good racket to focus on. Racketeering was the specialty of Mitkin's crime organization. The Russian Mafia's expertise was in the arena of prostitution, and it was in a very big way.

Mitkin's organization had grown to cover most of western Russia and reached far into Eastern Europe from where Mitkin's thugs and operatives would have easy pickings in the recruitment of young underage girls. The carrot dangled in front of young girls' eyes from impoverished towns and villages, would be the excitement of careers in the hospitality business as waitresses and hostesses in high class restaurants, bars, night clubs and discotheques where they could earn enough money to live comfortably and still help out their families they were leaving behind. The excitement and adventure to live in Moscow, St. Petersburg or Krakow was an irresistible lure to young country girls who had no real future to speak of. Once recruited, these girls were at Mitkin's mercy. The women would become virtual slaves for Mitkin and his organization to do with as he pleased. They were trapped. Any resistance to the Mafia's demand would be met by threats to harm the families the girls had left behind. Failure to comply with Mafia demands and resisting being placed into escort and prostitution service would result in harm coming to family members they left behind; young brothers, sisters, mothers and fathers possibly tortured or even killed. These women and young girls had no choice but to succumb and do what they were told.

This was the nature of modern sex slavery. Mitkin and his organization were experts at this having refined the process to an art. That was one side of the operation; Mitkin called it his "product," young underage girls forced into prostitution.

Mitkin understood that all good products needed a very high-class store in which to sell those specialty products. Mitkin had plenty of stores in several countries with large cities where his products were currently available but he was looking to upgrade and upscale his storefronts, and he had focused on the upgrades back home in Moscow. On the surface, Mitkin's official legitimate growing business name was the well-established, "Tsar Restaurants and Entertainment Company." The business consisted mainly of strip clubs, night clubs and discotheques. All his clubs promoted and thrived on prostitution of young girls he had working in his clubs. The women were allowed to keep just enough money to pay for their Mafia provided for lodging and their food and beverages along with some purchase of clothing and toiletries. Mitkin and his organization had pulled in enough hard currency over the past couple of years for him to open three very upscale and legitimate restaurants in Moscow, that employed no sex slaves or escorts and as a matter of fact were among some of the finest restaurants in the city. Mitkin had planned well. Tsar Restaurant's and Entertainment was making inroads of notoriety in the Moscow restaurant business and had gained the attention of the new hotel operators in the city, including the executive management of the Holiday Jewel Danamo and the new to open Red
Jewel.

Mitkin was in. His food and beverage business Tsar Restaurants and Entertainment had been successful in bidding on the tender for the restaurant and lounge lease operation inside The Holiday Jewel Danamo Hotel. This was the first western style luxury upscale hotel where his Mafia supported business enterprise had grown a foothold and what a hold it was! Mitkin's ultimate goal was to be leaseholder of the food and beverage operations in The Red Jewel and new upcoming Holiday Jewel Moskva Hotel and Casino but for now, he was very happy with the progress so far at The Holiday Jewel Danamo. His intention was to infiltrate these three hotels to their cores.

Mitkin had already placed his henchmen and Mafia operators into several other new hotels but not to this degree. The other properties only involved bought off security guards, who could easily be fired by the General Managers of the various properties, but with Holiday Jewel Hotels, Mitkin's aim was much more accurate and penetrating. Business was going well, he had already moved some of his girls into the operation, here at The Jewel Danamo, as he had throughout the city with Danamo's competitors, but with those other properties, he was strictly "an outside" operator. Here at Holiday Jewel Danamo, it was slowly at first. His girls were legitimately employed by his restaurant in the hotel, actually working in the positions they were promised when they were first recruited from rural areas of the former Eastern European block. They served tables and attended to 24-hour rooms service orders from the hotel rooms. Mitkin also managed the hotel lounge The Gorky Club, where his girls were dressed scantily but within the guidelines of the lease dress code clause, just barely.

The Gorky Club as it was known was very popular in the city with all business men; it was becoming a very popular place to meet and have some drinks and the women cocktail servers were most pleasing to the male eye. His business was picking up, and it was now time to act. His methodology: hook The Hotel General Manager first. Money could corrupt easily, and temptation was easily bought in Moscow. It was not The General Manager Marty Sabine he targeted with bribery but the hotel's Director of Security. He could be bought no problem. It may cost a few thousand dollars, but it was a drop in the bucket for the potential rewards. Mitkin's operatives had approached Misha Rudkin; The Security Director of Holiday Jewel Danamo with a bribe some months back. He was offered seven thousand dollars to look the other way for Mitkin's infiltration needs for the foreseeable future. From that afternoon on, when Rudkin took the cash, Mitkin's men had free rein to the hotel with Rudkin supplying "stand guard" service as the mafia thugs began their bugging process of The Holiday Jewel Danamo with Marty Sabine's private suite being the first on the list. Ironic as it was, Mitkin had no idea nor was he remotely aware of the clandestine bugging operation that his half-brother Bebchuk had already installed. This bugging being done by Mitkin was all on his own and totally separate, but unknowingly redundant.

What Mitkin had his men install into Marty's suite was video surveillance along with audio, but it was crude and easily detectable with even off the shelf probing devices.

Mitkin had done his homework. Before bidding on the food and beverage lease opportunity at Holiday Jewel Danamo, he had to make sure that the right General Manager was in place. There were two other properties in the city whose food and beverage operations were put out for tender, but it was only this hotel who had the right General Manager. It was Marty Sabine, a relatively young General Manager, just thirty-nine, he spoke Russian, but was an American. Holiday Jewel Hotels and Casinos had placed their trust into Marty Sabine to run the hotel with integrity and maintain the highest standards. Holiday Jewel Hotels and Casinos had become the force that it was in the hospitality business through a reputation second to none.

All General Managers who were fortunate enough to work for the company were among the industry's finest. Eldon's company adhered to a code of ethics that spanned borders no matter which country his operations were located. Employees working under the Holiday Jewel Hotel banner were known to deliver the highest service standards and utmost respect for the guests they served. "Compromise," was not a word in Eldon Barnes Davis's vocabulary when it came to delivering "service beyond expectations." The culture that followed emanated from Eldon's direction and company mission statement that all employees carried with themselves while on duty, etched into their name tags, and further championed by the property's General Manager on a daily basis.

"Service with Integrity" was the motto and cornerstone of Holiday Jewel Hotels and Casinos. Eldon believed that Marty Sabine was such a General Manager and thus agreed in offering Marty the Hotel General Manager position after being recommended by Louis James himself; Eldon's
Senior Vice President of International Operations.

Louis was certain Marty would do a great job. He was single and had been in Moscow now for almost six months having taken over completely from the opening General Manager. Alexander Mitkin was also sure he knew how to press just the right buttons at just the right time. After Marty Sabine's fourth month of nonstop work with only three days off, Mitkin figured Marty was about ready.

After four months of steady work, Marty Sabine would have more on his mind in Moscow than just running the hotel. Mitkin had found his target, Sabine and his situation was perfect, just exactly what he was looking for. Single young red blooded virile American, who for the past four months had been totally consumed by work. Mitkin was certain it was about time this young General Manager had some R&R.

The deed had been done; Rudkin had compromised the security integrity at Holiday Jewel Danamo, and Mitkin was in. He was not only in as the masked legitimate food and beverage operator of the hotel, but now he successfully penetrated the hotel security and gained direct access to the General Manager's residence. He was now set to start the games. Mitkin well knew that any betrayal by the General Manager of Holiday Jewel Hotels management philosophy, guidelines and integrity would result in immediate dismissal making that person's further career opportunities extremely difficult. The only option open to such an individual would be to come clean of any company betrayals and let the chips fall where they may or resign before word got out. Mitkin had a plan for that as well.

Two months before Viktor Orlov asked his Army General to blast away at Parliamentary Building Number 2 with Tanks, Alexander Mitkin put his trap into play with Eldon's Holiday Jewel Danamo Hotel General Manager Marty Sabine.

Marty was someone who enjoyed and took advantage of the hotel's room service. He found it relaxing not having to cook and being single it was easy to just pick up the phone, call room service and have his roast duck a la orange, brought up to his suite. It happened to be a weekend night, Saturday night just after 9:00 PM. Everything in the hotel was running smoothly and his night duty manager was usually left in charge to take care of matters. Saturday nights Marty tried relaxing and looked forward to taking every second Sunday off. Mitkin had ordered his people in the restaurant to be cognizant and to keep track of Marty's work routine. This had resulted in revealing to Mitkin, that Marty took every second Sunday off from work and did not show up at all until the following Monday morning. His duty managers would handle all hotel management issues in the meantime.

Marty picked up his telephone to place his room service order; his order would take approximately half an hour before it was delivered. Having placed his food order, he walked over to his upright refrigerator open it up and took out a bottle of ice cold Carlsberg beer. He twisted off the top and settled in loosening his tie, unbuttoned the top two buttons of his shirt, sat back on his living room couch, reached for the remote control and turned on the TV to kill some time waiting for the knock on his door from the room service waiter. He relaxed, savored the taste of the Carlsberg and started unwinding from his busy day. He felt good, wasn't tired at all… but glad the weekend was here.

Alexander Mitkin made certain that he would be in the hotel tonight with it being Saturday and this was the weekend that Marty was to be taking Sunday off from work. It was Marty's weekend to relax. Mitkin was going to help Marty with that.

Mitkin had arranged a few days ago to have his top two working gals available to deliver Marty's room service dinner order. Mitkin himself had instructed his top two money makers how to play this out and exactly what to say, and what to do and not to deviate from his instructions no matter what, and he would know because everything would be captured on video.

His top two gals were Anna and Ludmilla; they were his top two earners and they always worked together.

Anna and Ludmilla were identical twins. It was virtually impossible to tell them apart; the only visible difference was that Anna had a slight scar on the inside of her lower arm because of a childhood tricycle accident. It wasn't noticeable at all unless she actually showed it to you. Both Anna and Ludmilla were Russian but spoke broken English which made them both sound very sexy when attempting to speak English with their heavy Russian accents.

Both girls stood just over five feet eight inches tall, golden blonde hair identically styled, both wearing heels, and dressed in sexy cocktail lounge scanty uniforms. If one weren't careful, one would think they might be seeing double. The two women were absolutely gorgeous and looked like they were built for one thing only, and that was sex.

Marty's meal was prepared by the chefs working in the Tsar Restaurant's kitchen as normal, properly placed onto the white linen tablecloth covered room service table with a small narrow vase for a couple of longs stem flowers as to add a touch of class in the delivery presentation.

The Holiday Jewel Danamo did things up right in everything and anything that had to do with guest service. Tonight, this particular room service order came with a little something extra that wasn't yet on the menu, but if Mitkin had his way it would become a regular room service specialty item. When the room service table was fully prepared and ready to go,

Mitkin himself showed up in the room service delivery prep area and advised the staff that he personally would make the delivery to Mr. Sabine's suite. The table was ready to be rolled out of the kitchen and into the service elevator.

Mitkin wheeled Marty's room service table out. He had arranged for Anna and Ludmilla to meet him on Marty's floor and wait for him. The two girls did as they were told, they were there outside the elevator on Marty's floor waiting for Mitkin. Anna and Ludmilla, dressed in hotel lounge uniforms with name tags, looked like regular hotel employees.

The girls took over the table from Mitkin and were ready to deliver it to Marty.

Mitkin handed over the room service table to the Anna and Ludmilla, saying, "now don't you two bitches fuck up... do exactly as I said.

"*Vee understend,*" *Meester Mitkin, vee do goud jaub,*" Ann and Ludmilla said in unison.

"You bitches will be on video all the time; I will know."

The two girls wheeled the room service table to Marty's suite and knocked on his door.

The room service knock came, lightly at first. Marty could hardly make it out, then another very light knock. Marty got up off his couch and went to open his suite door. Upon opening the door, the girls immediately started wheeling the table inside his suite and having come fully through the door; Ludmilla closed it tight. He was surprised to see two waitresses

91

with his room service table and then realized suddenly that the two of them were twins!

"*Goud evening Mr. Sabine,*" Anna said smiling at Marty, "*dis iz my seester Ludmilla, she iz learning to be room service.*" Anna continued in broken English.

Marty's eyes were almost popping out of his head. Normally his room service order would be delivered by one of the gentlemen room service waiters. This was something new.

"Okay, nice to meet you two lovely ladies, can I have the check please I need to sign it" Ludmilla then spoke up, Marty turned to look at her. "She ran her tongue along the outside of her lips saying in a sexy voice, with the look of a vixen on her face. "*No check to zign today Meester Sabine, evreyting free,*" Ludmilla said with her Russian accent.

Marty found that to be just so damn sexy... damn! Just as she was saying that Ludmilla moved up to Marty pressing her body into his, reached down grabbing onto Marty's hand and pressing his hand in between her legs, letting out a moan that took Marty by such surprise he didn't know what to do. He was looking at Ludmilla when suddenly he realized that Anna had taken off her top, and she was pressing her breasts together and rubbing herself.

"*Meester Sabine, vee like you very mauch,*" Anna said, slipping off her lower section and standing there in front of Marty now naked except for her high heels. "*Meester Sabine, my seester Anna and me vee make sex you...yes, like?*" Ludmilla reached out again placing her hand onto Marty's crotch then kneeling down while reaching for his zipper.

Marty was taken aback so suddenly he was already in too deep, within two minutes of opening the door. Anna was already kissing him, his immediate reaction was to push Anna away, but her moist kisses and lips were just too much to resist, plus she was naked standing there kissing him, he pretty much just melted, while he found himself getting an immediate erection as Ludmilla was already performing fellatio on Marty. He was ambushed, but Marty wasn't resisting much.

Four months of straight work and no female companionship had worn his resistance down completely. He was overcome by these two expert women within two minutes. Anna started unbuttoning the rest of Marty's shirt, while Ludmilla already had Marty stepping out of his trousers, and within three minutes all three of them were stark naked. Anna grabbed Marty by the hand and brought him over to the couch, where she laid back spreading her legs, and Ludmilla said to Marty; "yes *Meester Sabine, you like...you fauk my seester... I like vaatch, den you fauk me okay, den you fauk Anna den you fauk me, goud Meester Sabine?*"

Marty thought to himself "I've just stepped into heaven and hell at the same time, too late now, may as well enjoy myself." Marty just melted hearing Ludmilla's Russian accent, saying "*fauk.*"

He was in, up to his neck! Marty woke up later the following morning at 3:16 AM. He was now in his bed. Ludmilla and Anna were still there with him snuggled up beside him.

"Girls, girls, you have to leave; you cannot stay here" Marty started saying.

Anna stirred and woke up...started kissing him all over again, Ludmilla was awakened as well, she moved on top of him and felt him, spreading her legs straddling Marty and taking Marty inside. Anna kissed him even deeper...Marty was not a fighter.

The General Manager's Saturday night room service dinners were delivered from that point on with the added menu items he had just experienced. Marty Sabine had become a Hotel General Manager with a new bounce in his step, who was now deeply inside the pocket of The Russian Mafia.

One problem, though, he was working for Eldon Davis. Holiday Jewel Hotels and Casinos was not for ever having to put up with organized crime.

**

Chapter Eight
King Eldon's roundish table

Louis James, Eldon's Senior Vice President of Holiday Jewel International Hotel Operations, was already on the case this morning. It was only 6:30 AM and Louis was busy determining what would be needed in coordinating the upcoming day's activities. Having received Eldon's midnight call just after Eldon and Kimberley arrived at the hotel, Louis was well aware that this would be a monumental day in the history of Holiday Jewel Hotels here in Moscow. After having talked to Eldon, Louis immediately called Marty Sabine and brought Marty up to speed in having him round up the usual suspects, meaning the "hotel's executive committee" for first thing in the morning meeting. Louis stressed to Marty that it was imperative that all executive committee members must attend, there were to be absentees from this morning's boardroom table meeting in the executive conference room.

"Marty, Louis here. Listen, Eldon and Kimberley just got in a few minutes ago, as you know Eldon flew in from the US. Kimberley has had one hell of an exciting day at the US Ambassador's residence earlier on; I'm sure you'll be updated about that, but Eldon is very concerned about events that took place here in Moscow earlier on. He wants an emergency exec-com meeting at 9:00 AM sharp. I want you to contact all committee members now, and make sure everyone is here. Yes, I know it's past midnight, but that will make it even more obvious for their absolute attendance." Louis said most emphatically.

"All right Louis, I am on it, should be one interesting day tomorrow." Marty responded.

Marty was up and about the hotel when Louis had called. Marty's favorite time in the hotel was between 8:00 PM and 2:00 AM, this was the time period when "things happened". All day long, hotel guests were checking out and checking in. The bell staff and concierge were looking after guests' luggage, making sure all bags got to the correct rooms, and the concierge was busy booking theater reservations to the Bolshoi Ballet and Moscow Symphony, along with arranging city tours. Rooms were being cleaned by the housekeeping department, and hotel maintenance was going on where needed. Meetings were being held, conferences were ongoing in most if not all the "breakout rooms", rooms reservations were busy with the sales and marketing department bringing in the business and the finance/accounting departments were busily consumed in looking after the assets of the hotel in terms of collections and payments; collecting on bills owed and paying vendors for services rendered and payroll department keeping track of employee hours and pay. Of course, the kitchen was busy all day long in prepping for meals to be served at breakfast lunch and dinner in the hotel's restaurants and bars, the hotel was ticking along like a Rolex. All very fine and good, but for Marty, it was after 8:00 PM that the hotel really came alive!

This was the period when the fine dining rooms and cocktail lounge was busy. Marty thrived on visiting the food and beverage outlets, interacting with hotel guests, asking if everything during their stay was in order or to find out how he could make their stay more enjoyable. This was time of day when Marty could have a complimentary bottle of wine sent to a couple's table who had been in the hotel for a few days; it was a way of thanking them for their loyalty, and it was fabulous public relations. Marty would do the same for several guests who frequented the cocktail lounge, complimentary drinks now and then from the GM would be remembered for many days and always bring the guests back to the hotel.

For Marty, the satisfaction of his guests at all times was paramount and after several years in the hotel business, he learned that all guests no matter who they were, loved being acknowledged by the hotel's General Manager. It was akin to being acknowledged and having their best interest at heart by the captain of a cruise ship. Marty knew well that any guest who was taken care of personally by the General Manager of the hotel would feel special and always without fail was sure to speak highly of the establishment and level of attention they experienced. This went a long, long way in developing good will and Marty understood that unsolicited word of mouth advertising was something no amount of money could buy.

Marty Sabine wasn't all about just the guests either; he felt equally responsible for making his employees feel like they were appreciated, valued and vital to the operation no matter what position they held or job they performed. Marty made a point to know each and every one of the five hundred and three employees by name.

One trick Marty had up his sleeve was to actually address an employee by name when the employee had his back turned to Marty. Marty might be approaching the employee from behind, walking down the corridor or stairs, and Marty would call out the employee's name saying hello even before the employee had a chance to turn around. This never failed to impress any employee, most definitely impressed the employee that Marty wasn't reading his or her name off their name tags. Marty was respected by all the Russian and expatriate employees of The Holiday Jewel Danamo Hotel.

Marty Sabine was a great Hotel General Manager, but Marty had a weakness now that he was trying to keep under wraps. Marty had fallen. He failed to uphold the honor and integrity entrusted in him by Eldon, Kimberley and Louis. Holiday Jewel Hotels' operating principles and "The Brand" could not ever be compromised. Marty knew that, but Marty also needed a job. To lose this job for having gotten the hotel involved into such deplorable activity was not going to bode well in any potential future opportunity should he need to seek other employment. Marty was doing his best to burn both ends of the candle while not getting burned himself. This task was going to be very difficult in the coming weeks and months. So far, he'd survived, but things were about to heat up, and it would start with this morning's executive committee meeting chaired by none other than Eldon himself.

Marty wasn't feeling so confident about things any more this morning; he had only managed six hours of sleep, and was feeling his betrayal starting to take an effect on his mental stability. He did his best to put it aside as he was shaving but still managed to nick himself and the seeping blood on his lower chin wasn't stopping. He felt it an ominous foreboding of things to come. Marty fumbled around his medicine cabinet for a styptic, finally found it and applied it to his cut. Marty thought to himself; "this morning's routine wasn't going well so far, he needed to get his act together."

The exec meeting that Eldon had asked for was about to get under way. The time now was just a little more than three minutes to 9:00 AM. A few of the executives were surprised to receive a call at home from Marty after midnight, but each and every one of them understood the urgency that had created this sudden call for the executive body of the hotel to meet. Everyone had already taken a seat around the polished oak boardroom table that was in the shape of an oval, it wasn't quite round, but did convey an atmosphere of King Arthur's round table. By no means was Eldon even thought of as a King, far from it, but he was in fact "the boss." The talk about the table was always referenced as "King Eldon's round

table" in the Alexander Pushkin Boardroom. The
boardroom was given the name in honor of arguably
Russia's most famous poet and literary genius
considered by many to be the founder of modern
Russian literature. The gathering this morning had all
nine members of the hotel's top management around
the table. Morning coffee and tea along with a
selection of fruit, croissants, danish, muffins and
yogurt were available for anyone who so chose to
partake. Most everyone had opted for coffee. It was
now a few seconds before 9:00 AM. The door to the
Alexander Pushkin Boardroom opened and in walked
Eldon with Kimberley.

Following Kimberley was Felix, Billy and Louis
James. Although this setting was far from a military
environment or atmosphere, as Kimberley and Eldon
walked into the boardroom everyone sitting around
the table stood and said, "good morning *dobroye utra*
everyone."

Kimberley walked beside Eldon to the top part of
the oval table and took seats on either side of the
curve. Felix and Billy took the two empty seats on
either side of Kimberley and Eldon. Louis James took
his seat at the opposite end of the oval. The boardroom
table was now set. There was complete silence in the
room, not even a cough or clearing of throats. All eyes
were focused on Eldon and Kimberley; these first
moments were filled with tension and anticipation.

The executive committee had the utmost respect
for Louis James, he was the head of all hotel
operations in Moscow, this property, the soon to be

opening Red Jewel downtown Moscow and the Holiday Jewel Moskva, still over a year out before that property opens, but there was much work to be done at all three properties, open or not. The committee members were closest to Marty Sabine.

Marty had gained the respect of every member around this table by showing and demonstrating excellent leadership qualities, ability in dealing with adversities that were unique to the Russian hotel market and especially the careful grooming of all employees that had resulted in achieving the highest service standards of any property in Moscow. Marty had accomplished this goal in spite of over seventy percent of the employees never having worked in a hotel before they started working at The Holiday Jewel Danamo. This in itself was a monumental accomplishment in a city where the idea of offering quality service was not part of the everyday fabric worn by Muscovites. The simple fact of having just formerly been a country built on communism that offered no incentives to excel, no entrepreneurial spirit in a totally socialist society, there was no need for excellence in service, because service was not a valued factor of daily life. It mattered not if a sales clerk smiled or didn't, so long as you were able to buy a pair of shoes, the smiles were not needed nor expected. This line of thinking or attitude towards customers, of course, had no place within the walls of any Holiday Jewel Hotel in Moscow or any other city in Russia. Service was the key ingredient to success. The new class and type of hotel guest now coming in throngs expected nothing less. This was one of

Eldon's gold standards, not to be diminished or compromised. Marty Sabine knew how to deliver on this one very golden rule which Eldon, Kimberley, and Louis had picked up on and recognized to be Marty's greatest asset. Marty was doing a good job. With Eldon and Kimberley now having arrived and taken their seats at the boardroom table, Marty couldn't help but think that the feeling he was experiencing must have been similar to what Judas Iscariot must have felt. He glanced around the table at his co-workers. Looking directly at Eldon and Kimberley, he felt very uneasy.

"Ladies and gentlemen, thank you for being here at this very important time in our hotel's brief history and this very important time in Russia's history which is being made even as we all sit here around this table." Eldon began his opening statement to his most select employees in Russia. He had everyone's attention, so he continued.

"When I was flying across the Atlantic yesterday, I received news of the shelling going on here just as we were leaving Bermuda on our way to London. Naturally, having received the news of what was happening here, I changed plans immediately and got here as quickly as we could. Why am I telling you this? I want to explain, that after having heard of the turmoil in the streets, my first thoughts of course were concerning the safety of my wife Kimberley and the safety of everyone sitting around this table and the wonderful people we have working for us here at Danamo, not to mention the affect this would have on

Muscovites in general. I have to admit; I had a certain feeling of regret which led to the thought of Holiday Jewel Hotels opening operations in Russia might have proven to be a mistake.

That, of course, was my immediate thought, only because of the dangers close by associated with Russian army battle tanks and artillery shells flying in the sky. That was my first reaction. But we were only in the air for a few minutes when I received the news and still had almost a three-hour flight ahead of us before we landed to refuel and then another five hours getting to Moscow.

Ladies and gentlemen, that was plenty of time for more sobering thoughts allowing me to see clearly and understand that what took place yesterday was a move that President Orlov was smart to have taken. Now I am not a politician by any means, but if it weren't for sweeping political changes here in Russia over the past three years, well as you can imagine, Holiday Jewel Hotels would not be a player today in the Russian hospitality industry. But because of the recent bold changes, we came to believe that the decision to invest here in Moscow and investing into each and every one of you to be a sound one. So far as I can tell, both investments have provided more of a return than we ever imagined as you have seen in your paychecks. Your dedication to this operation and commitment to consistently deliver services beyond our guests' expectations has positioned Holiday Jewel Danamo as the number one hotel in Moscow. We enjoy the highest percentage of occupancy, and remain the most desired property to stay at generating the highest returning guest ratio in all of Moscow." Eldon paused for affect, allowing a moment or two for his words to sink in.

"With Louis James's directions, and Marty Sabine's management, this executive committee is the finest, and most competent of any hotel in Moscow, and I want to keep it that way. I will let nothing come between us maintaining our integrity and service standards." Eldon was being sincere and with just having said the words "and I want to keep it that way" Marty felt a sudden shiver down his spine. Sitting directly across the table from Marty was the hotel's Director of Security. Marty happened to glance at Misha, and they caught one another looking eye to eye. To this day, Marty was still not aware of hidden video surveillance bugs in his suite or any other rooms and suites in the hotel, but he had an uneasy feeling about Misha Rudkin. The Judas Iscariot feeling was really starting to eat away at him. His palms became sweaty, and a bead of sweat formed on his upper lip. He wiped it away.

Kimberley then spoke up continuing where Eldon had just left off, but Kimberley continued in Russian. Most of the executive committee members spoke both English and Russian, with only a couple of them mainly Russian and broken English. Louis James only spoke English, but Louis fully knew what Kimberley was about to say. Kimberley wanted to make certain that her and Eldon's message came through crystal clear. In Russian Kimberley then said. "Two and a half years ago, Eldon and I decided that the possibility of expanding Holiday Jewel Hotels and Casino's business interests into the new Russian Federation would be a very exciting and wonderful experience. I am speaking in Russian now because I want no chance on how we feel about you all, and our business plans here in Russia to be lost in translation.

Both Eldon and I have a pioneering spirit that cannot be denied which leads us to seek out new and challenging opportunities the world over. With Russia, having opened its doors and offering a gateway to fabulous growth opportunities in a country with over a thousand-year history and culture, we both felt that the hotel business was the ideal vehicle for bringing international flow of tourism and business into this newly formed federation. In doing so, we believed in bringing the highest standard to the city that the hospitality industry could offer and so far, thanks to everyone's dedication, loyalty, and perseverance we have succeeded here at The Holiday Jewel Danamo." Kimberley then stood up from her chair and started walking slowly down one side of the table; as she walked she continued.

"Let me be clear, when Eldon and I settled on our decision to investigate business opportunities, we understood well, that we would face unforeseen pitfalls and unimaginable challenges, but we believed that the floodgates had opened, and it was just a matter of running the rapids in this new emerging government and business environment." She had just walked down the length of the oval and stopped beside Louis James and continued.

"We are not afraid nor do we shy away from challenges."

Standing beside Louis, Kimberley reached out and laid her hand on Louis's shoulder, leaving it there for a moment and then looking over at Louis, she said, "Louis James", she started walking back again to her seat, and before sitting down, smiled at the group as she laid her hand on Billy's shoulder, saying, "Billy Simpson, Felix Balon" as Kimberley said Felix's name, Eldon reached out and placed his hand onto Felix's shoulder as he sat next to Eldon, "and my husband and I," she moved behind Eldon and placed both her hands onto his shoulders and continued on, "have fought tooth and nail over the years in bringing integrity to all our resort and casino operations."

Kimberley then stood there behind Eldon, and waited. Her hands still upon the tops of his shoulders, and she waited another twenty seconds which seemed like an eternity. Then she continued. "You might know that my husband's late wife was murdered, and my husband's daughter kidnapped, held for ransom three years ago in an attempt to bring Holiday Jewel Hotels to its knees in extorting unrealistic labor union wages." There were glances around the room by everyone, looking at one another around the table.

This was new and very personal information about the owners of this company that most people around the table were unaware of. To divulge such personal life details was unheard of in Russian society, in a business setting. This was something new, something deep and meaningful; everyone was glued to Kimberley. She continued on.

"We overcame those challenges rescued our little girl, saved our company and we continued to grow. We did that because we are a team, with these fine gentlemen. We now look to you and welcome you into our Holiday Jewel family and hospitality team." Kimberley paused for effect.

The atmosphere in the room was one of amazement. Both Eldon and Kimberley could tell that everyone was stunned. The Russian contingent was not used to such openness, and straight forward talk. Eldon and Kimberley had just disclosed some of the most private and heartfelt incidents of their lives. It was very compelling and gripping.

"Ladies and gentlemen, we will not ever shy away from adversity. We want all of you here to understand that. Over the past two years, we have formed strong alliances with city officials here in Moscow as well as close ties with powers that be in The Kremlin. This was my main task, as you may know, my background is that of career diplomat with the US State Department. Let me tell you, the ties and relationships I have had the chance to build over the past fifteen years in international circles have helped out tremendously in our ability to doing business here in your wonderful country. Eldon and I wanted you to understand who we are as people, not just as your employer. We are not just a company which hires and fires people. We are a company that leads in the hospitality industry; we are a global force in the people business. We firmly believe in you, and without you, our company may as well be making beds in some factory instead of welcoming people to our beds at our fabulous hotels. You are not just another employee; you are part of our family, and we will take care of you. That is our promise to you. We only ask of your dedication to your job, and as our motto says, "service with integrity" is our mission statement; we will not be compromised, ever! Our coming here to Russia has proven to be a significant impact on the local economy already, and the future only looks brighter." Kimberley finished saying.

There was total silence in the room. An atmosphere of dedication and loyalty filled the air. The boardroom table had in fact taken on the life of King Arthur's round table, at this moment there was no dissent from any one individual, but two people sitting at this table did hold deep regrets for their actions.

Eldon then continued. "Thank you, Kimberley, my wife tends to be a bit dramatic sometimes, but I imagine nothing could be more dramatic than what took place on Arbat Street yesterday, and that is what prompted this morning's gathering." Eldon looked at the faces around the table.

"Our number one priority is the safety of our employees, along with safety and comfort of our guests. All of you sitting here and everyone working at the hotel, are now having to take into consideration the risks involved in coming to work and going back home. Let me assure you that we will do whatever is required to keep our employees safe while here in the building. If for any reason the situation may become more urgent, and your ability to travel to and from work becomes dangerous, rest assured that your jobs and everyone's jobs at the hotel will be here waiting for you when the dangers have passed. In other words, while the hotel is here, your jobs will be here. Should the situation become even more urgent and heaven forbid, civil war breaks out then the expatriates will be extracted back to your countries of origin in accordance with the "force major" clause in the work agreement, and it will be at no cost to you. Now, that is the down and dirty. As to what took place yesterday in the streets of the city, it is my opinion that it will result in a very positive reaction. But let me qualify that by saying that I am no politician, but I can be very analytic. I do think that President Orlov has reached a turning point. His actions of yesterday have seen Russia turning the corner so to speak and from today on, we, Moscow and Russia are in the clear. With the hardliners now eliminated, any opposition that may have existed has been wiped away. I am convinced that going forward, our struggles in doing business in Russia have become lessened and for you to maintain your jobs is now more of a long-term certainty." Eldon paused once again. He allowed his words to sink in. "Driving in from the airport last night, Kimberley and I commented on President Orlov's clear declaration to the entire world that the old guard is out, and the newly formed Russian Federation's light was shining brightly upon the land.

We were amazed at the way The President announced to the world that even during darkness, light will penetrate through as Parliamentary building number 2 was brightly lit up with the colors of the new Russian Flag. It was a genius piece of international statesmanship, the entire world now knows not to mess with Russia, there is a new sheriff in town. I believe Viktor Orlov's decision to hit the building was a brave and calculated move that will only end up benefiting Russia and confirm the invitation for new international cooperation. The Soviet Union is firmly no more. We are more than confident that with such an incredible group of managers as there is gathered around this table, we cannot fail. We are ready to take on the world, as top hoteliers here at The Holiday Jewel Danamo and soon to open Red Jewel." Eldon ended his comments by then handing the meeting over to Louis.

"And now Holiday Jewel Hotels and Casinos' Senior Vice President Louis James would like to address this meeting, go ahead Louis."

Just as Eldon finished speaking and Louis was about to. Yuri Garin, the Holiday Jewel Hotel and Casinos' Liaison Officer a Russian National stood from his chair and struck the air, shouting, "Bravo to Mr. and Mrs. Davis and Holiday Jewel", Yuri repeated it again, "Bravo Mr. Davis." with his heavy Russian accent.

Yuri's action then spurned on Irina Sopov the Human Resources Director to also stand up from her chair as then did everyone else around the table and the room was filled with applause. A number of the women executives started crying with joy and disbelief that for once in their lives their hard work and contribution in Russia was acknowledged and confirmed by the best company they could ever imagine working for in this new era. For the first time in their lives, they felt a real family connection to the group, to Eldon and Kimberley and were proud as could in being employees of Holiday Jewel Hotels and Casinos. The applause continued for another half minute, with Eldon and Kimberley looking at each other from time to time, being humbled by the graciousness of their dedicated staff.   Marty and Rudkin were standing as well, of course, Marty clapping his sweaty palms. Everyone had sat back down. Eldon then thanked his executive committee.

"Thank you, but that was not necessary. Both Kimberley and I felt your heartfelt sincerity. We are a team, we are leaders and working together, there is nothing that we cannot accomplish in this business. Louis...."

"I am very happy that Eldon called this meeting today. I think by what we have experienced here this morning we can all rest assured that going forward we can overcome obstacles that are still bound to surface. What I wanted to talk to you about this morning, is the current situation with our hotels, this property, and specifically The Red Jewel. I am sure everyone here is well aware that the overall progress at The Red

Jewel is coming along very well, and we are well within meeting our projected opening date. Some of you here have already been involved in the pre-opening phase of The Red Jewel. Mainly it has thus far been Irina Sopov our Human Resources Director, who has been doing an outstanding job in the recruitment of the opening staff, and providing the training necessary for the hotel to function with efficiency on day one. Along with Irina, I would like to thank Larina Kortnev for her hard work in mining the sales and marketing needs in ensuring The Red Jewel almost at full capacity on opening day. Larina has achieved remarkable success in capturing more; I do mean more than our market share available in showcasing our fabulous new property in the center of the city. Well done Larina." A round of applause erupted from around the table.

Louis continued, "and kudos to Jennifer Paige our Director of Finance for making certain that the new property management system and all IT functions required at the front desk, accounting and all point of sales outlets are up and running, have been tested, employees trained and we are ready to go."

Another round of applause from everyone at the table. Then after a longer pause, Louis looked around the table and said, "sometimes, promotional opportunities come quickly in this business of ours. I think that opening statement might have further gotten your attention. "Let me explain. Now that we have established ourselves as the premier hotel in Moscow, we must re-establish ourselves once again as the two premier hotels in Moscow and soon afterward as the three premier properties with the Holiday Jewel Moskva coming online in another year and a half, give or take a month or two. This would normally not be easy because we would, in fact, be in competition with ourselves. However, that is not how we will approach our business model. We will have three properties under one umbrella, with each property specializing in certain services and facilities. Only one property will have a Casino attached to it, being the Holiday Jewel Moskva. That alone will distinguish it as a different product but still under our brand." Louis paused for a moment, taking a look around the table. He was pleased to see that everyone was fixed on his update.

"Eldon and I have decided to market the three properties as separate but one. One of the ways in which we will achieve that concept is to offer all three properties when the reservation is created, but regardless which property is chosen; the guest will have access to all three as if all three were under the same roof. This will be partially accomplished by offering complimentary shuttle service first between Holiday Jewel Danamo and The Red Jewel, and eventually all three when open. So, if you happen to be booked into The Red Jewel, but wanted to have dinner at the Japanese restaurant located in The Holiday Jewel Moskva, you just hop on the shuttle and enjoy your meal at The Moskva, which would be part of your "meal plan" dine-around feature, allinclusive package. Stay at one property; eat at all three, as part of your Moscow visitation package. That example and change in how we will market ourselves is just one of the strategies we have. W are looking to put more attractive packages and plans together as we move forward. We anticipate a great deal of traffic flow among the three properties and spreading revenues among the three properties. The logistics and accounting for this has all been figured out and tested by Ms. Paige; there are still a few bugs, but nothing we can't deal with and have cleared up a few days before opening."

All executive committee members were nodding with unified approval of the new ingenious ideas that were being presented. A feeling of excitement filled the air. Louis continued on. "So, back to my opening statement about promotional opportunities." Louis looked at Eldon and Kimberley across from him at the opposite ends of the table. Eldon nodded to Louis indicating for him to go ahead.

"We have been very pleased with everyone's performance to date. The Jewel Danamo has done extremely well. Ever since our opening we have had the good fortune of high occupancy rates and we have been able to maintain top dollar in the pricing structure for our rooms. We owe this to all of you and wish to recognize your efforts. In some ways, we are fortunate that we happen to be the first Holiday Jewel to be built in Moscow because all of you here today coveted positions that could see you becoming regional directors in your specific areas. With the two new Holiday Jewel Hotels to come on line soon, the company here in Moscow will be too large for individual autonomous property management; we will be looking to create Regional Directorships.

Most of you here today will be offered the promotional opportunity to accept the position of Regional Director. In Ms. Paige's case, she would become Regional Director of Finance, that of course would not happen until we have found a replacement for her position, and the same would apply to everyone else. We will be creating our Russian Regional Headquarters inside The Red Jewel. The current construction and design of the building already include these regional offices. Naturally, for those of you who agree to move into a regional capacity, pay adjustments would be forthcoming. For those of you who prefer remaining in your current positions, we will honor your decision and look forward to our continued relationships. The changes will be made available to everyone here, except of course. Yuri, his position as you know is dedicated to our joint venture liaison with our Russian partners, who in our case happen to be silent partners, but Yuri keeps them abreast of what is going on. And Yuri has been doing a magnificent job of it, thank you, Yuri."

A round of applause from everyone erupted in the room once again.

"*Spasiba, spasiba*, Yuri said, waving his hand thanking everyone.

Louis then continued. "That is all I have for you today. We will be addressing these topics with everyone individually as the time comes closer, within the next two weeks. Now... let's see what tomorrow brings and how this firing off tank shells into buildings affected the hotel market. I'm hoping and thinking it did us all a lot of good!"

Eldon then spoke up. "Ladies and gentlemen, that will conclude our meeting for today. Everyone have a good day and keep up the great work." As the group was starting to leave, Eldon then said, "Marty I want you to stay."

Marty's heart then skipped a beat.

***

Chapter Nine
Gorky then and Gorky now

There are instances and decisions in the modern world when references and utilization of historical figures and names on the surface seem appropriate but with a little investigation turn out to be diabolically ill placed.

One example was the decision to utilize two Russian historical names being: Tsar and Gorky. The regime happened to be Tsarist, and the writer happened to be a Marxist socialist who openly opposed the Tsarist regime. That writer was Maxim Gorky. Now as history would have it, Gorky was exiled from Russia but then later returned upon receiving a personal invitation from Joseph Stalin himself; the living breathing personification of communism. Gorky was the famous Russian writer. Tsarism was defined as an absolute rule, dictatorship. The two were like oil and water; they did not mix. However, the two historic names so ingrained into The Russian language came together once again under the roof covering The Holiday Jewel Danamo Hotel. Here in this setting, the two names were just as ill combined today as they ever were in history, as coming events would prove.

The Holiday Jewel Danamo Hotel was already well known by the business and press crowd as having one of the most upscale chicest after work drinking holes in the city. The Gorky Club had fast become the place to meet and after 5:00 PM, and the place to be after 10:00 PM. If you were looking for a sexy intimate yet classy piano bar to wind down your day, after having been out to dinner or looking for a night cap, then The Gorky Club would be your choice, whether you were staying at the hotel or not.

Walking through the main entrance doors of the Jewel Danamo, the Gorky Club lounge was located across the marble stone lobby that led into an arched hallway with the words "Gorky Club" engraved into the top of the archway's marble stone. Walking farther down the arched hallway, a set of smokedglass doors flanked on either side by more smoked glass from the ceiling to the floor created a feeling of opulence and intimacy. On the right-hand side of the glass doorway, the smoked-glass was etched with a likeness of the famous Russian writer Maxim Gorky, and next to the portrait of Maxim Gorky was the company name of the leaseholder operating lounge, it read: The Gorky Club, operated by Tsar Restaurants and Entertainment Company. Tsar Restaurants and Entertainment was owned by Alexander Mitkin, in other words, the Gorky Club was now managed by the Russian Mafia.

Gunter Vogel, the vice president of sales for Kruger Machinery Works, headquartered in Frankfurt Germany, had become a frequent guest of The Holiday Jewel Danamo over the past year. Gunter would fly into Moscow once every six weeks to check on his current customers and pursue sales opportunities; participate in various trade shows where he would showcase his company's precision products. On this trip, Gunter had a few of his company's salespeople along for the trip and tonight they were looking forward to enjoying a few cocktails

in Gunter's favorite bar in Moscow, The Gorky Club. Gunter Vogel and his four salespeople had finished dinner in the hotel's gourmet dining room "The Mir" and made their way across the lobby, through the archway leading to The Gorky
Club.

The Gorky Club lounge manager "Vlad" was at the host podium, and greeted the now familiar hotel guest.

"Welcome back Mr. Gunter, so nice to see you once again visiting our fine establishment, and I see you have brought some of your friends along." Vlad greeted the five gentlemen.

"Yes, good evening" replied Gunter, feeling "special," about being recognized by the lounge manager, and being welcomed back.

"We are glad to be back in Moscow, and I believe a few drinks are in order for my colleagues and me. We are in a mood to celebrate a little tonight; your wonderful city has been very good to us this day." Gunter finished saying with delight in his voice and with a German accent.

Vlad, of course, was only too happy to show the five businessmen to a choice location in the lounge.

The day had gone very well with Kruger Machinery Works having signed more business contracts earning handsome commissions by all his sales people at the table tonight. Celebrations were in order, and what better way was there than with a few bottles of Dom Perignon Champagne to start. As the night went on, and the men celebrated, more drinks were ordered and the bravado loosened with the conversation flowing, taking on an "anything goes" attitude around the table, fueled by vodka chasers.

The lounge manager "Vlad" took note and had been watching the five all night long.

By 1:00 AM Gunter and his colleagues were feeling no pain and in very good jovial moods but to be sure with more than a few brain cells less than they had started out with earlier in the day.

The Gorky Club management, upon Mitkin's directions, remained discreet in their "after hours" activities but never missed an opportunity to recruit more members for their "after hours hospitality" membership.

Alexander Mitkin's top two money earners Anna and Ludmilla were also to work the lounge that evening but had yet to make an appearance. Anna and Ludmilla were always held back to this time of the night when the two of them could make the biggest impact by being the cherries on top of an evening out drinking and celebrating. Vlad, of course, worked for Mitkin and knew what to do and how.

He had kept a close eye on Gunter's table, and it seemed to him now to be the perfect time in sending Anna and Ludmilla over to his table. The time was now just after 1:00 AM and all five men were in a friendly mood. The Gorky Club lounge manager picked up the lounge telephone and called the private hospitality suite 2020 on the second floor that the club had been renting from time to time. Tonight, was of those nights when the hotel had a lot of corporate business guests, and it would be a good night for the hospitality lounge to be available for the "after hours club".

Anna answered the phone in the hospitality suite. "Anna speaking."

"Okay, you and Ludmilla come on down." Anna hung up the phone, motioned to Ludmilla who was sitting on the sofa with five other young girls. Not one older than seventeen; dressed scantily in sexy little skirts, one dressed as a waitress, another two as French maids, another as a nurse and another as a stewardess and all wearing pumps.

The young girls had been at this now for more than a year, and were now even at their young ages "pros". They had overcome their initial fears but were still under threat to perform for the sake of their families back in Romania, Moldova, and Hungary.

Mitkin was ruthless to the core, this was the way of the Russian Mafia, do or die, the young girls understood this well. Examples of failure to comply were very real, and so the young girls always did as they were told. Just a few days prior to this evening, all four young ladies had found out that one of the girls in their group who worked another hotel had resisted Mitkin's orders which sadly resulted in pictures delivered to her, showing her younger brother lying murdered in a ditch back home in her village. The young girl, Kati, no longer resisted, fearing that same fate awaiting her parents if she decided to cross Mitkin every again. Eventually, Kati had considered suicide to end it all, but even that was not to be risked, Mitkin had an answer to that solution as well. Suicide would only hasten the death of her family as Mitkin had made clear. There was, in fact, no way out, so they became whores for Mitkin.

They were prostitutes, but tonight they were upscale prostitutes having been promoted to working The Gorky Club with Anna and Ludmilla being their teachers and watchers. It was now their way of life and tonight, Kati, the young sixteen-year-old from Hungary was now part of the Gorky Club after hours entertainment menu. Everyone had their lot in life, and this was theirs.

Ludmilla and Anna had arrived via the service elevator to the kitchen and service area of the Gorky Club lounge. Vlad was there to meet them. He brought the two girls up to speed about the five businessmen from Germany.

Vlad had come to know Gunter over the months with Gunter being a frequent hotel guest, and had always treated Gunter with top notch service and attention, but tonight Vlad was to go the extra mile. Vlad had made sure during the night that the five men were provided with good table service but not too good, he didn't want them to be drunk, but most definitely feeling good, more than good maybe. He had also sent them complimentary hors d'oeuvres over the course of the hour and a half they'd been in the lounge, and now he was about to send over a complimentary bottle of Dom Perignon with Anna and Ludmilla, along with champagne glasses for all seven of them.

This was a total set-up designed to be a sitdown-invitation with the five men. It would be impossible to refuse Anna and Ludmilla's generous offer to join them at their table. So, Vlad sent them off. Anna carried a tray with seven champagne glasses, and Ludmilla carried over the Dom.

The two women were this evening dressed very elegantly, sexy for sure but with a touch of class; it was meant to be this way. It was all very strategic and very thought out. Of course, just the sight of Anna and Ludmilla walking together was a picture of erotica. The fact that they were identical twins was, even more, mind blowing! Both had a ribbon around their necks clasped with a diamond. Ludmilla's neck ribbon was red, and Anna's was black so that one could tell them apart, and both wearing identical outfits, white blouses with smartly cut embroidered red vests and black leggings with high heels. The two blondes standing five feet ten inches tall in their stilettos could not be missed no matter where one was sitting in the lounge, their presence alone overtook the entire room.

Gunter and his colleagues had been seated by Vlad with this in mind already when the five of them first arrived. Vlad had made sure to seat them in a semi-private area of the lounge in case they became a little too vocal and of course for this event to be discreet and private as possible.

As soon as the girls appeared on the floor in the lounge, the group of five Germans spotted them immediately; they were in fact like a pack of lions watching as two antelopes approached their table. Ludmilla and Anna walked straight across the lounge floor heading directly for Gunter's table, and just before the two women reached Gunter's table, there was a sudden realization by all five men that the two women were most definitely coming to their table; one carrying seven champagne glasses and the other carrying the Dom.

Well, instinct kicked in, and before the women reached the table, all five men rose to their feet in respect. They were German, and chivalry was in their blood.

Approaching their table, Ludmilla and Anna stopped, with big smiles on their faces, and in broken English with her heavy Russian accent, Ludmilla said; *"goud evening gent le men, I am Ludmilla, and dis iz my seester Anna. Ve have kum to say hello and breeng you a tokhen uv our appreesheeashen for veezeting da The Gorky Club veet dis kompleementari tchampayn "*

Anna began placing the champagne glasses down onto the table in front of each man."

The five men were speechless; they were still all standing. Ludmilla handed the Dom Perignon to Gunter who took it from her automatically.

Ludmilla then said smiling at Gunter, *"vood you please doo da honors Meester. Gunter and pop da korkh?"*

Gunter was so pleased that Ludmilla she knew his name; he had never ever met her before. He was impressed.

Anna then said, *"may ve join you, gent le men?"* Gunter was a little tongue tied but got it out. "Ladies, absolutely, our pleasure to have your company."

Gunter's friends all spoke up, "yes ladies, yes, please sit, what a pleasure."

Gunter then proceeded to introduce his colleagues, still while everyone was standing, he went around the table gesturing towards each man as he called out their names, "Werner, Franz, Hans, and Otto, yes, yes, please sit down ladies."

Gunter stepped aside allowing Ludmilla to step in between himself and Otto, and Werner stepped aside allowing Anna to sit between himself and Franz. Gunter then stood and poured champagne for Anna and Ludmilla, thereafter for his colleagues, and they all toasted to a great night.

Ludmilla engaged Gunter in light conversation, pleasantries as did Anna taking turns talking. Within two minutes, all five men had totally forgotten what time of night it was, and their attention was totally focused on these two elegant women.

Then Anna started speaking in her broken English but perfectly understandable.

"Gent le men, it iz so nice for my seester and me to meet you all tonight. Ludmilla and I vood luv for you all to join our "after hours hozpitality kloub". Ve voodd be delighted in having you az members. Let me assure you, membersheep to our kloub iz very excluseev, and vuns you join, you are entitled to enjoying all ov our feetures and akteeveeities."

The guys listened to Anna. As Anna was talking she placed her hands into Werner's and Franz's, turning and smiling at both. Ludmilla did the same with Gunter and Otto while running her tongue around her lips; looking at Hans. The girls left no one out in their proposal to have them as members.

Ludmilla then continued; taking over from Anna.

"Our after-hours hozpeetaleety kloub opens in a few meeneets at von tirty and goz on till da vee hours in da morning. Ve hav sum entertainment for you tonight, very nice young laydeez who viill be very happy to have you join dem for dreenks and how szoould I say," she then paused for a moment... and after a few seconds said slowly and very sexually "akteeveeties." *I don't theenk I need to explain vat "akteeveeties" are I'm sure."* Ludmilla then puckered her lips and moved her upper body in a very sexual manner. All five men caught onto that body gesture without any difficulty, it was very obvious and telegraphed clear as a bell. Ludmilla was such an expert at bringing the woman inside her out all over the table with just one motion of her body. "

"Natchoorally, Anna and I veell be dehr az vel, vhere ve koud get to know each odher much better. Membersheep includes everyting, and it iz a membersheep fee only."

The guys all listened smiling; Anna had now moved her hand onto Werner and Franz's thigh. Ludmilla did the same with Gunter and Otto.

"So, tell me Ludmilla, how does one become a member?" Hans was already willing to be a member, and he wasn't even touched by either woman yet... but he was eager to becoming one.

"Oh itz so simple, ve know who iz a member and who izn't, ve axsept kahsh or krehdeet khard and da membersheep iz only five hundred dohlars and itz goud for a whole munt!

Remember gent le men; itz a kloub membersheep fee and nuting more. Kan ve kunt on you to kum up? Tonight, vood be exkluseevlee for you five gent le men onlee az new members. Our "after hours kloub" iz da hozpeetaleetie sveet on da sehkund floor, sveet number tvhenty tvhenty."

Ludmilla then moved her hands along Gunter's thigh and Otto's...smiling at them. Hans wished he was sitting beside her; he felt left out. The five men all looked at one another, making faces, driven by the drinks they consumed and decided that it would be worth checking out.

Gunter then said. "I think we could look into this, what do you say men?"

They all nodded, and then Anna chimed in saying, *"vhahnderful, so glad to hear ve vil have your kompanee. ve kan settle up da membersheep fee in da hozpeetaleetie sveet."*

Anna then took her champagne glass and held it out and toasted the agreement, as they all clinked glasses together and drank the last drew drops of their Dom. Ludmilla and Anna then left the table and made their way up to the hospitality suite. As the two women were leaving, they turned and blew kisses back at the five men. Gunter and his colleagues looked around at each other as the girls left the table.

"Well, are we going to do this?" asked Gunter. "I don't have a problem with it." Gunter continued saying, "it wouldn't be my first time, to be honest, and wow those two are hot!"

Franz was hesitant. Although he was intrigued and wanted to, he backed out." Well, you guys go ahead, I'm going to pass."

"Okay, suit yourself Franz but you're going to miss out on some major fun, I know that,"

Otto was game; he was in for sure. Hans didn't have to think about it at all; he was in even before Anna and Ludmilla sat down.

Then Gunter spoke up, but in a low tone, "Look, we all know what this is, there is no question about that. The five hundred per person membership is all right with me, and as the girls said, this is a membership officially, nothing more nothing less. Whatever happens inside the hospitality suite is part of the membership privileges, she made that clear, and I believe it's like that to make things legal. Do we all understand?" Gunter wanted that to sink in, it was all above board, membership to clubs were no problem.

Everyone nodded, and the four of them were in. Franz wasn't, he was going to opt out and go back to his room and go to sleep.

Gunter motioned for the lounge waitress to come over with the check. Gunter took the check for the drinks and signed it to his room for his account to be charged.

"Okay boys, let's see what this is all about, I can't wait."

Gunter and his four colleagues were on their way out walking across the lounge, passing a table with two other gentlemen who had been sitting there when the five of them first came into The Gorky Club. The five men nodded at the two gentlemen as they made their way out the lounge.

Felix Balon and Billy Simpson looked up from their seats, nodding back to the five men from Germany, politely saying "good night."

Billy and Felix had watched the whole thing go down from across the room; it was very revealing.

***

Chapter Ten
Tour Bus to Misery

The route would be one thousand eight hundred ninety-three kilometers or twenty-four hours drive time, but it would take thirty-six hours to arrive at the final destination. It was an older Volvo tour bus with seats for fifty-two passengers. On this trip, forty of those seats would be occupied by young girls ages fifteen to eighteen with eighteen years of age being the oldest ever to occupy a seat on Alexander Mitkin's milk run bus to misery. The starting point for the "Misery Tour" was the city of Debrecen in Hungary.

This secondary city of two hundred thousand residents was located in the agricultural outskirts; a central point to the surrounding farming communities. Mitkin's Mafia recruiting thugs were Hungarian nationals paid by Mitkin to prey on girls living in this area. They were to locate and recruit young girls from poor families in rural towns who had no real futures or potential income prospects. The offer to work in glittering Moscow, to earn good money that would enable the girls to help their families back home was hard to refuse. That sort of opportunity was not to be missed. On this recruiting effort, the local recruiter was able to find seven girls ages fifteen to eighteen who were picked up in the surrounding towns and taken to the meeting facility in Debrecen from where Mitkin's bus would transport them on their thirty-six-hour trip to Moscow and into the unknown.

Each girl was allowed to bring one suitcase only and a handbag or purse. There were no exceptions.

FRANK JULIUS

Birth certificates were all that was necessary. Being a Hungarian Citizen granted them automatic working rights in the former Soviet Union with Hungary having been a former satellite of Russia. Three of the girls knew one another, and the other four were to meet for the first time at the meeting facility, which turned out to be Mitkin's bus, parked in an open field outside of town.

The Hungarian girls were; Kati, a sixteen-yearold from a family of five, two younger brothers still in elementary school. Kati's parents were poor farmers and the thousand dollars that Mitkin's thugs gave to Kati's father as an advance on Kati's earnings was a godsend to the family since it would carry them through the coming five months of winter.

So, Kati's parents allowed her to leave and seek her fortune in Moscow. Still, her parents felt like they had just sold their one and only daughter to a slave master, but on the surface, they believed in the greater good and hoped Kati would find her future in the glitter of Moscow's elite.

The scenario was much the same for the other six young girls, Margie, Sylvie, Este, Maria, Ildiko, and Zusza. They all arrived in Debrecen and were put onto Mitkin's bus. They hadn't been on the bus for more than a few minutes when the driver showed up. He came onto the bus, told the girls they could sit anywhere they wanted to since they were the first ones there. He then told the girls that they should go to the bathroom now because there wouldn't be a stop for another four hours.

He then pointed at Kati and motioned for her to come with him to bring in some boxes. Kati complied. A few boxes of food had been dropped off, nothing fancy, crackers, salami, and three oneliter jars containing pickled hard boiled eggs and some Hungarian dry sausage along with a few loaves of bread and bottles of water.

Kati brought the boxes inside the bus. She was told to place them on to the first four seats. The driver then explained that the food was for everyone on the bus, but the meal periods would be assigned at certain times only. The food was not to be touched. Water could be had any time, but that was it.

"Okay ladies, we are leaving in a few minutes, if you need to go to the bathroom go now, there are some bushes just on the other side of the bus, that will be fine." The driver said in a very "hurry up sort of tone."

A few girls decided they better do that. The bus was not equipped with a toilet. Five minutes later, the seven Hungarian country girls were off on their journey to Mitkin's world. The trip would take them through to The Ukraine where the bus would pick up another fifteen girls. Then continuing to Belarus, another ten girls would be boarding the bus, and once having entered Russia another stop. Eight more girls; Russians would join the group heading to Moscow.

Kati looked out her window as the bus had started moving out onto the highway. She wondered if she had done the right thing. She was only sixteen, she had endured watching her family struggling her whole life. The money for her parents is what made her do it. She was only sixteen, but this was a chance to help out her parents and younger brothers. The money would be so important for her family, and maybe she would do well in Moscow, perhaps she would become rich, and maybe she could help them even more. But she teared up anyway and started crying silent tears, feeling tightness in her throat with a huge lump. Sweet little Kati watched the light poles going by as she was leaving Hungary and her sixteen years of life behind.

***

Chapter Eleven
Too much hospitality in the hotel.

The Holiday Jewel Danamo Hotel's executive committee was in the process of leaving the boardroom. With Eldon, having asked Marty to stay behind, Marty remained in his seat, but Eldon wasn't happy with the seating arrangement after most of the chairs had been vacated.

Eldon then said, "Marty come on up here to this end of the table so we can all be together." Louis had already gotten up from his chair at the opposite end of the table to Eldon and had sat down beside Felix. The boardroom table now had Louis, Felix, Kimberley, Eldon, Billy, and Marty with no unoccupied chairs between them.

No one spoke, everyone anticipated Eldon to start speaking immediately as to what this private secondary meeting was all about. Marty was antsy about his nervousness. He couldn't help thinking it would show through. He wasn't sure what this was all about. It could be anything, from the volume of business being generated by tour consolidators to slow collection of the outstanding accounts receivable to Eldon's opinion on the current service level throughout the hotel. Marty, however, couldn't discount his reason for worry being his infidelity in maintaining a clean property, and by "clean" he wasn't thinking about the hotel's housekeeping standards.

Naturally, Louis, Kimberley, Felix and Billy knew exactly what this was all about. On one hand, they all hoped that Marty did not know what this was all about, and yet if Marty had no idea, that too would not be a good thing. The subject had to be addressed; it was much too important to leave alone.

Eldon had a certain way about him in the manner in which he addressed certain situations and how he approached sensitive topics. It was his personality and an art, combined into one attribute that could be very intimidating to whomever it was being directed towards. Of course, the intimidation factor was only felt if someone had something to hide. Otherwise his demeanor and delivery were quite serene. He was the epitome of calm under stress but always thinking and always playing out scenarios to the end game. In terms of hotel management, the one thing that annoyed Eldon was finding out potential problems about a property from someone other than his property's Hotel General Manager. He however; was not one to be jumping to conclusions or decide with knee-jerk reactions, he was willing to listen and to "let one go" but just once, not twice. So long as the situation was rectified, Eldon would be okay with things. The information he received a few hours earlier this morning from Billy and Felix had him and Kimberley very concerned. Concerned to the point where he thought it not out of the realm of things already to be spinning out of control.

Eldon reached out to the plate of scones and croissants. He picked up a scone, then a knife and cutting it, slowly buttered one-half of his scone while looking and watching what he was doing, not looking at anyone, he started to say, "when my wife

Kimberley and I decided to venture into Russia and take a stab at making things happen here with our company we were very excited."

Everyone listened. There was complete silence as everyone watched Eldon buttering his scone. "We are still very excited about being in Russia and as we have just discussed, let's hope the events of yesterday turn out to benefit us all, and I do mean all the hotels including our competitors." Eldon finished buttering his scone, took a bite of it, and after a few seconds started in again, now sitting back in his seat and looking around the table.

"Last night we had, let me call it... "an observation" shall we say, that is indicative of things to come or perhaps things already having come into our hotel. I will not get into the details at this time; I will let Louis elaborate on it afterward. It is enough for me to say that we as hotel operators need to take action and by that I mean a thorough investigation into our hotel's food and beverage lease operations." With that, Eldon looked directly at Marty. He continued on.

"I have never been much of a proponent on leasing out the food and beverage operations. I don't believe it adds nor does it hold over time to the overall management philosophy of hotel operations, not to mention how difficult it is to bring an outside operator on board who is in tune with our mission statement and overall objectives in perpetuating our company motto, "service with integrity."

Eldon continued on. "We agreed in having Tsar Restaurants and Entertainment take over our food and beverage operations knowing the well-established reputation their other restaurants and supply chain have in the city, but I fear that we as hotel operators failed in our due diligence, vetting Tsar Restaurants to a deeper level than we did. We do have a lease agreement with them, however."

Eldon then stopped talking and picked up his coffee cup, looked over at Louis, nodded his head and Louis then continued moving forward after Eldon's preamble.

"So, we believe our hotel has already been infiltrated by unwanted elements. Marty, you know our priority in operations is to maintain a clean customer product. Misha, our Director of Hotel Security and his team, are your front-line barriers to keeping out unwanted elements. We believe Misha may have already been compromised by the activity witnessed last night in The Gorky Club by Billy and Felix, in fact, it's a virtual certainty that The Holiday Jewel Danamo is, let's use the term "infected."

As a Hotelier and Senior VP of this company my number one priority is to make absolutely certain our hotels and product, "the guest stay experience" that we aspire to deliver on a consistent basis is fail safe and not open to compromise. As Eldon, has already mentioned, the problem is in the Gorky Club, but it stems from porous security and we believe it then spreads to the floors of the hotel after hours. We have been down this road before in a number of other properties we own in The

Caribbean, and we know how to deal with it.

We have a good idea of what is going on, but we cannot at this point prove it. Once we can, and we have the evidence, then Tsar Restaurants and Entertainment will be in violation of their lease agreement, and they are out, immediately. Marty, I want you to take the lead on this, and get to the bottom of things, and we need to have it done quickly."

Eldon then interrupted. "Marty, we mean right away. Louis, Billy, and Felix will fill you in as to how this needs to be dealt with. Now Kimberley and I have a meeting to prepare for this afternoon with select members of The Duma, The Mayor, and US Ambassador Albert, so we'll leave you to it."

Eldon and Kimberley got up from their chairs and were leaving the boardroom when Eldon turned and said most emphatically in a low but piercing voice that was heard as clearly as if he was shouting from a mountain top...

"I'm looking for results, and fast, the hospitality in this hotel is getting out of control. The associated risk factors with this sort of activity are huge; it threatens the very existence of our hotel. I want you to stop it. Marty, I'm counting on you."

And with that Eldon and Kimberley left the boardroom.

Marty knew he had his work cut out. He wondered to himself; "how on earth was he ever going to deliver?"

***

Chapter Twelve
Eagles, Bears and Doves

Anton Marat, the Mayor of Moscow, had his offices located in City Hall, but of course, on this day the meeting with city officials and select members of the Duma was to be held in The Kremlin. The reason for holding mainly a "city" meeting in the Kremlin was because Viktor Orlov's wife Svetlana had taken on the official position of Travel and Tourism Minister in Viktor Orlov's new Cabinet.

Svetlana Orlov's command of the English language coupled with her education abroad in the USA had positioned her to be a viable and suited person to hold this now very important position. With Svetlana also attending this afternoon's meeting, deference to hold the meeting on her grounds was deemed appropriate rather than the city offices. This afternoon's get-together was turning out to be a major event that would result in reaching an understanding and agreement between the newly formed Russian Federation and the rules and regulations governing the fast-growing hotel and tourism industry in Russia but especially in Moscow. This final meeting to sign pending agreements had been in the works for a long time, with edits and revisions being refined over the last year or so. Terms had come to mutual satisfaction for both sides being; the hotel owners and operators and the City of Moscow with The Russian Department of Travel and Tourism.

Meeting behind Kremlin walls dictated certain protocols that went with the venue. Eldon and

Kimberley had been through the process a time before having met Viktor and Svetlana Orlov when Holiday Jewel Danamo was first opened. A reception for new Russian joint venture companies was held at The Kremlin. The invitation to that reception was extended to Eldon and Kimberley by her friend and university colleague; Svetlana. It had been a good opportunity for both Kimberley and Eldon to meet The President of The Russian Federation and his wife on a semi-personal basis. It was at that first meeting with President Orlov and The First Lady that the naming of Eldon's new hotel "The Red Jewel" was discussed. Eldon had won over Viktor Orlov in obtaining his approval for naming the hotel "The Red Jewel."

Eldon recalled how Orlov had been opposed to the name at first, but Eldon's reasoning and logic had convinced Viktor. Ever since that night, The President was in full approval and favor of the name. That first meeting although very brief and focused had gone well. Both parties felt good about having met.

Viktor Orlov wasn't scheduled to attend this meeting, but Svetlana would be. She was a gracious hostess and an effective calming element like a dove among the American eagles and Russian bears that would be gathering at this very crucial meeting to seal the deal for the foreseeable future. This was to be a business meeting today, not a diplomatic event. Although Frankie Albert, the US Ambassador to The Russian Federation was to be in attendance, formal arrival protocol was not needed nor expected. All guests of the Minister of Travel and Tourism were whisked through Kremlin security without fanfare this afternoon. The usual guards of the Kremlin were present throughout the various structures, halls and facilities but once cleared for admission everyone was free to move about the building as needed but with a Kremlin guard in tow.

Svetlana Orlov had arranged for one of the Kremlin's spacious meeting rooms "Pushkin Hall" to be utilized. Eldon and Kimberley found this a bit ironic having just left their own meeting also held at Holiday Jewel Danamo's Pushkin Boardroom.

"Maybe it was a sign of things to come," Kimberley thought.

As the attendees walked in and down the large wide corridor leading to Pushkin Hall where the meeting was set in U-Shaped style, Eldon and Kimberley walked together in full business style but also as husband and wife representing Holiday Jewel Hotels and Casinos. There was a reception area just outside the large French doors leading into Pushkin Hall. Eldon and Kimberley stopped by the reception area and began exchanging greetings with others who had already arrived.

Eldon recognized it right away as did Kimberley; they glanced at one another with approving and surprising facial gestures, both their eyebrows being raised in amazement as they approached the standing crowd outside of Pushkin Hall.

Americans were mingling with Russians and Russians were engaged in small talk with Americans.

This was a huge improvement. The last time some members of this group had gotten together each side pretty much kept to themselves and not much mingling or interaction had taken place. Now however almost half a year later, it seems there was more commonality between the Americans and Russians than ever before. It wasn't just Russians and Americans; there were corporate executives present from Germany, France, England, Canada, and The Netherlands as well, mainly from the hotel sector but representatives from tour consolidators and major airlines serving Moscow were also present.

It was Svetlana Orlov's house so to speak that this meeting was being convened at, but it was all about the city of Moscow. In truth, it was The Mayor of Moscow; Anton Marat's meeting. He stood next to Svetlana Orlov by the large open ceiling to floor French doors leading into Pushkin Hall. Both officials extended their warm welcome with handshakes and appropriate greetings to all the arriving participants. Svetlana was first in the twoline greeting party.

Eldon and Kimberley walked up towards the entrance to Pushkin Hall, and immediately Svetlana's eyes lit up with a huge smile forming on her face as she saw Kimberley coming into view.

"Kimberley, oh I was so looking forward to this meeting today knowing that you and Eldon would be here. It's been much too long since we've seen each other." Svetlana spoke perfect English with just a hint of a slight Russian accent as the two women, and close friends gave each other a hug and kissing gestures on both cheeks.

FRANK JULIUS

"Eldon, so good to see you again," Svetlana said reaching out to shake Eldon's hand offering her warm welcome.

"Svetlana, both Eldon and I are so glad we have this opportunity to meet again, as you say it's been much too long.

"I look forward to catching up with you. Perhaps after this meeting is done we can all have a few minutes together, I would like that very much," Svetlana said.

Kimberley responded with a reassuring commitment to follow up on their special friendship after the meeting.

"I would love that Svetlana; I hope we can make time.".

"Kimberley, you and Eldon know our Mayor his Excellency Anton Marat." Svetlana motioned towards her co-host standing at her side.

Eldon and Kimberley greeted Anton Marat. He welcomed them as well and showed them into Pushkin Hall directing both Kimberley and Eldon to their designated seats at the large U-shaped table. It was set to seat fifty with two rows of chairs; one for the primary attendees and a second row directly behind for their aides and supporting staff members.

Eldon and Kimberley did not have supporting staff members, they would not need any, Eldon and Kimberley were well prepared and handled everything in person without the need for aides or staff, not even Eldon's Senior Vice President of Russian Operations, Louis James was on hand.

Eldon and Kimberley would handle it all and then issue company directives to Louis James for things to start happening and stay on track.

Most everyone who was to be at this meeting had already arrived and had taken their seats inside the hall. Ambassador Frankie Albert had met up with Kimberley and Eldon about the same time arriving at the Kremlin but then Ambassador Albert was taken aside with special greetings of other Kremlin officials, and as Eldon and Kimberley walked into Pushkin Hall, Ambassador Albert caught up from behind.

"I finally got away from those pesky little mandatory hand shakings, now to get on with business."

Eldon and Kimberley could tell from Albert's comment that sometimes he detested the protocol required by his presence, no matter where he went, he had to extend the obligatory diplomacy that his title carried.

The three of them walked into the hall and as it turned out Ambassador Albert's support embassy staff had already taken their seats directly behind The Ambassador's designated seat with his sport marked "The United States Ambassador Albert".

Eldon and Kimberley found their seats designated beside Frankie Albert along one side of the U-shaped board room table. The room had been set up very professionally. Moving around the table the designated spots were marked with the name tags of the attendees; there were several. All western interest hotels now operating in the city of Moscow were represented by their corporate CEO's and in some cases the Russian joint venture partners. Holiday Jewel Hotels and Casinos joint venture partner was not present. Eldon's Russian business partner was a total silent partner. All management needs and decisions were addressed by Holiday Jewel Hotels and Casinos management as they best saw fit. That meant Eldon, Kimberley, and Louis James. In addition to the western interest properties being represented, the representatives for two major tour wholesalers operating out of Chicago and London England were also present as well as V.P.'s from a number of international airlines; the USA, England, Germany, Holland, and China.

Not to be left out was the neglected, but still operational Russian National Hotel Company. Up until two years ago, it was State owned and operated but now transitioned as a subsidiary of Russoflot Airlines; a Russian Federation government owned airlines, operating as a government corporation. The Russian Hotel was doing its damnedest to be a viable contender among this new group of exclusive hoteliers. They had succeeded in renovating two of the Soviet "wedding-cake" architectural style buildings with the modernization of all rooms, positioning themselves as an inexpensive "Russian" option. But they were having a tough go of things now having to compete with the new kids in town. Eldon and Kimberley had garnered most of the attention in the hall as the dominant players among this group. Not counting the Russian hotel factor, Holiday Jewel Hotels and Casinos properties will command the largest share of rooms available from one company.

The rest of the rooms' availability was distributed among the seven other properties operated by companies from England, Germany, Canada and The Netherlands.

As Kimberley, Eldon, and Frankie Albert walked into Pushkin Hall, before taking their seats, they took their time in walking around the boardroom and greeting everyone. Some had already taken their seats while others were still standing and milling around in small talk with their colleagues and fellow attendees. It was another fifteen minutes or so before they had made their way to the head table area of the U-shaped boardroom where the Moscow City Officials, members of the Duma, Moscow Mayor Anton Marat, and Svetlana Orlov were to be seated and chairing the meeting. It was customary to mingle with the hosts last. Thus the hosts being the first to meet the arrivals in the welcome line, and once again, the last to meet with before the meeting got under way, it was another diplomatic process showing respect. Kimberley and Eldon knew well how to play the game.

The large French doors of Pushkin Hall were being closed. Two Kremlin military guards were posted on either side of the doors outside of the hall. The meeting was to get under way as indicated by the faint sound of a Tchaikovsky composition being piped into the meeting room. Everyone took their seats around the boardroom. The music stopped, and silence filled Pushkin Hall, all eyes front, and center onto the head table. It was Anton Marat's meeting. The Mayor of Moscow stood up and walked center to the lectern and spoke in not perfect but acceptable English.

"Ladies and Gentlemen, I ask for your consideration to a few moments of silence in respect to those who perished yesterday in our efforts as a new government in establishing freedom and democracy in our growing new country. Ladies and gentlemen, please rise."

No one expected the Russian National Anthem to be played, not even Albert, everyone was caught by surprise, having no option but to stand, and they did on his command.

As Anton Marat finished saying those words, the National Anthem of Russia played through the piped in sound system. All Russians at the head table held their hands over their hearts as the Tchaikovsky composed Russian Anthem played. Everyone around the boardroom stood in silence with heads bowed. The anthem finished, it was a powerful moment, and Marat continued on..."it is with sadness and sorrow that we lost our citizens who could not or would not see the new ways of our country and democracy, and it is a tragedy that the action needed to win them over was not short of violence. These too, are the growing pains of a new nation and grow we shall, let us not make a mistake about that! The city of Moscow will grow in spite of these pains. We will evolve into the coming twenty-first century as a world center for commerce and tourism. Moscow will be rivaled by the likes of London, Geneva, New York, Tokyo, Montreal, Dubai, Beijing, Rio de Janeiro, Seoul,

Riyadh, Shanghai, Berlin, Chicago, Paris, San Francisco, Vancouver and the rest of the world."

Anton Marat's words filled Pushkin Hall. Just by him calling out the world's major centers brought a sense of belonging. Moscow had already been established as a major power center on the global economy, but now positioned to soar even higher than ever before with unlimited potential.

"Ladies and Gentlemen, Moscow is open for business and you all seated around this table will be the co-hosts to our greatest city in Russia."

Here at this point, Marat stopped speaking for a few seconds and looked around the table, not so much at everyone at once, but let his eyes travel down one side of the table and back up the other side, getting everyone's eye contact. Eldon and Kimberley looked at each other with knowing eyes, in agreement; it was a terrific opening statement. Marat had captured the attention of everyone in the room. The room erupted into applause with everyone looking around the table nodding in agreement.

Eldon thought to himself; "Marat had done a masterful job."

The Mayor continue on saying, "I wish to thank The First Lady of The Russian Federation and President Orlov's Cabinet member as Minister of Travel and Tourism; Svetlana Orlov, for allowing and arranging this meeting to be held here in this most historic and famous of all Halls in The Kremlin. We are pleased to have you all gathered here this afternoon for what both Minister Orlov and I are sure will be a most informative and welcomed session.

Today we will review the policies put together by our esteemed members of the Duma, The Ministry of Travel and Tourism, and our City Government. These covenants, as presented by The Ambassador of the United States of America, and select members of the Travel and Hotel Industry gathered around this table.

I am confident these agreements will result in a fruitful union between our governments and your companies operating in Russia. These rules, regulations, and laws, we believe will enhance our abilities in meeting operational requirements and projected profitability for this sector of our local economy. We look forward to exceeding those projections for the Travel and Tourism industry anticipated over the next decade for the Moscow market and extending out into other major urban centers throughout Russia.

Once again, it is my pleasure as the Mayor of Moscow to welcome you to Pushkin Hall on behalf of Minister Orlov. I will now take the pleasure of introducing you all the attendees of this afternoon's meeting. I ask that you stand as I call out your names as participants to the resolutions being presented and signed in agreement between the City of Moscow, Department of Hotel and Tourism and your companies and organizations as signing members."

Marat then took a moment and looked over to US Ambassador Frankie Albert and then continued on.

"Before I go on with the general introductions and reading of names, I wish to make special mention and acknowledgment of the hard work and persistence that Ambassador Ferenc Albert of the

United States has brought to meeting our objectives. It is my belief that without Ambassador Albert's tireless efforts, in presenting our case to the US Congress and the United States Department of Commerce; the foundation enabling this understanding of things to come would have been impossible.

Ambassador Albert championed our request as a unified group of hotel operators, spurred on by Mr. and Mrs. Davis of Holiday Jewel Hotels and Casinos. The Ambassador's avocation in having the European Union and the United States of America designating our region a special exemption as an International Free Trade Zone, thereby paving the way to Corporate IRS expense exemptions status for all conventions and meetings held in the Free Trade Zone. The Free Trade Zone being the entire city of Moscow, to include all hotels, and convention centers. This then allowed growth in the hotel sector, and free enterprise to begin its flourishing expansion throughout our new democracy.

This we owe to Ambassador Frankie Albert and the business acumen of Holiday Jewel Hotels and Casinos."

Having finished saying those words, Svetlana Orlov stood and started applauding, directing her gratitude at Ambassador Albert, Kimberley, and Eldon who were all seated together as a party of three. Everyone else, upon Svetlana's initiation of applause, stood and joined in.

Eldon, Kimberley, and Albert then stood and bowed in appreciation to the group's acknowledgment. This was a very significant and bold accomplishment; opening an avenue to kickstart this new emerging economy enabling added invitation of foreign investment. The Moscow Hotel Association could now begin acting as a catalyst and conduit of hospitality enabling the coming together of minds, money, and know-how of the international entrepreneurial, free enterprise spirit of expansion.

As the applause subsided and everyone seated, Marat started in with the introductions going around the table.

"Representing the Patriot Hotel Corporation from Amsterdam The Netherlands, Heidi Veenstra. Ms. Veenstra is the CEO of Patriot Hotels and is currently operating the three hundred forty-seven room Patriotic Hotel at the Moscow International Airport. Welcome, Ms. Veenstra."

Heidi was in her fifties, Dutch to be sure through and through to the core and one hundred percent business. Heidi brought to the table a legacy of the Dutch East India company, with Patriot Hotels founders having historical and ancestral ties dating back to one of the greatest global entrepreneurs in history. Heidi Veenstra stood as Marat finished introducing her and spoke into her tabletop mounted microphone.

"Thank you, Mr. Mayor. It is with great pleasure that we can participate as a corporation in your new economy and we, at Patriot Hotels look forward to contributing as good corporate citizens in Moscow.

We are now actively engaged in due diligence looking for possible expansion opportunities here within the city limits. We are very excited for what the future holds in terms of our company; Patriot
Hotels, and the city of Moscow."

Anton Marat continued with introductions down the length of the table and over to the other side where Kimberley, Eldon, and Albert occupied the last three seats adjacent to the head table where Marat stood at the lectern. Svetlana was to his right with two members of the City Duma flanking Svetlana and two other members of the Duma to his left.

Representatives from four other multinational companies operating hotels in Moscow took their turns with short statements, all with positive outlooks and encouraging operating results.

Eldon and Kimberley had not yet been called upon nor announced. Marat continued introducing CEO's from four major airlines now serving Moscow. The airlines executives confirmed that business had already increased threefold over and above their projections with two of the major air carriers calling for the expansion of the current airport since there was a vital need for additional gates and luggage handling facilities. These were all very well recognized requirements for the coming influx of tourism and business class travel.

The tour operators and wholesalers were now being inundated with the desire to visit Moscow and Russia. It had become increasingly clear to everyone around the boardroom table that things were moving along much faster than anyone had anticipated.

Marat then looked over at the last two remaining guests, and that was Kimberley and Eldon. "Ladies and gentlemen, Mr. and Mrs. Eldon Davis of Holiday Jewel Hotels and Casinos, and I am certain, no introduction is necessary."

Eldon stood up. "Thank you, Mr. Mayor, and Minister Orlov our heartfelt warmth and thoughts are with you and your City Mr. Mayor for the tragedy that unfolded yesterday. It is our hope, Kimberley's and mine, and all our employees at Holiday Jewel Hotels that the outcome of yesterday's events will have paved the way forward in lasting peace and prosperity for many years to come."

Eldon had "his people" from Holiday Jewel Hotels corporate offices in Ft. Lauderdale work on a tactile, visual project specifically for this afternoon's presentation. The past ninety days had seen close cooperation between Mayor Marat's office and Eldon's architectural design division back at his
Florida corporate offices. Eldon had suggested to Mayor Marat a center block presentation that Eldon's team would put together; a scale model of the city of Moscow showing the impact that the new hotels had on the city and how just the hotels alone had changed the Moscow skyline showing the expected total impact that the new spirit of commerce and changing political climate will bring overall.

Marat had agreed to this project and had supplied Eldon's team in Florida with cooperative information. Marat's team and Eldon's team had been busy putting this presentation together, and it was now ready for unveiling. The only change had been the venue. This meeting was originally to be held at Marat's City offices but with Svetlana now hosting at The Kremlin, the location was moved. The presentation platform and mechanics were now in place, situated in the center of the U-shaped boardroom table that currently contained a huge flower arrangement and vase. The large vase and flower arrangement was now to be removed in the coming few minutes.

Eldon didn't lose a beat; he went right on and into his presentation.

"Ladies and gentlemen, the good Mayor's office and my company have been working closely over the past few weeks in order to present to you a visualization of what we as a group in this room have accomplished over the past four plus years or so. As you can appreciate, we have all undergone a variety of growing pains, obstacles, interruptions, red tape so to speak, and I don't mean Soviet tape, I do mean "red tape" as in bureaucratic annoyances. Such as; needing five approvals for one small, simple little thing."

He paused looking around the table and up at Marat, members of the Duma and Svetlana Orlov. Some nodded in acknowledgment, others raised eyebrows but everyone agreed one way or another.

"We all know what I am talking about, and we have all survived these past few years. All of us have seen our hard work flower into blooming success stories. We intend to carry this on for many more years to come, to be a vital element forming a vital section of the economy, to showcase Moscow and Russia to the world as never before, and ladies and gentlemen, I do mean as never before."

Eldon then nodded to the two porters standing along the back wall of Pushkin Hall. The two porters walked to the center block inside the U-shaped boardroom table and removed the large flower arrangement and vase, along with the tablecloth covering the platform.

"Ladies and gentlemen allow me to show you what we as a group have accomplished in these few short years."

Eldon paused and picked up a remote-control unit and doing so, pressed a button. The top layer of the centerpiece platform which appeared to be about the size of two full sized pool tables came alive with the top piece splitting in two then one-half of the top retracting across and down, wrapping and hiding along the inside of the structure.

Eldon pressed another button, and the open half of the tabletop saw a three-dimensional scale model of Moscow rising. It was a large presentation; an exact replica of the city. The scale model was as Moscow appeared with its skyline as of 1991 just after the fall of communism and prior to the existence of the new Russian Federation.

The city nevertheless even in 1991 was very impressive. The Kremlin complex dominated the city center, with its huge open space promenade and St. Basil's. Another was Izmailova complex which did hold a huge hotel and another large internationally funded hotel built during the Soviet era by an American oil magnate and industry maverick; the late Armand Hammer.

Eldon was not Armand Hammer, but Eldon and Kimberley certainly carried and emulated the entrepreneurial spirit of the legendary visionary and most individuals sitting around this table were starting to come to terms with recognizing another true Maverick in their midst. Eldon and Kimberley Davis had taken that mantle and tradition without ever officially being offered the baton by Mr. Hammer, but Eldon never needed a hand me down or a hand over in taking things to the next level. Eldon and Kimberley were a team like no other. Eldon continued on.

"What you see here is an exact replica of Moscow as it appeared in 1991 just prior to the formation of the new Russian Federation. As you can see, it was even back then a very impressive capital city." Eldon looked over towards one of the porters still standing by the back wall and nodded towards him. The Porter moved to the dimmer switch and slowly started dimming the overhead lighting of the large chandelier and perimeter lights of Pushkin Hall.

Eldon walked down to the end of the U-shaped table and into the centerpiece area where the display now came into full view, as the interior lighting of the model began turning on. Eldon took from his pocket a laser light pointer and aimed it at a receptor that lit up the section of the scale model depicting the Ring Road, a circular thoroughfare around the main city of Moscow.

"We've all traveled the Ring Road; we know it well."

Next Eldon pointed the laser at the bell tower of The Kremlin and the entire complex of the Kremlin lit up bright, with all buildings being outlined in light. With the lights dimmed in Pushkin Hall, the scale model was turning out to be a very eye catchy presentation.

"Now, let me highlight the reason we are all here."

Eldon then pointed the laser at several locations one at a time as the buildings started lighting up and being outlined on the Moscow City model. Eldon had highlighted eight other buildings all being hotels that existed up until 1991 and some still in operation. These were large building, for example the Rossiya Hotel, still the largest hotel in Europe, being twentyone stories with three thousand two hundred rooms was a massive building, being one of the "seven sisters" structures. These seven "skyscrapers" of the Soviet Era of which three were hotels with thousands of rooms, unfortunately, although thought of as state of the art five star properties during the Stalin era no longer measured up to the standards now in demand. Not only had these hotels lost their dominance in occupancy, but these buildings themselves represented Russian oppression of The Soviet era and were avoided by just about everyone who came to Moscow.

Once all the hotels were selected and lit, the skyline of Moscow took shape in the darkened room, and it was impressive. Eldon then moved away from the city model and backed up far enough to stand clear of the centerpiece as he activated the other half of the structure. The same identical model rose up beside the one already lit, this too lit already as the first model, but then things started changing.

"And this is how far we have come in the short time we have had" Eldon finished saying, and then pointing his laser light at where the very first Western joint venture hotel opened in Moscow, that being Heidi Veenstra's company: the Patriotic Hotel at Sheremetyevo International Airport.

As Eldon pointed his laser at the empty spot where there was no hotel, a panel slid open, and the exact replica of The Patriotic Hotel now rose up to fill the spot. It was very impressive. Everyone started into applause right away seeing the rise of the Patriotic Hotel at the airport.

It was a tall building and looked very impressive on the scale model. Eldon once again, hit the hotel model, and Patriotic Hotel lit up with lights throughout the building. This now caused the room to explode once again into a round of applause; the lighting of the hotel sparked an emotional reaction from everyone. It was the first Western hotel and it marked a new era that then brought in everyone else around the table including Eldon and his company Holiday Jewel Hotels and Casinos.

He then did the same for the remaining eight new properties that came into existence. Each time Eldon pointed his laser onto the newly risen replica; the old buildings were lowered and replaced with the new hotels coming to life with their brilliant lighting as each rose.

With each new rise of each building, Eldon identified the new hotels, stating the number of stories, the size of the hotel in terms of footprint on the landscape, the number of rooms each property offered.

Although Eldon was only in charge of Holiday Jewel Hotels and Casinos, just his own interests, he knew and understood the competition as if it was his own operation. None of the others around the boardroom had any knowledge or heads up about this presentation to be taking place except of course Mayor Marat and Svetlana Orlov who were both fully aware of this event to take place.

It was quite evident how impressed everyone was with his knowledge about their properties. It was almost as if Eldon was the de facto CEO for all companies being represented at today's meeting. The last two remaining spots on the scale model were his two properties still to be opened, but Eldon did something a bit surprising. The Holiday Jewel Moskva was not scheduled for completion for at least another year but he shined his laser on the Jewel Moskva location instead first. The existing buildings receded into the model and the massive Holiday Jewel Moskva Hotel with its adjacent casino complex filled the open space along the Moskva River and as the model filled in, the lights came on throughout the structure lighting up the scaled river bend. The scaled model was looking very impressive now with all the new hotels being lit and outlined in blue light.

Eldon left the final effect for the city center and then verbally added.

"And ladies and gentlemen, my wife Kimberley and I, along with all the employees and business associates of Holiday Jewel Hotels and Casinos are very excited and proud to be opening our flagship property within weeks, which is as you all know The Red Jewel. It will be the tallest building in the city, and the tallest structure in Europe." He paused, having just uttered the words "and the tallest structure in Europe" was, in fact, a historic statement all on its own. He let that sink in.

"We believe that the Red Jewel will mark a new era in hotel design and level of service never seen in the city, and that is notwithstanding all competition. We at Holiday Jewel Hotels and Casinos, welcome and respect our competition here in Moscow and worldwide. We believe competition keeps us all sharp and cutting edge hoteliers."

And with that Eldon aimed the laser into the center of the Moscow City Center. The old buildings disappeared receding into the model, and the towering scale model started to rise slowly, but already lit and outlined in red, with the words "The Red Jewel" with a shining Ruby Red LED light at the top.

The Red Jewel dominated the Moscow skyline, and when it reached its total height, Eldon pressed his remote one last time, bringing to life the red laser beam that rotated over the scaled city model of Moscow. With the lighting of Pushkin Hall being dimmed, the scaled model of Moscow with the laser from The Red Jewel created a stunning presentation.

When the ruby red laser began its rotation, everyone stood up and applauded.

"Bravo, bravo" some around the table yelled. It was a visual site to behold. Eldon had accomplished what he intended. There was no denying, Eldon and Kimberley were not only pioneers of the new Russian hotel industry, but they were visionaries and promoters of the new Russian Federation.

Eldon looked over at Kimberly; she was applauding as well, as was all who sat at the head table, all the Duma members along with Svetlana and Anton Marat, were all standing. The image was dramatic. The contrast between the two skylines of Moscow was like night and day. The addition of the new hotels had totally changed the skyline of the city; Moscow had become an overnight sensation with architecture to be rivaled by other world capitals.

Eldon, thanked everyone for their attention, motioned to the porter standing by Pushkin Hall's dimmer control and had the lights come back up. With that, Eldon took his seat beside Kimberley. Kimberley reached up and hugged his shoulders, pecking him lightly on the cheeks and smiled proudly at him so the whole room could see. It was a moment of both husband and wife affirmation of their admiration for one another and an appropriate gesture of "great job honey…" for everyone to envy. The two of them were a duo to contend with and perhaps more importantly not to mess with, and everyone knew it.

Svetlana Orlov, stood and thanked Eldon saying, "thank you, Mr. Davis, for that wonderful and visually stunning presentation. Together with our Mayor's select team and your company's most capable architectural scale modeling expertise; you have highlighted our city and its progress in a way that no one could possibly misinterpret. The city of Moscow and the Russian Federation is most fortunate to have such a distinguished collection of western corporations representing and contributing to the growth of our economy leading to our mutually rewarding prosperity."

Svetlana then took a minute and raised a glass of champagne in making a toast to Eldon and Kimberley.

"May I say on a personal note, that I am so pleased indeed that life's events sometimes bring about the most uncanny and unpredictable situations. It was in my years as a university student studying abroad at Rutgers University in New Jersey USA that I was blessed to have met Mrs. Kimberley Ashton-Davis. We happened to be unwitting classmates, and now several years later we find ourselves sitting in this most historic of halls in this new Russian Federation."

Svetlana looked towards Kimberley and raised her glass, saying, "Kimberly, I could not imagine anyone more suited or more pleasurable to work with and call my friend than you, and now your most charming husband. We are pleased here at The Kremlin with all that you and Holiday Jewel Hotels and Casinos have brought to our country and the leadership your company has demonstrated; a standard of excellence for all in this room to espouse and adopt." Svetlana then completed the toast to

Kimberley and Eldon taking a sip and directing a warm smile at her friend Kimberley. Everyone around the table toasted Kimberly and Eldon, and they toasted back. It was a very fitting moment.

The First Lady continued.

"And now ladies and gentlemen, may I bring your attention to the future of our travel and tourism industry. As you all know, tourism is an "export." When we welcome travelers, be they genuine tourists to this great country of Russia or be they entrepreneurs or corporate business people, the impression and results they experience is what they take back home; and that is the "export" of our country. Our culture, our hospitality, and our legacy, yes they all take a little bit of Russia back home.

We export a little bit of Russia every time a plane lands and a plane leaves. As Minister of Travel and Tourism, my number one responsibility is to promote this country to the world and with such a professional group of hoteliers, travel experts, travel agents, and airlines as are gathered in this room, I cannot expect anything other than great success. Our Russian culture is ready and open for the world to visit. Our business opportunities are like nowhere else on earth, and you all will be the hosts to great things ahead for your companies, our companies, our government and the Russian people."

Svetlana took a pause and prepared to surprise the group with her next statement. Before speaking, she looked at Kimberley and winked.

Kimberley picked up on it right away, it was a sign between the two that they both instinctively understood, a surprise was about to happen. It was their private way of communicating that whatever Svetlana had special and unexpected up her sleeve, she was about to reveal to the group now. It was something that only Svetlana being The First Lady of Russia could have pulled off... and did she! And here it came.

"With that ladies and gentlemen, I would like to introduce to you, my husband, Viktor Orlov, President of The Russian Federation."

The large French doors to Pushkin Hall opened and in walked Viktor Orlov. The surprise and amazement in the room could be felt in the air. No one had expected The President to be attending this gathering, but now it became evident as to why the venue was moved from the city hall to The Kremlin. Viktor Orlov wanted to be part of this; he obviously felt this meeting needed his input. It was a great honor to the group that The Russian President would make his appearance and give his approval.

Everyone stood as Viktor Orlov walked in. Dispensing with protocol, Viktor did not approach the head table; he walked directly into the center of the U-shaped table and stood beside the scale models of the two Moscows so that he was front and center for everyone around the table to see. Viktor was not shy; he liked and actually craved being the center of attention but was in no way a time waster. Viktor motioned to his wife Svetlana; she then left the head table and came down into the center, joining her husband.

As everyone in the room understood, Viktor Orlov did not speak English well, so Svetlana would be his crystal-clear translator.

Viktor came straight to the point. The feeling around the table was electric. This was turning out to be one incredible afternoon. This, in fact, was history making. This, in fact, should be filmed, it was momentous. For the Orlov's to be co-presenting to such a group of businessmen and women...well this occasion was worthy of international news, but no, it will be for this select group only and perhaps one day, it will be released. No one around the room doubted that everything was being recorded, the entire afternoon, all the speeches and now this incredible final event of the afternoon, Svetlana and Viktor together in Pushkin Hall, decrying the past and embracing the future.

Viktor Orlov started in.

"Yesterday pcoplc dicd because their ideology was in contrast to the future of our nation. It is with great sadness the events of yesterday morning had to happen, but we are on a new pathway to the 21st century and obstacles to our newly formed democracy, and emerging economy is too great a price to pay. Unfortunately, our Russian Brethren chose to pay with their lives." Viktor paused and allowed for his wife to translate.

As Svetlana spoke, Viktor looked around the room at everyone at the table. Viktor did not smile; his look was deadpan serious.

Viktor then continued. "It did not have to be that way, but it was their choice, and we fulfilled it for them, with the strength of our will and the loyalty of our military. What we have here in front of us this afternoon," Viktor pointed and gestured towards the Moscow City Models, "is the past, present and the future depicted by Mr. Davis and Mayor Marat." He paused again, allowing for Svetlana to translate.

Viktor then reached into his pocket and extracted another remote-control device, and the room lights dimmed again. The new scale model came to brighten again with the new hotels, The Red Jewel's laser rotating around the model's perimeter and Viktor pressed some buttons on his remote and continued speaking as additional changes started taking place on the model.

"The next few years will see the skyline of Moscow change even more dramatically than what Mr. Davis has so expertly demonstrated." He paused again, as the scale model started taking on changes. Everyone was amazed at what was happening. Entire sections of the city, complete city blocks were being removed and replaced with futuristic modern skyscrapers to rival those of Dubai, Taiwan, and Beijing.

Svetlana translated as the new skyscrapers started rising in the center of the city.

Viktor went on.

"This ladies and gentlemen is the future of our great city. Yes, the Red Jewel is a jewel, not to be discounted, but there will be other jewels in this city to come. We have seven major new buildings going up in the next five years. Already the skyline has changed with the new hotels, but the coming changes, planned by the new government will be... in simple terms, groundbreaking. We will be the city of the future."

Viktor paused again, and Svetlana filled in.

"Moscow will be the center of the world for business, trade, commerce, military might, and yes as my wife so eloquently declared, a travel and tourism destination not to be outdone by anyone or any country. We are Russia, we are Moscow, we are the New Russian Federation and on behalf of the Russian people and our new government, I welcome you to Russia."

As Viktor finished, the scale model also finished making the changes: Svetlana was now finishing Viktor's final words, and now the difference between the old Moscow model and the new Moscow model with the new hotels and the new buildings was like night and day.

The new city was unrecognizable. The only giveaway that it was, in fact, Moscow Russia was that The Kremlin still dominated the center of the city, and nobody on earth could mistake The Kremlin complex and St. Basil's with any other spot on earth than Moscow Russia.

As Svetlana finished translating for Viktor, everyone stood and applauded. Viktor had scored and scored big with these corporate magnates.
Svetlana then continued.

"The President wishes to thank you for attending and looks forward to many years of cooperation in business as well as cultural exchanges. My husband has a full schedule of events to attend and wishes you all a pleasant visit to the city and looks forward to meeting once again in the near future as our city and country grow. The President wishes you all a good afternoon and welcomes you to enjoy the city and the new era of history as brought in by Viktor Orlov's Russian Federation and its entrepreneurial spirit. Good afternoon ladies and gentlemen, *spasiba*."

Viktor Orlov, The President of Russia, left Pushkin Hall as quickly as he entered. Eldon and Kimberley looked at one another;
Eldon said to Kimberley, "wow!"

***

Chapter Thirteen
House of Lace and Pain

Kati tossed and turned. She could not sleep. No matter how hard she tried ridding her mind of the horrors back home delivered with the photograph of her little brother's murder, she simply could not. Mitkin had delivered the nightmare that would now forever haunt her young mind, and that was several weeks ago. Now that Mitkin had Kati in his full control, he ordered her to answer to Ludmilla and Anna, two of Mitkin's whore runners, who were also the young Kati's teachers and sub-masters. Anna and Ludmilla were paid well by Mitkin. They had long ago succumbed to their fate surrendering to him and settled in to face their lot in life, trying to make the most of things, day in day out, night in night out.

It was getting close to noon, and Kati would need to rise, she had errands to run today. Last night had been a long night with Kati having serviced several men during the orgy that ensued after the first round of drinks at 2: AM in the "after hours club". Kati lay in her bunk. She hadn't showered yet, and the smell and odor of alcohol and cigarettes were all over her and in her bed, she hated it. She closed her eyes and pulled her legs up to her stomach and lay in the fetal position. Her eyes teared up, and in her mind, she prayed, she prayed to God. She put her hands together and with her eyes closed and her lips only moving in mimicking the words in her mind she prayed to God that he help her somehow.

Kati still believed in God although these past few weeks had her questioning her devotion, but she prayed. In her heart, Kati knew that God would show her a way out, and maybe all her Hungarian friends who were caught up in Mitkin's net. She only had to keep asking and one day God would hear her and show her the way.

Marty Sabine sat there waiting for what was next. Eldon and Kimberley had made it clear that things would need to happen and happen fast! Marty did his best in being the team player and leader that Louis James was looking for, and Eldon demanded. So now, sitting around the boardroom table at the "infected" Holiday Jewel Danamo Hotel were only the four of them, Louis, Marty, Billy, and Felix.

"Marty, I don't want you to feel like you are bearing the weight of this alone. We understand the situation and we are here to help. We can and know how to exterminate this virus that has entered our operation. What we will need to do is in medical terms, is introduce an antibiotic.

The wheels have already begun turning this morning Marty even before we came in for the meeting, and here is what we are doing about it." Louis finished saying, looking directly at Marty.

Felix then added; "we've been in operation for many years in the Caribbean as you know and from time to time we have run into the same sorts or similar sorts of problems there. Just so that we are not mincing words here, and to be crystal clear, what we are talking about is prostitution running rampant throughout the hotel.

Marty, we have a number of people in the company on whom we call in situations such as this, and they have already been contacted this morning, as a matter of fact very early this morning just after Billy, and I left the Gorky Club Lounge. What Billy and I had witnessed was a test case scenario that was systematic and typical evidence as to what is already going on. What we witnessed would have to have been well established and perfected for a long time running, for it to have gone down as well as it did. It, in fact, took place last night at that table of business executives from Germany." Marty just sat listening to Felix; not saying a word.

"Yes, we know who they are, and we also know that in order for this level of penetration to have taken place inside the core of our operations; it would have required assistance from the inside. By that, we mean our first line of security which happens to be our Department of Security, and that means the direct involvement of our Director of Security, Misha Rudkin." Felix finished saying in a very professional and knowing manner. Felix had been down this road a number of times, as had Louis James.

Prostitution wasn't just the oldest profession of the world only in the Caribbean, it was the oldest and probably one of the first professions the world over. But now it was time for Marty to shine a light on the situation before it ran away from him leaving Marty to become just another General Manager, a "has been" statistic. It was time for Marty to make a serious attempt at saving his tarnished and deceiving career.

In his heart, Marty knew that he could not come clean, because if he did, Eldon would let him go. Marty's ties to Louis James were much closer than it was with Eldon. Marty was hired in the first place on Louis's say so. Louis had gone out on the limb for Marty and in all respects, Marty up until a few weeks ago, had been doing a marvelous job. He got the hotel ready and brought the occupancy up to where it should be, not to mention Marty's ability in stoking the flames of employee morale, he was very good at his job. Where Marty wasn't so good was his weakness in succumbing to the pleasures of the flesh, and that could take him down, the hotel down, and Eldon's efforts in Moscow down.

Eldon would surely not tolerate his continuance. So now, Marty did what he had to, he made a valiant effort here and now in front of Louis, Billy, and Felix in adding to the understanding and solutions required in ridding the hotel of the virus. Unfortunately, Marty was a key protein that made up this virus now living inside and slowly beginning to destroy this "living cell" know as; Holiday Jewel Danamo.

Marty started in, utilizing his most inner depth General Manager wisdom, letting it be known that he understood just exactly what was at stake with the potentially grave nature of the prevailing circumstances.

"As Eldon was saying on his way out, the associated risk factors are huge and threaten the very existence of the hotel. Yes, Eldon is absolutely correct, and I understand the severity of the situation. The thing is, that with something like this infiltrating our operation, it is not only the guests we are placing at risk with the introduction of nefarious elements such as prostitution, but the tentacles that can be and in most cases, are attached to such criminal activity, being drugs and the black market." Marty was trying his best in voicing his understanding of the situation; he continued.

"I know we have to weed out this intrusion. I am making it my mission as of right this minute to get to the bottom of it." Marty put his best effort in, even invoking Eldon's name in front of Eldon's three most trusted souls sitting in front and beside him.

Marty wondered; "did it work? Did they buy his sincerity or could the three of them detect that maybe, just maybe Marty had overplayed his cards and was sounding just a tad too righteous?"

Marty supposed time will tell, for now, he had given it his best shot, and it looked for now as if the three men were embracing Marty's declaration of professionalism while having enhanced his loyalty to the integrity and level of service expected from him by Eldon and the Holiday Jewel Hotel family.

"So, Marty here's what's going to happen," Louis said. "As Felix just mentioned, we have a number of people who handle these types of situations for our hotels, and they have already been contacted and made aware of the urgency. You will be expecting four gentlemen to be arriving next week Friday, that's almost two weeks from today, for the weekend, two Canadians from Toronto and two Americans from

Detroit. They will be arriving to attend the International Moscow Auto Show being held next coming weekend and are posing as auto industry executives. The companies they may be with do not matter, but the detail on their accounts will specifically state they are convention attendees. The four of them will be in the hotel for about a week or as long as we need to have them until they get a hit, and you know exactly what I mean by "a hit." Trust me, Marty, these guys know what they are doing."

Marty was listening to Louis's every word.

"The four will meet up here in the hotel and they will be visiting all the hotel's food and beverage outlets and making good use of the bars especially the Gorky Club and The Lobby Bar. All four are Holiday Jewel Hotel and Casino employees, Marty; they work in our corporate security department, and this is what they do. They seek out vice and fraud within hotel operations. Although they specialize in our Casino operations division, the hotels and casinos are in most instances linked both physically as buildings as well as operationally in terms of gaming and lodging.

Marty, you will not be making contact with these people until you are needed. You and they will stay away from one another so as to not arouse any suspicion of familiarity or any prior knowledge of anyone in their party knowing the management of this hotel. The farther apart you stay from them, the more flexibility they will have allowing for their autonomy and private goings on here in the hotel without hotel management involvement. We may need you as things progress but initially you will not interact.

It will be a setup, and you will be integral Marty in making certain they are left alone to do as they please, got it?

"Absolutely," Marty replied. "I understand. So, they will be acting as bait for them to be hit on, and once they are targeted we can then act with certainty. Is that the idea?" Marty asked.

"You got it Marty" Billy Simpson chimed in. "That is how the cookie will crumble here at Danamo."

"Marty here are the names and pictures of the four guys arriving to the hotel. They will be in private suites; all will seem perfectly normal. Reservations have already been taken care of." Louis continued saying and handed Marty an envelope containing four snapshots of the men coming in and their assumed names.

"Their hotel rooms and incidental charges are to be billed, the information on the billing arrangements are attached, make sure that it's all set up in the property management system so there are no glitches at check-in and check-out." Louis finished saying.

"Sure, no problem, consider it done," Marty responded.

Louis went on, "but that's not where it ends Marty. We have gone the extra mile on this one, and we are bringing in some insurance and extra discovery capability. We also have two young ladies fly in, also to be attendees to the auto show." Marty sat listening and thought, "this was becoming very interesting."

"As you know, auto shows and large conventions act like honey to a bee, in this case, hookers to a convention. These two ladies who will be flying in also work for us in security and vice, coming from our Casino division. They too are experts at what they do. The two women's photographs and assumed names are also in that envelope, they too are to be left alone so they can operate as need be. They naturally will be posing as ladies of the night here in the hotel, mainly concentrating on the lounges and bars. They know how to conduct themselves posing as high-class prostitutes, naturally only to entrap the clients and to sniff out the operation leading to additional information gathering. We strongly believe that the security department in this hotel has been severely compromised. We believe Marty that Misha Rudkin has taken a bribe and allowed Holiday Jewel Danamo to be infiltrated by Mafia operations. Make no mistake; the hotel is still in good standing in terms of service and reputation, but unless we find and stop these goings on, in no time will it deteriorate to the point of no return. What the two women will do, is bring the corruption of the security department out into the light."

Louis paused for a moment, reached for the coffee carafe and poured himself a cup. Marty did the same. Marty was fascinated by the efficiency and serious attitude not to mention the quick action being taken by the company to ferret out the problem.

Marty, in fact, was now becoming nervous, and as he poured coffee into his cup, his hand trembled a bit and he realized it had been a mistake in opting for a cup of coffee. Being nervous at this stage of the game was not something he wanted on display; he was hoping no one noticed his jittery pour. To Marty's relief, Louis continued on. Both Felix and Billy, Marty had noticed were making notes as Marty was pouring so, Marty figured all was good, as Louis went on.

"The two women will make it known in the lobby bar and The Gorky Club that they are in a discreet but in no uncertain terms here to attend the convention and offering their personal escort services to gentlemen who might need the services of a woman. They will only be interacting with the four men from Toronto and Detroit, and never any real hotel guests. Naturally, this will all be for show to get the attention of the hotel security and perhaps Security Director Rudkin's attention.

The four gentlemen will continue on with a deeper investigation as to what is happening in the Gorky Club as well. We think Mitkin's girls will hit on the four of them without question." Marty was now finally getting the full picture; all was now coming into view.

"So, you get the picture now Marty?" Felix jumped in.

Marty picked up on it right away. "Yes, sure do, it is a nice sting operation or at least an operation to ascertain collusion with hotel security. If I get this right, what this operation will reveal will be the outright encouragement of the security department in enabling certain girls in the Gorky Club and our lobby bar as well, who are known to security as "working girls" allowed to carry on their business, and "working girls" who are not allowed to do so."

"Yes, exactly, that is how it works Marty." Louis said and continuing on, "naturally, if the security department is on the up and up, doing their job as required, all attempts at prostitution and escort services, essentially amounting to the same thing will be stopped, and the women asked to leave the hotel and be barred from re-entry.

But if it turns out that it's just our planted women being asked to leave, and regular girls allowed to stay, then it is a sure thing that security is compromised, and you will have to take action, Marty." Hearing Louis say those words "you will have to take action Marty" almost caused Marty to soil his pants. "That means you may have to start replacing the security team, and it will have to start with Misha Rudkin himself."

Marty was doing his best in keeping his composure. This was serious shit going down. Marty in his heart of hearts knew it the moment he set his foot inside the boardroom that this day was not going to be a good one, and surely his feelings were confirmed.

Marty thought to himself; "to get rid of Rudkin is going to be a huge problem, maybe for Marty, maybe for everyone." Marty wasn't sure yet how all this would play out, and maybe there was a solution, but his gut feeling told him that things were going down the toilet and real fast.

Marty then enthusiastically responded to Louis, "excellent planning! This should be a most interesting and revealing set of events unfolding in the next few days. Hopefully, we can clean the hotel and get things back on track the way everything should be. But even with security being replaced, we will still need to find and rid the hotel of the beast itself, and that as you have already eluded will be the determination of where the Mafia operation is centered in the hotel and who controls it. I'm sure everything will come to the surface in due course."

Marty almost choked on his own words, but in fact, he was forecasting the true future. He was sure he was not far off as he himself described events to come. He could only hope that somehow, he escapes it all and comes out smelling like a rose. He would take things one day at a time.

"All right then; that is it for today." Louis stood up and started packing up his briefcase as did Felix and Billy.

"I have a meeting scheduled in a short while with the chief engineer at The Red Jewel, so I'll say goodbye, and Marty I'll be talking to you shortly. Great job on the numbers by the way this month. I see you have exceeded budgeted occupancy, and the house profit looks good Marty. Now if we can transfer your expertise in hotel management to The Red Jewel and Holiday Jewel Moskva, we will all be in good shape."

Marty was relieved to receive a compliment from Louis; it relaxed him some after the tense morning. Louis smiled at Marty and patted him on the shoulder as he left the boardroom. Marty motioned to Felix and Billy as he held the door open for them; they all walked out and went about their business.

Misha Rudkin was standing by the front desk as Marty exited the elevator. Marty caught Misha's eye. There was an unmistakable look of "don't mess with me" coming from Misha's glare directed at Marty. Marty walked towards Misha and within ear range asked; "everything ship shape Misha?"

"Yes Mr. Sabine, all is in order," Misha replied.

***

Chapter Fourteen
Money, Traitors, and Vice

Misha Rudkin was a specialist in his field that being Hotel Director of Security. He had earned his stripes as an investigator in the Russian police force before joining the management staff of Holiday Jewel Danamo and as most career law enforcement officers he had a built-in sixth sense that set off alarms when things weren't feeling just right.

This morning's meeting had that sort of feel about it. No, it wasn't something that Misha Rudkin could actually put his finger on, but the feeling tore away at his gut which prompted him to act. That is the reason he was sitting in Alexander Mitkin's private booth at Gentleman's Stork Club, just one club in his many clubs that made up his local strip joints owned by Mitkin that made up most of his Moscow prostitution ring.

Mitkin rarely appeared at any of his clubs, but one table was always held in reserve in case he showed up or had one of his "private booth meetings" come up suddenly. This was one of those nights.

It had been no accident that Misha Rudkin was Director of Security at Danamo. He was handpicked by FSB and as the agreement between the new hotels and the joint venture Russian side, the Chief Engineer or Director of Security was to be a Russian local and in some cases even the Director of Human Resources. But even FSB operatives were lured away from duty and allegiance by the power of the Dollar. No, not the

Russian Ruble which was internationally worthless, but hard western currency that people such as Rudkin could sock away and live comfortably on during retirement, and of course adding to that was the human condition called greed.

Mitkin had bribed Rudkin, and now Rudkin was indebted to Mitkin, all while still being an FSB agent working as Director of Security at Holiday Jewel Danamo. Things don't get much more complicated in an ex-Russian Police investigator's life than this, and Rudkin was in neck deep now.

He was becoming anxious and sought out Mitkin for advice as well as endearing himself to Mitkin in alerting him of a possible detection of his operation at Holiday Jewel Danamo. It was all very tense, and Rudkin needed some reassurance that his association with Mitkin would not filter through to The FSB. It was all very Russian and all very complex, and now no doubt to become even more so.

Rudkin sat nursing his vodka and beer. When Mitkin showed up with his bodyguard, Rudkin stood up immediately in greeting Alexander Mitkin, but Mitkin motioned for him to remain seated. The booth was in a darker back wall of the lounge, far enough away from the other patrons and table dancing girls. Mitkin slid into the booth while his bodyguard remained at the booth's end, standing. No doubt his bodyguard carried a Micro Uzi sub machine gun underneath his jacket, as did the bouncer at the entrance to The Gentleman's Stork Club.

Mitkin himself was never armed, but his bodyguards and club bouncers were required to carry the Micro Uzi. It was small, but this weapon was designed to maintain strong automatic firepower albeit through handgun dimensions. It was the perfect personal defense weapon which in Mitkin's case was more of an offensive tool.

The Gentleman's Stork Club, in reality, was a sleazy establishment but managed to attract more than its fair share of patrons, mainly foreigners from oil-rich Azerbaijan and Kazakhstan. Mitkin had his tentacles throughout the former Soviet States which were now independently governed countries, but overnight stops were still required in Moscow since most flights to those outlying countries were routed with connecting flights the next morning through Moscow. Mitkin and his organization had his girls working the rich oil field regions throughout the former Soviet Union, and his clubs were well known to all who sought out his special brand of R&R.

"Misha, you are fortunate I am in Moscow for the next few days," Mitkin said to Rudkin. Mitkin did not shake hands with Misha; he just sat down opposite Misha in the dark booth, almost hidden by the lack of light. He nodded to his bodyguard who already had the bartender's attention. Alexander Mitkin's beverage of choice was prepared within a minute of his arrival. One of the scantily dressed waitresses brought over Mitkin's drink; Mitkin was never to be kept waiting, it was a glass of ice water, fresh spring water from the Urals. No, Mitkin did not drink an alcoholic beverage which was incredibly rare for a Russian.

"You are even more fortunate that I planned on visiting this club tonight for my usual monthly business meeting. Otherwise, I would have had to make a special trip here just to see you."

Misha's heart sank, having heard Mitkin's apparent annoyance with his need to see him. Then Mitkin let out a loud laugh breaking the sudden tension. Misha to this point hadn't even said a word yet and already he was feeling intimidated. Alexander Mitkin was good at being able to do that.

Misha wanted to get a word in, even if it was just edge-wise. "There are developments you need to be made aware of Alexander; I thought it best the sooner you knew, the better for us both." Misha finished saying.

"For us both!" Mitkin replied most emphatically, at the same time, looking up at his bodyguard, as his bodyguard then looked over at Misha. Mitkin was questioning and making a statement at the same time with his tone of surprise. Mitkin was toying with Rudkin; he could tell that Misha was very uncomfortable with this meeting, but it was Mitkin's nature to take the high ground in all his dealings with anyone he ever talked to. When Mitkin felt that the intimidation had grabbed hold, he would back off a little and have his prey move in a little closer, winning his confidence and attention, then pounce if necessary. It was his style; he was very good at it.

Even before Misha could start in again, Mitkin motioned to his bodyguard who reached inside his overcoat, took out an envelope and handed it to his boss.

"Misha, I know why you are here, and I expected this day to come, just not so soon," Mitkin said in a very matter of fact way.

"Not to worry, this will solve everything," reaching over the dark table handing the envelope to Misha which Misha took all the while nervously looking at Mitkin.

"Yes, that is what you think it is Misha, it is a video tape of our good Hotel General Manager. Not only does that videotape contain episodes of our girls fulfilling Mr. Manager's every sexual fantasy, but it also contains several of his most important hotel guests and clients employing the services of our wonderful young ladies. I'm sure Mr. Manager would not wish for that tape to be made available to the employers and wives of those gentlemen on that tape. Make good use of that tape Misha. I want you to place that videotape in Mr. Hotel Manager's room. Make sure he gets to see it. We will be in contact with Mr. Marty Sabine in a few days, just to let him know how much we care about his health and wellbeing, you know what I mean Misha?"

Misha nodded at Mitkin sitting across from him, saying "*da, da…* yes, yes."

With that Mitkin raised his hand, and flicked his fingers in a "come here" gesture towards the bar where his lounge manager was standing and watching Mitkin's booth like a hawk, indicating to him that he was now ready for some late-night company.

His lounge manager then pointed at two girls sitting waiting and watching for his sign at another table. Immediately the two young ladies, entertainers of the lounge came scurrying over to Mitkin's booth. Mitkin slid out and let one of the girls in who was now on the inside and the other young lady sat on the open end of the booth snuggled up beside Mitkin. Misha just watched as the young lady on the inside opposite him looked out at Misha and smiled while leaning in and down, all the while Misha could hear the sound of a zipper being undone and the young lady's head disappearing down in front of Mitkin.

Mitkin leaned back, and said to Misha, "I believe we are done here" as he closed his eyes while the young girl on the open end of the booth slid out of her panties and prepared to mount Mitkin in the darkness of the lounge, his bodyguard standing watch while Mitkin was being entertained.

Misha stood up and left with tape in hand as Mitkin's women continued servicing him.

Mitkin's usual monthly business meeting was now under way. His girls knew their business, and how to please him, they had no choice. Mitkin sipped his Urals water.

***

Chapter Fifteen
Crossed Wires

Feeds from the eight properties throughout Moscow were being captured now on a daily basis. *Raul* was functioning flawlessly. FSB's Black Bear project had secured the procurement of RUL technology and with *Raul* watching and listening for the past years at the eight hotels, a great deal of information in video and audio format had been collected, cataloged and now stored in the most secure section of FSB headquarters.

The storage of RUL information captured by FSB was categorized by the following computer menu groupings; Property, Date, Guest Name(s), Home Country, Company Name, Topic(s),

Corporate, Private, Duration. Those were the main category headings, all computer files with subcategories under each main menu item.

Everything could be cross-referenced with easy find, as well as indexing from one hotel property to any other on the network. In some instances, meetings were held at several hotels covering the same topic. This would occur mainly when several individuals were scheduled to meet at one particular property, but the attendees were staying at various locations. FSB's *Raul* surveillance would then coordinate and bring together information gathered from various locations, subsequent conversations, decisions, and follow-ups that could then be consolidated allowing for greater cohesion and subsequently joined as the "fully completed" picture captured and put together by *Raul*.

It truly was an ingenious example of FSB espionage intelligence gathering capability, all, of course, brought about and made possible by the American "*Raul*".

All the western joint venture properties having been built just within the last three years had been fitted with latest fiber optics technology for communication and television cable needs. The city itself was undergoing revitalization in this area, and all new buildings were tagged with this leap in communications capability. Without the fiber optics, *Raul* was not possible. It was the fiber optics that carried both the video and audio data that was then decoded by super encryption that only *Raul's* software was able to decode and then convert into a standard video signal and output, along with decoded audio.

The key and core of RUL technology lay in the ability of the associated software to convert the light source captured by the fiber optics and the sound source captured by laser resonance frequency interpretation.

Raul's ultrasound component capability was an added enhancement feature that would flesh out the image gathered by the radar tech, and the three working together generated the data required for *Raul's* software to create the images and audio.

With fiber optics leading to each property, it was just a matter of fitting the specific television sets with the fiber optic extension that was part of the television screen, along with the radar and ultrasound. The three types of tech data delivered and then recaptured by the same fiber optics, one being an output feed and the return an input feed. *Raul's* software would take over afterward, decoding the radar, the laser resonance and modulation that was picked up from the window panes fitted with a microscopic sized *Raul* data transceiver along with the ultrasound imaging.

This was top secret in the US military arsenal and now standard CIA issue utilizing *Raul* in their information gathering needs. The FSB now had it in their possession, was making use of it, fully. FSB technicians understood the theory of the technology but lacked the know-how of the software algorithms and complex data interpretation required to turn the data into intelligible information. But so long as the American software was doing its job, well FSB would live with the mystery of it all for now.

Sasha Bebchuk, FSB Director, was very happy thus far with what had been gathered, in fact, was very impressed with *Raul* but befuddled as to why his scientists and codebreakers were thus far unsuccessful in their efforts to reverse engineer the entire system and make their own FSB version.

CIA was very good at what they did. He would not underestimate the CIA ever and now understood not to underestimate Eldon Barnes Davis; the head of the company that designed *Raul*. Ironic as it was, that Eldon happened to be the owner-operator of The Red Jewel, now equipped with FSB's operation "Black Bear" *Raul*.

Bebchuk was indeed very pleased, once again he chuckled to himself, thinking how brilliant this plan had been and how incredibly well it had been deployed and now working for the past two plus years. Soon, the Red Jewel would become operational, and that would be his very own icing on Eldon Davis's cake. Bebchuk chuckled some more.

The past week had gone well. Sasha gathered the material provided to him by Vasily. The intelligence package had been put together most professionally providing a complete breakdown of all meetings held for the past two years in all the new hotels where *Raul* was watching and listening. Sasha's upcoming meeting with Viktor Orlov would be a review session of the information already having been gathered and cataloged and now the new updates and some of the new players involved in the business transactions conducted between the western companies and the Russian joint venture sides of the businesses. This information; being the private internal conversations of executives and how things would pan out with their companies coming into light with *Raul's* information gathering capabilities, now in the hands of the Russian FSB. Corporate secrets were no longer that secret, and this gave Orlov's government the upper hand when it came to upcoming and new negotiations with the western side. Sasha was pleased with himself.

What Sasha did not know however was that his organization wasn't the only one with eyes and ears already planted in the various hotels, that other body, of course, was none other than Sasha's half-brother's organization known by all as The Russian Mafia. In fact, Alexander Mitkin had been gathering information, video, and audio and then blackmailing almost on a regular basis, this would explain some anomalies detected by fragmented business dealings picked up and revealed by *Raul*. Sasha had wondered about the fragmentation but wasn't too concerned; perhaps he should have been.

***

Chapter Sixteen
Special Delivery

Misha Rudkin left Mitkin's booth at the Stork Club and walked outside into the cold winter night. He had tucked the envelope containing the videotape inside his overcoat's pocket. Having walked outside, he stopped on the curb and lit a cigarette, inhaling and then exhaling the cigarette smoke that now mixed with his cold breath forming a cloud in front of his face. Tiny thick flakes of snow fell obscuring the street lights. There was stillness in the Moscow air. The falling snow clouded his vision as his mind too was cloudy and thick with uncertainty as to what the outcome of all this would come to be.

Misha felt the chill in the night air and wanted to get on with things. He made his way over to his car, got into it and reached under his seat, pulling out a small bottle of vodka. He took a swig which seemed to revive him; he felt its heat going down his throat, and it felt good. The cold winter night didn't seem so cold now, he started the engine and drove off heading for Holiday Jewel Danamo.

It was late at night now, past midnight. If there was ever a time for Marty Sabine to be given this tape it would be now, tonight. It was always best to receive bad news in the middle of the night; it would be a much bigger impact, making things just a little direr than things might look in daylight.

Misha thought to himself, "yes, Marty would be wondering what the hell had just happened, but he for sure would watch the tape almost immediately, the curiosity would be overwhelming not to mention the bad omen to be broadsided so unexpectedly at such a late hour."

Misha would make certain that Marty got the tape without delay. Traffic was light even in Moscow this time of night, early morning just after midnight. He increased his speed; Holiday Jewel Danamo was no more than maybe a twenty-minute drive. It was almost 1:20 AM by the time Misha arrived at Jewel Danamo's front doors. No doorman was working the front doors during the graveyard shift, but there was ample security around at all times.

Two of Misha's security guards were stationed at all times in the lobby area of the hotel and with a car driving up to the front door at this hour, one of the security guards was always on hand. "Director Rudkin, this is an unusual hour for you to be her Sir, is there anything wrong?"

Misha replied, "No nothing is wrong at all, but there is some urgency in the works which Mr. Sabine needs to be made aware of," Misha replied.

The young security guard looked perplexed, with concern on his face, and attentive to Misha's every move as he made his way in through the front door of the hotel.

"Come with me," Misha said. The young security guard snapped to attention and followed Misha in step, wasting no time briskly walking through the lobby heading for the elevators. Misha reached into his overcoat pocket and extracted the envelope containing the videotape.

"Evi, I want you to take this envelope from me, and I want you to deliver it to Mr. Sabine's room now. It is very urgent, but I want you to do it. Come with me; I will escort you to Mr. Sabine's floor, and I will wait for you by the elevator while you go and knock on Mr. Sabine's door. When Mr. Sabine answers, just hand him the envelope, do not say anything other than, this is for you Mr. Sabine and have a good night, and then leave, got that Evi?"

Yes sir Mr. Rudkin, I just hand it to Mr. Sabine, and say have a good night and leave." replied Evi.

"Yes, that will be fine; I will wait for you by the elevator." Rudkin finished saying.

The elevator door opened on Marty's floor; it was in an alcove and two steps ahead one could turn either left or right accessing the entire length of the floor with the elevator being in the middle. The doors to the rooms were also receded one foot in from the walls so one could not see who if a door was open or closed by looking down the length of the corridor, it was well planned out for privacy purposes, a well-designed hotel. Evi walked down the hall and having reached Marty's suite stopped and knocked on Marty's door with greater than normal force thinking Marty might be sleeping and knocked hard enough to wake Marty.

Hearing the knocking on his door, Marty thought this to be unusual; he was already in bed and just about asleep when the knock came. Marty put on an evening robe and opened his door to see Evi the security guard standing there. Before Marty had a chance to ask, what the situation was, Evi stuck his hand out with the envelope but said nothing.

Marty, of course, reached out immediately and took it from Evi, and having done that, Evi said "Have a good night Mr. Sabine", turned and left.

Marty couldn't help it; he stepped out and looked down the hall in both directions, all he could see was Evi walking away and back towards the elevators. Marty shrugged and closed the door to his suite with envelope and videotape in hand.

Normally this would never happen; that Marty would be woken up to have a package delivered to him in the middle of the night. Even packages addressed to his attention via courier could wait until the following morning. Marty knew that "something was up" and he wasn't feeling too good about what that something might turn out to be.

"No point in overreacting," he thought to himself, but there was no way he could wait until the morning to open the envelope and see what was inside. It was one of those large padded bubble wrap reinforced mustard colored envelopes, a large one. Marty wasn't real sure what it was that was inside, but as soon as he broke the seal and reached inside, he knew by just the feel, it was a video tape. There was no way that he could put this viewing off until the morning. Marty became so nervous and overwhelmed by the need to view the videotape that in his haste he even inserted the tape backward…naturally it wouldn't go, but he kept trying instinctively realizing moments later that he was trying to fit a square peg into a round hole. Finally, he inserted the video cassette tape and sat on the couch, and pressed play.

It didn't take long, within seconds Marty was watching himself. This obviously was an edited version of events that had taken place over the past few weeks and couple of months. It was a compilation of Marty's Saturday night dinners with Ludmilla and Anna and just over the recent few Saturday nights; it had been several other women provided compliments of Alexander Mitkin including young Kati and her small group of Hungarian bus mates from Mitkin's Misery Tour.

Marty sat watching and now started feeling sick to his stomach. The video captured Marty and the young girls he had been taken advantage of in all sorts of sex acts and pleasures of the flesh not only in the living room area of his two-room suite but all throughout his small apartment.

In the kitchen, having sex on the kitchen counter, the island block in the kitchen, the bedroom, and even the hallway floor. Always two women serviced Marty. Marty now realized that his suite had audio and video surveillance hidden throughout the rooms at various angles which meant that his unit was either bugged with several devices, or it was being moved around from time to time to avoid his detection. It was plain to see that Marty was in big trouble. The videotape was not meant to be delivered for any other purpose than to make Marty fully aware that he was now totally indebted to the infiltration of his hotel by the Russian Mafia. Marty was about to shut the tape off since he'd seen more than enough of himself when the tape suddenly switched to completely different locations in the hotel.

"Whoa!" he cried out audibly to himself. "What was this?"

This was something he did not expect, but the sad realization sunk into his head that the virus in his hotel was not limited only to his suite but several others throughout the hotel. What Marty was watching now were scenes captured from the hospitality suite used as "The After Hours Club" and a continuing compilation of clips showing some of his hotel guests' and clients' activities in the hospitality suite. The clips captured all sorts of sex scenes with the very same girls as well as a few others that Marty had engaged as his personal dinner guests for the past several Saturday nights.

Marty immediately recognized the hotel guests in the video. They were the German sales executives, the Vice President of Magnus Oil Corporation out of France. There was also a clip of another gentleman from his own hotel suite, where a young lady was providing sexual favors, this gentleman happened to be an Evangelist who Marty himself greeted upon the troupe's arrival. That had been some three weeks ago. The religious organization's entire camera crew and church delegates were staying at the Holiday Jewel Danamo on a crusade mission of faith, preaching the gospel to an entire sports stadium full of faithful Russian Christian Evangelists.

Mitkin had managed to work his special talent with his women and poison the hotel entrapping a wide variety of his hotel guests in his web of prostitution. Marty was amazed at how easily Mitkin was able to do this and how weak a lot of his guests had been allowing themselves to be entrapped by and to the pleasures of the flesh.

Marty looked inward and thought to himself "he was no better" and just as weak and even weaker when it came to such pleasures as these poor bastards he was now viewing on the tape. Marty also understood that a video tape with this sort of content was something these executives would not ever wish to have made public, or presented to their corporations and much less to their wives.

This material was poison to the hotel's operations, even to its ongoing survival and Marty knew it. He was now in oh so deep; in such deep shit that he wasn't sure what he could do about all this, but he had to do something. Marty sat there on his couch for a while after the videotape had ended, thinking to himself... "what could he do?"

He wasn't able to get past that one question in his mind, "what could he do?" Answers would not come to him. For now, he could not see a way out or even so much as a temporary solution.

"Man o' man, was he ever screwed!

Although Mitkin's Mafia organization had managed to quite handily bribe security at the other hotels, and already planted his crude audio video bugs into the other seven properties, it was only the Holiday Jewel Danamo where Mitkin had the General Manager personally involved in his ring of crime. There was a reason for that, and the reason would soon become evident should the situation spiral out of control requiring more serious measures. Mitkin figured it had not yet come to that, but the arrows were pointing down that highway. Time would tell how things would pan out. In Mitkin's mind, it was now up to Marty.

Alexander Mitkin, however, had never really understood or grasped Holiday Jewel Hotels and Casinos' extermination capabilities when it came to ridding their properties of such infestation. In this case, it would be a matter of fighting fire with fire.

A "backburn" would soon take place. Eldon Davis would light that backburn. Eldon's backburn scorching technique would start with Holiday Jewel Danamo and then extend citywide snuffing out Mitkin's wildfire not one hotel at a time, but all properties in one dragnet maneuver right across Moscow. It would come upon him like a lightning bolt. Mitkin was about to find out for himself in the not too distant future.

The finishing touches on The Red Jewel downtown Moscow had been going very well over the past week, so well in fact that the hotel was almost ready to open from a building and facilities standpoint. The restaurants were ready to go, as were the lounges and the housekeeping department. Furnishings had been arriving all week long and with a full contingent of housekeeping staff already on board, the guest rooms were ready to receive hotel guests.

The only one thing holding up the entire hotel from actually opening its doors for business was the operations end of things. The points of sale transaction terminals were not yet fully programmed. So even though the kitchen had the ability to prepare a meal, it did not yet have the ability for the order to be generated by the food and beverage service staff. In addition, the menu items still needed programming into the restaurant and lounge point of sale system. But this would all be attended to and solved within days. It was not due to a lack of ability, it had all to do with scheduling the expertise in setting up the property management system and the integration of the property-wide point of sale to the front office system.

The technicians and property management systems implementation experts had been scheduled for these tasks months ago. To reschedule them earlier was a logistics modification being handled by the corporate controller; Ms. Paige who was doing a remarkable job in seeing that the I.T. Department moved along faster than planned. The Red Jewel was ready to open in just a few days' time now. Louis James would move things forward and surprise the night sky with activation of The Red Jewel's rotating ruby laser beam that would signify its opening. That would happen much sooner than planned.

Eldon was very pleased with the progress at The Red Jewel; it had been a week since the executive committee meeting held by Eldon and Kimberley.

FRANK JULIUS

Several individuals seated around that boardroom table on that morning had already been offered regional positions as was promised during the meeting and some had already relocated to the new offices inside The Red Jewel. Things were moving along well.

But there remained some housekeeping duties to be performed, and the cleaning needing to be done was not in the nature of dust, but in the nature of vice and prostitution.

The four gentlemen and two ladies had arrived for the coming weekend and longer. The planned sting operation at The Holiday Jewel Danamo was to get under way today being the Friday after the board room meeting and the laying out of the plan by Louis James, Felix, and Billy to Marty. This sting operation had to be successful. Eldon, Kimberley, and Louis were counting on the expertise of their undercover agents. It was crucial to the integrity of Holiday Jewel Hotels to act quickly and resolve the situation before the opening of The Red Jewel took place. Eldon wanted to make certain that The Red Jewel was clean and free of any possible prostitution even before the first guest set foot through the front doors of his new hotel.

***

Chapter Seventeen
Silent Prayer

Little Kati lay still as she could be in her bed, with her knees pulled up tight in the fetal position, she continued praying to God in silence. She had tried sleeping ever since getting back to her quarters late in the morning after having serviced several men the night before in a wild sex orgy at the Gorky After Hours Club. She was exhausted with her body having been ravaged. She was young, and she would recover only to be abused again night after night.

Mitkin was in charge of her life, Kati wanted to desperately end her young life and be done with it all, but she couldn't, she wouldn't because that would bring about the death of her loving mother and father. Mitkin had made it clear, by committing suicide and crossing Mitkin, death would come to her parents, so Kati continued on and now she prayed quietly and deeply. She cried as she said the words in her mind and forming on her lips, in Hungarian she prayed.

"*Kedves Jo Istenem*, My Dear God, please hear my prayer. I beg of you on my little brother's life, please show me a way out of here, please show me a way out of this misery, and please show me a way to take my dear friends with me, out of this life. I pray to you and ask for your mercy with love in my heart, My Dear God, please hear my prayer, Amen."

Kati said those words so softly on her lips while holding a picture of her murdered little brother close to her heart. She continued sobbing till she ran out of tears.

It was time to get up and out of bed. She would need to get on with things and get ready for another day and night of her miserable existence.

***

Chapter Eighteen
A Backstage Visitation

The afternoon's meeting in Pushkin Hall at the Kremlin had come to a close. It had gone well, exceeding everyone's expectations. Although the meeting was over, for Kimberley and Eldon there was to be a brief follow-up or perhaps better said an "encore."

When Kimberley and Eldon had first arrived this afternoon, and were greeted by Svetlana Orlov, Svetlana had mentioned briefly to Kimberley that she would love to take a few minutes and do some "catching up." Well, Svetlana was true to her word and as the meeting was breaking up a Kremlin usher, a young man dressed in a ceremonial military outfit and wearing white gloves approached Kimberley and Eldon. He handed Kimberley an official Kremlin envelope. Kimberley accepted the envelope from the smartly dressed young usher saying
"*spasiba*, thank you."

Eldon was standing right beside Kimberley. She looked up at Eldon, raised her eyebrows, and then started to unseal the envelope and extract its content. The young Russian Kremlin Usher had taken one step back and respectfully stood at attention while Kimberley read the invitation.

The card inside the envelope read: "My dearest Kimberley. I hope I am not imposing on your valued time. Viktor and I would be honored to have the company of you and Eldon in The Kremlin Library. Please follow your escort, he will show you the way.

The invitation card was signed in ink "Svetlana".

Eldon and Kimberley both read the card at the same time and having read it, they both looked up at the young usher and nodded okay. With their agreement, the young usher then said in English "please" and motioned for Eldon and Kimberley to follow him as they walked out of Pushkin Hall and down the corridor leading outside onto the sprawling courtyard and over to the building that housed the Kremlin Library.

The young usher led the way. A Kremlin Guard followed a respectable fifteen feet behind to ensure security. This was The Kremlin; nobody walked alone.

As Eldon and Kimberley followed the young Russian usher outside and across the courtyard, the snow had started to fall again but just lightly. By four o'clock in the afternoon, the light was already starting to fade; being close to six in the evening daylight was replaced with darkness.

The courtyard lights had come on illuminating the falling snowflakes. Stillness was in the air, as the American hotel moguls walked the grounds of the Kremlin. It was about a forty meter walk across to the Kremlin Library building. Knowing that the Davis's were to meet with The President and the Russian First Lady, the courtyard sweepers had been instructed to clear the cobblestones of snow for Eldon and Kimberley.

Eldon put his right arm around Kimberley's shoulder as they walked slowly. He embraced Kimberley closer, and leaning in towards her, gave her a light kiss on the side of her forehead, then whispered into her ear; "this ought to be interesting."

Kimberley turned her head towards Eldon and wrapping her arm around his back as they walked, she replied, "yes babe, this will be interesting for sure. I wonder what else this day will bring?"

Kremlin Military Guards were positioned to flank the entrance to any building that was at any time occupied by The President of Russia, this was strictly internal protocol and by no means intended as security although the guards were trained to guard The President if ever the need arose. The Kremlin was already well-secured perimeter wise. The Kremlin Library building's main door was this evening designated with a pair of guards on either side.

As Eldon and Kimberley made their way to the entrance the guards snapped to attention as if the Russian President himself was to walk through the library building doors. It mattered not who was to enter the building, knowing that The President of The Russian Federation was to receive guests, anyone, and everyone entering was greeted by the same protocol and deference being guests of The President. Eldon was quite impressed with the show of respect not so much to him and Kimberley but for the atmosphere of power and tradition that the motions conveyed and projected. It worked very well.

The office of the American Presidency currently occupied by President Fenton was considered to be the most powerful seat in the world. Eldon was sure that sentiment or opinion was not one that was shared in The Kremlin.

As they approached closer, there was no knock on the doors needed, the guards flanking either side of the entrance opened the doors and in walked Kimberley and Eldon with the young usher stepping to the side. Another two ushers were present inside the library, and one of the ushers took Eldon and Kimberley's coats while the other motioned for them to follow.

Kimberley and Eldon were shown to an open doorway just down the foyer hallway and as they turned to walk through and into the library, there stood Viktor and Svetlana Orlov looking over a huge model of Moscow laid out on a large table enclosed with a glass dome set in the middle of the large open room. As Eldon and Kimberley entered, Viktor and Svetlana looked up from the model towards the entrance. The Orlovs started walking towards them, with Svetlana reaching her arms out to hug Kimberley and kiss each cheek with a warm embrace. Both men allowed a few moments for the two women to greet one another as old college friends of many years gone by.

Having greeted one another, Svetlana reached out her hand towards Eldon, and shaking his hand she said: "Welcome to The Kremlin Eldon, it is such a pleasure to have you and Kimberley join Viktor and me this evening, thank you for coming." With that, then Svetlana continued on, "Eldon Davis, my husband, Viktor."

Eldon then responded, "Mr. President, my pleasure to meet once again." Eldon extended his hand. Viktor moved in a step and reached out as the two men shook hands, Viktor much to Eldon's surprise spoke up in English!

"Mr. Davis, it is also my pleasure to meet once again, in much less formal surroundings and to know you in person, and please, today it is "Viktor."

Eldon was much surprised. With The President speaking up in English Eldon could not help but glance over to Kimberley showing an impressive expression causing Svetlana to speak up.

"Yes, my husband has been studying the English language and has mastered a respectable level of conversational English. Officially, of course, we maintain protocol and government translators are provided and accompany all Kremlin related matters." Svetlana finished and smiled at her husband; The President of The Russian Federation.

"Mr. President", Kimberley reached out to shake Viktor's hand.

"Thank you for your kind invitation. Naturally, we couldn't wait to make your better acquaintance; it is such a pleasure."

Viktor then once again responded. "Please Kimberley, Viktor this evening, perhaps next time it will be Mr. President but today it' is Viktor."

Kimberley well knew what Viktor Orlov meant by "next time" being in a public setting or diplomatic gathering. It was most gracious of the Orlovs to have them in their company as friends (in quotation marks, Kimberley thought) this evening.

As the four stood greeting one another and with the few words of pleasantries having been exchanged, Eldon noticed and noticed very clearly that Viktor had a sense and aura about him that could not be mistaken even in this most relaxed atmosphere. Even in this very personal setting, being the Orlov's home, albeit inside The Kremlin but nevertheless The Russian President's home. He projected power, strength, and conviction. When Viktor Orlov looked at you, he not only looked at you but looked into you. Eldon felt it, his eyes pierced into Eldon's and cut into the fabric of his American entrepreneurial spirit.

Both men were sizing up one another. Only in this instance size was not to be a measure of how tall one stood. Viktor Orlov was barely five feet seven inches tall, but make no mistake about it; any man lacking self-confidence would be reduced to that of a worm in Viktor's presence. Orlov was only five seven in height but carried the might of a world nuclear power, perhaps the most feared nation on earth at this time and on this given day if for nothing else than the country's current state of volatility.

With the snap of his fingers, Orlov could put the entire world on alert. This Eldon knew and understood, yet Eldon had a sensed "an atmosphere of need" that Orlov projected and that need was aimed at Eldon. Viktor needed Eldon and Kimberley to help shape and carve out his new country's international posture and subsequent status.

Eldon decided that wisdom with caution would be the recipe for success this evening. Eldon was almost six feet in height, but he most definitely saw eye to eye with Viktor Orlov. This sizing equation contained parts consisting of achievement, ability, vision, and action. Those parts of the equation equaled the constant that was Viktor Orlov.

At this time, Eldon sensed a level of comfort laced with a healthy dose of "keep your friends close and your enemies even closer" feeling.

Eldon could only hope there was a mutual amount of respect and understanding with Viktor that would see their relationship grow and prosper over the coming months and years. He hoped his initial gut feeling was right. Eldon sort of liked Viktor or maybe, for now, he was just fascinated with The Russian President, especially after having witnessed Viktor's surprise presentation at this afternoon's meeting in Pushkin Hall.

Viktor was very impressive. With all that had happened in the last forty-eight hours here in Moscow, The Russian President no doubt had urgent matters to address behind the scenes. Eldon was keenly aware that Viktor Orlov thought it a priority in making time for this brief encounter. Obviously, a relationship with Holiday Jewel Hotels and Casinos, him and Kimberley was on top of Orlov's list. This fact did not escape Eldon or Kimberley.

Eldon could hardly wait to speak with Kimberley about the events of today and now this most unusual but important evening with the Orlovs that was about to get under way. Eldon figured this would be short but poignant.

Svetlana spoke up: "Please, come, see the selection of traditional Russian delicacies our chef has prepared. It is almost dinner time. I'm sure you and Eldon must be thinking of food by now, come, please let us enjoy this fine selection. Viktor and I regret that we weren't able to make this a dinner invitation. Viktor will have to break away shortly with other pressing matters, but we both most definitely wanted to take these few precious minutes in having this intimate private visit." Svetlana finished saying as she moved towards a decorated buffet table.

A smartly dressed Chef was tending to the buffet table and assisted in plating the selections as the four walked down the length of the table. The buffet table was adorned with delightful Russian delicacies. The hors d'oeuvres and appetizers consisted of pickled cucumbers, raw slices of bacon, fermented sour cabbage, meat jelly or aspic. There was salami with Russian black bread, pickled mushroom and marinated herring, caviar, of course, pickled tomatoes, and not to be left out was famous Shashlik, known in the western world as shishkabob. To top things off, Foie gras imported from France.

The table was very elegant, but neither Eldon nor Kimberley was fond of Russian appetizers. The Holiday Jewel Danamo served these appetizers on a daily basis, and the sales were very good but neither of them ever really developed a taste for pickled herring or meat in aspic. They both did however enjoyed Foie gras and arranged a small plate of the delicacy with Russian black bread and asked the Chef to split a skewer of shashlik between the two of them. Having made their selections, they moved to a round table with settings for four. A Sommelier came to offer a selection of either red or white wine, both from the wine growing region of The Black Sea. Eldon selected red as did Kimberley, Viktor, and Svetlana.

Viktor did not stand, but he was the first to speak. "Mr. and Mrs. Davis, Eldon and Kimberley, it is mine and my wife's pleasure to have you at our table this evening. We trust this to be the roots of a long-lasting friendship from this day forward. Here I make a toast to great successes and inroads to be realized for us, for you and your company." Viktor reached out his glass and toasted Eldon, then Kimberley as they all touched glasses and sipped the Black Sea Russian wine. Svetlana could not help but look on with great pride in her husband and eagerly anticipating Eldon and Kimberley's reaction and response.

Eldon decided to take on this effort in mutual understanding and an invitation to a much deeper relationship between the two families. What Eldon found most interesting in these first few minutes were the contrasting projections, "the powerful and not to be messed with" President of The Russian Federation, contrasted now to Viktor's casual demeanor that perhaps one might expect from a trusted lifelong friend. Eldon wasn't sure what to make of this... perhaps Viktor was trying too hard to win over Eldon and Kimberley or maybe this was the real Viktor Orlov in his private world, which he momentarily allowed him and Kimberley to step into.

Kimberley was quite adept in these types of situations. Her expertise with diplomatic situations having learned and honed the proper responses to any event in any venue presenting or requiring proper etiquette was well within her realm but in this case, she knew it was Eldon's turn to respond and already she was impressed with Eldon's counter not even having uttered a word yet.

"Mr. President." Eldon paused, "Viktor, both Kimberley and I are very pleased and honored for this opportunity to meet with you and Svetlana here in this privacy of your home. Please accept our condolences for the Russian compatriots who chose to lose their lives in the struggle of your nation finding its true pathway. We understand that even the loss of citizens with opposing views can diminish the overall strength of a nation knowing that dissension and disagreement within a democracy can make "a people" stronger. It was unfortunate that there could be no other way out." Eldon paused again.

"I respect your invitation this evening was to hinge on a lighter note, but the obvious cannot be ignored, and both Kimberley and I extend our heartfelt feelings and concern that these recent events have no doubt brought about a need for wisdom. We both believe that your actions will bring about the peace and prosperity the world now expects and waits upon from the new Russian Federation."

Eldon raised his glass, extended it towards Viktor Orlov and said; "Viktor; to the victor" and with that the four toasted once again. Kimberley sat beside her husband, so proud, so pleased and so American.

Viktor Orlov then decided to engage in a little conversation.

"Eldon, I was watching your presentation this afternoon from a remote location. I have to commend you on your knowledge of our city and the detail you possess concerning the hotel business in terms of our needs today and for many years to come in the future for Moscow and Russia. I am very pleased as is my wife in your decision to expand your operations into our new Russian Federation. I know that with the opening of The Red Jewel, your crowning achievement will have been accomplished. I understand that the opening date of the Red Jewel has been moved up to be just a few days or perhaps weeks away."

"Yes Viktor, we have made much better progress than anticipated, and a great deal of the credit is due to your excellent construction work crews and engineering team that made this building and project possible. We are in fact very much ahead of schedule and look forward to our grand opening. Our executive team will announce the official opening date within the coming week and it will be our honor if your schedule allowed for your and Svetlana's attendance." Eldon finished saying, reaching over towards Kimberley and taking hold of her hand, signifying their joint effort in making this most important and landmark hotel come to fruition in Orlov's city.

"Eldon, I will make it a priority in doing what we can to being there for your grand opening. I trust you did not mind the modifications our electronics modeling team had made to your Moscow city model presentation. I know you were unaware of the further modifications that were added and brought about in order to reshape the future of Moscow as presented by the new buildings in addition to your crowning jewel to the Moscow skyline. It will be a day to remember and to be marked when The Red Jewel's ruby laser light comes to life piercing the Moscow night sky inviting the world to visit." Viktor finished saying and taking a finishing drink from his wine glass.

"Mr. President, Viktor, it was a most unexpected and very impressive presentation and vision of Moscow. Your presence focused the attention and determination to the reshaping of Moscow, the international efforts put forth in attracting new commerce and prosperity to come." Eldon responded and Kimberley added, "absolutely Mr. President."

Having said that, and having just heard what Viktor had finished saying, Eldon couldn't help but think to himself; "I wonder what other modifications have been going on without my knowledge?"

But Eldon left it to the side for now. There was a sense of caution though that Eldon now paired to every word Viktor spoke. This meeting with Viktor and Svetlana had proven most interesting and in Eldon's mind brought about a need for reflection and review.

"I'm afraid that time has come for my husband's need to step away from our visit. Viktor has an evening meeting scheduled with his national security advisers." Svetlana said disappointingly, standing and extending her hand to Kimberley, signaling the end of this evening's brief encounter. Pleasantries were exchanged, and the four parted ways with the young smartly dressed Kremlin usher showing up all of a sudden to escort Eldon and Kimberley back outside the Kremlin and out to their vehicle in the Kremlin visitor parking lot. Eldon and Kimberley's day and evening had come to an end at The Kremlin. They walked silently together arm in arm back across the courtyard on the freshly swept cobblestones, following their escort.

Eldon's driver and bodyguard had been waiting the entire afternoon and now evening for their return. The Kremlin had a "driver's lounge" where Maxim had relaxed most of the day taking in a Russian Roman Greco wrestling competition on television, so he was well entertained during the wait. Now however Maxim was ready and waiting for Eldon and Kimberley's arrival, making certain that he was there to greet them, and he was. Eldon and Kimberley got inside their Beemer, and Maxim headed out driving into the Moscow night air. Eldon and Kimberley sat in the back; Kimberley snuggled up to Eldon, neither saying a word. There would be much to discuss later.

After a few minutes, Kimberley took Eldon's hand into her lap and whispered to Eldon. "I love you so much honey."

Eldon then put his arm around Kimberley's shoulders, brought her in closer to his side, and the two of them watched the street light poles passing by in the Moscow night. The snow fell, the star on the Kremlin tower shined brightly, and across town, Mitkin's sex slave, little Kati from Hungary was applying her makeup, preparing for another miserable night at The Gorky after hours club.

***

Chapter Nineteen
Setting the hook

The four gentlemen who were to act as bait for the internal sting operation had arrived by 2: PM this Friday afternoon to Holiday Jewel Danamo. Before coming checking in to Jewel Danamo, they had already scoped out the city's other hotels having arrived four days earlier on the previous Monday. The two from Toronto, Ken, and Harry flew in via Frankfurt and the two from Detroit, Stu, and Cameron flew into Moscow International earlier on in the morning having caught the red-eye from Heathrow.

Check in process at the hotel went very well, all was in order, and their in-house reservations status was flagged in the computer guest history file as "auto convention attendees."

The two women who were to pose as "escorts and ladies of the night" were also already registered but no mention of convention attendance, their status indicated "business visas". Millie and Frances knew how to attract attention but only when the situation required. Upon arriving and checking into the Holiday Jewel Danamo, both women wore business attire and drew no unwanted attention. Attention getting will be at a later time this evening.

The two ladies had already made their presence known in city's other western style properties having rendezvoused with Ken, Stu, Cameron and Harry. They had run their bait and tackle with hotel security officers throughout the city. It was only the men who changed hotel accommodation having checked into different hotels each night testing the properties active prostitution rings. For the past week, Millie and Frances were working out of the six hundred eighty room mega hotel The Royal British House. From there, the two ladies would meet up during the night with the four men stationed at various properties posing as targets for Millie and Frances to hit upon, thereby undercutting the local ladies of the night if in fact, any were present.

As things had turned out, every hotel in the city had Mitkin's fingerprints all over them. The prostitution ring was pervasive throughout the western properties. Frances and Millie were asked to leave each and every hotel in which they made their presence felt, with two property's security guards manhandling both women grabbing them by the arms and forcibly removing the two from the hotel. The guys, of course, were welcome to stay. No sooner had Millie and Francis been removed, Harry and Cameron were immediately approached by inhouse hookers working for Mitkin and watched over by hotel security. This had been happening all week long at every property, but it was only at one of the hotels; The Universal Hotel where the two ladies got a bit roughed up, Harry and Cameron made sure they weren't abused by security, just removed.

The in-house computerized property management system which held the front office system for The Holiday Jewel Danamo was the key data source for all hotel operations. The information it contained was for all intents and purposes confidential and in essence meant to be utilized for the benefit of all guests and hotel management. This data, however, as with all data, could be used in nefarious ways if in the hands of the wrong people, or in this case in the hands of management staff who happened to have been bought off by Mitkin and his crew.

One such individual making up the management committee of the hotel was, of course, Misha Rudkin; the head of security for the property. Misha had full access to all guest related information held by the property management system. He could look up information about any guest in any room no matter if they were in-house at the moment or had stayed at the hotel a year ago, or had reservations waiting a year out in advance. He had access to everything, which normally would be a good thing, but his main reason for accessing guest information was to determine which hotel guests were associated with which companies so that he could channel the desired information to Mitkin thereby enabling Mitkin to hit upon the most vulnerable and potentially most lucrative investment opportunity to be pursued after the guests' departure.

The investment, in this case, would hinge and center on blackmail and extortion, which was to kick in a week or two after the guest had departed, and meant to come as a sudden unexpected shock that resulted in panic thereby inducing emergency action by the individual being infected.

It was classic and genius Mafia textbook operations, proven over and over again wherever their tentacles reached around the world and yet to this day never being overcome.

Mitkin, however, had never dealt with Eldon Davis's Holiday Jewel Hotels and Casinos crew. He was about to learn a new lesson.

Billy Simpson, Eldon's personal pilot and one could even say protector of Eldon and his family, along with Felix Balon; officially Eldon's Public Relations Manager, were Eldon's two closest friends and business associates.

Yes, both were in Eldon's and now Eldon's and Kimberley's employment but with very special status within the company. So, special was their relationship with Eldon and Kimberley that Eldon had both Billy and Felix added into his last will, as beneficiaries. Of course, neither Billy nor Felix had any idea that Eldon had filed a codicil to that effect.

The four actually formed a group, an unbreakable and cohesive unit. From time to time, both Billy and Felix found themselves involved in situations that only they could understand and know how things needed to be dealt with. Officially they had their duties as employees and key members of the company, but unofficially they were family and whatever the situation demanded to ensure and solidify the integrity of Holiday Jewel Hotels or the safety of "the family" and those under the umbrella of the company, well... Billy and Felix were always there.

They both were true to the core, dedicated and acted with love and desperation when needed. Now may be one of those times. With the pending sting operation to be getting under way, both Billy and Felix were prepared for just about anything, even if it meant having to deal with life-threatening situations. Felix and Billy both well understood that Russian Mafia thugs were not to be taken lightly. Billy had done his research and Felix; well he was just in the know of all things. Eldon himself never failed to be amazed at how sometimes Felix seemed already to be one step ahead of Eldon, and that was no easy feat.

Eldon and Kimberley set the pace for things to come set and defined the pathway. Felix then provided the paving to make things a smooth ride in the expansion of Holiday Jewel Hotels and Casinos.

Today with the arrival of the sting operatives, Billy and Felix would be ready, knowing that both of them would be called upon.

Billy Simpson, congressional medal of honor recipient and ex F14 Tomcat fighter pilot, a veteran of the Gulf War and savior of Eldon's darling little girl Cathy, was someone not to be fooled with. Billy Simpson could rip the beating heart out of an opponent with one blow to the chest cavity. Billy was a docile man in his own heart, but make no mistake, never ever underestimate Billy Simpson, he could and would if necessary eat you alive.

Billy was prepared to lay his life down for Eldon, or Felix or Kimberley and most especially for Cathy, his darling little co-pilot.

"Take me flying Billy-Bob... take me flying up with the birds, I love you so much Billy-Bob." Billy could hear Cathy singing in his head still from five years ago. Billy experienced no greater joy in his life than on the day when he and Eldon broke down the door to the cottage where Cathy was held hostage. That day Cathy was reunited with Eldon, back into her father's loving arms. That was some five years ago on a deserted Bahamian Island, and since that time Cathy had grown but still loved to fly with Billy every chance she could. Billy was Uncle BillyBob to Cathy and Billy's heart melted just thinking of Eldon's baby doll. Eldon knew of the love Billy and Felix had for his little girl; his family was in good hands in all four corners of this loving and dedicated relationship. Not long afterward, Kimberley became part of Eldon's family and stepmommy to Cathy.

Stu, Cameron, Harry and Ken left the hotel and rendezvoused with Billy and Felix later that afternoon at Izmailova flea market, a good hour drive from the hotel. This was very neutral ground, very pedestrian and very discreet. There Billy then distributed five pagers to the five of them including Felix. All pagers were synchronized to Billy's and Felix's pager with dedicated ID's for each one. Stu was code 11, Cameron Code 12, Harry Code 13, Ken code 14. Billy's pager ID was code 00, and Felix's 01 The activation of the pagers placing a signal to Billy's unit would only ever be initiated in a situation of emergency whereby Billy was needed on the scene immediately due to trouble. At all times during the sting operation, Billy would be aware of the five's approximate locations, communication prior to engagement of an operation and the location of the sting was always preset. The four operatives were now ready. The two ladies would be handled in the same manner, both Millie and Frances were met by Billy at Danamo Metro subway station where the ladies were equipped with pagers, codes 16 and 17 respectively, following the same protocol. No further meetings for now, would be necessary between Billy and the operatives.

Felix also had a pager but probably wouldn't find himself in a position to need it other than receiving a signal that the sting was in play, but better to err on the side of caution. Felix would come into play where help of a different nature was needed, one of compassion and sanctuary. Eldon's special team of men and women were now ready to do what they came for. It was now Friday late afternoon; the sun was setting. The hotel was starting to come alive.

The bars had started filling up, the restaurant was solidly booked with reservations, The Gorky club would be hopping tonight; Marty was sure about that.

The scene was set, the players were in position, and little Kati was sitting on the subway train, making her way into the heart of the city, changing trains at Mezhdunarodnaya midtown subway station and heading to Holiday Jewel Hotel Danamo, just a fifteen-minute ride on the jam-packed train.

It was Friday, the convention was in town, Kati's dreaded day had arrived, she sat silently on the train seat, her eyes watering slightly, in the inside pocket of her overcoat she carried the cherished photograph of her family back home in Hungary. She felt the train coming into the station; she stood up as it slowed, wiped a tear from her eye and stepped out, onto the platform making her way to the Metro station escalators. It was a quarter mile deep underground, the ride up to the surface had two change levels, Kati emerged on street level, took in the cool winter night air and walked through the snow towards her destiny.

***

Chapter Twenty
Black Bear

Viktor Orlov's meeting with his National Security Adviser was with none other than Sasha Bebchuk his Director of The FSB. The topic for discussion and update tonight was project "Black Bear".

Having just finished meeting with Eldon and Kimberley Davis, The President found it ironic having had the kingpins of Holiday Jewel Hotels and Casinos at The Kremlin Library, sharing appetizers and pleasantries. 1 hotel magnates while now a few minutes later, he and Sasha Bebchuk would, in essence, be spitting into the eye of the red ruby laser soon to come alive atop The Red Jewel Hotel.

"Black Bear" had been operational for a good length of time gathering and siphoning information derived from this government contrived corporate espionage snooping endeavor. It had paid off in ways neither Sasha nor Viktor had predicted, thanks to the eyes and ears provided by Eldon Davis' very own surveillance technology and CIA controlled RUL "*Raul*".

There had been many small victories so to speak leading to nothing more than gaining insight into the corporate climate and structure shaped by key company executives. That type of information could prove very significant when the right opportunity presented itself, not always in the near future but bound to come in play perhaps several years down the road. All information could at one time or another prove useful, was just a matter of when and where and why. But there were also some major victories attained without the opponents even knowing about it, all due to the RUL technology, *Raul's* listening and watching capabilities. Just exactly what was meant by that?

The most recent victory came about with *Raul* picking up an executive gathering's conversation of The Swiss drug giant "Qurit Corporation," looking to partner with a Russian company in expanding into the Russian market. *Raul* had picked up a definitive conversation that specified the very top percentage that the company was willing to offer to the Russian partner. That conversation had taken place behind closed doors at the Patriotic Hotel. The information was then passed on to the executives at the Russian company by FSB operatives who enabled Robek Pharmaceuticals, the Russian potential partner to offer conditions acceptable to the Swiss corporate executives. The deal was done, and *Raul* had paid off big in that espionage insight.

"Yes Sasha, that was well played." Your information gathering efforts and most importantly the follow-up was handled beautifully. I have no doubt that Robek Pharmaceuticals will be indebted to us for many years to come, and we can count on their generous financial contributions to our political party." Viktor commended his FSB Director.

"Thank you, Mr. President, as this one particular success depicts, we have several more situations similar to information that enabled the partnership between Qurit and our Russian Robek Company. We are currently working on notifying the Russian entities on the other opportunities." Bebchuk finished saying with more than a little pride in his voice. Bebchuk lit another Cheyenne cigarette.

"That is very good Sasha. So then, we have eyes and ears in all Western hotels now. Is that right Sasha? Viktor anticipated Sasha's answer to be affirmative but asked nevertheless.

"Yes Viktor, we have eyes and ears on every property, and even as we speak, the final workings have been completed at The Red Jewel. As soon as the new hotel opens, we are in operation there as well." Bebchuk answered definitively.

"Excellent Sasha, excellent I knew you were the man to make this happen. It has taken almost four years, but you saw it through with your crack team of experts. I believe The FSB has evolved into a most formidable agency outdoing itself in these times of covert surveillance techniques. Well done Sasha. Continue with your operation; let us glean as much as we can while we can."

Viktor then said. "Sasha, I believe that will be all for now. I will be attending the grand opening of The Red Jewel. It will be an ironic day for our government and The FSB. I understand the announcement of the opening day will be made in
the coming month."

"Yes Mr. President, the Red Jewel will open soon, and we are always close-by with our Black Bear control center located just two buildings down from the new hotel at 6 Krasnaya Ulitca (Red
Street).

"The motherland thanks you and your team of experts for your dedication and ingenuity." Viktor then stood and toasted Bebchuk with a cling of rock glasses. Bebchuk sipped Kentucky bourbon and The President of The Russian Federation drinking twelve-year-old Scotch on the rocks. Both Bebchuk and Orlov had acquired international taste buds in their preferences for alcoholic beverages.

Viktor Orlov was most pleased with the progress of his FSB Director. Their meeting had come to an end, but before departing, Orlov commented to Bebchuk: "keep that "black bear" sniffing around, make sure it does not hibernate." "Yes, Mr. President, the bear is out on patrol," Sasha replied.

***

Chapter Twenty-One
Ladies of the night

The Moscow International Automotive Show was to kick off tomorrow morning, Saturday. The past week, however, had been party week with all the hotels in the city being almost to capacity, not just the western style hotels but even the older Russian hotels, enjoying good occupancy. The Holiday Jewel Danamo Hotel had a full contingent of staff, with extra labor on hand to make certain all hotel services were humming at maximum efficiency. Hotel management had planned ahead. Upon entering the lobby of the Danamo, one was greeted with a historic display of the International Automobile Industry. The lobby featured real cars dating back to the first steam driven carriages, along with models manufactured during the Soviet era, spanning the industry from 1929 to the dissolving of the Soviet State in 1991.

It was all Marty's idea to set the lobby up in this historic fashion in honor of the automobile industry over the years. He made sure to contrast the past with the advanced modernization of the industry and the huge pending international trade in auto parts and sales including the top manufacturers of the world from Mercedes and BMW to the upcoming Formula 1 races to be held in Moscow. This coming week's auto show would be a boom for the city and a boom for Mitkin's ladies of the night along with a contingent of foreign working girls flying in to work the convention floor itself.

Mitkin with his prostitution empire, however, was going to do all he could to make sure the visiting prostitutes would only be left with scraps from the table. Mitkin and his crew of young women would be sure to sweep up the cream of the crop gentlemen who were looking for his brand of entertainment; Mitkin had all the hotels covered. Millie and Frances were busily and artfully applying their more than friendly makeup. The two women were pros at transforming themselves into high-class escorts. Although they had no doubt that every man in the hotel looking for their type of women, would be looking to "hit" on the two of them, they would be protected under Ken and Harry's wings. Then of course in case things were to get out of hand, it was just a matter of a pager tweet, and Billy Simpson would appear practically out of nowhere.

The time was now close to 11: PM. Marty noticed the lobby lounge had become full of customers. The hotel's gourmet dining room had been to capacity with two complete turns of the 95 seats. They had served almost two hundred people in the dining room, with the first seating at 7: PM and second around 8:30 PM and now the dining room was starting to thin out although the kitchen remained open until 11: PM for the late comers. Marty had no doubt that the kitchen would end up preparing meals this night for 250 covers and at an average check of sixty-six dollars and fifty-four cents, the restaurant stood to generate revenue of seventeen thousand dollars in food sales alone, not to mention another expected forty percent of that amount in beverage sales. It was a good night for the hotel.

This was good for Marty, but with Marty now having both feet firmly planted one being in hell and the other in heaven, Marty knew he was caught between a rock and a hard place. Marty was told not to interfere or to make contact with the sting team. He didn't. He kept his distance but couldn't help himself wanting to know just exactly what was going on. Marty was told that he would be contacted by Billy or Felix when the need arose.

Marty wanted to be ready but being afraid of what was to come down the pike wasn't bolstering his bravado, no, in fact, Marty was feeling sheepish. It would only be a matter of time before this group of experts uncovered and exposed the prostitution ring that had ingrained itself into Marty's hotel operations and possible his implication. Marty walked throughout the hotel like a lost soul, he didn't have any idea how he was going to get out of this, and how the hotel would not swallow him up in the revelation that was sure to happen and soon.

Marty walked about from restaurant to lounge, to the banquet halls. He stopped by the front desk, pretended to be looking at the computer system reviewing guest information but in reality, he was lost and probably looking a little rattled. He decided to go up to his suite for a while and try calming down. Before he went to his hotel suite, he decided to check in on The Gorky Club, sure enough, Vlad was just showing Stu and Cameron to a table in a quieter corner of the lounge. It was 11:PM, the Gorky club would be ripe and ready for Stu and Cameron.

Marty had no doubt Anna and Ludmilla would soon be working their charms on Cameron and Stu. It was now just a matter of time. Marty thought to himself "well, the chips will fall where they fall." Tonight, would turn into tomorrow and tomorrow is another day. All he could do was to take each one at a time.

Eldon and his crew had handled this type of situation a number of times in their other hotels and resorts. This type of special handling need arose from time to time in the Caribbean properties. No matter how vigilant casino management was, eventually working girls found their way into his casinos and from time to time his casinos needed "weeding out."

Eldon had insisted that in approaching these situations, it needed to be both extermination of the organization and the rescue of women and young girls who in some cases found themselves forced into the world's oldest profession. Eldon had no misconceptions that in Russia some of the criminal world's hardest and cruelest conditions prevailed over the lives of women who were caught up in the net of organized crime.

Eldon's operatives, in this case, Ken, Cameron, Harry, Stu, Frances, and Millie were to ferret out the organization and if possible offer an out for the ladies of the night who found themselves trapped and forced into an unwanted situation.

Granted, some ladies had chosen and pursued these opportunities openly, but some were caught up in the whole ungodly deplorable situation with no way out. Ken, Cameron, Harry, Stu, Billy, and Felix would see to it that those unfortunate girls would have an avenue of escape; at least those working out of the Jewel Danamo. This was how Eldon wanted it done; exterminate and if at all possible offer asylum and liberation from the chains of desperation placed on the innocent.

The Lobby Bar at the Jewel Danamo was a bit more of a bar than just a lobby bar. Its seating capacity was certified for 47 occupants by the Moscow Fire Department, but it was well situated, spacious yet intimate enough to have a nice cozy drink after coming in directly from the cold winter air, or perhaps take in some people watching for an afternoon or evening. A good cross section of the world's ethnicity could be seen passing by even here in a hotel lobby situated in Moscow. Mainly continental Europeans then Brits, then Americans then Israelis and Turks, Indians, Japanese, and most recently Arabs from The UAE (United Arab Emirates) and of course the Chinese were making themselves known recently.

The bar itself in The Lobby Bar was a U-shaped design equipped with arm-rest bar chairs placed around it. Millie and Frances sat in two of the chairs. Each lady nursed a glass of white wine; it was a standard "lady of the evening" indulgence. Sitting directly across from Millie and Frances was Valeria, one of Mitkin's girls who was looking more than a little agitated with the presence of the competition being Millie and Frances.

Valeria couldn't yet be certain about Millie and Frances although all the signs pointed to the two being "working gals" but Valeria had to be sure before calling on assistance from hotel security in getting rid of the freelancing competition. Valeria was seasoned in her craft and had been allowed to work on her own by Mitkin for the past few months. Valeria's domain was The Lobby Bar, with regular hotel security guards well aware of the need for keeping Valeria's potential clientele hers and hers alone.

The confirmation factor that Valeria needed would not take long. Ken showed up a few minutes later while Harry waited in the wings, sitting comfortably in the hotel's lobby, pretending to be reading the local English language paper until the scenario with his partner Ken had played out with Frances.

Ken took a seat situated at the end of the U-shaped bar and ordered himself a vodka tonic on the rocks with an olive. Ken made sure to ask the bartender for the check right away which he made very clear to be "signing to his room" which then further confirmed him to be a hotel guest, staying in the hotel. It certainly looked like he was on his own. This was a "key" invite for "company or female companionship" as far as "the girls" were concerned, and Valeria didn't miss a beat having picked up on that immediately. She noticed both Millie and Frances had also picked up on the gentleman at the bar signing the bar check to his room, and so now the game among whores was on, so Valeria thought.

Valeria made several glances towards Ken doing her best to garner his attention while still trying to remain discreet but adjusting her body language in encouraging his coming over to say hello, even swiveling her chair into his direction. Wearing a very short skirt, she slightly spread her legs while sitting, a very daring and obvious move on her part not being discreet in doing that, but she was desperate, she needed this "John". Make no mistake; Valeria was very high class looking lady of the night, and she well knew that she was scraping the gutter with that slutty move.

Unfortunately for Valeria the lure of the two independent freelancers who both teased the gentleman at the bar with their double girl power was too much for Valeria to overcome, the existing challenge of the freelancing whores was just too great.

She watched as Millie and Frances made eye contact with her soon to be stolen client.

Frances glanced at the gentleman, swirled her tongue around the outside of her lips while looking at her wine glass then glancing at the gentleman.

Valeria was right! It didn't take long; he obviously was in the right store to make this purchase. Ken got up from his bar chair and made his way over to Millie and Frances. Valeria was not mistaken, they were ladies of the night all right, no doubt about that. She couldn't make out exactly what Frances was discussing with the man, but the giggles and the right gestures for playfulness were most definitely going on. Ten minutes after the gentleman had approached Frances, the two of them left the bar together with him having picked up Frances's bar tab.

No sooner had Ken and Frances played out the game, Harry made his way over to the bar and took a chair a few seats down from Valeria, but she could already see Millie making eye contact with Harry as he walked up to the bar. Although Valeria was just a few seats down from Harry, it was Millie who was able to make the eye contact since she had a direct view of Harry who sat straight across from her. Harry too ordered a drink and at the same time sent a drink over to Millie.

This was not turning out to be Valeria's night. Valeria was fuming inside! Valeria felt like she had just been robbed by the first lady and now she was about to be robbed again! No this was not good, this was Valeria's bar and domain. This was a prime night, and she was seeing no action!

Mitkin would not be pleased; She would already be in trouble having made no money yet this night. Not long after while Valeria was caught up fuming about her bad luck, Harry and Millie left the bar together leaving Valeria all alone without a client.

There was nothing she could do at the moment but sit and wait. Almost an hour had passed, and much to Valeria's amazement Frances was back and sat down again in the very same seat she was sitting on just an hour ago. "Oh no, this would not do...not one bit." Valeria thought to herself. "It is time to get rid of this bitch and her friend."

Valeria was already a seasoned prostitute and had become hardened over the past two years in Mitkin's service. She too, however, was still under his thumb. Although Valeria was Russian, her situation was much the same as all of Mitkin's crew. Valeria was a native of the Siberian western plain from the average city but forgotten capital of Siberia; Tobolsk, in the Tyumen region. Mitkin swept her up in his crime net when she was only sixteen having paid her poor collective farm worker parents the equivalent of a thousand dollars in Russian Rubles for a chance to have Valeria find her fortune in the glitter of Moscow.

Alexander Mitkin had her turning tricks a month after she arrived in Moscow. She would do her utmost in helping to support her family back in Tobolsk the best she could by spreading her legs almost nightly so that her family could eat more than borscht and potatoes. Every once in a while, she would send a little money back home to her mother and father so they could buy meat for the dinner table. Valeria had a good heart, but now she was Mitkin's whore. She earned her freedom to operate on her own, but still very much under Mitkin's thumb, yes, she was still trapped and enslaved to do with her as he wished.

She got up out of her chair and went to the lobby looking for hotel security. She found the security officer she was looking for and updated him on the situation. Misha Rudkin had educated his security crew on the matters of the ladies of the night working the hotel. Security was well acquainted with Valeria and her need in having no competition. Valeria having informed security returned to her seat in the lobby bar and watched as two security officers showed up five minutes later and asked Frances to leave the lobby bar. About a half hour later hotel security then removed Millie after she returned. Millie and Frances had the confirmation they needed that hotel security was well involved. To make things airtight, they followed up with Ken then changing places with Cameron in the Gorky Club. Cameron, a new face for Valeria to consider, made his way over to the lobby bar, ordered his drink and waited for Valeria to make her move. Having had two potential clients practically snatched right from her arms, Valeria was now desperate to make some money, and she made the first move on Cameron.

He made it easy for her, he sat two seats down from her, glanced over towards her and smiled. She smiled back and then he asked Valeria if he could buy her a drink. Valeria accepted his generosity and upon her accepting his drink, she bravely asked, not wishing to waste any time, if he would like her close company for the evening.

He asked her just exactly what she meant by that; "well that is a very interesting thought but what is it you mean, I am in your company now am I not?" Cameron asked.

Valeria then replied with a Russian accent, smiling and playing along, "yes you are in my company, but I would like to get very much closer to you, very much closer. I could tell you and show you in person for three hundred dollars," Valeria said smiling all along and being just a bit too forward but she had to press, she wanted to make Mitkin happy by not coming up empty handed all night long.

Cameron had his confirmation; she was hooking, and she was being supported by hotel security. Cameron then said. "Yes, I think that would be lovely."

Valeria was suddenly elated! This was not to be a lost night at all; she would, after all, do well. "Yes, very good, I will meet you in the lobby in five minutes, we can settle up the fee in privacy later."

"Okay, that works for me," Cameron said. Cameron paid the bartender for the drinks walked out into the hotel lobby and beeped Felix Balon. Felix felt his pager vibrating, he was ready for this but wasn't sure it would come to pass tonight, apparently; it was happening.

He and Billy were in Cameron's suite going over the strategy and how to handle things should things move quickly. With Felix's pager coming to life, things were now moving quickly. Millie and Frances were already in Cameron's suite as well. This is where everything with Valeria was to go down. Tonight, was either going to turn out being Valeria's sanctuary and a night of salvation or a ban from ever entering any Holiday Jewel Hotel property in Russia. The same would apply to the other working girls fortunate enough to be swept up in this dragnet under operation by Eldon's sting team. Eldon and his team were not out for revenge, Eldon's extermination team was to offer sanctuary, and a cure for what infected his properties, both was about to happen soon.

Valeria too had her instructions with designated contacts inside of the hotel, and that was the Mafia paid and bought for corrupted hotel security officers reporting to Misha Rudkin the Director of hotel security.

Valeria met Cameron in the lobby and the first thing Valeria asked Cameron was the room number to where she was to meet him. Next, she told Cameron she needed to powder her nose. On her way to the ladies' room she passed Cameron's suite number 3070 to the select hotel security guard who then verified Cameron's room number, all seemed clear and good to go for Valeria.

The Mafia also had their need to keep tabs on Valeria and her whereabouts. They needed to know of her location, not so much for her safety, as far as Mitkin was concerned, the girls were expendable but more so to secure payment for a girl's services should payment not be forthcoming. Valeria too had her pager exactly for such possibilities. Valeria's pager would also be put to use this night for one last time.

Vlad, the manager in charge of The Gorky Club, had seated Stu and Cameron at a corner table overlooking the lounge. Cameron was replaced by Ken, and with Ken and Stu having had ordered a couple of drinks, Vlad now had their room numbers and complete access to their in-house guest files. Seeing that the two gentlemen were convention attendees made them qualified targets for an invite to membership in the After Hours Gorky Club and a potential trip to the hospitality suite.

Naturally, Billy and Felix had briefed the sting team on the process they had witnessed almost two weeks ago with the group of five from Germany. Anna and Ludmilla had worked their magic on the willing Germans. A couple of those German hotel guests would be getting very nasty rude awakenings as to their activities at The Holiday Jewel Danamo, that rude awakening to be reigned upon them in the coming days from Mitkin himself in the form of blackmail and extortion.

There was still some time before Mitkin's Mafia swords of pain would find them back home in Germany but only a few days, Mitkin usually acted within the same month as the membership was recruited. The time now was well past midnight. The lounge was starting to thin out some already, and Vlad had decided it was time to bring Anna and Ludmilla down from the hospitality suite to entice Stu and Ken.

Stu had grown a little concerned that they may be passed on this evening since there was only the two of them. Stu's concerns were soon put to rest with Anna and Ludmilla showing up in their sexy attire, Ludmilla carrying a bottle of Dom and Anna carrying a tray with four champagne glasses. The ladies had this procedure down pat by now and were, to say the least experts at their game. Anna and Ludmilla once again filled the lounge with their presence as they walked across the floor and approached Ken and Stu's table.

The two men pretended like they were total greenhorns and captivated by the two girls' charms. Yes, they had charms to be sure, charms that were to cost a thousand dollars for the two memberships. It was rare that the girls failed in their quest. Ken and Stu made certain to be very intrigued by the girls and after a half hour of coaxing and champagne, Ken and Stu agreed to become members of the Gorky After Hours Club.

Anna and Ludmilla had made it clear to the two men that all treats in the hospitality suite were at their beckoning call in whichever ways they chose to partake and of course Ludmilla and Anna would also be on the membership's list of tantalizing menu items to be served till the wee hours of the morning. Anna handed both Ken and Stu a business card each. Anna said they would need to show the business cards to be admitted to the hospitality suite.

The twins left the lounge. Ken paid the drinks tab, and the two men made their way up to the hospitality suite. From time to time, the hospitality suite would be at opposite ends of the hallway, depending on the need and booking availability. Mitkin had made sure to have the suites booked under the names of different companies and individuals so as to not establish a routine booking, and thereby keeping it in a transient status rather than a regular recurring reservation that would bring attention. Most months it was only booked for three nights maximum, but when considering there were six properties already operating after hours clubs at different hotels, the money was rolling in not to mention the follow-up extortion and impostor lawsuits brought about by Mitkin's cronies.

Eldon would become very aware of that special maneuver in the coming days as Felix would bring to light.

This day, however, would prove to be a major upheaval in the finely tuned workings of Mitkin's Mafia operations. Yes, the fly in Mitkin's ointment would turn out to be one huge stink bug, which was about to embed itself into his After-Hours Gorky Club right now with Ken and Stu's arrival.

It was Suite 2020 on the second floor. Ken beeped the suite number to Billy's unit as to where they were headed. Suite 2020 was a full hotel suite, almost an apartment but lacking a kitchen. Kitchens were not parts of the suites when the hotel had full dining facilities and looked for food and beverage revenues. The suite had a large living area holding three sets of couches, love seats and sofas. There was a hallway leading from the living area with more separate bedrooms. It was perfect for a large family; in this case, it was perfect for this purpose.

For the members to use the private bedrooms an extra charge of one hundred dollars would apply, so no opportunity was missed in maximizing potential revenues to be made in the illicit prostitution ring. Most members took advantage of the available women right there in the main living room area which in most cases could have rivaled episodes of carnal knowledge with scenes directly taken from the sexually deviant Roman Emperor Caligula's autobiographic marathon orgy adventures.

Harry, Stu, Ken, Cameron, Felix, Billy and the two ladies, had all been down this road a few times having to deal with similar situations in the Caribbean, mainly at hotels with adjacent casinos. Here, however, the stakes were far greater because the ladies of the night were captives, forced into sexual slavery. Billy especially well knew the workings of the underground here in Moscow. One of the main concerns in building new hotels was to build them clean immunized from prostitution, but try as hard as they could, this element had a way of finding its way into a property and it all had to do with greed. Hard currency now flowed in Moscow, and hard currency, US dollars, British Pounds, and Deutschmarks were far too attractive not to be pounced upon, and every security guard in the city was a mark for the taking. It was time to break the circle of corruption.

Stu and Ken took the elevator to the second floor and made their way down the hallway towards suite 2020. There was a heavy set burly strapping Russian man dressed in a suit sitting on a chair just inside the alcove leading to Suite 2020's doorway. He was obviously part of Mitkin's gang and acting as a screener/bouncer and guard all rolled into one.

As the two approached, the guard stood. Ken noticed immediately that the guard's suit jacket had an unusual bulge inside and underneath the left arm. Obviously, the guard was packing a weapon, probably an Uzi. Ken and Stu presented the business cards given to them by Anna. The guard gave both men the once over, patted down both Ken and Stu and being satisfied that the two were clean, opened the door and let them inside.

It was just women inside no other men had been recruited for membership this night. This was good. What wasn't so good was the obvious sex slave factory the Mafia was operating in The Holiday Jewel Danamo. Sitting on the sofas in the room were five other ladies. Actually, they were teenage girls, not one looked older than maybe sixteen or seventeen but all trying to look older. Little Kati was one of the girls making up the group, and the rest were her friends who were all recruited in Hungary and had made their way together on Mitkin's misery tour bus from Debrecen several months ago.

The girls were dressed in skimpy outfits, all wearing stilettos. Having entered the suite, Anna and Ludmilla got up out of their chairs and approached the two, greeting both with smiles. Then Ludmilla asked to have things settled up. Ken paid Ludmilla one thousand dollars in cash, and having taken the money Ludmilla, and Anna then took hold of each their arms and brought them over to the ladies sitting on sofas. As Ken and Stu approached, all the girls stood up off the couch. Anna introduced the girls to Ken and Stu going down the line of girls standing on display calling out their names as she pointed to each one, each stepping forward as their names were called."

Then Ludmilla, said with her heavy Russian accent, "*ull da girls speak a leetle inglish but very leetle, eenuf so dey understand you, okay, vy you don't you gent le men make urself komfortabal and git to know the ladies, I know dey vud very mutch like you, you vil see.*"

Ken then asked Ludmilla about privacy, explaining that he wanted to take two of the ladies with him into the private room. Ludmilla, with a sexy smile, said, *"Oh, yoo are very horny Meester Ken. I know the ladies vil like make sex for you."* Ken then paid Ludmilla another hundred dollars for the private bedroom and looking over at the row of ladies standing in front of him, he smiled at each one, and they smile back, knowing that their time had come to earn their keep. They all wore red lipstick, and all seemed to be eagerly but forcefully looking to meet his every need.

Ken focused in on one of the young girls who happened to be on the left end of the line; it was Kati. Kati had the most beautiful green eyes and shiny straight ebony hair down to her shoulders; she really was a little goddess, but a goddess with a look of fright and terror combined with surrender, yet willing to please.

It was a most unusual look, one that Ken had never seen in his years working vice in hotels and casinos for Eldon. Ken was a man with hardened character, not easily moved and yet, looking at young Kati, Ken's heart melted. Ken right there and then decided he would do everything in his power to save this young girl before it was too late for her, there was still time in her life to leave all this behind, but she couldn't do it on her own, no she couldn't.

Ken had made a connection, maybe a one-way connection for now, but nevertheless, Ken's determination to see this through had all of a sudden taken on a state of urgency. The young girl who stood beside Kati moved in closer beside her indicating that he should pick the two of them, they obviously were friends. It was like telepathy and Ken knew in his heart it would be these two ladies of the night to whom this morning he would offer sanctuary.

He then turned towards Ludmilla and said, "Okay, I will take these two beautiful women."

"Luvlee choozing Meester Ken" Ludmilla answered and waved the two girls forward. Ken then was lead down the hallway and into one of the private bedrooms; Kati and Ildiko followed Ken inside. Kati closed the door behind her. The three of them were now in behind closed doors, and both Kati and Ildiko were getting ready to undress for "*Meester*" Ken.

Stu was left with the three other Hungarian young sex slaves, Maria, Zusza and Este. "They were so young, only seventeen maybe eighteen at the most." Stu thought they were the same age probably as his gorgeous daughter back home in Traverse City Michigan. Just being in the presence of these young ladies, Stu developed a personal need and crusade as did his partner Ken in changing these girls' lives. But it wouldn't be up to him alone, the girls would need to want it, and he knew that very well. Tonight, this morning, however, they would have that opportunity. Holiday Jewel Hotels and Casinos, with Eldon and Kimberley's mission statement, "service with integrity" would shine brightly on the ladies of the night on this day.

He then turned to Ludmilla and Anna who were awaiting his desires. Anna spoke up saying to Zusza, *"Vy you don't make sex now here, kom Zusza, make Meester feel goud... show him vat you kan do."*

Anna then asked Zusza to step forward and start performing fellatio on Stu. Before Zusza could even get close to Stu much less his private parts, he raised his hands.

"No, I want to take all three girls into a private room as well, I will feel more comfortable with them there, he turned and said to Anna.

Anna then addressed the girls like a mother hen, *"No prublem Meester Stu, kom girls kom, ull you, yes for Meester Stu, you make him happy yes!"*

Ken and Stu now had all the After-Hour's Club's ladies of the night behind closed doors, except of course for Anna and Ludmilla, but they would deal with the twins soon enough.

Anna and Ludmilla were not to be left out. The two senior women were obviously the young girls' immediate bosses and getting the girls away from the twins was vital in allowing them not to be pressured when presented with the opportunity to rid themselves of their chains. It was going to be now or never for the Hungarian girls; they were Kati's compatriots; all enslaved to Mitkin. Perhaps as of this night, no longer. It would be up to the girls, and a very key turning point opportunity in their lives.

Kati had prayed this morning before leaving her humble abode, living under Mitkin's thumb, but on this day, Kati's prayers were to be answered.
Guardian angels Ken and Stu had arrived.

◇◇◇

Cameron had gone up to his suite 3070 ahead of Valeria. She was to follow in five minutes' time. Valeria waited the five minutes, and made her way to the elevators, taking one of the cars to the third floor. She exited, walking down the hallway not even having to check in which direction the room was, she already knew the layout of the building having visited several hotel suites at The Jewel Danamo. Halfway down the hallway, there was a mirror on the wall where she took a moment to check her makeup and lipstick for one last time. Everything looked good. She walked up to Suite 3070, knocked lightly while holding her pager at the ready in her left hand. Cameron opened the door; Valeria stepped inside and was immediately overtaken by shock.

There in front of her stood Millie, Frances, Harry, Billy Simpson and Cameron along with Felix Balon. Cameron then closed the door to Suite 3070 behind her.

In her sudden shock and fear, not knowing what to do, she pressed her pager's panic button and as nervous and shocked as she was, the pager slipped out of her grasp, dropping to the floor. Billy knew just exactly what that meant.

Although she did yet not know it, in these coming few seconds, her life was to be changed forever. Valeria was for the first time in a very long time safe.

***

Chapter Twenty-Two
Betrayal of the innocent ones

It was by no means a State Department dinner, no not at all, but it could have been since Ambassador Frankie Albert and his wife Marika were present. The dinner this evening was not at the US Ambassador's residence; Spaso House but rather in the gourmet dining room of The Holiday Jewel Danamo Hotel; The Mir Dining Room, named in honor of the Russian space station Mir, launched on February 20th, 1986.

The Mir Dining Room was first opened serving the very first dinner guest February 20th six years later. The Ambassador and his wife were the invited dinner guests and hotel guests this evening sitting at Eldon and Kimberley's private table, Louis James, Eldon's senior vice president of hotel operations, made up the round of five. The Ambassador and his wife would be the occupants of the Jewel Danamo's Presidential Suite this night, courtesy of Eldon and Kimberley Davis.

Translated from Russian to English, Mir was "Peace or World" both aptly applicable since no better names could have been chosen in breaking bread with international clientele and guests from the world over who found themselves dining together at Jewel Danamo's gourmet dining room.

The hotel's Mir Dining Room was adorned with scenes from the Russian space program. Stunning photographs of planet earth artfully placed along the walls. These photographs of Planet Earth showed how connected we are as the human race, without lines on maps separating countries, yet proclaiming the pioneering spirit of the Russian people and their achievements in space exploration. A huge colorful ceramic mosaic covered one entire wall depicting the first man to journey into outer space on April 12th, 1961, Russia's Yuri Gagarin, flanked by cosmonaut Alexey Leonov in his spacesuit, floating weightlessly in space; the first human to spacewalk on March 18, 1965. Other photographs showing milestones in Russia's space program added to the overall theme and atmosphere of the restaurant.

The Mir restaurant had a smaller intimate room just off to the side of the main dining area, still very much part of the restaurant but very private, separated by smoked glass French doors, with a dedicated captain and waiter to meet the needs of the guests in this reserved area. Tonight, it was the hotel owners; Eldon and Kimberley making very good use of the private and exclusively intimate setting.

"So, I understand from Kimberley that The Red Jewel is well ahead of schedule," Frankie said.

"Yes, things have been moving along much quicker than we expected. In fact, we are way ahead of schedule. Our building project manager attributes it to the excellent weather conditions the Moscow region has enjoyed over the past few months and to far less equipment failure and downtime than we had planned for." Louis then chimed in. "It's taken three years to build the hotel, and usually, there are delays upon delays, but we've been very fortunate with this construction project. Everything seemed to fall in place properly with the time-lines assigned to each phase. We've only had a few hiccups with not having on time delivery concerning some window panes, but for the most part, it has been a flawless construction process. We are very happy with the Russian side of things. Louis paused, almost acting surprised with his own statement complementing the Russian construction industry.

"The local construction crews and companies have turned out to be much more efficient than we had thought, seeing all the problems we experienced with building this property,"

Eldon added. "We really did learn quite a lot about the whole construction industry in Moscow. With the Jewel Danamo, we were fortunate to acquire this building already erected and all we had to after we signed the joint venture agreement, was to finish the inside and turn it into a Holiday Jewel Hotel. The Jewel Danamo, before it was the Jewel Danamo had been sitting unfinished ever since the 1980 Olympics. Originally it was built to form part of the athletes' village complex, but with the boycott of the games, the building wasn't ever completed. It sat here Frankie, empty for over eight years. It took almost two years to complete it and turn it into one of the city's finest hotels." Eldon then stopped. He reminisced a little to himself and continued.

"Yes, we had decided to go ahead with this bold move, coming to Russia even before the new Russian Federation was born. Kimberley and I believed that the loosening of the rules here with Gorbachev's new policies, those being Glasnost and Perestroika, a new era was taking hold in Russia, and we decided to jump in on the gamble. Actually, to be honest, what really sold me on coming to Russia, was Margaret Thatcher's comment." Eldon stopped and looked at Frankie, then glanced at Kimberley. "Remember what it was she said, Frankie?"

Frankie answered right away. "You mean her statement about doing business here?"

"Yeah, that's right. It really was an eye opener. Sure, it was a long time ago, several years even before Kimberley and I met, but I had not forgotten Thatcher's words when she said that "she liked Mr. Gorbachev, and we can do business together."

Well, it sort of shocked the whole western world. That Britain was okay in doing business with "the enemy". But Thatcher was right; she had vision. Then with the wall coming down in Germany, and us already being here, well we knew we had made the right move. By that time, we had made great progress in finishing this building and with the new atmosphere that Gorbachev's Perestroika policy and Glasnost had brought about, we applied for The Red Jewel's building permit, and it was granted." Eldon finished saying looking around the table.

"And so, a year later, we opened this hotel, our first property, with all the growing pains having been overcome. Now, the Red Jewel is about to cast it's light over the city and much sooner than we anticipated, thanks to the incredible progress this city has seen.

Yeah, we learned quite a bit with this building, which led to anticipation of complications ahead of time, and thereby we avoided some pitfalls this time around. With construction now booming in Moscow, the competition among contractors has been fierce, and we were lucky in securing the expertise of several companies vying for our business. We really believe that they've caught on here." Eldon said with some conviction and excitement in his voice.

He continued on, "the local construction companies gradually understood that they now had competition internationally, and shoddy workmanship or delays would not be tolerated. So everything has improved." Eldon finished saying.

Then Kimberley picking right up after Eldon, added: "It's all part of the free enterprise competitive spirit, newly found everywhere one goes throughout Moscow, and it's no different for the hotels here in the city."

It was evident that the three hoteliers were all singing from the same song sheet when it came to their excitement about the hotel industry in Moscow.

"Well, I must say, you have done an incredible job on this property, and this dining room, my goodness, it takes my breath away just walking in here. It's so modern and yet full of history." Marika then added.

"You know Marika; we have had some very nice comments on the design of this room. We were reluctant at first about the whole space program theme. We didn't think it would be appropriate decor for a fine dining room. For a theme park, perfect, but for a hotel and dining room not so much. But then we were presented with some of the concept drawings, and room layout. Eventually, we decided to go with it, and as you can see, it turned out to be quite pleasing." Eldon explained.

"Yes." Marika added, "and the food is out of this world!"

Frankie raised his glass in offering a toast, "beautiful job done on this room and the hotel Eldon. I'm sure you and Kimberley are very proud of what Louis and his team have put together here. I am sure that The Red Jewel will even outshine this property, Moscow should be proud to have such a hotel as this, and well, then a year from now your Jewel Moskva will be completed. Just incredible Eldon, just incredible." Frankie exclaimed.

Kimberley then said, "Well yes, thank you, but things are not as incredible as you might think, we have some major concerns of late Frankie. Actually, I'm not very comfortable talking about it, so I'll let my husband explain."

Kimberley looked over to Eldon sitting beside her, reaching out and placing her hand on top of Eldon's.

"It's not something that we haven't come across before Frankie, so we think we know how to handle things. You know our properties in the Caribbean from time to time go through ah… how should I put it, "an infection" of sorts."

Frankie and his wife Marika sat there intensely both with a look of concern on their faces, hinging on every word Eldon spoke. "What could have gone amiss at this hotel that would be put across in such gloomy terms?" They both wondered.

Well, Eldon was about to ring Frankie Albert's bell loud and clear, although Eldon had no idea that he would be a "bell ringer", only Frankie would hear that bell causing the ringing in his ear to last for days and maybe even weeks. Eldon was about to take his hammer and hit that bell with a loud thundering crack. Frankie and Marika sat waiting for the next word to be spoken by their friend, with whom Frankie had partnered on behalf of the US government allowing Holiday Jewel Hotels and Casinos to gain expansion into Russia.

Frankie had cleared obstacles for Eldon and Kimberley through his diplomatic connections in Russia, and Frankie had cleared a few other things as well that was now about to come back and haunt him.

The dining room captain came by to take their dinner orders. The wine had already been served. Eldon extended the invitation for Frankie to pick the red wine selection for dinner. The Ambassador went with a red from Chateauneuf de Pape region of France, a ten-year-old wine bottle. Kimberley ordered the white, a Mouton Cadet Blanc from the Bordeaux region of France, both excellent choices.

With the captain at the table, their conversation was briefly curtailed as they informed him of their choices. The Ambassador and his wife had both chosen a Hungarian dish, "chicken paprikas."

The Mir dining room was one of the few restaurants in the city that offered an international dish menu. Both Frankie and Marika enjoyed a traditional dish from their home country whenever possible. Eldon and Kimberley settled on the duck a la' orange and Louis James went with the Chilean sea bass as his main course.

After the captain, had taken their dinner orders, the five sat quietly as Eldon started in again. Kimberley still held onto Eldon's hand resting on the white tablecloth. Frankie took a sip of his wine and then Eldon taking a deep breath, raising his eyebrows, began saying; "yeah, we have a situation. We had hoped to stay clear of this, but I suppose it's just the nature of the beast in the hotel business and no matter how hard we try watching for it, eventually it takes hold and then it's a matter of acting." Eldon said, almost "matter of factly" expressing the serious nature of a problem needing to be dealt with, but at the same time sounding routine about it all.

Frankie and Marika both weren't clear yet on what Eldon was referring to, but now would be.

"Yeah, even as we sit here this evening, our dining room is full, the lounges are doing well, and with the auto show convention in town all hotels in the city are to maximum capacity and right about now, Louis's crack team of experts are about to take action. To most people looking in on the hotel and its atmosphere this evening, I suppose, everything appears normal, even rosy, but the sad truth is that the hospitality has gone a bit, well not a bit, but a whole lot overboard in the past few months. It has become so acute, that some of our guests and I emphasize "some" may, in fact, be in danger by being taken advantage of. Mind you those "some" are willing participants, it's their own doing, but we have unwittingly become the facilitators."

Eldon looked over at Louis, acknowledging his organizing the sting operation about to go down this night at the Jewel Danamo.

Eldon continued, totally owning Marika and Frankie's attention.

"What am I talking about?" Eldon asked rhetorically, all the while with Frankie and Marika being spellbound by Eldon laying out the scenario.

"So, what I am talking about is widespread prostitution that has ingrained itself into every hotel in the city, including this bastion of hospitality; The Jewel Danamo."

Marika was taken aback by Eldon's blunt and candid way of telling it all. Eldon continued.

"Yes, this evening, later as the night goes, Louis has his crack team in place, running a sting operation throughout the hotel. We anticipate being able to uncover and close in on the prostitution ring being run right out of this hotel." Eldon paused for a moment and took a sip from wine.

With Frankie and Marika now processing the information, there was time for a quiet moment as their dinner choices were being brought to the table and served.

The mood had quieted down some around the table, but Eldon felt it was important for Ambassador Albert to know what was going on in the city regarding this epidemic that had spread throughout all the newly opened properties. The situation had the potential to have devastating effects on tourism not to mention huge liabilities from corporate clients visiting the city. The liability aspect had already hit the Jewel Danamo, which Eldon was still having investigated to determine its legitimacy. Eldon had asked Louis to look into the matter with Felix in the next day or two, but it was not looking good. For now, Eldon shelved the matter till Louis and Felix reported back to him after a full review of the situation was completed.

"Oh, that is such awful news," Marika said quietly under her breath.

"We had a very similar problem in Hungary with Budapest hotels that started right after the Berlin wall came down. As we all know Eastern Europe had become very much liberated soon after that period and even a year or two before that momentous occasion. Business was picking up and with that, prostitution became a problem throughout the city, especially in the posh hotels. Back then I had just met Frankie, and I always dreaded having to rendezvous with him in hotels. I felt it cast the wrong shadow, but we had no choice since I couldn't yet freely meet with the US Ambassador to Hungary at his residence. We were still considered a communist country; I could have been viewed as a traitor or spy, so we met in secret at hotels. I was always so uncomfortable with that, thinking what others might be thinking."

Marika then reached out and took Frankie's hand, smiling at him; she kissed him on his cheek. "And so, here we are, together in Russia, in the new federation, and history repeats itself in this most unusual way, with "hookers" no less."

Marika finished saying while looking around the table at Kimberly, Eldon and Louis, raising her eyebrows, tightening her lips, and gesturing with a "so there you go" look.

"Wow," Kimberley was impressed with Marika. She really liked the way Marika was so candid about it all and how even after just two previous meetings between the Davis's and Alberts, she was so open with everyone at the table. This was the first time that Marika had met Louis James, but that didn't seem to stop her from being open about her past or for that matter, The Ambassador's.

"Well, it goes much deeper than just the ladies of the night." Eldon then said referring to Marika's casual "hookers" quote.

It was obvious that Marika did not understand the gravity of the situation, but Eldon had not expected her to. Marika was a violinist in a symphony orchestra, she did not travel the roads of prostitution, how could she know, she was the cream of the crop culturally speaking, although she did have street smarts as she told of her hotel rendezvous story meeting Frankie.

Eldon responded, "I had heard about that Marika. My hotel company was fortunate having started in two years after on the property we developed on Lake Balaton. We just opened the Csardas Jewel on Balaton last summer and happy to say, finished the final touches converting it into a year-round resort operation. The Csardas is only a small resort, only seventy-five rooms but it's right lakeside with a wonderful patio lounge and restaurant. This winter it operates as a winter resort taking advantage of the frozen lake, which we use as an ice rink for figure skating events and ice hockey. Eldon said to Marika and Frankie.

Marika then added, "yes, and I've heard snowmobiling has become very popular in the Lake Balaton area. Your resort will probably enjoy some good winter business from those enthusiasts as well.

"Indeed, we already have excellent bookings for coming winter." Louis James responded. The Csardas Jewel on Balaton has had a very successful first year and a half, and no, we've had no such problems as we do here in Moscow, happy to say that!"

Eldon continued, picking up from Louis. "So, in Hungary with our one little property we are good, have no concerns there, and the Hungarian people have been wonderful to work with." Both Marika and Frankie took that to be a personal compliment from Eldon.

"The problem however here in Moscow is inhouse." Eldon said while cutting into his duck, "Frankie; Kimberley, Louis, and I believe this is important vital information for you to have."

Frankie Albert looked up from his dish, glanced at Marika, placed his fork down onto his dish, and taking his wine glass in hand took a sip, giving Eldon his undivided attention.

"Go ahead Eldon, I'm listening," Frankie said calmly.

Eldon started in on his duck, taking a bite, and then went on to say, "we believe that the situation as we said already has become a city-wide epidemic. The reason you will need to know will become clear should we need to take drastic action citywide. When that time comes, and it might not, but if it does, I will look for your support. My VP of public relations Felix Balon will fill you in next week.

Frankie, I have no doubt you are expecting full disclosure from me now, but let me assure you as your friend and fellow American, I need to be discreet. The reason for that is to protect your integrity, yours, Marika's, and the US Embassy here in Moscow. But like I said, Felix Balon will fill you in next week when we have confirmation and if we don't, well, then nothing to worry about, but either way, Felix will update you fully in the next few days, you have my word on it."

Frankie sat there in his chair almost like a stone, not moving, having heard what Eldon had just said had given him reason to pause and raise his own question in his own mind.

"What did these three people know that he didn't know, and apparently, it was something that could hurt him and his Ambassadorial status, this was not sitting well at all with Frankie, he was feeling butterflies now. In another minute Frankie would forget about the butterflies. Eldon would soon ring that bell, and his hearing may be damaged forever. Frankie would hear the bell soon enough, probably before he had time to finish his "chicken paprikas."

He glanced over towards his wife; she too was sitting quite taken aback.

Eldon continued on, "already we have signs that the situation has taken a turn for the worse which probably involves a number of other properties.

Frankie, I'm talking about extortion on joint venture hotels in the city being conducted by," and Eldon stopped for a moment, taking another sip from his wine, "The Russian Mafia."

Frankie and Marika looked at one another for a moment, glancing over towards Louis James who was nodding his head in silence confirming Eldon's suspicion and concern. This wasn't making Frankie feel any better, seemed like the more Eldon talked, the more Frankie felt a threat coming on, not an intentional threat of course, but secrets hidden for years were now starting to rumble in his mind. Frankie's appetite seemed to be subsiding. Eldon then went on, telling his dinner friends of the problems he and his company were facing.

"Stems from the lease agreement we have with the food and beverage operator and Management Company for the hotel. Although I was fundamentally against the idea; that being to lease the food and beverage operations, I agreed to it since it made the opening of the hotel easier and it took some of the pressures off in finding the skilled Russians in operating our kitchen. Remember, we had several setbacks in the building and finishing off of this property. We not only had labor disputes with carpenters and electricians, but we had some really bad weather that had us delay construction for almost three months in all. We needed to find ways in expediting the schedule and bringing the opening date closer to the original targeted date. Having a local lease operator also meant that they already had the inroads to the local market and suppliers of the food and beverage inventory we would need to have on hand. Establishing new business relationships with suppliers and the further assurance of top quality product would be taken care of with the lease operator who already had all this in place. We had a number of companies bidding on the leasing rights. We decided to go with your recommendation Frankie, well, let me back up a minute." Frankie looked at little surprised, not understanding just exactly where Eldon was coming from by Eldon then saying, "*to go with your recommendation Frankie.*"

"It was on the recommendation of your custodian and manager of Spaso House." Frankie now had a "what are you talking about" look on his face. So, Eldon continued, satisfying his look of intrigue.

"You see, apparently, Tsar Restaurants and Entertainment Company, centered here in Moscow is the supplier to Spaso House for your food and beverage items. I need not tell you that those items end up being served to diplomats and Department of State officials, I believe President Fenton and his family has had dinner at Spaso House in the past, and everything had always been top-notch and of the highest quality. Your Chef confirmed that actually when we called to get his opinion on the quality of produce from Tsar." Eldon, stopped and drank from his wine glass, just long enough for things to sink in.

"He told us there was none better in all of Moscow. That actually sealed our decision to go with Tsar as the lease operator for our restaurants here at The Jewel Danamo."

Eldon then took another bite from his duck, paused for a few moments and looked around the table. Yes, everyone was busy eating dinner, but at the same time, very tuned in to what Eldon was saying.

Frankie Albert on the other hand, well he was very fortunate that he happened to have swallowed his mouthful of chicken before hearing the words "Tsar Restaurants and Entertainment Company." Surely Frankie would have choked on his chicken hearing Eldon Davis say those words. Even now as he sat there, his heart rate increased and started racing.

He was struck, the bell had rung, and the anvil in his ear rang loud enough to make his heart skip beats. He knew he had to excuse himself from the table. Frankie Albert wasn't sure what to do, but he knew he had to get a grip on things and regain his composure. It would be a miracle in itself for him just making it from the table to the restroom without collapsing. He paused a moment or two, waiting for Eldon's words to sink in around the table.

"My apologies, but I've been trying to put it off for the past several minutes, I'm afraid I need to excuse myself to the restroom." Frankie Albert got up out of his chair, smiling at everyone at the table, trying to hold it together, and made his way to the men's room. He thought he might even be a bit wobbly walking there; he hoped he wasn't. He reached the door to the men's room, turned the door handle and walked in. There was a front room where a washroom attendant was ready with fresh hand towels and a variety of fragrances, colognes, and toiletries. Frankie accepted a fresh hand towel from the attendant, and said "*spasiba.*"

He immediately made his way over to the granite counter-top sink and began running cold water. Frankie bent over the sink and brought the cool fresh calming cold to his face. That then seemed to have a cooling off effect for his entire body, just the feeling of the cold water on his face helped. He did it again and again. Frankie reached for his towel and dried himself. He then braced his body over the counter-top propping himself up on the base of his palms, looking into the mirror.

He stared at himself for a minute or so. Thinking, thinking to himself; "almost all the dots are on the page, it's only a matter of time before more dots appear on the page of revelation. Eldon and Kimberley are sure to uncover all the dots. The lines connecting those dots will magically appear; it will be so obvious," he thought to himself.

"Perhaps all the dots were already on that page, only needing another look, to make the connections, he couldn't be sure, he wasn't sure; he didn't know!" But Frankie Albert knew one thing. Nothing could stay hidden forever, nothing!

He looked up at himself in the mirror and said; "this is your life Ferenc Albert, deal with it!"

He calmed down, regained his composure, walked out of the men's room and sat back down in his seat at the table. Frankie took hold of his wife's hand, smiling at her as he did, and picked up his wine glass, took a sip and said: "Sorry for the interruption, so where were we?"

The atmosphere over the dinner table had become very serious. Kimberley and Eldon were at this point still very open and up front about everything that was going on in the hotel, but now there was a sense of "what's next to come" anticipation around the table.

"Normally we would conduct in-depth due diligence even for such a process as deciding on a lease operator for our food and beverage outlets. We, however, faced a fast approaching deadline. With an opening date for the hotel that was in favor of going with a lease operator rather than taking the extra time in hiring our own kitchen staff; chefs, bartenders, porters, room service staff, cooks, service staff and everything else that goes along with such management needs for restaurants. Tsar Restaurants and Entertainment could have things ramped up and ready to go within a couple of weeks' time."

Eldon paused again, looked around for the waiter, didn't see him, picked up the bottle of red and asked who would like topping up. Louis raised his glass as did Marika; Eldon poured and then topped up his own.

"So, that's what we did, we signed an agreement with Tsar, thinking since they already did business with the United States Embassy here in Moscow, that surely the embassy would have vetted the company thoroughly before engaging their services in supplying all the food and beverages to the residence of the US Ambassador. We believed this would save time, and we had the word of Spaso House Manager as to the top notch second to none quality provided by Tsar. In fact, we to this day have no complaints in that area. It's to do with another area that sees us at this juncture." Eldon finished saying and turned to look at his wife. She took his cue, and Kimberley continued where Eldon left off.

"A few days ago, we had our suspicions that Tsar was, in fact, running the prostitution ring out of their food and beverage operation here at our hotel from The Gorky Club. It had come to our attention, as we admit, it should have a long time ago to our General Manager's attention, but it didn't or it hadn't until just recently that indeed, we had a problem emanating from the Gorky Club. Well, I decided to do some research, and this is where things get a little uncomfortable."

Kimberley picked up her wine glass and took a drink of the Mouton Cadet; it was still her favorite wine. Before she placed the glass back down on the table, she swirled the wine inside, looking at Eldon, and then around the table, still slowly swirling her wine glass. Both Eldon and Kimberley had a flair for the dramatic, it was their way, they not only explained but they added visual drama to whatever they had on their minds. Kimberley more-so than Eldon, and her ways never failed to impress and put people on edge, either in a good way or a bad way, all depending on which side of the fence the listener happened to be on.

"The sad thing is, that we also have a lease agreement with Tsar to operate the food and beverage needs of The Red Jewel which is about to open shortly. The other problem we will have because of this is that we will have the right to immediately cancel the lease agreement for violation of the "morality clause" and failure of the operator to upholding the mission statement and slogan of our company that being "service with integrity". I think it's pretty plain that the proliferation and promotion of prostitution within the walls of our hotels is not in keeping with our mission statement and morality clause. That one I'm quite sure we will win. The bigger problem along with this, however, comes to light in terms of Tsar Restaurants and Entertainment Company's ownership."

Kimberley wasn't about to mince words at this stage, she aimed her words squarely at Frankie Albert, saying to him while looking directly at The US Ambassador.

"Frankie, Tsar is owned by Alexander Mitkin, who happens to be the former assistant director of the Russian KGB. This is where things become somewhat complicated and messy. We have a "sting team" now in the hotel. They are running an operation tonight, but they've been in town for a week already checking on the other properties as we've already mentioned. They've reported back Ambassador that there is virtually an army of young underage girls from Hungary hooking in all the hotels in the city.

Ambassador, they are young Hungarian girls, some maybe not even sixteen years of age. We believe Mitkin is running an international sex slave operation, preying on young girls from Hungary who have no foreseeable future. We hope to catch Mitkin's operation red handed tonight here at our hotel and with some luck, tonight, this morning will be the beginning of the end for Mr. Mitkin."

Frankie looked on, gazing around the table; feeling like a knife had just been thrust into his heart. Hearing that Mitkin was enslaving young teenage girls from his homeland almost made Frankie sick to his stomach, it ate away at his core. He took a deep breath and said to Kimberley, "Wow, what else have you got?" Kimberley then looking at Eldon for a moment continued.

"Both Eldon and I thought you would want to know that. I know this is not the sort of dinner conversation you wanted, but its both business and personal, and we wanted to let you know of this, with Eldon, me and Louis being your friends whom you can count on.

Mr. Ambassador, Frankie, I will never forget how you protected me at Spaso House; how you instinctively placed your body on top of mine sheltering me from possible shrapnel on that morning. I will never forget that, and as we sit around this table tonight, we as a group need to know that this is happening in our adopted city, and we will need to act." Kimberley reached over to hold Eldon's hand once again. Having done so, Frankie reached and held Marika's hand, and the four of them all sat at the dinner table, pondering what tomorrow would bring.

Kimberley, however, continued on; she wasn't about to let this moment pass when it was ripe for the taking.

"Now we all know that The KGB is no longer, but really, come on now, it's still The KGB but with a different name. Give it some different initials and all of the past is wiped away? I think not; KGB is now FSB. Granted, Alexander Mitkin is no longer working for The KGB, but let's not kid ourselves, once in The KGB, always in The KGB; that will follow you around the rest of your life.

A person such as Mitkin will continue reaping rewards of loyalty for the rest of his life, and will always enjoy a special status in whatever he finds himself involved in. Sadly, the real truth is, that he will also find himself having immunity in activities for which most common people would face criminal charges, not Mitkin, he most likely would be given a pass.

Mr. Ambassador, after much digging with my former contacts in the State Department, confidentially speaking, I believe as does my husband, that the American Embassy here in Moscow is being supplied goods and services and god knows what else by the Russian Mafia. We tell you this now so you know what may be coming down the pike Frankie. Keep your eyes open and ears to the ground. We suggest that you immediately bring in a "clean team" and have Spaso House wiped for listening audio and video devices. Naturally you should immediately discontinue the vendor relationship with Tsar, as we are probably about to do ourselves here at the Jewel Danamo and re-neg on the contract with them at The Red Jewel." Kimberley then said, "Frankie we are so sorry to have to bring this news to you, but these are the facts, and we will no doubt have more news tomorrow.

The good news is that we will soon know just exactly what we are dealing with and just exactly who all the key players are." Kimberley added smiling.

Kimberley's smile had no easing effect on Frankie, quite the opposite hearing her say "we will soon know just exactly who all the key players are." Frankie felt like his chicken had turned into a "cooked goose."

The dinner event in The Mir restaurant had come to an end. The Alberts made their way up to their Presidential Suite at Holiday Jewel Danamo. Frankie and Marika were not having the sort of night they had hoped for staying at a lovely luxury first class hotel in The Presidential Suite. They did not talk much after retiring for the evening. When The Ambassador and his wife went to bed, Marika kissed her husband goodnight, knowing that Frankie must have the weight of the world on his shoulders with calamity running through his mind; she turned and went to sleep.

Frankie Albert, American-Hungarian, lay silently beside his Hungarian wife, in the darkness looking up at the ceiling, seeing nothing but blackness and thinking to himself. "Mitkin, Hungary, Budapest, his cousins, and his nephew. Marika's sister; Olga, The KGB, Hungarian Defense Minister Farkas, and of course, Mitkin's thugs, what a mess!"

Frankie was caught between a rock and a hard place. It would soon be time to decide between "country and family."

He was the United States Ambassador to the former Soviet Union and had been The Ambassador to Hungary and the Hungarian people, his flesh and blood were still living there as was Marika's. Frankie Albert stared into the darkness. He searched within himself, to the core of his being and the essence of his soul, but no, inside his darkness, he could see no light.

***

Chapter Twenty-Three
Sanctuary

Billy Simpson bent down and picked up Valeria's pager right away. The red transmission LED was still flashing indicating that pager was in the sending mode. Billy realized that whoever was receiving this pager signal, it would be a signal of distress which would result in almost an immediate response. The ironic thing about it all was that Billy considered this a "good thing," they had just gotten themselves a lucky break! Valeria had done on her own what Billy Simpson thought he might have to do if Valeria had a beeper or a pager, she did!

"Perfect," Billy thought, as he picked up Valeria's pager. "Soon they would be having an expected, "unexpected" guest, probably barging in on this little party that was to get under way."

Valeria was standing there, actually trembling. She wasn't sure what was about to happen. Then something did happen. Suddenly the door behind Valeria sprung open, and a man dressed in a track suit, brandishing a gun in hand barged into the room almost as if the door had been wide open.

About a half a second after barging in, he found himself lying on the floor, squirming with pain, convulsing, face down and immobilized. It was Lev; one of Mitkin's thugs barging in with gun in one hand and holding the key card in his other hand. Billy Simpson was holding a stun-gun in his hand, and as Lev barged in, Billy, standing right beside the door frame, zapped him on the back of his neck with one hell of an electrical shock, sending Lev to the floor and dropping his gun while convulsing in agony.

The hotel security guard still standing outside the open door, saw it all go down and was about to make his exit when Billy Simpson yelled out to him, "no no... you stay!"

The security guard froze. Billy then told the guard to get in the room and just to sit in the corner and stay out of the way. The security did as he was told. He was harmless, but still, Billy wanted him to stay. Billy and Felix would deal with him later.

This had all happened within the first minute after Valeria had entered. She was now shaking more than ever, totally being freaked out. But not to fear, Frances and Millie came to her rescue. As Valeria stood not knowing what to do, the two women approached Valeria. Before she had a chance to react Frances hugged her, embracing her as Valeria started crying. Frances knew Valeria was in shock, she caressed Valeria's head softly brushing her hair with her hand, all the while saying, "it's okay, it's okay, you don't have to be afraid, don't be afraid, I am here to help you, we are all here to help you. What is your name sweetheart?"

She whimpered back, "Valeria."

Valeria couldn't stop crying; she thought her life was in deep danger now. There laying on the floor was her protector or better said her "watcher" the one who made sure her clients paid up, and if they didn't well, her clients would have better days. Lev was mean and dirty, if her client wanted a reduced rate or was unsatisfied with her services, and refused to pay; Lev would beat the living daylights out of him and then he would pay. Now with Lev on the floor, surely Valeria would receive the beating of her life from Mitkin. None of this would have happened if it wasn't for her! Mitkin would not let this one go.

Mitkin had trained his women so that anything and everything that could and did go wrong, ever, was always the fault of the girls, they were to blame for all mishaps, and this was the biggest mishap ever to happen to her. So thought Valeria.

Billy Simpson watched as Frances and Millie calmed Valeria, her tears running down her face smearing her cheap mascara. Frances wiped her face clean as if a mother was cleaning up her child's face. Frances was a caring woman. Millie took Valeria by her arm and helped her over to the couch. Valeria followed and sat down, with Millie then embracing her also, holding Valeria and telling her, not to worry.

"Valeria, darling, don't be afraid, we are here to help you." She took Valeria's hand into hers and said, "your life can change tonight forever Valeria, we can help you change it. That is what we do, that is our jobs, Valeria, to help you and all your friends." Millie looked at Valeria. She could see the fear in Valeria's eyes.

"I know you are very worried about many things now Valeria, but we know what to do, nothing can touch you now Valeria, you are safe for the first time in a very long time, I know that. Valeria, I want you to sit with me, here sweetheart, have some water; don't be afraid, you will see, everything will be good. We work for Mr. Davis, he owns this hotel Valeria,

and he knows about you, he is a good man Valeria."
Valeria started calming down some.

Then she started to sob again. "But you don't understand, my mother and father at home, they will be in trouble because I am making this happen. Mr. Mitkin will be very very angry." She sobbed lightly. Millie could sense the fear in her voice and motioned for Billy to come over. Billy Simpson came over to the couch and sat down beside Valeria. Millie then said, holding onto Valeria's hands in hers, "Valeria, this is Mr. Simpson, he is a very close friend of Mr. Mrs. Davis the owners of this hotel, do you understand?" She asked Valeria gently.

Valeria looked up at Billy, and said: "yes, I understand, Mr. Simpson is a good man too."

Then Millie said looking at Billy, "Valeria is afraid for her mother and father, she thinks they will be harmed because of what happened here tonight."

Billy then put his strong hands on Valeria's shoulder and looked Valeria in the eye and said to her. "Valeria, right, that is your name?"

She nodded her head,

Billy then continued, "where are you from Valeria, where is your home sweetheart?" Billy asked Valeria with a very gentle voice but a reassuring voice.

"I am from Tobolsk, a city very far away in Siberia," Valeria answered.

"And you are afraid for your mother and father's safety is that right?" Billy continued asking gently.

"Yes, Mr. Simpson, very afraid Mr. Mitkin will bring bad things for them, look at Lev on the floor, I will be in much trouble too." She started to whimper again.

"Don't you worry about Lev, he will be let go in a little while, we don't want him, we want you, Valeria, we want to give you a new life sweetheart, how old are you, eighteen nineteen maybe? Billy asked, continuing in his gentle manner.

Valeria looked at Billy with tears in her eyes and asked. "You would do that for me? Nobody ever does anything for me, why would you do that for me?" Valeria was confused and now very humble.

Billy then said, "yes Valeria we would do that for you, and not just you but everyone of your friends working this hotel as you were before we found you. Valeria this is what we do, and to show you how much we mean it, we will take care of you here at the hotel until your life is figured out, and your mother and father are safe. Will you help me do that Valeria? Billy asked with a look of great comfort and safe haven in his eyes.

Valeria reached out and put her arms around Billy, and started to cry..."oh thank you, thank you so very much, I don't know there are people like you in the world", she continued crying and holding onto Billy, he had become her personal Savior this day. No, Valeria was no longer a hooker, and in Valeria's heart she never was, just a beautiful eighteen-yearold young lady. She had been a sex slave, but a slave no more.

Billy then said, "Valeria, I want you to go with Millie and Frances, they will show you to your room here in the hotel, a very special room where you will stay for the next few days, with us Valeria. We will take care of everything for you. This will be your new home for a little while. Both Frances and Millie will be with you and watch over you; you need not be afraid anymore. You are safe now. Go with Millie okay? Billy finished saying to Valeria what she needed to do.

Valeria looked back at Millie, and she then hugged Millie as well and said: "I will go with you, thank you."

Billy watched as Millie and Frances took Valeria to her new accommodations courtesy of Eldon and Kimberley Davis.

Sanctuary had arrived for Valeria; now it would be Kati's and her friends' turn to embrace their opportune moments in time.

With the door, having been shut behind Kati, Ken then looked Kati and Ildiko in the eye and asked. "So, you girls have to do as I say, is that right?"

Kati replied, "Yes *Meester*; we do anything you want." as they both started undressing.

Ken then said. "No, no, keep your clothes on. I want you both to sit on the edge of the bed. Yes, come here, you Kati, I want you to sit right there, and you Ildiko, right there beside Kati, yes, just like that. Ken motioned for them to sit.

The two girls did as they were told. Ken then went and got himself a chair and placed it right in front of the two girls who were sitting down now beside one another on the edge of the bed and he too

279

sat down into the chair, just within arm's length from the two young girls.

Ken then said. "now listen to me, and listen to me very carefully, do you understand me? I know you speak a little English do you understand?"

"Yes, *Meester*, we understand." Kati replied with a look of "what's going on" in her eyes.

Ken then reached into his pocket and took out a photograph. It was a picture of Eldon and Kimberley with their daughter Cathy. The photo showed two loving parents, with their little girl, perhaps only five or six years younger than Kati and Ildiko.

Ken knew this would be the draw; it always worked with young underage girls like Kati and Ildiko were. Girls trapped as Kati and Ildiko were trapped; always thinking of their home. Still young and still almost children, who had grown up much too fast and robbed of their innocence.

With both Kati and Ildiko sitting on the edge of the bed, Ken then asked Kati and Ildiko to hold hands, the two girls did.

He then reached out and took hold of the two girls hands into his, and said, "don't be afraid, I am not here to harm or to hurt you, I am here to show you something."

Kati and Ildiko then became nervous; this was a bit too out of the ordinary for them both, but there was something about this man that was different, they did as they were told, they listened. Ken then held up the photograph of Eldon, Kimberley, and Cathy.

"You don't know these people, do you?"

Both girls shook their heads, Kati saying, "no who are they?"

"This is a picture of the man and woman who own this hotel. They are Mr. and Mrs. Davis. That is their little girl Cathy, I think that is your name too, but in Hungarian is that right Kati? You and she have the same name." Ken said, looking at Kati, smiling. Kati was intrigued as was Ildiko.

Kati nodded, "yes that is my name, Kati," she said, gazing at the picture of Cathy Davis. The photo immediately triggered thoughts of Kati with her parents back in Hungary. Kati was all of a sudden lost in her head, thinking of her family back home and how much she missed them.

"Oh, if she could only hold them again and sit with them as this Cathy in the picture was sitting so happily with her parents."

Ken went on. "They love her very much. One day, their beautiful daughter Cathy was taken from them by bad men, and they had to find her and rescue her." Ildiko looked at Kati, not knowing what to make of all this. Ken could see that the girls were mesmerized.

"They did, they found their beautiful daughter Cathy." Ken then paused and let that sink in, but just long enough for the girls to catch their breath. Then he continued.

"And now I am here because of Mr. and Mrs. Davis, who own this hotel, they both asked me to find you, to rescue both of you from this terrible life you are forced into."

Both Ildiko and Kati immediately started crying. The two young teenage girls were overwhelmed, totally overwhelmed.

Kati then asked, "but how, how you make this happen? How do Mr. and Mrs... know about me, about Ildiko about my friends, how they know?"

Ken went on saying, "Kati" looking straight at her, "honey you and Ildiko have to trust me."

For effect, Ken took out a security officer's badge from the USA which was in his wallet and showed the girls.

He then said. "I am a personal agent for Mr. and Mrs. Davis, who own this hotel, we know everything that goes on here. I am here to help you out of this, but I cannot force you, you have to agree.

If you agree to come with me, I can make sure you will be safe. Mr. Mitkin will no longer bother you or your friends; his business will be over, and you will have a new life and good jobs, working for Mr. and Mrs. Davis. But you have to agree. If you do not want it, then you will have difficulty, because you will be on your own here in Moscow. Girls, Kati, Ildiko, this is your chance today. Take it and come with me."

Kati turned to Ildiko and started speaking to her in Hungarian. Ken could tell that both were nervous as hell and unsure about the whole thing. This was just too much and too out of the ordinary, yet that photograph of Cathy with Eldon and Kimberley was too much of a draw for both girls to ignore.

"How do we come with you, what do we do?" Kati asked.

Ken then said, "that is nothing to worry about, we leave this room, you do not pick up any of your things, you just follow me. Do you understand?" Ken asked.

Kati and Ildiko started talking to one another in Hungarian again and then hugged each other. "Okay, we come with you."

As soon as he got the okay from the girls, Ken pressed his pager, and Billy's unit came alive. He knew where Ken and Stu were; Suite 2020 and Billy was on his way.

The suite was only a minute away if that. Billy Simpson arrived on the second floor and headed down the hall to the suite. As he walked down briskly, he could tell there was a large guy sitting on a chair at the end of the hallway. Billy thought to himself; it must be the guard posted there to screen any person wanting access. Billy walked down the hall, and the guard stood up.

As Billy got closer, the guard eyed Billy and asked: "can I help you?"

Billy then said, "no its okay, I'll help myself" and with one strike as quick as a lightning bolt Billy took out the guard with a Karate blow to his larynx. The guard grabbed at his throat trying to breathe but was having great trouble. Billy then handcuffed him, hogtied his feet and relieved him of his Uzi from under his jacket. The guard wasn't going anyplace. Billy opened the door to the suite with his pass key card and dragged the guard in.

Ludmilla and Anna seeing Billy enter suddenly jumped up off their chairs. They had been watching TV when Billy burst in with the guard in tow.

"Vhat, vhat's happen, vhat's go on?" Ludmilla demanded of Billy.

Billy having dragged the guard in then turned towards the two twins and said. "Ladies, ladies, sit back down, nothing to worry about, your night is over. We are in charge now." Having said that, Billy looked to see down the hallway as Ken was walking back with Kati and Ildiko.

"Okay, these two young ladies have agreed to have our help, Billy, this is Kati and this is Ildiko" Ken introduced them to Billy. The two girls couldn't believe their eyes. They were too dumbfounded to really comprehend just what was happening.

Mitkin's guard was tied up lying in the middle of the floor, gasping for air. There was a strange man being introduced to them who reached out to shake their hands like real people do.

Anna and Ludmilla sat quietly like little doves, no longer their sex masters. But no sign of the other girls; a minute later, Stu then showed up with the other three young Hungarian girls.

Stu had used the same tactic on the three young girls he took with him into the other room. Only Este was willing to go with Stu, while the two others said they were too scared that Mr. Mitkin would be very mad and hurt their families back home. As much as Stu tried to explain to them that their lives could now change forever and that Mitkin would no longer be a threat, they did not agree as far as Stu could tell. The main problem was the language barrier, but there would be a solution for that to come as well. Stu wasn't giving up on the ladies just yet.

Billy, Stu, and Ken were now trying their best to comfort the girls including Anna and Ludmilla. When the three girls with Stu came out and saw what had happened to their guard who was currently tied up and laying on the floor, all three girls gravitated to Stu, and now the two reluctant ones told Stu they wanted to come along now. Ken and Stu both understood that the girls were very shaken and scared. Communication was an issue, but for now, the girls were safe and from this day forward, the services of Gorky After Hours Club had come to a screeching dead stop.

Billy then went to the phone and called for Marty Sabine. It was late in the night, already morning well past midnight. Marty was in his suite but was in no mood for sleeping. He knew the sting operation was to go down this night. He had been on pins and needles the whole day. When Marty's phone rang, his body jumped almost as if someone had spooked him. He instinctively knew this phone call would bring him into the mix. He answered: "Marty Sabine."

"Marty it's Billy Simpson," Marty listened carefully, while his heart beat quickly, pinned to every word Billy spoke.

"The sting operation has been completed; I want you to bring a contingent of hotel security with you to hospitality suite 2020. We will have to take care of a few matters right away."

"Okay, Billy will be there shortly, will need a minute or two in rounding up a few security guards. We have a full house tonight as you know and with the convention in town, we scheduled extra security so I should be able to bring a couple of guys with me." Marty answered.

"Yeah, well, try to get at least four of them, we will need as many as you can round up, we're here in the suite waiting for you."

Both Billy Simpson and Marty well knew where the hotel security guards' loyalty lay. In the end, they all needed jobs.

By now it was very apparent and obvious with what had gone down that hotel security was in on the prostitution ring, but only because they were under the thumb of Misha Rudkin, the chief culprit, and head of the security department. If any one of Rudkin's staff were to refuse his instructions, he would let the person go, and not one of his staff members wanted to lose their job. The hotel paid well, better than most hotels in the city.

With all this having gone down tonight, Rudkin was nowhere to be found; only his assistant was on duty. Misha had decided to take the weekend off; he had become very skittish of late, especially after having been handed the videotape by Mitkin. Ever since, Rudkin had kept his profile low.

Rudkin too had a sixth sense about things. Lately, his confidence level was beginning to erode. Marty was still the General Manager of the hotel and security reported to Marty over and above anything that Rudkin every wanted. Marty was with whom the buck stopped, they all knew that. Marty was the one who signed their paychecks, not Rudkin and not Mitkin.

Security would do what Marty ordered; there was no question where loyalty lay when push came to shove. Same went for any other people bought off by Rudkin including the front office staff or even other members of management who would eventually be rooted out. Billy had no doubt about that, and neither did Louis James or Eldon. It was still their hotel, and in the end, Eldon and Kimberley called the shots; now to clean up this mess, and get on with business.

Marty rounded up the four security guys and had them follow him up to suite 2020. Marty used his pass key card to enter. Billy in the meantime had called in Maxim, Eldon's bodyguard and former KGB agent who also, being an auxiliary constable carried a Moscow Police Badge. It was rare, that Maxim was called upon for police duty, sometimes when the city experienced large political demonstrations he would be called upon for crowd control, but that was about the extent of his police involvement. Tonight, his police badge would come in very handy.

In walked Marty with four security officers. With Maxim and Marty, the Hotel Manager now present, the rest was all for show, mainly for the guard who was still handcuffed, and to some extent for the girls who were for the moment thinking they were being arrested by Moscow Police for solicitation of prostitution. In fact, that would not have stood up in court since the whole thing set up as a club membership, but with underage girls being present, sex crimes would take precedence over the club membership loophole.

Maxim pulled out his police badge and informed all the girls in the room and the guard, that they were being placed under arrest for violation of city ordinance laws covering illicit activities. With the girls thinking that Maxim was with the police department, they all panicked once again thinking that they really were being arrested. The effect was exactly what Billy and the Sting Team wanted to convey to the guard who was now seated in a chair, handcuffed and listening and watching everything very carefully. It was playing out exactly as Billy and Felix had hoped it would. Everything was very official. Hotel security was ordered to take the girls into custody and to hold them for the police department to arrive and to be taken to jail. This, unfortunately, was one final fiasco the girls had to endure. Later, Billy, Ken, and Stu would explain to them that it had to be done, to send a message to Mitkin that they were all under police custody and were being repatriated back to their points of origin.

Mitkin's guard was removed by Maxim and taken to a holding room where hotel security would watch over him until the morning at which time he would be released along with Lev from Valeria's case. They no doubt would be reporting back to Mitkin that the girls had been detained by the Moscow Police in a vice squad operation.

Mitkin well knew that all underage girls, caught in the sex trade, especially non-nationals would be repatriated to their countries of origin as per the UN treaty among nations signed in the summer of 1989, to protect and eliminate sex trafficking and exploitation of the innocent.

The girls would be safe; Mitkin's reach would have been severed forever. The girls, however, had no clue that such a law existed, they just lived in fear day in day out. For tonight they would just be relocated to a different section of the hotel. The first thing that Billy needed to do for them was to remove the girls from the environment of entrapment and forced sex.

Eldon and Kimberley had made it clear that the girls needed a comfort zone, and leaving them in the hospitality suite where they had been enslaved would not do. They needed reassurance, and one huge element was one's environment that in most cases dictated activity or condition. So, for now, the girls were moved to a different section of the Jewel Danamo.

Ludmilla and Anna would be separated from the rest of the girls; they had not yet been offered sanctuary. They would be, but in private from the other girls. If they wanted the sting teams help, and go down a different pathway in life, then they would be united with the girls, if not, then they would be forever banned from entering any Holiday Jewel Hotel and Casino property for the rest of their lives.

Eldon and his team already had their best interest in hand with a plan to making their lives whole again. It was all part of the sting and extermination process in fulfilling the company motto, "service with integrity" and that cut deep into all that Eldon and

Kimberley's company stood for, here in Moscow and internationally wherever their hotels operated.

Kimberley was very adamant about preserving the dignity of all who fell victim to this blight that seemed to run through their business from time to time.

Kati and her four Hungarian friends were asked to get dressed back into their street clothes. They would be taken to a section of the hotel that had interconnecting suites. In all, there were four bedrooms between the two suites. There they would meet up with Valeria and the eight of them along with Millie and Frances would all spend the rest of the night together, safely resting in sanctuary for the first time in a very long time. When morning came, a plan from Holiday Jewel Hotels, courtesy of Eldon and Kimberley would be unveiled and offered so they could all have new lives if they so chose. Decisions would need to be made, but definitely, the road would be theirs to take.

Ludmilla and Anna were taken away by Maxim and Billy. In private, once separated from the Hungarian girls, Billy and Maxim offered the twins sanctuary as well. Both women after a long discussion and time, since they were twins, accepted Billy's offer. They too would now be rid of Mitkin forever.

There remained one problem however which the girls did not know how to handle, but it would come out eventually. Both Ludmilla and Anna remained quiet; the problem was Mr. Sabine.

Seeing Mr. Sabine in the hospitality suite with Billy and Maxim had confused the girls, all of them.

But as young as they were, and as innocent as they were in their hearts, all of them had "street smarts". The girls knew when to speak up and when to remain silent, they all thought best to be silent for now. Yes, indeed, Marty knew the twins and other girls in ways that Billy was not aware of, not yet, and the girls had picked up on that, in particular, young Kati.

She remained confused and skeptical, and as she was being relocated she started to cry again, thinking of her little brother, mother, and father.

"What could happen to them?" In her confusion and anxiety, she grabbed onto Billy's arm as she was being shown to her new accommodations, walking down the hallway, she started in on Billy pleading with him but in Hungarian, she reverted back to her native tongue, she pleaded and pleaded crying to Billy "*segitcs a csaladomat.*" Billy, of course, didn't quite understand, but he did comprehend that this young lady was desperate for help and needed to be understood. Help would come to Kati in the morning, in a big way.

Kati was reunited with all her familiar friends in the connecting suites, all eight ladies now including Ludmilla and Anna. The twins shared one bedroom to themselves; the other six girls took up the rest of the bedrooms with Millie and Frances sleeping on the sofas in the living areas of the two suites. Everyone was comfortable and had bedded down for the night, with Millie and Frances acting as comforters and mentors to the girls, and two security guards posted outside the suites until morning came.

Kati had settled down; she was in her bed opposite Ildiko. For the very first time in their lives, Kati and Ildiko slept in hotel beds in a normal way, sleeping by themselves, enjoying the plushness of the pillow-top mattress while taking in the fresh scent of the clean sheets and the comfort of the luxurious pillows.

Kati prayed once again, holding onto the photograph of her little brother and another of her family asking God, "that soon, soon, she could see their faces just one more time, just one more time please lord," and she fell asleep.

***

Chapter Twenty-Four
Say it ain't so

The room service order had been prepared to the highest possible standards of excellence and presentation. The kitchen and service staff of the Jewel Danamo was impeccable. Ironically Mitkin's Tsar kitchen and service staff were second to none in that department, and their skills showed in the final results. The room service waiter knocked on the door. Ambassador Frankie Albert answered the knock, greeting the waiter as he wheeled in breakfast for The Ambassador and his wife.

Marika and Frankie had already showered and fully dressed for the day but had decided to stay in and relax with room service rather than doing the morning restaurant routine downstairs. Well, Marika was relaxing, enjoying her breakfast; Frankie Albert, not so much. He hadn't slept much, and when he did, he tossed and turned.

"Darling you didn't sleep well last night, I can tell, are you okay?" Marika asked her husband as she sat across from him at the breakfast table.

"I'll be okay Marika, just have lots on my mind with this situation from dinner last night," Frankie answered his wife. Frankie poured himself a glass of freshly squeezed orange juice. Looking back at his wife across the table, Marika went on.

"Yeah, really something, isn't it? But it sounds like the Davis's know what they are doing and have been down this road before. I think it was good advice about cutting ties with our food supplier, and then there is the whole thing about getting in a "clean team."

O' my god, I don't even feel like going back to Spaso House. Frankie, the whole building, could be bugged! Who knows?" Marika sounded alarmed.

"Yes, well I'll make the call to Washington and have them send out a crew to scan the embassy, don't worry it'll be taken care of immediately."

Marika then remarked, "maybe we should stay here for the next few days till it's taken care of Frankie, I'm sure Eldon and Kimberley would be okay with that."

Frankie then answered, "well for today anyway, then let me see how things pan out."

Just as Frankie was answering his wife, the phone sitting on the desk next to the dining room table rang. It was within arm's length reach, and not even having to stand up; Frankie was able to reach it.
He picked it up and answered. "Albert."

"Ah, yes...good morning Mr. Ambassador, it's Kimberley." I hope I'm not disturbing you, but there is something I need your help with." Kimberley said politely.

"Well, it's already quarter after nine Kimberley and we are just having breakfast, so we're good my dear, what is it I can do for you?" Frankie, although sounding very interested in helping Kimberley in whatever she may have in mind, wasn't exactly too enthusiastic about it all, but did not let on.

"We have a little situation in which I could really use a translator. Frankie, we have a young lady in the hotel here, she is frantic Ambassador, she's a Hungarian girl who apparently keeps going on and on about her little brother and her parents back in Hungary.

Ambassador, I thought you or Marika might like to talk with her, and find out what is making her so frantic. She's been crying most of the night, and she is on her own. I could really use your help."

"Okay Kimberley, I'm about done anyway, give me a few minutes, and I'll come down to your suite."

"Ambassador, I really appreciate this, it will be a great help to us knowing what this young lady needs to tell us. I will have Billy Simpson come and escort you to our suite; I'll send him over in ten minutes? Is that all right? You've met Billy right Ambassador?" Kimberley asked.

"Yes, I know who Billy is, I think just about everyone in the State Department knows who Billy Simpson is Kimberley, I'll expect him in ten."

The Ambassador then looked over to his wife, and in Hungarian, he said: I'm going to see a young Hungarian girl this morning to find out what she is so excited about, Kimberley needs a translator. I'll be back shortly. When I get back, it should be close to ten, and we will need to leave for the auto show soon, you may as well get ready; I'm pretty much set to go."

Marika then said, "a Hungarian girl, here in the hotel? Kimberley needs a translator, and you're going without me? Not on your life! I'm coming along, she might need the voice of a caring Hungarian woman, besides, I may be able to get things out of her, that you can't. I bet this has everything to do with what we talked about at dinner last night. I'm coming!" And that was that. Frankie was told.

Marika was not to be left out. Frankie then thought to himself; "well, you might as well come, I'm sure in the end you will be just as involved as I am, may as well get you prepared for what's coming."

And with that, Billy Simpson knocked on The Ambassador's door.

Eldon had heard enough. He had just been fully briefed on what went down last night and early this morning with the sting takedown team. The three of them were back in the Pushkin Boardroom. Louis James, Eldon, and Marty Sabine.

Marty, as usual, was trying his best in keeping his composure; he was doing all right, managing to hold it together.

Eldon spoke. "So, Misha Rudkin decided to make himself scarce this weekend. It's one of the busiest weekends the hotel has had since opening and our Director of Security decided to take the weekend off. If I didn't know any better, it's almost like he's got a sixth sense for what was going down last night. Well, it doesn't matter; Marty I want you to call him in."

Louis then added, "that should be no problem, as per his employment agreement he is on call twenty-four seven."

Eldon then continued, "call him in Marty and I want you to fire him on the spot. With the six security guards coming forward this morning after being questioned by Felix and Billy, they have all confessed to Rudkin paying them off to look the other way and act as "watchers" for the girls working the hotel. Fire him, and take his security officer's badge. He is done. Got that Marty?"

Marty answered. "Okay Eldon, consider it done. I'll call him right now." Marty got up from his seat, went over to the phone in the boardroom, took out his day-timer pocket planner, looked up Rudkin's home phone number, dialed it, and called Rudkin into the hotel right there and then in front of Eldon and Louis.

"He will be here in a half hour Eldon, I told him to meet me in my office," Marty said, looking back at Eldon and Louis.

"Okay then, for now, we are done here. Marty, let me know when you've fired Rudkin. I also want you to call the Director of Human Resources and our Russian Liaison Officer. I want them both here when you fire Rudkin. You will have Rudkin wait until the other two have arrived, so they are witness to Rudkin's termination. I want all our "i's" dotted and "t's" crossed. Make certain you are letting him go for violation of the company's code of ethics and for participating in the facilitation of prostitution and organized crime. Got it?" Eldon was pissed, and Marty knew it.

"Yes Eldon, I fully understand, I'm on it." Louis and Eldon got up and left the boardroom, leaving Marty by himself. Marty sat there for a moment, took out his day timer planner once again and called both Irina Sopov the HR Director and Yuri Garin the

Russian joint venture Liaison Officer for the company. They would both be there within the hour.

Louis James also had an office in the Jewel Danamo; he rarely used it. Most of the time Louis was in meetings with a number of his executives at one time discussing hotel-wide policy and procedures so the Pushkin boardroom was where Louis would spend most of his time when it came to meetings. After having met with Marty this morning, Louis did return to his office with Eldon. Felix was to meet them both in a few minutes there. Passing by the concierge desk in the lobby on their way to his office, Louis asked the concierge to call room service and have pots of fresh coffee delivered to his office, both decaf and regular. He knew that Felix was a several-coffees-a day kind of guy, but Felix only drank decaf, good thing too Louis thought. Otherwise, Felix would be bouncing off the walls after his eight cups every day.

Felix was already there in Louis's office when Eldon and Louis arrived. Louis had a nice oak executive desk, with a high back chair behind it. But he did not sit there.

All three men took seats at a round table with board room style chairs set around it. The coffee came, the waiter placed the tray with the hot silex coffee pots in the center of the table. Felix reached for the decaf, poured himself a cup, added some sweetener and was ready.

Eldon then said, "How can you drink that crap?" Eldon looked at Felix like he was nuts or something, but jokingly.

"Well, I like it," Felix answered back. Eldon then just let out an "hmm" shaking his head at his close friend.

"Okay Felix, what have you got for me?" Eldon was referring to the potential bad news already on top of last night's bad news regarding Tsar's ownership being Alexander Mitkin. Felix then reached into his briefcase and extracted a manila file folder. He placed it on the table. The file folder had the company logo on the front of it. "HJHC" with a recently updated artist's drawing of The Red Jewel. It was now the company's flagship business hotel. Eldon knew right away it was from his corporate offices back in Ft. Lauderdale.

"Eldon this came in yesterday via courier from our legal department in Lauderdale, it's not good news Eldon," Felix said.

"Okay, let me have it, just say it, Felix, I've had so much bad news lately that one more will probably not make a difference, may as well pile it on top of the growing heap." Eldon was at this point prepared for just about anything, "just about" but not quite for this.

"Seems we had a Mr. Gunter Vogel staying with us a couple of weeks ago Eldon. He is from Frankfurt Germany, Vice President of Sales for Kruger Corporation. Eldon, Kruger is a large manufacturer of precision machinery and tools. Mr. Vogel has been a regular repeat guest of this hotel for the past eight months with frequent visits to Moscow. Anyway, Mr. Kruger is suing Holiday Jewel Hotels and Casinos in the amount of ten million two hundred thousand dollars. The two hundred thousand for direct damages suffered by Mr. Vogel. Being hush money paid to prevent images of Mr. Vogel engaged in compromising situations (specifically sexually explicit) of him, reaching his wife. And ten million for punitive damages suffered by Mr. Vogel due to the direct negligence of Holiday Jewel Hotels and Casinos, namely The Holiday Jewel Danamo Hotel in Moscow in keeping his activities private and confidential while staying with us, that was two weeks ago. You see Eldon; I told you this would not be good."

Eldon didn't say anything. He just sat looking at Felix. After fifteen seconds or so, he asked. "And this came via courier yesterday from Florida?"

"Yup," Felix replied. "Okay, then that means Mr. Vogel is suing us in Florida as a Florida corporation and not here in Russia correct?" That's right Eldon. Felix answered.

"So, then he is actually suing the corporation, and not the hotel itself." Eldon was already onto the strategy.

"That's right Eldon; he isn't a dummy. He knows he has a better chance of collecting from the head office than he does from the hotel. Without civil damages defined here clearly in Russia, it's doubtful that he would even be successful here. Hell, there might not even be a lawyer or judge for that matter who could be competent enough to represent the guy much less hear his case. Things are pretty up in the air here as you know, nothing seems to stick to the wall when it comes to civil lawsuits; it never used to exist here under communism. The State was the be all and end all. You pretty much did as you were told. People were happy enough to make it through the day without being ratted on by someone for looking at you the wrong way."

Eldon thought about it a while. "Well, this puts us in deep shit. First, it tells me that Mitkin has surveillance set up in this hotel and who knows how many rooms and which rooms are bugged. This also means that it isn't just him, there may be a lot more of these lawsuits coming our way, and I would venture to say, we are not the only hotel in town that's been targeted and hit like this. Okay, Felix, tell the legal team back in Florida to deal with this and also tell them that I personally will be making a trip back home shortly, and I will come in to talk with them, all right? Eldon looked at Felix, making more of a statement than asking a question.

Then with a very "pissed off" and "have had enough of this" manner Eldon remarked; "We are going to need to take some action, this whole Tsar, Mitkin thing is getting totally out of hand. I'm about to rattle someone's cage and rattle it big, big enough to shake the demons out and clear this shit up once and for all!"

Eldon walked out and headed up to his suite. Billy, The Ambassador, and his wife Marika were also heading there. Kati would be brought up to Eldon and Kimberley's suite shortly by Frances.

Irina Sopov the human resources director for the hotel as well as Yuri Garin had already arrived and were sitting in Marty's office. Marty had just briefed them on the situation having advised Irina that the decision to dismiss Misha had been made by Eldon himself, and there was to be no reconsideration. Misha was to be fired today.

Marty had laid out the clear reasons for doing so, and Irina had already prepared a separation certificate indicating dismissal for cause. Dismissal was justified because of Rudkin's direct violation of hotel policy, and willfully compromising the integrity of the hotel, thereby jeopardizing the safety, and privacy of the hotel's patrons. This was more than adequate for immediate termination of employment without recourse.

Misha Rudkin arrived and knocked on Marty's office door, and walked in. There were two security guards already in Marty's office, these were guards who Misha had personally paid off, but now that wasn't so important anymore since loyalties lay with job security, not with Misha Rudkin. Misha wasn't someone who was born just yesterday; he knew of the risks involved when he capitulated to Mitkin's bribes. The security guards stood up, the two of them were the most strapping and physically dominant men on the security force. Misha would not be wise to tangle with them.

"Take a seat Misha," Marty said.

"What's this all about?" Misha asked, but he knew what this was all about. It was standard procedure to have security present when dismissing hotel employees. They would need to be escorted off the property. It wasn't something that happened often, but it did happen, mainly for theft, stealing hotel linen and cutlery and of course guests' personal property.

Irina Sopov then looked at Misha and said very matter of factually, "Mr. Rudkin, your employment with Holiday Jewel Hotels and Casinos is officially terminated at this moment. Here is your separation certificate. That is all. The hotel security guards will escort you out of the hotel and off the property. You are never to return to this property or to any other hotels owned or operated by the company. Have a good day."

Irina reached out to hand Rudkin an envelope with the termination papers. Misha's face turned beet red, and they could all see his temper start to rage. He did not accept the envelope from Irina Sopov, instead started shouting at Marty.

"You son of a bitch, you're going down with me..." and even before Misha could get the next word out, both security guards tazed Misha and he went down hard, falling onto the edge of Marty's desk splitting open his forehead, bleeding onto the carpet. One of the guards radioed for a first aid kit immediately. Misha was convulsing on the floor having been hit with two stun guns at once. Another security officer showed up with the first aid kit. Misha's forehead was bandaged, and the three guards then carried Misha out of the hotel and off the property, having placed his envelope inside his jacket. The security guards then put Misha into his automobile and allowed him to recover in the driver's seat. Three-quarters of an hour later, Misha's security guards watched as Misha Rudkin drove away, never to return again.

"Ambassador Albert, Frankie, Marika, I'm surprised to see you here this morning, to what do we owe the pleasure of your company?" Eldon asked as he walked in and entered his living room. Frankie and Marika had just sat down before Eldon walked in.

"Oh honey, we have another little situation, that I asked The Ambassador to help us with this morning," Kimberley said, walking up to Eldon and taking hold of his hand.

"I've been having all kinds of little situations already this morning, so what is it that Frankie and Marika are helping us with?" Eldon asked, looking at his wife.

"It's one of the young girls Eldon, Billy suggested we see her, she is frantic Eldon, but she's stuck on speaking Hungarian only. She understands little English and Billy tells us she's terrified Eldon. I asked Frankie to come and translate for us, and Marika was kind enough to come along just in case the young girl needs some comforting words from a Hungarian mother figure. Frances will bring the girl here; Billy just went to get them. She's spent the night with Frances Eldon, she's safe, but I think she could use our help, honey." Kimberley said to her husband.

"Okay, excellent sounds like this girl may have good reason to be scared, I don't doubt it." The door opened and in walked Kati with Frances and Billy.

Kati looked so scared; her eyes were bloodshot from crying just about all night long. She was a beautiful young lady. Now without the cheap mascara and makeup, she looked like a little angel, an angel tainted by life, and scarred by fate. Frances walked Kati over to Eldon and Kimberley who were both still standing. Frankie and Marika were sitting on the sofa in the living room. Kati was only four feet ten inches, a little angel with bright green eyes.

Frances then said, "this is Kati, Kati is from a little town outside of Debrecen Hungary, Kati this is Mrs. Davis and Mr. Davis."

Kimberley then said to Kati, "Kati, don't be afraid, I, we are here to help you, Kati." Kati understood that much, and as Kimberley reached out taking Kati's hand, Kati looked up at Kimberley. Seeing Kimberley's face clearly, her eyes widened, and in her amazement said to Kimberley, whimpered, "it's you, it's you" with tears forming again in Kati's emerald green eyes. This time, however, Kati's tears were tears of joy, as Kati looked at Kimberley, and then at Eldon, recognizing both from the photograph Ken had shown her earlier this morning. She lost it; couldn't help herself, she hugged Kimberley like she was hugging her own mother back home in Hungary. Kimberley was taken aback; she wasn't really sure what was going on. Kati had never felt safer in her life than being in the arms of the woman who found and rescued her own little girl Cathy. Kati was now her

Kati; she cried into Kimberley as Kimberley hugged her back, feeling that this lost soul had just found freedom and salvation from being enslaved and forced into enduring unspeakable torture. Then Billy said, "I think she just recognized you and Eldon from the photograph that Ken showed her last night.

Kimberley then exclaimed, "oh my god, this girl, this child has been through Mitkin's hell." She hugged Kati, then held her arm out to Eldon, he moved in closer to Kati, bent down, and looked her in the eye again.

"I am Mr. Davis, Kati, you are safe now." Kati didn't know Eldon, only from the photo, but she put her arm around his neck as well. Eldon knew then and there, without a shadow of a doubt that what he had instructed his sting team to do was the right thing to do. They had to uncover the evil, and then to complete the circle; they had to save the young girls.

Eldon felt the presence of his daughter Cathy through Kati, the love and the longing for being relieved from captivity once again echoed in Eldon's mind. Eldon hugged Kati back and said. "We are here for you Kati and all your friends." Eldon wasn't sure how much of what he said Kati understood, but he said it anyway.

Kimberley teared up, and a moment passed, a moment in time never to be forgotten by anyone in the room being a witness to human frailty being turned into human strength. Marika and Frankie looked on, with Marika having tears in her eyes as well. Frances sat on a chair, with her hand on her heart, it was such a touching moment. Billy, the big man, thought back on the time he and Eldon found Cathy in the cabin on Conch Island in the Bahamas, and how Cathy hugged Eldon crying "daddy, daddy, daddy as Eldon found his darling daughter reuniting his family with Kimberley.

"Come darling... this is Mr. Albert and his wife Mrs. Albert, they are Hungarian Kati," Kimberly said to Kati, motioning her to come over and sit on the sofa between Frankie and Marika. She looked over at The Ambassador and Marika and walked over sitting between the two. Frankie Albert then addressed Kati in Hungarian, saying. "Don't be afraid, you know we are here to help you, Kati, you never have to fear Mr. Mitkin ever again. Do you understand Kati?

Kati then took out the picture of her killed younger brother lying in a ditch that Mitkin had given her after she had become a problem not wanting to prostitute her body. She showed Marika and Frankie.

Kimberley came over as did Eldon, and Kati started crying again, "that Mitkin would now kill her other brother and maybe her mom and dad."

Thoughts ran through Frankie's head now, seeing Kati's young brother laying in the ditch, his face bloody and his body dumped like road kill and left no doubt to rot. "

Ferenc Albert, Hungarian national, born in Budapest, checked himself and asked just exactly who and what had he become over the years. "Was this his doing? Was he in fact somehow implicated in this girl's daily agony?" Frankie thought about those dots on the page in his head. "Some dots barely visible were becoming well defined. Had Frankie become a

307

traitor to both the United States of America and to his birthplace, his country Hungary, had he?" Frankie couldn't help but wonder what this child's life had to do with his, just how intertwined were they? This sixteen-year-old who appears from nowhere and him, a life's journey leading to this moment."

Frankie's stomach turned, his heart raced, his soul bled, his destiny would soon be revealed. "Was he a failed human being? The dots... the dots." Frankie thought.

Kimberley then said. "Can you imagine what it took for Kati to come forward like this, with her brother slaughtered and dumped into a ditch? The bravery it took for this traumatized child to come forward, thinking all along that her actions would further put her parents in peril by Mitkin's ruthless thugs. Kati has been going through hell I'm sure. Every night forced into being raped."

Marika then embraced Kati and told her that she has nothing to fear, Mitkin will no longer have any power over her or her family. Marika then talked to Kati about her home outside of Debrecen, Marika was from a smaller town as well not far from Debrecen and just with the familiarity of another Hungarian woman close to Kati; she calmed and for the first time in days, Kati smiled. She smiled at Marika, and Frankie and hugged Marika back. Kati really was just a child, sixteen years old. A baby. Marika thought.

Eldon then told Marika to tell Kati that he and Kimberley would see to it that Kati goes back home to her mother and father and that Kati would be given a job as a waitress in a real restaurant in Eldon's Hotel the Csardas Jewel on Lake Balaton. Like this, she would be earning good money, and would be on her way to making a good living and back to a normal life.

After hearing Marika translate Eldon's offer; Kati got up and walked over to Eldon, wiping her face from the tears and hugged Eldon saying, "thank you, Mr. Davis, thank you, Mrs. Davis, thank you, everybody, you are so good people, thank you."

"Kati, we will be talking to all your friends who are with you, please go back now with Frances, and I want you to tell your Hungarian friends that we will be looking after all of them, and they can all work at the same hotel on Lake Balaton with you." It will be new a life for all of you Kati, will you do that for me?" Kimberley said, brushing Kati's hair softly with her palm, looking at Marika for translation. Marika did, and Kati had a huge smile on her face.

"Marika, tell Kati that I want to borrow her two photographs. Tell her we only need them for a few minutes and she can have them back before she leaves this room, we need to make copies; it will help us catch the bad men." Kimberley said.

Kati complied, and Billy went to make copies in the next room. Kati had her photos returned within a couple of minutes. Frances showed Kati back to her hotel suite with the other girls. It had been a very good morning for Kati.

It was not a very good morning for Frankie Albert however. No, Frankie Albert still harbored secrets of the past. A storm, however, was brewing on the horizon, a huge and powerful hurricane, threatening the piers holding fast Frankie's secrets in his not so safe of-late harbor.

The weekend had come and gone. The hotel did very well with full occupancy and excellent revenue from both room sales and high revenues from the restaurants. It was the middle of the week. Monday morning, Eldon had legal documents delivered to Tsar Restaurants and Entertainment with notice of lease cancellation. The legal documents were hand delivered and to be effective immediately. Eldon had his HR Director send out notices to all food and beverage employees working for Tsar, that they would be locked out of the hotel as employees of Tsar. If any Tsar employees wished to keep working at The Holiday Jewel Danamo, they would need to quit immediately, and they could be hired on the same day by Holiday Jewel Hotels and be back working their same jobs. Everyone took the option. There was no interruption in service whatsoever. Tsar was out, and Holiday Jewel Danamo now ran and operated their own food and beverage services. The Tsar Restaurants and Entertainment lettering was removed from both the Mir Dining Room entrance as well as the entrance to The Gorky Club. Tsar ceased to exist in the Jewel Danamo.

Mitkin was fuming mad about it all. He had been cut down and thrown out of his largest and most lucrative operation in Moscow. He had no cards to play, Eldon and Kimberley had pulled the rug right out from under him and his operations.

"Someone's got to pay." Mitkin said out loud to nobody. Mitkin put a contract out on Marty Sabine's life.

On Thursday night Marty Sabine drove his car into Moscow city center on his way to the Bolshoi Ballet. Marty parked his car. He got out of his car, was about to walk across the street to the theater, and with the street crowded; a man dressed in a heavy overcoat, walked up behind Marty.

The man reached inside his heavy coat and pulled out a pistol with a silencer attached and put a 38 bullet in the back of Marty's head. Marty Sabine fell to the sidewalk and bled out. He had played his final act. His ballet of life had its curtain drawn tight on the stage of a snow-covered Moscow street.

***

Chapter Twenty-Five
Woman to woman

The day was Friday, and it was morning. Kimberley had made up her mind; it was time to take serious action on her part as well. Eldon would do what Eldon did best, running the business and looking after the hotels. Kimberley had her own talents, and this talent would now rely on friendship and test the mettle of character, revealing where and how the real convictions lay in this new Federation of Russia. It was time to test her friendship with Svetlana. Kimberley had Svetlana's private line number. Svetlana Orlov was the Minister of Tourism and Travel, and this matter surely would be of great interest and great concern. Kimberley dialed Svetlana's number.

"Svetlana Orlov" she answered.

"Hi Svetlana, it's Kimberley, how are you?" Kimberley replied.

"Good Kimberley," Svetlana replied adding, "so early you called, it must be something."

"Well yes, Svetlana, it is something, something I need to see you about in person and it's urgent."

"Kimberley, I'd love to meet with you, but I'm tied up in meetings all day, and …."

Kimberley cut her off. "No Svetlana, I need to see you today; this morning. It's of the highest urgency that you can imagine. I cannot stress this strongly enough. Whatever meetings you may have going on with your people, you as Minister of Travel and

Tourism need to meet with me, I assure you, nothing you have to meet about today is more important than what I have to talk to you about." Kimberley pushed, she pushed hard, maybe too hard. This was after all, not just the Russian Minister of Travel and Tourism, hell; she was the wife of the Russian President for god's sake. Nobody talked to
Svetlana as Kimberley just had, nobody."

Svetlana Orlov listened after having been cut off. She paused after Kimberley's plea to meet with her. Kimberley listened; there was no sound on the other end. Still, nothing,

"Svetlana, are you there?" Kimberley then finally asked.

"Yes, I am here," Svetlana responded. "Are you at your hotel Kimberley?" Svetlana asked.

"Yes Svetlana, I am here at the hotel," Kimberley answered.

"All right, I will be there in one hour. I have canceled all of my meetings for you and Kimberley."

"Yes, Svetlana. Kimberley replied.

"This better be good," Svetlana said and hung up.

With the first lady of the Russian Federation coming over this morning Kimberley wanted to make certain that hotel security was aware of her pending arrival. She called Marty's office, and all she got was voice mail. She then called the concierge and asked for Marty Sabine. The concierge told her that they hadn't yet seen Marty yet this morning. Kimberley was starting to get agitated.

She then called Louis James's office. Louis answered.

"Louis, Kimberley, I've been trying to reach Marty, but no answer and nobody has seen him this morning."

"Yes, I know Kimberley, I was wondering myself where he was until about two minutes ago. Kimberley, I have some very sad news, Marty Sabine was found dead last night in front of the Bolshoi Ballet Theater. Kimberley, he was shot in the back of the neck. I have just been informed by Moscow Police. A Police Officer is in my office now." Louis finished saying. "Oh, my God, oh my God." Kimberley couldn't believe her ears. "I'll be right down Louis."

"No Kimberley, best if you stay put for now. Let me handle this, no really I mean it, I appreciate your concern, but for now, I believe it will be best to have as few people involved as possible."

"Of course, Louis was absolutely correct." Kimberley then realized. "Okay Louis, of course, you are right, update me when you can okay?"

"I will Kimberley." and Louis said goodbye.

Just as Kimberley hung up, her phone came to life again, ringing, it was Svetlana Orlov calling from her chauffeur driven Kremlin limo.

Kimberley, I was on my way, when our secret service advised me that we cannot complete the trip due to some police matters at your hotel. My security people tell me that your General Manager has been murdered, and I cannot be present at an associated or secondary crime scene. Secret service will not allow me to go there; the risk factor is too high. What in god's name is going on?" Svetlana asked with bewilderment in her voice.

"Svetlana, I just now found out myself, my Vice President of Operations here in Moscow Louis James just informed me, I didn't know myself till a minute ago, but Svetlana, this I am sure has something to do with what I wanted to talk to you about. I will come and see you instead, where can we meet? Kimberley asked.

"All right Kimberley, come to the Kremlin, and meet me in the Kremlin library where we met the last time with you and Eldon, is that something you can do?" Svetlana answered. "Yes Svetlana, I will be there in one hour's time, is that good?" Kimberley asked.

"Yes, I will inform Kremlin Security to whisk you through directly to the library building, you will not need to leave your car, your driver can bring you right to the library's main entrance, see you there," Svetlana replied. Kimberley was out of the hotel a half hour later heading to the Kremlin with Eldon's driver and bodyguard Maxim at the wheel.

On the way to the Kremlin, Kimberley usually had the car radio tuned into the English language local radio station "Moscow One". This ride was no different. No sooner had Maxim driven five minutes, the breaking news of Marty's murder was everywhere.

"We interrupt this program with breaking news of the murder of Marty Sabine the Hotel General Manager of the Holiday Jewel Danamo Hotel. Marty Sabine was found after having been killed on the street in front of the Bolshoi Ballet building at

approximately seven forty-five PM last night. Mr. Sabine apparently was on his way to attend the 8: PM ballet performance that evening. Mr. Sabine was found with a theater ticket in his possession. According to the head usher of the theater, Mr. Sabine was a weekly attendee of the ballet and a familiar face at The Bolshoi. We are still awaiting comment from Mr. Sabine's place of work, The Holiday Jewel Danamo Hotel. Stay tuned to Moscow One for further updates; as soon was we have it, you have it. Maggie Harlow reporting for
Moscow One."

"Oh, my god, it's all over the news, this will go international in the next hour." Kimberley thought. "AP and Reuters already have it, she had no doubt, and soon it would be on CNN and VNN and everywhere else. "Felix will be fighting off the news media all day long," she thought.

Maxim drove up to the Kremlin vehicle entrance checkpoint. "Kimberley Ashton-Davis for Svetlana Orlov," Maxim said to the Kremlin gatekeeper, handing over his and Kimberley's ID. The Kremlin guard verified the credentials and motioned Maxim to proceed. A vehicle with a rooftop mounted flashing amber light showed up in front of Kimberley's Beemer and Maxim was instructed to follow it across the courtyard. They were brought directly to the main entrance of the library building. Kimberley got out and went through the front door. Maxim followed his escort vehicle to a parking area where he was to wait for Kimberley.

"Svetlana, I got here as soon as I could. I cannot tell you how much I appreciate you doing this." Kimberley said as she was removing her overcoat. The two women and longtime friends from college hugged with the traditional greeting, but this was business and serious business at that.

"Well, you certainly have my curiosity peaked, now I know this is urgent, after hearing about your General Manager being found last night, and murdered! My god Kimberley what is going on in your hotel?" Svetlana remarked.

"Svetlana, I'm afraid it's much bigger than my hotel, the question isn't what is going on in my hotel, the question to be asked is "what is going on in your city? And Svetlana, that is why I am here, there are things you need to know about if you already don't and this is where we must trust one another with full disclosure, a great deal is at stake Svetlana, a great deal." Kimberley said, looking her college friend and wife of the Russian President in the eye.

Svetlana, looked right back at Kimberley, now with a questionable look in her eye. "Was this some sort of warning or threat from Kimberley?" Svetlana thought. "Was Kimberley telling her that there are things going on in the city that her government and people don't know about? Was Kimberley implying that Svetlana and her people were in the dark?" Kimberley's comment did not sit well with the Minister of Travel and Tourism.

"Kimberley, why don't you come and sit down here, tell me what's on your mind that's so urgent. I'm sure we can sort things out." Svetlana said, not looking at Kimberley, but turning her back on Kimberley, walking away, a move and gesture acting to minimize the serious nature of Kimberley's concern.

Kimberley picked up on this tactic, and wasn't about to be upstaged with this chess move; she would call check on this queen, even if she was the first lady of Russia. Kimberley was not to be second guessed, after all, this whole damn thing comes back to a former KGB official; Alexander Mitkin.

Kimberley followed Svetlana to a sofa and a chair. Kimberley sat down in the chair and then realized in her haste that she had made a mistake coming here. Kimberley's mind was all of a sudden racing, thinking of all the alleys and backstreets of cheat and deceit that had gone on with the situation in Grenada and Cathy's kidnapping. The internal double crossings by the CIA and the complications involved with operation Island Hop, and the whole Caribbean Initiative.

Kimberley suddenly realized that her disclosure to Svetlana, here and now, may in fact somehow place her college friend in harm's way. Kimberley thought that if deceit and corruption can run rampant in her own government back home in the good ole' USA, there is nothing to say that it cannot happen here, especially with this new Russian Federation being in its infancy.

Yes, indeed Kimberley had done the wrong thing coming here. She had no doubt that whatever was openly discussed here at the Kremlin, no matter which building it may be in, everything would be listened to.

Nothing would be private, not this conversation, not any conversation in any building except for maybe in Viktor and Svetlana's private units within the Kremlin.

Kimberley was now trapped, she couldn't tell Svetlana what she came here to tell her, she would now look foolish.

Kimberley thought and thought as she took a seat beside her friend. "She would have to just tell her the truth, that she couldn't tell her the reason she was here, not here. This in itself no doubt would test their friendship beyond any question. Okay, she had to go with it." Kimberley decided.

"Svetlana, you know I am not here because I want to have a cup of tea with you." Svetlana's gaze at Kimberley was "right, get on with it girl" look. Kimberley did.

"Svetlana as I was just now walking here behind you to sit down and tell you why I am here, I suddenly realized that I cannot. You've heard what happened to our General Manager. You know that my coming here is of the greatest urgency. I know Svetlana that our friendship is strong, we are like sisters in many ways Svetlana, I think we understand each other." Kimberley said with conviction and honesty coming through with every word she spoke.

Her friend looked back at her, and she smiled. "Yes Kimberley, we go back a long way, I have trust in you. This day today is unlike any you and I have ever had in person." Svetlana said with a more understanding look in her eye now.

"I realized late but not too late that what I tell you here will not be heard by your ears alone." Svetlana wasn't sure how to react but understood. She reached out and took hold of Kimberley's hand, then said; "wait a minute Kimberley, I know what to do."

She got up off the sofa, went to a desk nearby, opened its drawer and took out a pen and notepad. Svetlana wrote something on it and handed it to Kimberley; it read: meet me in Gorky Park, I will be there in half an hour by the entrance to the "fallen monuments."

Kimberley read it, and looked up at Svetlana, leaned in and gave the first lady of Russia a hug.

Svetlana was a quick thinker. She understood that no matter how assuring she would be to calm Kimberley's suspicions about the Kremlin's ears, Kimberley would not be satisfied, and Kimberley would withhold the information. Svetlana now wanted to know what Kimberley knew, and rather than fight it out of her, Svetlana thought it simply best to meet Kimberley on her own turf, a neutral turf, none better than an open-air park. She was sure Kimberley would be good with that, and she was.

Kimberley stood up, got her coat and walked out not saying another word. The guard at the entrance to the Kremlin Library building summoned Maxim. Within two minutes, Kimberley was on her way to Gorky Park.

***

320

Chapter Twenty-Six
A quick sweep

"Officer, please excuse me for a moment, I will be right back, I have something to attend to, please make yourself comfortable. Also, I should bring in our company's VP of Public Relations, he will need to hear this from you as well. Be back in a minute or two." Louis James said to the Moscow Police Officer sitting in his office.

Having to leave the office to get the VP of public relations for the company was a good excuse for Louis to have a moment of privacy, he needed to get in touch with Eldon, Billy and Felix immediately. Louis went to Eldon's suite, knocked, and Billy came to the door. They were already discussing what needed to be done as Louis was walking in. Having heard about Marty, and with Eldon already having been informed by the assistant head of security, that the Moscow Police were in to see Louis. Eldon was already up to speed.

"Louis I'm glad you are here," Eldon said. "This is such terrible news, hell it's already on VNN and all over the TV. Felix is on top of it, don't worry yourself about it, Felix knows how to deal with the press better than anyone.

I've already had Billy and Felix scour Marty's suite for things we might want to keep or hold onto," Eldon said.

"Yeah, that is exactly the reason I came up here, was to ask Billy and Felix to sweep Marty's room for anything that may be significant, before the Moscow Police get in there," Louis said.

"Well, that's the same thought we had, so that's been taken care of," Eldon said.

"So, did you guys find anything interesting or significant?" Louis asked.

"Well, we don't know yet but are about to find out. Felix found this padded envelope containing this VCR cassette tape. Felix found it with the envelope, just like this, tucked away inside one of Marty's suitcases. So, we are about to play the tape," Eldon said, as Billy had just inserted the cassette into the VCR player and pressed play.

"Well, damn, I can't stay to watch this; I have a Moscow Police Sargent in my office, waiting for me to come back with Felix. I told him our PR rep would want to be in on his visit." Just as Louis had finished saying that, the tape came to life with Marty and the girls, it took only a few seconds and everyone's jaw dropped.

Well, not Eldon's so much; he already had his suspicions about Marty, but gave him the benefit of the doubt.

"Holy shit!" Felix exclaimed. The four men just stood watching the TV. About thirty seconds had passed, Louis had seen enough, and so had Felix.

"Oh, my God," said Louis, " he was part of it, all along."

"Well Marty's now dead, so let's keep his legacy as honorable as we can. He worked hard here for this hotel, who knows what demons ran in his mind." Eldon said.

"Okay Louis, take Felix with you and attend to the police matter, Billy and I have this covered. We'll get together later; now where is my wife? Had anyone seen her today?

Felix then answered, "saw her earlier on in the morning, as she was heading out, something about meeting with Svetlana." Felix said, looking at Eldon, "thought you knew."

Eldon looked back and commented. "Well, I'm sure she knows what she's doing, maybe she'll get something of value out of her, and they're good friends you know. I'm sure she's on a mission of some sorts; she has a way of coming up with things, she's a digger." Eldon said while still watching the video. Felix and Louis walked out.

Billy and Eldon had no choice but to keep watching the video. Suddenly the video changed scenes. Several video clips followed, obviously edited over a period of days and weeks joining a number of sequences featuring a variety of male hotel guests in their hotel rooms and a lengthy clip showing activities in the Gorky after Hours Club.

Sadly, the young Hungarian girls were all engaged in servicing these men. The video said it all; secretly captured video of hotel guests, entertaining prostitutes inside the Jewel Danamo obviously being captured without the guest's knowledge to be used in blackmail and extortion.

Eldon standing there, watching what was taking place on the TV screen knew that this was serious, very serious. Looking at Billy, Eldon thought to himself; "the courier package from Florida with the lawsuit has arrived with very sharp teeth, his company would have a very difficult time defending itself with videotape evidence such as this."

He would need to take action and right away. Something huge had to be done, this had to end now, it could bring down the entire hotel industry citywide not just the Jewel Danamo.

"Billy, this is serious Billy, very serious," Eldon said.

"What are you going to do Eldon?" Billy asked.

"Not sure yet Billy, but I'm working on it, I have an idea that might work. Might be the one and only solution, but it's going to take everyone's cooperation" Eldon answered.

Billy knew not to press Eldon at this point. Eldon was formulating his plan and working things out in his mind. Billy had no doubt Eldon would come up with the answer and something totally unexpected that would see all of this end, not just for the Holiday Jewel Danamo but every hotel operator in the city.

When Eldon decided on doing something, it was always the "scorched earth policy," nothing and no one having a hand in this would escape his wrath. This Billy knew beyond a shadow of a doubt.

***

Chapter Twenty-Seven
Frankie, Eldon, Mitkin, Bebchuk and *Raul*

There was a knock on Eldon's door. Billy and Eldon looked at one another with Billy showing a big question mark look on his face, wondering who would be knocking on Eldon's door. Billy walked up to the door, opening it to see non-other than Ambassador Albert standing there, with a security guard escort.

Eldon having a clear view, immediately called out, "Ambassador Albert, please come in.

"This was highly unusual," Eldon thought.

The Ambassador walked in, with a certain anxiety about his persona. Eldon picked up on it.

"Eldon, I wanted to come and express my condolences for the loss of your General Manager and to let you know that Marika and I will be leaving the hotel today and returning to Spaso House.   Our State Department clean team has been in, according to them, we are clean and never did have any bugs in the building. Marika and I thank you for your hospitality." Frankie finished saying.

He then glanced over to the TV.

"What are you watching there Eldon?"

"Frankie, that's our hotel's in-room activity. Frankie this hotel is bugged, both audio and video it seems. We found this tape in our General Manager's suite. The tape has several edited video clips of male hotel guests engaged in prostitution, right here in this hotel, secretly recorded no doubt by Mitkin and his crew." Eldon said and looked at Frankie like an infection had permeated throughout the building.

"Not only that Ambassador, this videotape evidence or tape similar to this, is being used as the basis for a privacy violation lawsuit against Holiday Jewel Hotels. We are in deep shit, Ambassador."

Eldon finished saying, looking at the TV, then pressing the stop button on the VCR remote. Eldon had seen enough, and he was sure Frankie had as well.

"Oh, my god, Eldon, things seem very serious. You will let me know if there is anything at all I can do, will you?" Frankie offered, but Eldon thought "not very convincingly."

Eldon was somewhat surprised that Frankie didn't remark on who was in the video. It was little Kati which in itself was gut wrenching enough having to see this little angel, whom both had hugged and given comfort to just a few days ago, and now seeing her engaged in the video, Frankie, seemingly to shrug it off. Eldon thought it strange that Frankie wasn't "shocked" by seeing his
Hungarian compatriot in such a dire situation.

"Kimberley and I will definitely call on your support should we need to Ambassador. I hope your stay in The Presidential Suite was to your liking. Please give Marika my best regards." Eldon reached out and shook hands with Frankie as then did Billy.

Frankie Albert left Eldon's suite. The Ambassador and his wife Marika then departed the Holiday Jewel Danamo Hotel. Neither Eldon nor Kimberley would ever hear from or see Ambassador Albert in person again.

◇◇◇

Frankie Albert sat in the rear seat of his limousine heading back to Spaso House. He was very quiet. He wasn't saying anything. Marika was very concerned that Frankie was torn about what happened at the Holiday Jewel Hotel over the past week.

Both she and Frankie were just horrified what the young Hungarian girls had been put through. Marika was so relieved with admiration flowing from her for Eldon and Kimberley in their efforts and determination to give the girls new respectable lives. It would be a big expense, but an expense that would turn into good-will that no price-tag could ever be attached to. She was totally amazed at Eldon and Kimberley's dedication to their craft. They were good people. Her husband Frankie was in good company. Marika was very proud of Frankie and the social circles he embraced.

Frankie Albert on the other hand, sitting quietly knew in his heart what had to be done. His diplomatic life had played out to this end game. Frankie felt deep to his core there was no other way out or escape. The only way out Frankie knew would be with the final solution, the final solution to all of life's problems. He sat in the back seat, reaching out for his wife's hand, looking over towards Marika, squeezing her hand, knowing time was close.

Having arrived back at his residence, Frankie wasted no time. Time, in fact, was now of the essence, he understood that well. His mind raced, thinking and questioning himself, "how, how would he do it?"

There was no question in his mind that it had to be done, but it must be in the right way. He then had it. "There was a section of road along the banks of the Moskva River that was high enough, and if he recalled correctly, the drop was a good fifty feet, and it was steep with only a wooden guard rail along the cliff side. For once Frankie was grateful that the road safety barriers were at best minimal in parts of Moscow. He thought it out.

"An automobile accident would be the right way." It would provide the cover and end it all. The conditions demanded he fall on his sword, for country and family. Frankie had chosen family over country in his diplomatic career. His actions had saved the lives of Olga, Marika's sister along with Frankie's three cousins and his nephew still living in Hungary.

Yes, Frankie was an agent, a double agent perhaps in terms of the spy game between nations. Really when examined it was not so much spying but the betrayal of his country the United States of America and as Ambassador to the new Russian Federation there would be no escaping, no way out. Frankie could not escape treason.

Frankie's long history of times past tied him to the chains wrapped around his soul by Alexander Mitkin. Frankie's Hungarian heritage had guaranteed his loyalty and devotion to the safekeeping of his family. In the summer of eighty-seven, while serving as Ambassador to Hungary, Alexander Mitkin had threatened to have his remaining family killed unless

Frankie capitulated and surrendered to the Assistant Director of The KGB's demands.

Frankie was recruited. To make matters worse, Frankie had been duped. The KGB had set up a Swiss bank account in Frankie's name with his signature obtained forcibly. Alexander Mitkin then deposited two million Deutschmarks into Ferenc Albert's Swiss bank account. The manipulation was complete. Mitkin threatened Frankie's family with their lives, and then Frankie would be further made to look like he sold out his country for two million Deutschmarks. Mitkin had forever set up framing Frankie Albert as a traitor and spy. Treason would be the charge. There was no way out.

Frankie had approved and authorized all procurement orders for *Raul* devices that the Hungarian Armed Forces had requisitioned. With Hungary, having been invited into the North Atlantic Treaty Organization (NATO), the Hungarian Armed Forces were a favored nation for technology transfers once approved by the State Department. All procurement orders by the Hungarian Armed Forces for (RUL Technology) *Raul* were approved and authorized by the State Department's US Ambassador to Hungary.

It had been all set up. The KGB, Mitkin to be specific in 1987 and subsequently Sasha Bebchuk still pulled all the strings of the Hungarian Defense Minister; Minister Farkas. Farkas would then redirect all approved *Raul* devices to Russian FSB Director Sasha Bebchuk, who then had them installed into all the Moscow hotels.

Alexander Mitkin, of course, had absolutely no idea that RUL was flowing into Russia, no not one iota of a clue. Mitkin had only provided the avenue for the flow of goods and information. Mitkin was long out of the picture, but the information provided by Mitkin, that being Frankie's availability as a double agent and a means of securing top secret limited export CIA "RUL" technology, well... that had been "alive and well" long after Mitkin had left The KGB. That avenue had remained open for Sasha Bebchuk to take as often as he needed.

But recently with Frankie having become Ambassador to Russia, he could no longer approve RUL orders for Hungary, but Bebchuk had already acquired enough while Frankie was still Ambassador to Hungary. The Red Jewel and the yet to be completed Jewel Moskva already had their designated units.

Frankie was torn inside. Earlier on in the day, Frankie did not let on. He could hardly stop himself from falling apart. The sight of little Kati and her friends on the video shocked Frankie to the core. Seeing the video, and knowing what he knew, Frankie had joined dots in his mind, even while standing beside Eldon and Billy; Frankie knew what he had done.

His hand was in this horrible thing that had now completely and utterly taken over his life. The dots he clearly now saw were of himself, Mitkin, Bebchuk, Eldon and Kati's little brother's death, all of his Hungarian compatriots, and other dots representing his betrayal of every Hungarian in his life, as well as the trust the people of America had put into his leadership and integrity. He was a failed Ambassador, this he knew. What did, however, give Frankie some level of dignity in his heart was his honest desire to keep his family alive, but in turn, unfortunately, sacrificing the lives of others such as Kati's brother and Marty Sabine. Frankie had a hand in it all. Frankie would pay.

Ferenc Albert went to his office desk, sat down in the US Ambassador's chair for the last time. He obtained a sheet of official US State Department letterhead, took pen in hand and started writing his final words, not to Marika, the love of his life to this very day, but to:

Dear Eldon and Kimberley:

***

Chapter Twenty-Eight
Gorky Park

Kimberley stood just inside the pillars forming the gateway to the area known as "monuments of the fallen." Once again, it was overcast in Moscow this morning and snowing lightly. It provided extra cover and dampening for private conversations. Maxim, Kimberley's driver this morning was nearby, watching over Kimberley and waiting.

Kimberley waived as she saw Svetlana approach. She was followed closely by two secret service agents. This was normal of course. As Svetlana approached, the two women did not hug, both just continued walking in step side by side, walking arm in arm which was the way many Russian and European female friends walked together. This was common and also afforded privacy in conversation, lower tones, almost whispers.

"Svetlana, thank you so much, I know this is highly out of the ordinary," Kimberley said.

"Yes, I know this is going to be very impacting news you have for me Kimberley, I am ready for just about anything now," Svetlana said. "I am sure you didn't have me come all the way here just for a walk in the park."

"Svetlana, this is very serious, we, you, hell for that matter the entire city Svetlana, we have a huge problem. I am going to just say it and then I want you to walk with me and think about what I said." Kimberley looked at Svetlana.

Her college friend nodded back at her, saying, "all right, let me hear what this is all about."

Kimberley couldn't help herself; she turned her head to see how far back the secret service agents were. They were close but not too close; they walked just far enough back to provide privacy.

"Svetlana," Kimberley held onto Svetlana Orlov's arm a little tighter. "We are certain our General Manager was killed by one of your former KGB directors Svetlana, Alexander Mitkin, wait, I am not finished. Alexander Mitkin is the owner of Tsar Restaurants and Entertainment, we, our company did not know at the time of agreeing to have them as our lease operators that Mitkin owned the company. I will just tell you the main facts now; details can be filled in later."

Svetlana felt Kimberley grasp onto her arm tighter as they walked, bringing her closer in to Kimberley. "You know that the love I have for you Svetlana goes as deep as my trust in you, I tell you this because I know you will do the right thing." Kimberley then glanced at her friend, and the two women renewed their special connection that reached back to their year together at Rutgers. Kimberley took a deep breath, let out a sigh and continued on, her breath freezing in the cold air.

"Mitkin has been running a prostitution sex slave ring with young Hungarian and Russian undcrage girls. He smuggles the underage Hungarian girls into Russia and then forces them all into sex slavery by threatening their families back home." Svetlana looked back at Kimberley with disbelief in her eyes.

"Just listen Svetlana, just listen... he tells them that he will provide good jobs and a career in the restaurant and service industry in Russia, in the glittering lights of Moscow that will enable them to make money to help their families back home. Then Svetlana, he places them into slavery. If anyone disobeys him, he kills their family members, if any of the girls decide to take their own lives he threatens to wipe out their whole family. These young girls Svetlana are trapped and in dire straits. Yes, we have evidence. We believe our GM was killed in revenge for us uncovering his sex slavery ring. We have also canceled his lease operator's contract, having delivered legal papers to him regarding the matter. Tsar is no longer in our hotel."

Kimberley then showed Svetlana the photocopied pictures of Kati's young brother in the ditch and a photograph of Kati and her family in Hungary.

"Svetlana that's not all. Mitkin is operating citywide. It's not just the Jewel Danamo it's every hotel in the city, every joint venture property. We had a sting team come in last week, and we did a citywide test and sweep of all hotels. Svetlana, I know you will have concerns about this.

As Minister of Travel and Tourism, this becomes a huge problem for you and the city. We are already dealing with things in our own ways. The young girls we have uncovered in our hotel, we have taken care of them all Svetlana. Eldon and I will ensure they are given every opportunity in making their lives whole again. They are young enough to somehow put this behind them, as tough and impossible as it may sound, we both know the human spirit is capable of soaring to new heights even after great adversity."

Kimberley looked at her college friend again and said, "Svetlana, we need to do the right thing. I will leave you now and allow you to think about this all, I have no doubt, you being my friend, The First Lady of The Russian Federation, that you will know exactly what to do in your own way and in your own heart."

Kimberley then stopped, moved in close, gave Svetlana a kiss on her cheek, placed the photocopies of Kati's pictures into Svetlana's hand, turned from Svetlana, and walked away, leaving Svetlana standing in the falling snow.

She looked down at the photographs once again, standing still, then looking up at Kimberley as she walked away, looked down at Kati's picture again.

Snowflakes fell onto the photo; it became wet. A tear dropped from Svetlana's eye onto Kati's picture; Svetlana knew what needed to be done.

***

Chapter Twenty-Nine
The Letter

The next morning, Eldon and Kimberley both rose early. It was only five-thirty in the morning. Neither could sleep, and both wanted to get on with their day. Their days had become very busy and filled with turmoil. Eldon had some very urgent matters to take care of. Not just the problem with Mitkin but now he had the pending lawsuit to deal with. He decided to visit his legal team back home in Florida over this matter as soon as he could get away. It would also give him a chance to see his daughter Cathy.

Kimberley and Eldon looked out over the city of Moscow. They had a good view from their dining area. Eldon sat drinking coffee. Kimberley and Eldon had just made love this morning. It was wonderful. Both needed relief from their stresses over the last few days. Their days and nights were much too full of problems and issues for any sort of intimacy to come into play.

This morning, however, it was time; they craved one anothers' touch. Kimberley walked up behind her husband as he sat, and caressed his face with her palm, moving her hand around his cheek, and down the front of his neck, and onto his chest. She bent down and kissed Eldon, "I love you, honey," letting her long shoulder length hair flow over the side of his face and neck, Kimberley said softly and lovingly whispering into Eldon's ear.

"I love you too babe, we'll get through this, we always do," Eldon said, kissing her back on her lips, reaching around and pulling her hips in close to him.

The radio was on just lightly, music playing, tuned to Moscow One. But it was just loud enough to bring Eldon and Kimberley's attention to; "This is Maggie Harlow, we have breaking news. United States Ambassador, Ferenc Albert was found dead this morning. Apparently, the vehicle Ambassador Albert was driving had lost control on the Moskva River Road and crashed through the guard rail barrier plunging fifty feet down the river bank. The Ambassador's car was retrieved from the Moskva River with his deceased body still inside. We will have more breaking news on this during the day. Stay tuned to Moscow One for more developments. When we have it you have it. This is Maggie Harlow reporting for Moscow One."

Eldon and Kimberley just stared at one another with both their eyes wide open.

"Oh, my God!" Kimberley exclaimed. "Oh, my God."

Eldon looked at his watch; it was just a little after 7. Eldon's phone rang. "Eldon Davis."

"Mr. Davis, this is Davidov, the hotel concierge. I am very sorry to disturb you so early this morning, but sir, there is a United States Embassy courier gentleman here. He has an envelope for you. He can only give it to you in person Mr. Davis."

Eldon then said, "tell the courier I will be right down." Eldon hung the phone up and was out the door in fifteen seconds. "We have an envelope delivered from the US Embassy by Embassy courier service; it has to be from Albert. " Eldon remarked to Kimberley as he bolted out the door saying, "be right back Kimberley, hold onto your horses."

Eldon was back in two minutes. He sat down beside his wife. She leaned in towards him, putting her hand on his shoulder as she watched Eldon opening the envelope, and extracting the official US Embassy letterhead. With Eldon holding onto the extracted letter, Kimberley and Eldon looked at one another and then the two of them together, read Ferenc "Frankie" Albert's last words.

Dear Eldon and Kimberley:

I must confess, in more ways than one. First being: I never expected my life to come to this end, but this is the exit ramp I must take. The deal I once made with the devil must now be paid.

That deal was in 87 shortly after being appointed as US Ambassador to Hungary, and this is where my second confession lies. "Lies" ironically is the operative in this case. I lied to the people of the United Sates, and I lied to the people of my birthplace. I know my countries will never forgive me, and I ask not for forgiveness; I ask for understanding.

In the liar, I was and am, I take solace in knowing I played a part in keeping evil at bay. The lives of my cousins and nephew in Hungary along with my wife Marika's sister has been spared. My accidental death will allow each to live their lives to their natural end.

The "Sword of Damocles" no longer hangs by a hair over my family's head. My death will set them free of Bebchuk and Mitkin's revenge. Therefore, I shall seek my maker with calm in my process and peace in my soul.

Eldon, I approved all purchase orders generated by Gabor Farkas; Hungarian Defense Minister. (still loyal to his former KGB overlords, Mitkin and Bebchuk) For the procurement of RUL Technology. With RUL being classified as experimental, distribution, as you know, was limited by the CIA to NATO members only through State Department authorization. I willfully violated the oath I swore to uphold and conspired with the enemy. I chose family over country.

RUL surveillance technology was then transferred directly from Hungary to the Russian FSB, specifically Sasha Bebchuk. RUL surveillance capture technology is widespread throughout all Moscow hotels including your property the Jewel Danamo as evidenced by our viewing of Marty's Sabine's video. It is now apparent his unfortunate end was implicated and entwined with Mitkin's operations.

I Ferenc Albert today fall on my sword for country and family. In so doing, I can only hope that this letter you burn and allow my legacy to live out with honor. The decision is yours. You now have the power in your hand to rule over The FSB if you play it out. I know you will find the way.

Frankie.

"The Russians have *Raul*," Eldon said looking at Kimberley.

"I can't imagine how torn Frankie must have been over the years. Bebchuk had him living in the same terror day in day out as Mitkin did with his sex slaves; do as we say or your family dies. I cannot imagine how any man or woman could deal with or handle such evil." Eldon whispered under his breath.

Kimberley then asked her husband; "Eldon, should we burn the letter?"

"I want to Kimberley; I really do, but let's wait. We can burn it anytime. For now, let's wait. I don't know yet how this may come into play if at all, but let's wait." Eldon said, holding onto Kimberley's hand.

"What are we going to do Eldon?" Kimberley was lost for a moment.

She totally deferred to Eldon. This one she couldn't yet grasp or deal with. Besides, it now involved Eldon's other interests, his technology division which Kimberley was not up to speed on. That truly was Eldon's area; she could only advise and comment in broad brush strokes.

"Well, I know we will need to get Nick Kovacs over here. I will tell him to be ready for a trip to Moscow. I know I will want him and need him here when the time comes.

Now here's something interesting babe. You know Nick was instrumental in locating Cathy's abductor, without his expertise we might not have found Cathy.

"Yes, I remember babe, I remember you telling me the story, about how elated you Billy and Felix were when Nick uncovered the hidden clues on the

340

video tape. Cathy's location was found by Nick's ingenuity. I recall you telling me that like it was yesterday." Kimberley said.

"Nick had worked for me a number of years before taking the position with NASA in Cape Kennedy. You remember it took all I could do to lure him back into working for us at Davis Technologies again. His dream was to visit the ISS, but Nick was passed over by NASA due to some sort of medical thing. But that allowed him to come back to Davis Technologies, and we were happy he took my offer. The funny thing is, Nick too is Hungarian, well, second generation, but it seems a lot of people nowadays in our lives are Hungarians. Kovacs is about as Hungarian as it comes when it comes to names."

"At this point, I don't care if Nick is a direct decedent of Attila the Hun!" Kimberley remarked. "Eldon, how do we get rid of this blight?" Kimberley asked.

"I know how," Eldon said. "It will take some doing for sure, but I think I know how. I'm calling Felix, and by the way, there is no way The Red Jewel is opening until I know all our hotels are clean. Actually, Kimberley not just our hotels but everyone in the city is clean, and I mean everyone." Eldon finished saying with conviction in his words.

Kimberley looked at Eldon and said. "Okay and how will you do that?" She asked.

Eldon replied, "watch me."

That was what Kimberley loved so much about her husband. She knew Eldon had a way when nobody else could see a way. She was not baiting him, by asking "Okay and how will you do that?" No, not at all, she just loved seeing and hearing his confidence, oh, she loved him so much! She saw it in his eyes, the determination, the drive, the need to succeed. She had no doubt Eldon would do what was needed.

"But not without her help," she thought, and that's what she loved about him. "All business, and all in."

"Kimberley, I need to get Felix involved, and I need to fly back home, to deal with the lawsuit. I will also need to see Nick as well about *Raul*. God knows, I'm hoping I can keep the CIA out of this for now. It doesn't appear as they are aware of any of this; let's keep it that way if we can for now. When the right time comes, we will have to let them know, then they can do whatever they need to, but for now it's only in this letter.

I think we should both fly back for a couple of days babe, just as soon as we can. Like that, we can see Cathy as well and your mom and dad. I think we both need to get away from this mess even just for a day or two. But before we go, we need to meet with everyone. I mean everyone."

Kimberley was momentarily perplexed. "What did Eldon mean by "everyone", everyone who?"

Eldon picked up his phone and called Felix's suite, all the while looking and winked at his wife, Felix answered.

Then Eldon said, "Felix come on over here will you, I have a job for you."

"What are you up to Eldon?" Kimberley asked of her husband. Looking at him with inquisitive eyes, seriously but perplexing.

"Something revolutionary baby, I will need you to be strong, this will test us both. He bent in towards her and kissed her on the lips, saying,
"Frankie will not have died in vain."

***

Chapter Thirty
The Orlovs

Svetlana sat down at the dinner table with her husband, Viktor. There was unusual quiet tonight between the two. The two had just watched the news. The US Ambassador was dead, as was the General Manager of The Holiday Jewel Danamo Hotel. These two facts alone caused an eerie silence to set in over their dinner. Viktor didn't say anything, he waited for his wife Svetlana to; he knew she would, and she did.

"Viktor something is going on, I don't know what it is, but I can tell you that we have a problem," Svetlana said, not even looking at her husband, but talking to her food on her plate instead.

Viktor heard her loud and clear; he was only two feet beside her. "Tell me Svetlana, what sort of problem do you mean?" Viktor egged her on.

"Viktor I am Minister of Travel and Tourism; we have a big issue. It's all over the news Viktor, the general manager of one of this country's largest and most prestigious hotels has been gunned down in front or our greatest cultural building, The Bolshoi Ballet Theater for god's sake, in the street! That is one hell of a problem for me and being your wife for you!"

Viktor hearing Svetlana scold him, then suddenly pounded the dinner table with his fist! "You do not talk to me like that Svetlana! You think I don't know; you think I am stupid?" Viktor responded.

Svetlana then stood up from her seat; she took out the picture of Kati's little brother laying in the ditch, face bloodied and threw it down in front of The President of Russia.

"Yeah, you know what is going on do you, do you? Tell me what this is all about then Mr. President, what is this?" Svetlana; now yelling at Viktor as she then threw the other picture of Kati and her family in front of him.

"That Viktor is the work of Mitkin, yes, Viktor, Sasha's half-brother. Viktor, Kimberley AshtonDavis gave me those photos today. Their hotel is infested with Mitkin's sex slave ring of prostitution. Mitkin...Sasha, Mitkin! Your FSB Director's halfbrother! Does that ring any fucking bells in your head?"

Viktor suddenly jumped up from his chair and backhanded Svetlana's face so hard she went flying across the room.

"Yes, so this is how you handle your bad news is it? By slapping your wife around?" Svetlana stood up, not about to let Viktor get away with this.

Viktor stood there looking at her; he was fuming.

"All right fine, so you hit me. Now go and hit your FSB Director, but hit him a hell of a lot harder than you did me, because if you don't, he might well come back at you!"

The First Lady yelled at her husband as she walked out, leaving Viktor Orlov standing in the Kremlin dining room alone, with Kati's photos staring back at him.

***

Chapter Thirty-One
Going Dark

"Felix, I want you to get on the phone and call every Vice President, President, Regional Director, and General Manager of every hotel company here in Moscow. Whoever is in town, I want a meeting with everyone tomorrow." Eldon said emphatically.

"Okay Eldon, this is going to take some doing," Felix said.

"Felix, tell them that Kimberley and I, head of Holiday Jewel Hotels and Casinos, have the most serious and urgent issue to discuss. Their longevity, their ongoing ability in continuing to do business in Moscow and their own individual personal safety are at stake. Tell them that I will host a meeting of all hotel executives tomorrow at 10 AM at St. Peter's Monastery."

Felix looked back at Eldon with a curious look on his face, saying, "you're having a city-wide hotel meeting at a monastery?"

Yes, Felix, it's all arranged, The Abbot at the monastery; the senior monk has agreed in allowing me the use their dining hall.

It is over a thousand years old, and the dining hall is carved right into the stone, it easily holds thirty people, I doubt more than fifteen will show up anyway, but that should be enough. I know that the monks' dining hall will not be bugged. That is the only place probably in all of Moscow in today's world you will find that is clean." Eldon remarked. ◇◇◇

"Ladies and gentlemen, thank you for coming on such short notice. I know this must have upset a lot of your schedules, but believe me, you would not want to miss this meeting as you shall soon see." Eldon said in his part opening statement.

"Allow me to take a moment in thanking you all for the condolences you have expressed to myself and our team here this morning in the passing of our Hotel General Manager, Marty Sabine. He will be missed, and for my fellow Americans in this room, I am sure the tragic loss of our Ambassador to the Russian Federation, Ambassador Albert's passing is an added burden for our country to bear. This has not been a good week for us, or for our adopted city, Moscow." Eldon said with both strength and sorrow mixed into his delivery.

"Sitting to my far left is Felix Balon, our company's VP of public relations, next to him is Louis James, our Senior VP of operations here in Moscow, and beside me is the love of my life, my wife Kimberley, Director of Holiday Jewel Hotels and Casinos.

I am certain there wasn't much need to further impress the urgency of this meeting. I know some of you no doubt are wondering why I picked such an unusual place to meet, but I'm sure some of you have already figured that out. As to the others, well, you may not know because you simply do not know. I assure you before you leave here this morning you will know, and you will have a major decision to make. That decision will need to be made this week. Urgency will become evident, never in your individual careers will the essence of time have been more urgent and become more important than on this day going forward." Eldon Davis, head of Holiday Jewel Hotels and Casinos said in his opening statement.

Eldon, Kimberley, Louis James and Felix had arrived earlier than the others and took up the front of the dining hall and were now facing their hotel colleagues, all fourteen of them. Every western joint venture property was present. The hotel companies operating in Moscow were all major chains with most having their regional vice presidents in the city. There was one corporate executive who flew in overnight on this short notice on a private company jet from Geneva.

Eldon and Kimberley commanded the attention of the international hospitality industry. It was now a well-known fact, that whenever innovation or major progress was to be realized within the hotel business, HJHC was in the forefront, leading the industry.

This one time and most stunning request for this immediate meeting carried the weight and impact of the global hotel business. With the recent developments in the past few days, that only added more weight and urgency for everyone contacted by Felix in making this meeting. All properties were represented with the appropriate corporate decision makers.

Eldon was impressed as was Kimberley. This was a room filled with competitors, all vying to outdo one another by capturing the largest market share possible, make no mistake, but this morning they acted as one unified body. Eldon and Kimberley were to lay out a plan today that would save the hotel business in Moscow before it crumbled beneath them all.

Eldon continued on, "we as a group are a force to be reckoned with. The approximate five thousand rooms we represent in the city of Moscow has given this city the ability to host the world. Our industry here has seen expansion and growth in all areas since the rise of the new Russian Federation, business has been good, maybe too good, but I will touch on that in a bit. Let us not forget that combined; our strength is formidable indeed. Our hotels bring in tourists and most importantly bring together business through our convention facilities enabling the exchange of ideas and commerce here locally and on a grand scale internationally.

We facilitate millions and billions of dollars in joint venture deals and agreements, providing the venues and platforms for these discussions and meetings to take place. Moscow has grown because we have grown, I think we are all in agreement with that." Eldon had everyone's undivided attention. He stopped.

Kimberley took the reins and continued on, not missing a beat. "We have been in this business many years. My husband's father Len Davis, as some of you may know was the founder of Holiday Jewel Hotels back in the early 50's. Moving throughout the 60's he had the vision and foresight to capitalize on the nationwide development of the interstate highway system that fanned out across the USA that then spurned the national travel craze with everyone taking to the highways in "discovering America."

Len Davis saw his small motor hotel "The Holiday Jewel Motel" growing into the nation's largest hotel chain almost overnight and to this day, we remain a leader in the industry, now being multinational.

So, that is all well and good. But ladies and gentlemen, no matter how long we have been in business, and I assure you, we know what we are doing; from time to time we get infected. I am not talking about an infection of bed bugs, but I am talking bugs." Kimberley paused, she let that sink in.

This was critical for Eldon and Kimberley. At this point, they watched closely for the room's reaction. They got what they wanted. The looks on their faces confirmed Eldon's and Kimberley's hunch. When Kimberley said "bugs" they all gasped, slightly but gasped nevertheless, it was a sure confirmation. They had all been compromised and they all knew it, but everyone to this point had kept it to themselves.

She continued on. "Ladies and gentlemen, we all have been compromised. We at Holiday Jewel Danamo signed a lease agreement with Tsar Restaurants and Entertainment. I will tell you right now, that we failed in doing our due diligence before we agreed to Alexander Mitkin running our food and beverage operations and we paid for our negligence in a very big way. We since uncovered his sex slave prostitution ring operating out of our property." She paused again.

Now the executives filling this dining hall started looking around at each other. Eldon and Kimberley had discussed their approach in opening this topic, and both decided that having Kimberley deliver this portion would have the biggest impact. To have a woman talking underage sex slavery would make everyone very uncomfortable.

Then scanning everyone's face in the room and making eye contact for a moment with each, she challenged each one to bring forth their integrity.

"Of course, we have proof beyond any doubt. We have already delivered legal notification canceling the lease agreement, he is out of the property, and all his employees agreed to remain on board as new employees of Holiday Jewel Danamo, so our food and beverage operations were not affected, we remain open. However, this infection in our hotel has resulted in a new level of danger. It threatens our survival as a business here in Moscow and unfortunately for our General Manager, a danger to his life and loss of it.

No one in this room is immune from such as fate, no one! Ladies and gentlemen, Mr. Alexander Mitkin, prostitution warlord and hostage taker of underage young innocent girls and slave master is former assistant director of The KGB. We are absolutely certain beyond a shadow of a doubt; we have confirmation from the US State Department. Some of you may know my background is the State

Department before joining HJHC." Kimberley finished.

"All right I will be the first to respond." Nigel Wright President of Royal British House Hotels spoke up. Nigel continued on. "I think I know where this is going, I will be the first to admit, we have had problems in our hotel for quite a long time with this exact sort of thing. Let me ask now, everyone in this room, who else has had the same problems?" Everyone, everyone without exception raised their hands.

"Thank you, Nigel, I am sure we all know one anothers' pain now," Eldon said.

"But that's not the worst of it. Here is the problem we have. All the hotels in the city are bugged both video and audio; we know that, and that has lead to another problem, one that will take us down quickly if we don't act." There was quiet in the room. Yes, you could, in fact, have heard a pin drop. Eldon went on. "We, Holiday Jewel Hotels are being sued for privacy violation and willful negligence. Some of our guest's in-room privacy has been compromised by the bugs and now we are facing million and millions in damages. The situation has become so severe that it requires my personal attention with our legal department back in Florida where HJHC's head offices are. So, my next question to you all is this: how many of you are currently being sued by your guests for privacy violation asking for damages suffered due to your property's negligence, placing your guests in compromising situations, anyone?" Eldon asked.

A few seconds passed, and the hands started rising. Every representative raised their hands.

"So, ladies and gentlemen, Mr. Mitkin has gotten us all in deep shit." Eldon paused, let it sink in. There was quiet in the room once again.

"I know how we can solve this once and for all, and never ever have this issue again in any of our hotels here in Moscow or anyplace else in Russia. I have to tell you, we must act as a group, and we must stick together once we start."

Everyone was hinged on Eldon's next words, everyone. This was coming from one of the greatest hotel and hospitality moguls the world has ever known and everyone listened.

"First, let us not fool ourselves, we are dealing with the former KGB and now The FSB, they go hand in hand, I think we can all agree on that. Whatever reasons they had in bugging our buildings they had, so that is water under the bridge now. Our task is to remove the bugs and remove the infection, and rid our properties of the prostitution ring, right?" Eldon stopped and asked, to receive the room's confirmation before going on. He needed buy-in as he moved the plan ahead. Eldon could see everyone nodding in agreement, so he continued on.

"Now, I will take a stab and assume we have all done very well in this market in Moscow, all of us had made good profits. I do not need confirmation on that; I know we have and so has everyone else. As to the young ladies who have been enslaved and put to work as sex slaves within our walls; I believe we owe them. We owe them for not being vigilant in our efforts in preventing this blight and we owe them for being facilitators in providing a place, to their overlords for carrying out their business.

We are to be ashamed of ourselves for that, and I believe we must do the right thing." Everyone once again agreed. All heads were nodding; no one was to escape or think differently on this line of reasoning.

"Ladies and gentlemen, we need to make these young girls whole again. I put forward the motion that each hotel company here, offer the girls sanctuary from their enslavement and offer them a way out. A small percentage of our profits can go in helping these girls; young teenage women sixteen, seventeen, lets offer them new lives. Offer them a way out. What we have done at our property, is we've provided temporary housing for them in the hotel and soon after repatriation to their countries of origin. Hungary for most women. Holiday Jewel Hotels will offer them employment. They are all still young enough to get through this, but they will need our help and dedication." Eldon asked once again with conviction in his voice.

Then Kimberley added, "Is this something we can all take up and pledge right here and now as a group?

There was a pause, and then one after another everyone agreed. There was unanimous consent for this one matter, no question about it. It seemed like all the hotel executives were, in fact, decent people as it was turning out. Or was it that Kimberley shamed them into agreeing. Mattered not, it was agreed to.

"Now for the hard part. We need all the bugs removed from all the hotels from all the rooms, from everywhere, and they need to remove them not us. I can tell you this; I have the ability and know-how through my technology division to verify that all the bugs have been removed. We know how to do that, but the key is to have the Russian FSB themselves remove it. This will give us oversight, in fact, we would be watching them, not them watching us."

Eldon was almost there; he had everyone's undivided attention. The big question on everyone's mind, how do we do it? The bombshell was about to be dropped in Eldon's next words.

"We agreed that we control to a great extent the platform to the purse strings of the economy and the emergence of this new prosperity to be realized in Moscow. We agree as a group correct?" Eldon stated and asked once again. Everyone nodded, and one vocalized. "We sure as hell do."

Eldon then said. "Good, we cut if off, we cut it all off, we go dark. We close our hotels next week, all of us, no hotel accommodation in Moscow. Business and enterprise come to a screeching halt. I tell you what, that will get the attention of The Kremlin and President Orlov. We can force his hand. He will have to hand over The FSB to us on a silver platter. The spigot to his economy will be shut off and the only way to open it back up will be for him to remove all the bugs and wipe out prostitution in our hotels forever!"

"Whoa! That is a bold move. That will cost us millions, millions Eldon! I don't know if I can do that." Immediately one of the execs from the five hundred room Whilton Manor commented. Some others, as Eldon saw, were in agreement with him.

"Look, Steve, I think I can help in that area as well. The thing is people if we don't do this now, we are going to be bled dry with lawsuits first of all, and we as a hotel organization will have failed, we will become nothing but flop houses eventually having to close our doors.

The Russian Mafia, call it that, will end up doing us in and the city in as well, they will devastate the economy for self-gain, they are a parasite onto themselves in the long run, and we need to rid ourselves of their feeding upon us. Do we understand each other?" Everyone nodded, but Eldon could see resistance still grabbing a hold in the room.

"So, here is what I am offering to you as a group. We, Holiday Jewel Hotels and Casinos is a very large a profitable company, but we do not take things for granted, and we work hard for where we stand today in the industry. We look at all sides of the business, from ensuring our guests' safety and our employees' as well as our company's safety in times of turmoil and upheaval. I believe these times would qualify us for that scenario.

We at HJHC have taken out interruption of business insurance. Our attorneys have reviewed the policy, and we will be able to make whole our business losses for the period of time we need to shut down in order to rid ourselves of the corruption invading our business model and jeopardizing the safety of our guests, employees, and company. I am willing to share the insurance claim benefits we would recover. Furthermore, we are a large hotel and with The Red Jewel scheduled for opening soon, the revenues we would have realized there we will also claim. Now with The Red Jewel not open yet, we, in fact, are not having any ongoing business losses, only potential losses which I am assured our attorneys can also secure. Our insurance provider will cooperate in paying our claim since will be able to show our efforts in minimizing any further or future risk going forward. Our hotels will be clean, free of vice, and free of surveillance." Eldon paused; let his offer sink into everyone's head.

"Eldon, our company, also has similar coverage, I would bet that more than you and I have such coverage in this room." Heidi from Patriotic Hotels then added. "I think Eldon has the solution, I am in full agreement with Eldon on this," Heidi said.

"Eldon added, look, we need to do this now. We need to force President Orlov's hand, his wife's hand, Svetlana is the Minister of Travel and Tourism for god's sake, this will not sit well with her, Orlov will cave. I can guarantee you he will cave within a week after we close our doors. One other thing, if we don't have a solution within ten days after closing, it will be up to you all as to how you wish to continue.

For those of you who want to reopen, well, so be it. I cannot ask you to remain closed much more than what I already have put forward. I am virtually certain the system will cave within three or four days. The key is, he, Victor Orlov must have his FSB people remove the surveillance devices, and only then will we be assured going forward. You can be assured, that Moscow Mayor, Anton Marat will be screaming for Orlov to do something, as will The First Lady, being Minister of Travel and Tourism. The whole world will be barking at her. Viktor Orlov has come much too far now to see his efforts collapse. He has declared democracy of his newborn society to the world, he will not take the chance of "egg on his face" he will reopen our hotels, you can count on it. He will reign in FSB. He will personally, I assure you make certain our hotels remain clean. No more KGB, no more FSB, no more enslaved foreign sex slaves, no more lawsuits from our guests, we can clean this city up. Are we in?"

Eldon waited, he got what he wanted. They were all in. Better to lose a few hundred thousand dollars now, than to eventually lose it all. That was the common thinking in the room. Everyone was in.

Eldon then remarked. "Now remember, we are closing the hotels, but not letting our employees go. They will still be paid, if necessary and if the burden is too great, you might want to consider classifying this period as "vacation pay" that will be up to your properties individually, I can tell you now, we are not going to do that. I can also assure you that The Red Jewel will not open unless it has been cleaned and that hotel is Holiday Jewel Hotels' crowning achievement, flagship property." Eldon finished saying.

Kimberley then picked up where Eldon again left off. "Our targeted closing date city wide is one week from today. Notify your guests that their departure is imminent, due to structural issues with the building that need immediate repairs as per city engineers, and all guests must vacate until further notice. That will be the reason all hotels will use for closing properties, are we all in agreement?" Kimberley asked.

Everyone agreed. "Okay then, I have a pledge document here, attesting to everyone's agreement to close next week, in seven days from today's date your hotels will be shut until further notice. Please, everyone, come and sign the pledge. You will also note that you are signing as per our discussion, all points and terms are listed herein, including the agreement in making the young girls lives whole again, to the best of your abilities as good corporate citizens."

Eldon wasn't quite finished, he had one final request of this group, Eldon added; "We have one last thing to agree upon. The key to this being successful is our unity." Eldon looked over the room; everyone seemed fine with that statement and in agreement. He went on.

"Therefore, in order for this unity to be effective, we must as a group speak with one voice. Right here and now, we agree to form our subgroup of hotels "The Moscow International Hotel Organization" as a sub-chapter of "The Moscow Hotel Association."

What makes us different?" Eldon asked rhetorically. "We need independence as a group from the former properties historically and physically part of the city before our arrival because we are a new group, with a new vision and code of ethics. With the signing of this pledge, our individual properties and companies become official members."

"This is exactly what I have been waiting for a year and a half now! I've always felt we had to differentiate ourselves as an organization from the past. I'm all for this." Sylvie Connors President of Sunwood Hotels then said. Her company had the seven hundred plus room mega property, a strong competitor to The Jewel Danamo.

Eldon welcomed her comment. "Who's with Sylvie Connors on this motion?" Eldon then piggybacked on her positive endorsement. Once again everyone's hands went up.

"Okay, good, then we are all in agreement." Eldon continued. "I have taken the liberty of drawing up our Charter that outlines our mission statement as an organization and code of ethics to which we all become signatories today. Can I get a show of hands one last time from those in agreement?" Eldon then asked. Everyone's hands went up instantaneously in response.

"All right then, and with our organization being formed this morning, I ask that any interaction, questions, inquiries, excreta from the city of Moscow or from the Minister of Travel and Tourism be directed to Felix Balon who will speak for The Moscow International Hotel Association. Allow Mr. Balon to handle the entire process and procedure. This will show our unity and strength as an organization, giving us the weight we need to see this through.

During this period, there will be a need to address the media, and answer hundreds of inquiries. I assure you, Felix is an expert in this field and will do us justice in dealing with the powers that be.

Ladies and gentlemen, let me make this clear here and now. This action we have agreed to take this morning will cause immense turmoil; it will be huge. Within a day or two after we close, I assure you it will make international news.

Reporters from every news organization the world over will want to book flights to Moscow in order to cover this story. Much to their chagrin, they won't be able to since they will have limitations as to where they may stay. You shall see, our action will cause much turmoil that will require quick resolve.

President Viktor Orlov will be the one who steps in to address our concerns. That is how we see it at Holiday Jewel. So, remember, tell your people to defer all inquiries to Felix Balon, Public Relations Director: Moscow International Hotel Organization."

It was agreed to by all.

The meeting was over. All Western joint venture properties in Moscow would close in a week. Eldon and Kimberley had just achieved the impossible.

"Now to see what Orlov will do. This will be on hell of a historic chess match." Eldon thought. "Perhaps, he had just redesigned the chessboard allowing for "checkmate" in two moves." with Eldon and Kimberley having made their opening move, Eldon eagerly awaited Orlov's counter.

Eldon and Kimberley were heading back to The Holiday Jewel Danamo. Eldon was thinking to himself and feeling somewhat homesick. He missed his darling daughter Cathy.

"Kimberley, we can leave this in Felix and Louis's hands. Let's fly back home tomorrow, I miss Cathy babe, I think we can take a couple of weeks away from this madness. I'm sure you want to see your mother and father as well." Eldon said, holding Kimberley.

"Okay Eldon, let's go home I miss her too, I think we've both had enough fun here for the past few days, let's go home, baby," Kimberley said and snuggled close in beside her husband.

***

Chapter Thirty-Two
Turmoil

Within a week after Eldon's St. Peter's Monastery meeting concluded, all hotels forming the newly established Moscow International Hotel Organization had completed emptying their properties of all guests. On the seventh day, all eight hotels closed.

On the eighth day, into the second day of citywide hotel closure, telephones started ringing throughout the Ministry of Travel and Tourism. The calls would not stop; chaos ensued throughout the Ministry. Svetlana Orlov was inundated with demands for explanations on what was going on in her city.

The world's major airlines, tour company operators, meeting planners, and most recently her colleagues in the cabinet were now questioning her Ministry's competence, especially the Ministry of Trade and Commerce, demanding answers as to what was happening. Commerce throughout the city was taking a huge hit. Nobody in the city government, not Mayor Marat, or even the head of the Moscow Chamber of Commerce had any idea or answers as to what and why the hotels had closed. The hotels had all gone dark overnight.

"Mr. Balon, surely you can supply us with an explanation as to why all hotels in your Chapter have closed their doors." The reporter from the British Broadcasting Corporation said in a televised news media piece, now airing on Moscow television.

"I'm afraid the best answer to your questions can be answered by President Orlov. I would respectfully ask that you redirect all inquiries to The President's office or to the Ministry of Travel and Tourism." Felix answered that one and only question.

That was all he needed to do, Eldon's first move in this chess game of power had been made. It was "Eldon's Gambit", sacrificing citywide hotel revenues amounting to millions in his opening move, then hoping to recoup his losses and save this industry with his next move. It was classic chess and classic Eldon. Viktor Orlov on the third day pondered his counter; the timer was ticking.

Svetlana was beside herself. She was at a complete loss for explanations; explanations that would suffice.

Svetlana was not stupid; she had a feeling, a sixth sense, a gut feeling; call it woman's intuition as to what the underlying problem was. She had suspicions this all tied back to Mitkin, Bebchuk and Viktor, but she had no clear view of the whole picture. Svetlana was in a haze; a blur overcame her Ministry, and she was not about to take this, not from Bebchuk or Mitkin or her husband, Viktor.

"Something had to be done. Moscow's and Russia's economy was taking a huge hit, one that would take time from which to recover. This could not go on. It had to end." She decided to once again confront her husband.

"Viktor, you have eyes and ears all over this city. We have eyes and ears in every corner of our country, and you hear nothing, see nothing? Viktor what is going on?

The spokesman for the Moscow Hotel group is telling the news media that only you have the answers!" Well for god's sake Viktor tell me at least, what in the hell is going on? We have come such a long way Viktor, your accomplishments and achievements have captured the attention and admiration of the entire world, and now this... this?

What's going on Viktor, the walls of the Kremlin crumble around us, while you, we, sit and wait!" Svetlana pleaded with her husband.

"What in hell are you waiting for?"

Viktor had had enough, but at the same time, he too was broadsided by Eldon Davis. His gut feeling also led him to Bebchuk and Mitkin. Svetlana had brought that to his attention very clearly the other day. Viktor had no firm answers for now. His trust in Bebchuk was unquestioned. Viktor was loyal to his friend; he owed his life to Sasha Bebchuk. Viktor needed certainty before he questioned his friend and FSB Director; that bond he did not care to break.

He decided he had no choice; he would do what he didn't want to, he would call Eldon Davis. Viktor understood that Eldon was waiting for his call. He was absolutely certain about that. Viktor was impressed. He now had himself a formidable opponent. "Too bad they had become adversaries; perhaps it was not too late." Viktor thought.

"Svetlana, I've had enough. Do you hear me? You will have your answer shortly. The past week has not been one I wish to relive. Svetlana, you are my wife, I am The President of Russia, be my wife and stand by my side, trust and do as I say."

Svetlana, The First Lady of the Russian Federation, looked at her husband. She sat and after a few moments, she calmly said to her husband. "Viktor be The President! Get to the bottom of this. I am your wife; I will do as you say."

She then reached across the table and placed her hand on top of Viktor's. "I will Viktor; we've come too far for this to get in our way, what would you like me to do?"

"I want you to set up a commission, an agency inside your Ministry in conjunction with the United Nations, to coordinate the efforts of the Russian Federation in eradicating the trafficking of underage girls into the international sex slave market," Viktor said to his wife. "And I want you to make an official statement announcing this new initiative." Svetlana couldn't believe her ears.

"Viktor, you have been looking into this matter, from dinner the other night! You really did do something! Viktor, that was the right thing Viktor. Viktor, I will get onto this right away." Svetlana had renewed admiration for her husband.

"He is The President of The Russian Federation" She must have more trust in her husband" Svetlana concluded.

***

Chapter Thirty-Three
Florida

Billy brought the Challenger 650 into Jupiter Private Airfield with a soft as marsh mellows landing. Kimberley and Eldon were home.

Billy taxied to the hangar. Kimberley and Eldon bid Billy goodbye for the next few days; they were all looking forward to some much-needed sanity. Billy was thinking about the raw bar down on the beach and some deep-sea fishing in the next few days off the coast of Jupiter Island. He'd already heard marlin and wahoo were hitting, and he wanted to get his time in on the big game fish.

Eldon and Kimberley could hardly wait to be reunited with Cathy. Seeing mom and dad would be wonderful, just to have the family together again. Kimberley knew that Cathy would be filled with joy to see her father. Cathy had become Kimberley's daughter over the past five years as if she was her own. There was a bond between the two of them now and a family bond among the five with Kimberley's mother and father assuming the role of Cathy's grandparents. She called them grandpa and grandma. Eldon's family was whole once again.

The next day was all about relaxation as were the following four. Tubing with Cathy on the Intracoastal waterway, ice cream on the dock watching the dolphins swimming by, and best of all playing with Eldon and Kimberly in the pool, swimming, laughing, and showing Kimberley her latest dives from the springboard. Cathy was becoming an aquatic princess. She lived in the water.

"Not sure mom, we are here for a few more days, but may have to return on short notice," Kimberley answered her mother.

The four of them, sitting in their backyard on the Intracoastal enjoying the afternoon sunshine, watching the boat traffic going by. Cathy was honing her skills on the trampoline while Eldon Kimberly and her mom Carol and dad Bob, did some catching up. Neither Bob nor Carol much questioned what was going on in Moscow but this morning's news on TV could not be ignored.

"So, what's this I hear that all the hotels in Moscow have closed?" Bob asked, looking inquisitively at his daughter and Eldon.

Kimberley then answered. "Well dad, we have some problems there, very severe problems, in fact, having to do with guest safety and corruption issues. We decided to act as a group dad, and all the properties have joined in together. We've brought the issue to a head. It's the only way we are going to fix it." Kimberley said to her father.

"That sounds a bit drastic wouldn't you say, dear?" Her mother commented.

"It is mom, but it will bring about the cure we need," Kimberley answered. "I'm sure you and Eldon will have it all figured out in no time." Carol then added, closing the subject.

"Well, we are just so glad the two of you are back even for a few days." Kimberley's dad said.

"Yes, Bob, and once we have The Red Jewel opened, then we will be done in Moscow for a while, and be back home. We just need to take care of some things. Felix is over there now holding down the fort. I'm sure all will be fine in the end."

Bob then said to his son in law, "Eldon come with me, will you, I want to show you something." Eldon looked over to Kimberley and said, "sure Bob," and followed his father in law into the house and to the kitchen.

"Eldon," Bob continued on, standing next to the kitchen center island, looking back out onto the manicured lawn and seeing Kimberley and Carol sitting out, sipping their ice teas, "you've lost your General Manager Eldon, it's been all over the news. Eldon, are you and Kimberley safe over there son? You know Carol and I are worried every minute you spend in Moscow. After hearing the news about Marty Sabine, well we were overcome with anxiety." Eldon could see that Bob was very concerned. He didn't want to lose his daughter. He had a legitimate concern. Eldon could not fault him."

"I think we are fine Bob, I think we are fine," Eldon answered. "Bob, we have to see this through, in fact, I, Kimberley and I are dealing directly with President Orlov now Bob, trust me, things will work out.

Yeah, all hotels are closed, and just watch Bob, in the coming days they will all reopen, and when that happens you will know we succeeded. We had to close Bob, and only Orlov can reopen us. Once he does that, all will be settled. Trust me; we know what we are doing. This is what we do Bob, Kimberley and I; we know what we are doing, and we have some of the best people working for us, you know that. When this problem is solved, you and Carol will be coming over for the grand opening of The Red Jewel. Both Kimberley and I want you there as well as Cathy. Now you know with me saying that everything will be fine, right? Eldon finished saying.

"Okay Eldon, be careful, I know you will be, it must be a very interesting game you play son, I don't honestly know how you and Kimberley do it. I love you both, you know that, as does Carol."

"I know dad, I know. Eldon responded, and hugged Bob. The two of them walked back out, both carrying a Heineken in their hands.

The day passed with the family being together and happy. The next day was Friday. Eldon went and had his head office meeting at eight, two of the company's lawyers were present. Eldon needed clarity as to the lawsuit brought about by Mr. Vogel. Eldon's attorneys stated that Vogel had a good case, but if Eldon could solve the existing problem in Moscow, Eldon should be able to recover damages suffered in the lawsuit from the Russian government. Eldon was good with that, another dagger for Orlov to endure. This information alone, as his lawyers pointed out was in itself worth the trip back home.

Next visit would be to see his friend and current chief engineer, Nick Kovacs. Nick still lived up in Cocoa Beach. Eldon had already given Nick a "heads up."

Eldon had told Nick that he might have to make a trip to Moscow for a few days, so Nick was expecting Eldon to come see him for a more in-depth briefing. But before Eldon flew up there he would take some time and visit Linda's graveside.

It was not often that Eldon visited Linda's grave. He promised himself to visit at least once every six months. These graveside visitations brought him a certain sense of peace and shedding of guilt by momentarily being at his murdered wife's side. He stood for a while longer, gazing, thinking, smiling a little as memories of their wonderful life flashed through his mind. Standing by her graveside, looking at her name he did his best in holding back his emotions but it was not to be, he felt his throat tightening, and he let out a tear and a deep sigh, as he stood over her grave grieving but smiling.

He bent down and took a knee, with his left hand he reached out and placed the flowers into the vase, brought his right hand up to his lips, kissed his fingers and touched her headstone, not moving his hand but feeling Linda's presence and everlasting love for him and Cathy.

Eldon stood and turned, his mind even now racing with current events unfolding as he walked towards the parking lot back to his car. The south Florida sky had turned almost black with heavy rains blowing in from the Gulf, now just minutes away. As he opened the door to his Jag and getting inside, his car phone rang.

He answered. It was Viktor Orlov, President of The Russian Federation.

"Mr. President, Viktor, I trust this call is to inform me that we have an understanding, and you will work with me exclusively in bringing this to a mutually satisfying conclusion. We both need to resolve this problem.

"Eldon, just exactly what is the problem?" Viktor asked. "Viktor as you are well aware, ears in the sky are always listening. I will have my VP Felix Balon come see you. He has my full authority to deliver our message to you and to bring back your response on my behalf. Kimberley and I will be back in Moscow the day after I hear a positive result from Mr. Balon, good day Mr. President." Eldon ended the call.

Billy landed the chopper on Nick Kovacs's Cocoa Beach yard. Billy had been here a number of times in the past. Nick had a nice spot cleared with a helipad designated area. Eldon got out of the chopper; Nick was there already to greet him and Billy.

"Hey, Nick, good to see you," Eldon said, greeting his friend. Billy too shook hands with Nick. "How's the family Nicky boy?" Eldon asked giving Nick a pat on the back as the three of them walked back to Nick's house.

"Family is good Eldon; they're all up in Nantucket visiting Elsie's mom this month. I'll be joining them as soon as I can get away; I had a few things I needed to take care of at the lab." Nick said.

"Beer?" Nick asked.

"Yeah, sure, I'll have one Eldon replied. "Nah..I'm good Nick, flying, you know, otherwise, I would." Billy said.

"Bud good with you Eldon? That's all I have on tap this aft. Nick remarked, "out of Heineken."

"So long as it's cold Nick," Eldon replied.

The three sat down in Nick's Florida room overlooking the bay.

"So, you want me in Moscow is that right Eldon? I know when you come like this, it's something big." Nick said.

"Yeah Nick, it's something big all right. About as big as it gets, I don't think in the history of my business career or even in your electrical and optics engineering career has it been this big."

Eldon took a swig from the bottle of Bud, sitting back in the rattan chair, looking over at Billy. Billy looking back at Eldon, raising his eyebrows, and nodding his head, calmly but with a worried look on his face.

"Jeez Eldon, what is it?"

"The Russians have *Raul*," Eldon said in one breath and stopped.

"Holy shit, are you sure about that?" As soon as Nick said that, he knew of course Eldon was sure about that.

Eldon sat nodding his head, looking at Nick, taking another drink of bud.

"So, Nick, not to worry about why and how we need to address "the what."

Nick responded, "You mean "what we can do about it?"

"Yeah," Eldon said, continuing. "What is it you, (we) can do to it, as far as turning it off, disengaging from it, sabotaging it, kill it for good." Eldon said.

"Well, we would need access to the fiber optics data control center. From there it could be turned off with reprogramming the encryption decoder so that it reads and turns the data into garble and gibberish. But that could only be done by direct access to the control center computer." Nick answered in no uncertain terms.

Eldon then said... "hmm, that may be a problem, time will tell."

Nick asked. "Have you identified the specific install points and locations?"

Eldon, glancing at Billy then said, "well sort of. We know the hotels RUL had been installed into, but we don't have specific rooms."

In addition, in case *Raul's* been installed into other buildings and business, all data flows back to central decoding, and once that is taken out of commission then the entire system will be rendered inoperative. Nick said.

"So, that will take care of it all?" Eldon asked.

"Yeah, that will take care of it all." I just need access to the building, and then a scan of the entire structure would identify the access points. After having done that, a removal of the windows panes and modified television sets would need to be done to completely remove *Raul*." Nick then finished explaining what needed to be done.

"So, what's involved for you to reprogram the central decoder?" Eldon asked.

Nick then responded. "Eldon, we have developed an in-house virus specifically for this sort of eventuality. All it would take would be for me to have access to the control center, upload or install the virus and *Raul* becomes non-operational, useless.

It's something we've been working in the lab this year to meet the needs of the exact scenario you just presented to me."

Eldon was astonished. The timing couldn't have been better. "So, then all you need is access to *Raul's* central control computer, and you can render it useless? Eldon asked.

"Yes Eldon, it could be done in a matter of minutes, just have to load the virus program, takes about ten minutes in all and done, system down."

Eldon finished his beer. "Nick, you should be prepared for a Moscow visit in the next few days, perhaps as early as tomorrow, in the coming week I would say."

"All right Eldon, you know I'm where you need me."

"Thanks, Nick, I can always count on you. You were there for Cathy, and now you will be there again to get us out of this Russian mess. Billy and I are going to leave and get out of your hair. I have a few more things to get done. We may be flying back to Russia in the next few days, depending on what Orlov has to say."

"Orlov?" Nick remarked. "This is serious, isn't it?"

"Very," Eldon replied, standing up and shaking hands with Nick.

Eldon and Billy were in the air flying back to Jupiter Island. So far Eldon had what he came for; answers from his lawyer and answers to *Raul's* cutoff in Moscow.

Now for Orlov to play his next move. Eldon would have to wait. But not long.

***

Chapter Thirty-Four
Demands

The Kremlin driver dispatched to pick up Felix Balon from The Holiday Jewel Danamo Hotel arrived at the main entrance. Felix met the Kremlin limo upon its arrival, got in and was whisked away; two escort vehicles, one in front, one behind with blue strobes flashing, the three-car motorcade sped through the Moscow streets heading to The Kremlin.

Not one stop, no stoplights, right through. Felix was amazed, with the bumper to bumper traffic, how easily the way was cleared for The Kremlin motorcade to fly on through without as much as even having to slow for a bird or pedestrian or anything! The motorcade flowed like rapids down a river, rocks and boulders on either side of the rushing water.

"President Orlov," it is an honor to meet you, Mr. President." Felix extended his hand, The President and Felix shook hands.

"Welcome Mr. Balon, it will be just the two of us, I speak English better than you might know," Orlov said, addressing his visitor.

"This way Mr. Balon," Viktor motioned for Felix to walk with him. Viktor showed Felix to a Kremlin room adorned with Russian historical statues and artwork. There were two chairs side by side with a small coffee table separating the chairs.

"Please Mr. Balon, have a seat." Viktor motioned.

Felix sat down, and Viktor sat in the chair next to him.

"So, Mr. Balon, tell me what it is that your boss Mr. Davis has sent you here to resolve. I understand you speak for the Moscow International Hotel Organization, correct?"

"Yes, Mr. President that is correct, but today I am more of a messenger than a spokesperson." Felix said. Felix could sense an air or interrogation permeating into the room. He was not comfortable. This being his initial visit inside The Kremlin, although it was, to say the least, incredibly ornate, he felt uncomfortable. It was just a building, but very Russian and Felix, well he was very American. Felix was thinking "KGB," in capital letters. But Felix was a trooper; he did his best in maintaining his composure and projecting Eldon's position.

"Your group has managed to bring economic chaos to our city, Mr. Balon. Was there no other way in addressing your concerns? Was it necessary to bring about this financial calamity and international embarrassment upon The Russian Federation?" Viktor challenged Felix, admonishing the organization he represented.

Felix sensed a "feeling out process" taking place; gamesmanship. Viktor calculating and trying to get a sense on how Felix would and could handle the situation. This was not the reason Eldon had him visit The Russian President. Felix was this morning in the truest sense of the cliché "just a messenger" and Felix let Orlov know it.

"Mr. President, Sir, if I may, with the greatest respect. This visit is not about me or how or even why the organization chose to act in the way it did. I am not a representative of the organization; I am a person carrying a message only, and my visit here is purposed in safely delivering our message to you Mr. President. If you allow me to proceed I shall do so in earnest."

Viktor sat listening and looking at Felix, nodded his head; Felix continued. "Mr. Davis, who speaks for the group assures you his full cooperation in the group's desire for mutual resolve. I have here with me Mr. President a pathway to that end. If I may Mr. President;" Felix motioned towards his leather attaché folder.

Orlov stood up out of his chair extending his hand, indicating to Felix his agreement in accepting the attaché folder, but at the same time a clearly silent gesture saying in no uncertain terms, "Okay let me have it and get on your way, I'm done with you."

Felix handed the leather folder to Orlov. It contained the prepared documentation and other sensitive information directly from Eldon meant for Orlov's eyes only, specifically stating the action needed to bring about resolution.

Viktor accepted the folder, and asked, "This is it; everything is in here?"

"Yes Mr. President, it is complete, Mr. Davis prepared that himself before he left for Florida." Felix said.

"We shall see Mr. Balon." Viktor cocked his head slightly at an angle, raised his eyebrows, and then said, "tell Mr. Davis he will soon have my answer, it will be with either tanks or doves." Viktor smiled and stared at Felix.

It was not a threat at Felix, it was a threat directed at the entire organization meaning, "if this is some sort of game, and if this proves a folly, then their time in Russia will end in rubble, but if they are within their rights, doves will fly."

Felix got the message, loud and clear.

"You may leave now Mr. Balon, good day."

The President left the room through a side door while at the same time a Kremlin usher showed up out of nowhere and escorted Felix out.

Two days later, the phone at the Davis residence on Jupiter Island was ringing. The time was 12:20 AM in Florida and already 7:20 AM Moscow time.

Eldon answered the phone. "Eldon it's Felix, we have word from The President." Eldon then replied. "Yes, I know, you cannot discuss this now." "He tells me he has an answer for you, Eldon. He wants you to here in Moscow before he acts. I told him you were in Florida." Felix said.

"Eldon, his response to me was; get him back, that's it and the conversation was done. I'm pretty sure he's pissed and wants you back here." Felix replied. "One more thing Eldon, he said his answer would be with either tanks or doves."

Eldon replied, "Tanks or doves eh? I don't doubt that he's pissed. Maybe it's not us he's pissed at. All right Felix, the four of us will fly out immediately. I'm bringing Nick Kovacs with us; he's already here in

Jupiter. We were waiting for your call Felix; I knew it would come soon. We are leaving in the next couple of hours so we should be arriving your time around 10: PM or so. Okay, Felix, get word to Orlov
that we're on our way."

"Safe flight Eldon, I guess the end game is on," Felix replied.

"That it is, Felix, that it is, see you soon." The conversation ended.

***

Chapter Thirty-Five
Orders from The President

Russian Federation Army General Boris Kutosev was back in The President's office. Back sitting in the same chair, he sat in just a few weeks ago when President Orlov issued orders for Kutosev to destroy Parliament Building Number 2 on The Arbat.

"General Kutosev, your orders are clear. At exactly one minute to midnight, you will open fire with your battle tanks on all the buildings simultaneously, and destroy them all, bringing every brick to the ground. You will leave nothing; all will be turned into rubble. Do you understand General?"

"Yes, Mr. President. I will have our tanks destroy all buildings, nothing will be left, Mr. President."

General Kutosev saluted Viktor Orlov and left The Kremlin.

***

Chapter Thirty-Six
The Answer

The flight across the Atlantic from Florida to Moscow is a long haul. This trip Billy once again refueled in The Azores and continued on to Moscow International. Eldon and Kimberly arrived at The Jewel Danamo, but it was very strange indeed.

Neither Eldon nor Kimberley had ever entered one of their hotels that were closed. They did operate a few hotels that were seasonal, closed for the winter; two smaller properties that were strictly summer resorts, but to arrive at a major city hotel without guests or staff was very eerie. It felt like the building was dead when they both walked through the front doors.

Felix had met Eldon and Kimberley at the airport. There were two hotel limos with drivers, one car for Eldon, Kimberley and Felix, and the other for Billy and Nick. Both vehicles had privacy windows separating the driver from the rear section.

Maxim led the way, as front escort security vehicle and another security vehicle bringing up the rear behind Felix and Nick. During this period in Moscow extra precaution was the prudent road to take.

"Well, I can tell you that Viktor Orlov was not in a good mood," Felix said. He's had a couple of days to consider his response Eldon; he can be one hell of an intimidating dude... you know that?"

"Oh yeah, I know Felix. On the other hand, I think a lot of that is show. I am hoping that deep underneath somehow someplace he walks tall. One can only really do that knowing their virtue won over their greed and deceit. We're all human Felix; let's hope there is decent humanity in this man's core. We shall see." Eldon said to Felix and to himself."

"Did The President say or mention as to when he will get back to us?" Kimberly asked.

"Actually, I got a hold of The President earlier today to advise him of your ETA, and I asked him that very question, Kimberly." Felix paused and looked across the seat at both Eldon and Kimberley, then said. "We will know his answer; he will not need to call."

"Okay, now this scares me some." Eldon was suddenly alarmed. "Felix, you did say that his answer will be with either tanks or doves did you not?" Eldon asked.

"That I did Eldon, those were his exact words and something to do with ending in rubble. Not very comforting, is it?"

"Hell no, not at all! Orlov can be very unpredictable." Eldon exclaimed.

"Easy honey, trust me, I know how these things go. Diplomacy is an art, Eldon. I can assure you, Viktor Orlov is an artist. Let's all not panic just yet, give him a chance." Kimberley being the career diplomat she was; calmed the atmosphere. She took Eldon's hand, sat back and said. "It'll be all right," paused and then added. "I hope."

Having arrived, they all went to their suites and agreed to meet in the morning. The time was now 11:30 PM.

The three men, Billy, Felix and Nick, had decided to stick together, sharing a large suite. They cracked open some beers and sat in the living room talking about recent events in Moscow and how things got to where they stood.

Kimberley and Eldon felt bad about leaving Cathy behind again, but once this was over, Billy would fly back home and bring Kimberley's mother and father and Cathy over for the Red Jewel's grand opening.

Eldon could only hope that things would go their way. But right at this moment, he had to admit; he wasn't feeling it. Apprehension took hold, and it ate away at him.

Eldon's phone rang in the living room. The time was 11:50: PM. Eldon answered it, "Eldon Davis."

It was Felix. "Eldon look out your window," Felix said with alarm in his voice.

Eldon then walked over to the large window that overlooked the main street in front of the hotel and pulled back the drapes. His heart skipped a beat and terror filled his heart. "Kimberley!" Eldon yelled. She came running; stopped and cried; "Oh my God Eldon, Oh my God!"

Two T-90 third generation battle tanks had pulled up and stopped in front of The Holiday Jewel Danamo Hotel. A further battalion of tanks drove past the two already stationed in front of Eldon's hotel. The vibration from the heavy war machines, as they rolled by could be felt throughout the Jewel Danamo.

Eldon's phone rang again. This time, it was the director of security for The Red Jewel Hotel; he had Eldon's number for the private line to his suite. "Mr. Davis, there are tanks in front of The Red Jewel, my men and I are vacating the building." The call ended.

Eldon turned on the TV. Sure enough local news was breaking in, showing the movement of battle tanks spotted in various parts of Moscow, and now there was an update stating that tanks were on the move in a number of cities; St. Petersburg, Novosibirsk and Yekaterinburg specifically. All three of those cities had Western joint venture hotels.

Eldon and Kimberley stood watching the TV, and at the same time wanting to run out of the building.

The time had come. The minute hand on the Tower Clock of the Kremlin moved to one minute before midnight. Eldon and Kimberley held onto one another as they stood frozen looking out their window, expecting the inevitable. There was no time to run, no place to go.

"With two battle tanks positioned beside The Red Jewel Hotel, and battle tanks throughout Moscow placed into positions as instructed by President Orlov, General Kutosev gave the order and simultaneously all tanks opened fire at once, sixty seconds before midnight.

Thunderous noise could be heard throughout sections of Moscow. In all, seventeen tanks opened fire in unison across Moscow and another twentytwo throughout Russia. With the clock striking midnight,

Moscow time, a new day had arrived once again for the second time to be ushered in with the sound of the battle tanks.

Falling into heaps and piles of rubble were all of Mitkin's dens of sin; every one of his free-standing restaurants and all his strip clubs. Kutosev's T-90 tanks demolished all of Mitkin's houses of prostitution, brothels, and dungeons of enslavement.

Orlov had found them all. Viktor had his special Secret Service, independent of The FSB and Sasha Bebchuk to ferret out all of Mitkin's businesses and dens of sin and evil found in all of Russia's major cities.

Mitkin and his empire fell and were no more. Kutosev's army, having cleared each building of people inside, took one minute to destroy every building and every venue Mitkin had ever touched with his brand of terror and sins. A new day had arrived at the stroke of midnight across Russia. Mitkin's Russian Mafia had fallen and was no more.

The two tanks stationed beside The Red Jewel opened fire at one minute to midnight, targeted on building number 6 on Krasnaya Ulitca, (6 Red Street) blowing the headquarters of project Black Bear to smithereens. The T-90 battle tanks had created another pile of rubble that had once been The Black Bear control center. It too was demolished.
Nothing was left of 6 Krasnaya Ulitca.

The Red Jewel Hotel stood unscathed beside the rubble, untouched, not a scratch mark on it Eldon and Kimberley stood frozen looking out the window as the thunder around the city roared. They waited frozen in time holding onto one another, looking out at the tanks, expecting their end. It did not come, what did come was remarkable, incredible and pure Viktor Orlov.

The thunder stopped. Quiet enveloped the city. Eldon, Kimberley, Billy, Felix and Nick all stood looking out their windows and what took place in front of their eyes left them speechless. Suddenly the black night was lit up with high intensity white, blue and red flood lights in the color of the Russian flag, shining upon the two tanks and surrounding space. The pair of T-90 battle tank's turret platforms opened on both in unison and out flew one hundred white doves. Their escaping flight was bathed in light of the new Russian Federation colors; it was magic. It was remarkable. Orlov knew Eldon and Kimberley would be watching. Kimberley started crying for joy.

President Viktor Orlov's machines of war had brought peace and freedom from enslavement. Eldon and Kimberley were left totally speechless. There were no words fitting to say; none. Kimberley cried on, wiping her face from tears of pure joy; she couldn't help herself. Her emotions went from certain death to sudden elation and salvation. The emotional roller coaster she had just been put through had overcome her in a way she had not known before. She stood holding onto Eldon, crying but happy. Eldon watched as the doves' white wings fluttered as they flew into the black night. He held onto his wife.

Viktor Orlov had answered, with both tanks and doves.

***

Chapter Thirty-Seven
Bebchuk

The time was 11:40: PM. Sasha Bebchuk sat in The Russian President's Kremlin office. Two Kremlin military guards stood on either side of Sasha Bebchuk. Viktor Orlov entered.

"I know everything Sasha, everything. I know about RUL; I know about Ambassador Albert, I know how Mitkin enslaved the man, and I know how you brought about the procurement of RUL.

I know how Mitkin your brother, half that he was, but your brother, enslaved underage girls in the sex trade. I know that you knew but looked the other way. I know you and Mitkin had The Jewel Danamo Hotel general manager killed. I know how you conspired with Alexander in extorting payment by blackmailing hotel guests. I know how you used RUL's video surveillance to entrap corporate executives, showing them with Mitkin's sex slaves. I know how you looked the other way when Mitkin killed children. Mitkin is nothing more than cockroach droppings. You Sasha are not much better. I know how you conspired with Alexander in extorting payment by blackmailing hotel guests. I know how you conspired in using RUL's video surveillance to entrap corporate executives, showing them with Mitkin's sex slaves. You used project
"Black Bear" for your own personal gain."

Orlov was relentless; he was fuming and would have only minimal mercy for Sasha.

"Mitkin, your half-brother has been detained

and arrested for crimes unspeakable. He will not see daylight for the rest of his life. You Sasha, you, I will spare, only because I would not be alive if it weren't for you pulling me out of that hellhole in Afghanistan. That I owed you for, so consider this repayment."

"Viktor no, no!" Sasha yelled and was about to say more, but Viktor cut him off. The two Kremlin Guards moved in on Sasha. One of the guards placed the tip of his pistol on Sasha's temple.

"No! You are not to speak!" Viktor yelled back at Sasha. "You shall never speak to me again! You are to be banished Sasha; you will not live out your life in Moscow.

The old Soviet ways had some uses it turns out, yes, for people of your type. You are to be exiled to Siberia, where you will live out your days as a peasant. Goodbye Sasha, if there is a God; you may want him to be with you. Take him away." Viktor ordered.

The two Kremlin Military guards took hold of Sash Bebchuk and removed him from The Kremlin and Moscow.

***

Chapter Thirty-Eight
It isn't what it is.

"Yes, Viktor agreed to everything Kimberley. As a matter of fact, he insisted he pay for the hotel organization's business losses! Yes, even that! He also provided files from The FSB showing every RUL installation in every hotel, and on top of that, he agreed to the costs in refitting the hotels after the removal of RUL from all the buildings." Eldon looked at and told his wife.

"Eldon that is wonderful Eldon," Kimberley said smiling at her husband.

"Yeah babe, everyone is very pleased, things turned out well. As far as the blackmail and lawsuits are concerned, Viktor will cover most of that as well. We have some details to work out there, but in the end our expenses in bringing this blight to a close will be minimal, and all hotels will be open for business as of today!" Eldon continued.

"I am announcing the opening of The Red Jewel in two weeks' time following this Saturday. That will give us plenty of time for the invites. The Red Jewel will be ready, and open sweetheart. It will be a grand day!" Eldon was excited. Things had gone well.

Svetlana Orlov and Viktor made their entrance into the grand ballroom of The Red Jewel. As the Orlov's walked in the room came to a halt. The five hundred invited guests all stopped, and applause filled the ballroom.

Svetlana and Viktor walked arm in arm through the ballroom and to the head table. It was a historic moment. They stopped behind their chairs and stood, acknowledging the standing ovation they received upon their arrival. The applause continued for another full minute. Finally, Viktor motioned with his arm for quiet. Viktor and Svetlana took their seats, and having done so, both Eldon and Kimberley sat back down. The opening ceremonies were about to get under way.

The time was two minutes to midnight, and the large digital countdown clock mounted on the wall behind the head table had begun its two-minute countdown sequence. Eldon and Kimberley had invited Viktor and Svetlana to join him and Kimberley in honor of opening Holiday Jewel Hotels and Casinos' flagship property; The Red Jewel.

The countdown clock was now at the last minute. The ballroom full of people waited anxiously for the last ten seconds to start. At the eleven seconds marker, everyone took a breath and like a choir of five hundred, they counted loudly and with one voice.

"Ten, nine, eight, seven:" Viktor, Svetlana, Eldon, and Kimberley placed their hands on top of the huge Red Ruby button mounted in front of them, and got ready to push it down.

"Six, five, four, three, two, one," and the four together, pushed the red ruby; instantly turning on the red laser beam; piercing through the dark Moscow skyline, casting its laser beam of light in the night sky forever. The huge television monitors inside the

ballroom, carried the live feed from overhead
helicopters that transmitted the television coverage of
opening ceremonies and the lighting of the red ruby
laser that split the Moscow night. The room erupted
in applause! It was magnificent.

The Red Jewel was open! Champagne glassed
were clinking throughout the ballroom, as Viktor,
Svetlana and Eldon toasted one another and the
success of the most significant and important mega
luxury hotel in all of Russia. Next to the head table
was a table for the Davis family. Kimberley ran over
and hugged Cathy; she was so excited for her daddy
and Kimberley. Eldon hugged and kissed Cathy,
Carol and Bob were so proud of their daughter
Kimberley and their son in law Eldon. It was a
remarkable night.

Things like this were possible even in a world like
this with all of its shortcomings. Well, it was the hotel
business, the people business. Good people, bad
people, all people. Eldon and Kimberley knew about
people, more than most people did.

Nick Kovacs meandered over to Eldon once the
ballroom settled down and people started milling
about, socializing and enjoying the free-flowing
complimentary bottles of French and Russian
champagne. Nick moved closer in next to Eldon; they
clinked champagne glasses, and then Nick said, just
loud enough for Eldon to hear.

"You know the videos weren't from *Raul*," Nick
said under his breath.

Eldon looked at Nick. "Huh, what do you mean?" Eldon asked wrinkling and holding tight his forehead and eyebrow muscles with astonishment. "Yeah," Nick said, it wasn't video captured by *Raul*, the quality of the video was way too inferior, RUL would have had superior images, much better than what Viktor thought was obtained through RUL surveillance set up by Bebchuk. No, it wasn't *Raul* Eldon. It turns out that during our dismantling of the entire system throughout the hotels, we discovered secondary video and audio bugs, those I am certain would have been planted by Mitkin himself and his thugs to capture the sex scenes."

Eldon was listening, in amazement.

Nick continued on, "yeah, that filthy bastard Mitkin was taping the girls with different guys doing the deed throughout the city, and then blackmailing them to pay up, and also using that video as evidence for the lawsuits, but no, RUL had nothing to do with those videos. It doesn't really matter in the end, looks like Viktor bought it, when you told him it was RUL.

The thing about it is Eldon; it looks to me like Viktor had no idea, that Bebchuk had no idea that Mitkin had no idea that they were independently obtaining surveillance that ended up doing them all in. Kind of funny and ironic if you ask me. But in the end, it was you Eldon, who tied the fools together."

Nick started chuckling. Then Eldon started in laughing too. Then both men hysterically started laughing, a big belly laugh.

"The mighty KGB and FSB; how hard the mighty do fall! Eldon said laughingly. Another clinking of the champagne glasses and the tears started rolling down their cheeks from laughter.

Eldon looked around for Kimberley, found her and shouted over to her.

"Hey babe!"

She heard her husband. He rarely ever called out her name so loudly, it startled her, but she could see her husband and Nick were busting their guts laughing about something.

She too started laughing a little; it was contagious for sure even from far away, she wondered what it could be that was so funny. Eldon laughed, but never like this!

"Kimberley, come here, will ya." Eldon then found Billy, Felix, and Louis and waved them over. Everyone gathered.

"You guys have to hear this!"

Thirty seconds later, all six of them were busting their guts laughing and laughing.

Eldon then reached around Kimberley's waist, pulled her in close and kissed her. Everyone raised a glass, watching Eldon as he laid a nice big "wet one" on Kimberley.

It was a fabulous hotel opening and ending to it all. They formed a small intimate circle, raised their glasses once again, and toasted one another as the red ruby laser beam split the Moscow night from high atop The Red Jewel.

The End

FRANK JULIUS

FRANK JULIUS BOOKS

READER COMMENTS AND REVIEWS ARE
WELCOMED

POST YOUR COMMENTS ONLINE

TO MY WEBSITE / BLOG

@

WWW.FRANKJULIUS.COM